Early Praise for Persian Dreams:

Persian Dreams, Tabibzadeh's quietly powerful debut novel, weaves the stories of various Iranian women in the early twentieth century trying to gain rights in a strictly patriarchal society. The story's heroine, Nosha, wants to become a medical doctor—an ambitious desire in an era governed by conservative tradition. Tabibzadeh delicately takes the reader through a personal history of Iranian women's rights: from the years of traditional obedience at the mercy of their husbands and fathers at the turn of the century to the 70's, when it was common practice for women to vote, go to college, and choose their own spouses. Each story uniquely manifests the courage of women brave enough to protest against a violent, abusive, male-dominated society. At the same time, the author presents the beauty of Persian poetry and its role as the voice of an oppressed nation crying for change.

Tabibzadeh's elaborate and lavish descriptions of places, events, and characters take the reader into the heart of Persian culture; with the book's conclusion comes a real understanding of the struggle Iranian women have gone through, and the history behind their hard-won rights so far!

Shahnaz Peyman
Pal Alto, California

"A sweeping tale of romance and adventure." That's often what we hear with regard to works depicting foreign lands, broken hearts, and love unrequited. Maryam Tabibzadeh incorporates so much more in her achingly visual recounting of life in Iran across the vivid political and cultural span of the last century. She gives voice to the struggles of women wanting to be heard, to be counted, and to be loved and offers answers through the eyes of men shaped by a nation that no longer exists. The stories - and there are several - are wrapped in the lilting poetry of Persia. I suggest you read it in a quiet secluded place, so you can hear the movement of the sand...

Alexis Dobbins
CEO, writeRelations.com

Persian Dreams

To Mona Garret
I hope you enjoy it
Maryam

by
Maryam Tabibzadeh

Persian Dreams

Copyright © 2005 Maryam Tabibzadeh. All rights reserved. No part of this book may be reproduced or retransmitted in any form or by any means without the written permission of the publisher.

Designed by Sheila Mahoutchian

Published by DreamBooks®
1300 N St. NW #017
Washington, DC 20005 U.S.A.
www.dreambookspublisher.com

International Standard Book Number: 978-0-9794112-0-5
Library of Congress Control Number: 2005903433

2nd Edition

Acknowledgements

I would, first of all, like to acknowledge the efforts of my daughter, Sheila Mahoutchian, who inspired the creation of this book. She painted a picture of the day my book would be published and asked me how I felt about it, as if it really happened. This inspiration was what stirred the book that follows. She also put forth much effort throughout the process of creating it, from designing both the cover and interior to overlooking the editing process. I am proud of her persistence, and her artistic and thoughtful work.

Many thanks to Shahnaz Peyman, Alexis Dobbins and Maggie Campbell for their early readings of my book and their helpful insights and suggestions. Also to Iraj Shamas for helping my research on Persian poets in preparing the reference at the end of the book.

Finally I'd like to thank the rest of my family and friends for all the encouragements and love I received before and while writing this book. I especially thank those friends who gave me positive feedback on my Persian publications and the special one who told me, "You have to write more, because you can make magic come true."

Dedication

I dedicate Persian Dreams to my daughters, Sheila and Tara, whose encouragement and love gave me the courage and inspiration to write.

Also:

I deeply dedicate this book to the memories of my father, Aboo-Jafar Tabibzadeh and my brother, Saeed Tabibzadeh, upon whom the characters Babak and Navid are based.

Prologue

Let's travel, travel back in time and go back a century ago. Then pass over the oceans, mountains, and deserts to a faraway land. A land whose old name is biblical and famous but whose new name is very controversial. Over there, we cross the country to the south, then east of Persia, the birthplace of Cyrus the Great, and settle down in Pasargad. We get to know the people and travel with them over time. Get to know the culture, and observe their passion and love. Share their pain and loss. With them grow older and gradually travel back to present time.

Pasargad is a city as old as the Persian empire and as famous as her ruler. But in 1904 she is a forgotten small town. Life in Pasargad did not change much through the last five hundred years. The population consisted of landowners, government workers, merchants or business owners, the servants and peasants (in the villages), and of course the clergy, with one exception from the ancient Persian era. At that time, the clergy was Zoroastrian; but currently they are Shiite Moslems. At some time in Iran's long history they converted to Islam. These people kept their culture, as long as it did not conflict with their new religion, to which they were devoted. In this small town, there was little religious diversity as opposed to the rest of the country, which consisted of Moslems, Christians, Jews, Zoroastrians, and so many sects of Islam and Bahaism.

In Pasargad, there were only Shiite Moslems and Jews. In the majority of Moslems there were three main different levels of religious devotion:

Very religious: the clergy, businessmen, and their families.
Believers but not devotees: peasants and servants.
Nonbelievers: mostly young educated men.

The religious differences did not have any significant effect on people's relationships. Social status did. Although there were no restrictions regarding conversation and friendship between different social classes, marriages were mostly within the same class, and if there were any exceptions, there was so much oppositional pressure from society that most people did not go through with it. But in the stories that follow, we will see exceptions to restrictions such as these, and the difficulties presented to the courageous people who tried to tear down centuries of traditional restrictions.

Book I
Talah

Talah

She was born in a well-to-do family. Her beauty and good family name brought her many marriage proposals from the families of men in the city.

None of these men had ever seen or talked to her, but their mothers or sisters would tell them about her, in the context of an arranged marriage, as was customary. For men, this was the way life went. Some won by finding attractive and good-natured wives, but others did not, either because of his lack of interest or hers. Marriage, they said, was like a watermelon you buy: you don't know what's inside, until you take it home. It could happen that he got a wife that he did not like. Or she was not happy with him and they would fight. There were no other choices, however, in a country where all women were covered from head to toe. As a result, men did not have the opportunity to see the women who would be their brides, until the day they married them. For women, things were not so, they could see their potential husbands, but only from afar, and had to depend on their families to choose their future mates for them.

It was the same for Talah when she saw him arrive at her house. There he was, a bachelor from a good family. He was a landlord with servants and good wealth. That was enough for her parents to approve. What they wanted for her was a life that was secure. But she was young and wealth was not important to her. However, when she saw him, what she saw was enough for her to be excited.

He was a tall handsome man. His black eyes were deep and penetrating. His smile showed straight white teeth, which made him look much more handsome. He had black hair on a white complexion, which made a lovely contrast.

Talah was raised to get married at a young age. After puberty she was ready for marriage. So when she saw him the day he came to her house to speak with her father, she felt like she was looking at the man of her dreams. Her heart was pounding, and she felt a strange warm sensation spread throughout her body. Meanwhile, her mother noticed a trace of blush on her white skin, which made her look so beautiful that she wanted to pick her up and hold her as she did when she was a child. She dismissed the urge, since a twelve-year-old was considered an adult who could be kissed only on special occasions, like holidays or after long trips. But she smiled and sighed with relief.

Traditionally, a groom's family would see a girl from a distance and look for her good qualities. Being from a good family or being from the same socio-economic class was the first criterion. Second in line was beauty, and finally, it was the girl's demeanor and politeness. If the groom's parents found these criteria to be sound, then they first told their son about her, and upon his approval they visited the bride's family and proposed the marriage.

This was the drill for Rashid, Talah's suitor, as well. He was told by his mother that Talah was pretty and polite. She told him of her golden hair and her green eyes. He felt his heart beating much harder when his mother talked about a sweet girl with dancing green eyes. He was most excited about the love and lust in his future, and his life with her. He was madly in love with what he heard, even never having seen her. And as a result, he could not wait to have her.

Finally, the day came. The day where Talah found herself in the middle of a huge production, full of fussing women working on her hair, her dress, and her make up. She was amazed at all the gold and the other jewels they brought for her to wear. This was the day that she knew she would never forget, her wedding day.

Then he came in too and as the teenage girl looked at her future husband, she felt very proud. He was so handsome and her heart was full of awe that she was getting married. There was so much commotion. She was sitting on a chair higher than everyone, so they could all see her. Below her, the women were dancing and chanting. She liked her gold bangles.

And she liked all the dances. Everyone was telling her that she was a beautiful bride and that made her proud. The cleric came and, behind the curtain, asked her if she agreed to marry Rashid.

True to tradition, she asked where her father was, as he had to agree first. Then she told the cleric that her mother had to agree. They gave her their blessings and then she agreed herself; and then finally, at the ripe age of twelve, she was married.

Married Life

For the next few months it was a beautiful time for both of them. She still lived with her parents and he came and went as he wished. They were married officially but not socially. It was customary to have a waiting period for the newlyweds to become acquainted. During this time, they were considered engaged and they were not to have sex until she moved into his house. The more they knew each other, the more they fell in love. Her joyful way of seeing the world and her beauty made him love her madly. She loved him too, as he was calm and loving. His love and passion for her made her love him all the more.

Every day he came he brought her a present—either a piece of jewelry or an outfit—which was chosen so tastefully that she could not have chosen better. The gifts were not only for her; he would send fruits or cookies to her family as well. She was quite surprised when he had several trays of cookies sent to her house on the dawn of their new year. "Why did they send so many cookies?" she asked her mother.

"Well it is your first new year as a bride," was her mother's reply. She enjoyed all this attention and his never-ending love. She started to look forward to living with him as his wife.

Then one night they put her on the palanquin with a sheer cloth covering her. There was dancing and clapping. There was happiness and laughing. She was happy too, since she knew where she was going to go. They took her through narrow streets and alleys. Then they stood by a big gate like door and put her down. This was her wedding night and it was truly a joyful time for both her and her new husband.

She started her married life when she was only twelve. Soon she was pregnant with her first child. The joy of feeling her child was tremendous, and she glowed when she felt her child move inside.

Her life felt perfect. She would sit and be sociable with the other women, and work did not keep him far away from her; he did little more than tend to his lands or go hunting occasionally. But he did plenty when it came to love. When their baby was born she was thrilled; he was proud. The beautiful baby was their pride and joy. They named her Shiva and dreamed for her the best life that she deserved. But life is like nature: there are many seasons that change, there are Springs and there are Autumns. There are Summers and there are Winters. Talah's first seventeen years were the first Spring of her life. She had all the things she needed to be happy. She had loving parents, a beautiful child, and a passionate love.

But the next few years were tough for her. She saw the first Autumn come swiftly. She lost her parents due to an epidemic, and her happy heart grew sober and sad. Losing one's parents when you are so young is a disaster, but fortunately, she had a very passionate love for her child combined with the love and support of her young husband. His caring and sympathetic ways carried her along this terrible time and through it she clung to him as a person who is drowning clings to a rock. At age seventeen she was suddenly an orphan who had only two brothers and a husband to lean on. But at the same time, her little child needed her to be strong. She did not want the sorrow of her loss to disturb her child's life. So she stood tall, and told herself to be cheerful and strong.

And as life goes, time passed and soon she was fine. She recovered and was eventually free from the sadness of this loss. But a year later, the first Winter of her life arrived. This Winter was cold and cruel, one so cold that even she did not think she could endure. There it was—another bad disease that nobody knew how to cure and of which no one could make any sense. Everywhere people were sick, and every day there were funerals to attend. Then the worst happened, her husband got sick and became bedridden. She prayed day and night, begging God to spare his life.

She was strong-willed and she was in love, but she was scared of another loss. She looked at his cheeks red and hot, and so beautiful like the roses in her yard. Those big eyes looking so weak. Her tall man was in pain. She was sad and she was worried. But, she could do nothing but pray. She begged God to spare him and told him that she would rather be sick instead of him. *If I die my daughter has a father and she will have a good life. If he dies what can I do? I will be lost with-*

out a doubt. She was telling herself all this constantly, staying close at his bed and caring for him. She looked at those beautiful lips that had given her so much love. She remembered all the caring he gave her when she was sad. The loss of her parents she had endured, but this one she could not imagine that she would be able to sustain.

Days and nights passed, but slower than normal days. She could not bear to see his skin get pale. She watched sadly as she cared for him, without being able to prevent what she inevitably knew would happen. Then came the day she dreaded. That day, holding his hand, she found him dead. She called to him but there was no answer, and when she looked at him, his eyes were closed. His hands were cold and stiff. She looked outside and told her still husband, "I am so amazed that you are dead but the sun still is shining! You were my sun and your love was the only thing that lit up my earth."

Then she got mad and told the angel of death, "You're a bloodthirsty angel, you are the enemy of love! Why? Why did you kill this beautiful light and steal his warm breath from me? When he was alive his beauty gave color to roses and his breath was what gave pansies their perfume. As cruel as you are, all the generation will curse you, I am sure! Is it possible that you make wine of people's tears? So this is the reason that you are stone-hearted? This is the reason you make people cry, so that you can drink their tears?"

Then she began to kiss his cold face and lips and let her warm tears pour onto his face. From her wailing the servants and relatives came in saw that he was dead. They took her away from his body and to another room. Then they took him away to prepare the body for burial, and soon they all went to the cemetery for his memorial service.

As the men gathered around his tombstone, women wearing black covers from head to toe gathered around her as they stood at a distance, to try and keep her calm and to prevent her from running to the grave. The women were not allowed to come near the grave, because they were thought to be very emotional, and delicate. This was the way it often was at memorial services, men near the deceased, and the women at a distance.

For the next three days people came, and for the entirety of theses days and nights she could do nothing but simply cry. She could not understand why this had to happen to her, and nothing would calm her down, except her beautiful child. With her, Talah was calm and hugged her and caressed her. She could not bear her sadness but she knew she needed to stay strong in order to protect her daughter from the harshness she would suffer in life from this tragic event.

What could she do? She could not work or make money. She was well off when her husband was alive, but now with him gone she did not know which way to go. What would happen to her? She had no idea.

Dead of Winter

She had no insight into the work her husband did or how money was spent. She also did not know what the future would hold. As hard as it was, those days ended and in time she realized a month had passed. It was time for her to know that her bad luck was tougher than she thought. Her brother-in-law stopped in one day to say that by law, he had custody of his niece.

"She will live with me and all her belongings, the house, and the farms will be managed by me," he explained.

Talah could not believe what she heard. She felt such a sharp pain in the middle of her chest. With trembling voice and tears on her face, she said, "Without her I will be dead. I do not care about the house and all her things, those you can have and take care of. But, please, if you have any heart at all, let me stay with her."

He answered in an angry voice, "I am her uncle and she will be in my care. Please pack whatever you have here."

"What happens to Shiva; do you care? She just lost her father, and now you want to separate her from her mother?"

He coldly replied, "I am her father now and my wife will be her mother."

"I was the one who carried her in me and gave birth to her, I was the one who cared for her and raised her, now your wife is her mother?" asked Talah incredulously.

"Yes, that is God's will. My wife will be her mother," he said.

"God said that mothers have no rights? What kind of God is he?" she replied bitterly.

He said, "Bite your tongue and do not blaspheme. Since God is great and He knows better than us, I am obeying God's will that after my brother's death I have custody of my niece."

She could not argue or say any more. She could be whipped to death if she told him what she felt. *God is not just and that's a fact*, she told herself. But then she remembered that she would be burned in hell if she continued to think that God was not just and continued to ask why women have to go through so much. *Ungrateful witch*, she told herself, *did you forgot how happy God made you these last several years? Are you unaware of the other families who lost several of their children? But you have yours and she is alive and well. You can visit her in her uncle's house. So thank God and do not ask any questions of him*, she told herself, as she sat looking at her brother-in-law, crying.

She strongly believed in devotion to Islam and was taught to obey the rules of God no matter how harsh they were. She could not understand the reason behind this law at all, but she was not supposed to ask any questions related to the Islamic laws. Suddenly, she was startled by Shiva's arrival into the room, and the child's unexpected anger toward her uncle.

"How dare you call yourself my Baba! My father was kind and considerate. Who are you to make me call you my father when you want to separate me from my mother? I will not go with you! You cannot take me from my mother!" Shiva shouted.

Had she heard their entire conversation? Talah did not know, but she could not believe her ears. Shiva was a very polite girl and always respected her elders; it was so strange that she was shouting at her uncle! But Talah could understand her pain. She was only six years old and still in shock over losing her father.

Talah wished that she had had time to explain the matter to her before she heard the news. But Shiva was furious and was shouting and crying uncontrollably. She tried to hold her to calm her down, but then she was filled with horror when she heard her brother-in-law's voice.

"You little devil. How dare you talk to me like this? You can not live with this stupid woman, look how she has trained you to be disrespectful to your elders," he shouted as he lunged at Shiva.

The little girl, now scared, fled into her mother's arms with tears covering her face. Talah held her tight and said, "Please forgive her and let me explain it to her. She lost her father for God's sake; you can not expect politeness from a grieving little girl. She will be polite and respectful soon, you can be assured."

He said, "All right, you have an hour to talk to her and pack." Then he left.

She held her trembling six-year-old tight, kissing her wet face.

For a while they just sat and cried; then she dried the tears from Shiva's face and said, "Listen my dear sweetheart. How can you make me so sad by shedding tears from those beautiful eyes? Don't you know that I can not bear seeing you in tears?"

Shiva looked up and said, "How can I be calm and not cry? How can I not be sad when I don't have a father? And now I find out that you are leaving me too! I just can't understand. Why can't I be with you *Maman*? Is it too much to ask?"

"My dear child, you have to understand. God gives and God takes. The things are not what they seem. God knows what is best. We have to be patient. And in the good days we have to thank Him for His blessings."

"Was that His blessing that my father died? Or for me to stay with a mean uncle? Is this a blessing?" Shiva practically shouted.

"Oh honey, don't say that! All this blasphemy will take us to hell. Your father died; we do not know the purpose, but we know that he came to earth by the will of Allah and with the will of Allah went back to Him. He is in heaven, but he can not be happy to see his dear child cry. And he will not be happy if you blaspheme."

Shiva looked at her mother, with her brown eyes wide open and said, "My father can see me? Tell me how."

She replied in a calm voice. "Yes he can see you from above. When people die they do not vanish. Their body gets cold and is buried. But their soul does not die or vanish. Your father's soul is in heaven but he is worried. He wants to see you as beautiful and happy as he saw you last. You do not want your father's soul to be unhappy and worried, do you?"

"Oh no, no. I didn't know father's soul was watching me," Shiva answered and then she smiled. Talah thought to herself wondrously how much children were like the springtime. The same way that stormy days do not last long in the spring, sadness does not stay too long in a child's heart. She saw Shiva's smile, and like sunshine after a stormy day in the spring, her smile was just as beautiful and magnificent.

So she said to Shiva, "Yes my darling, he is watching you and wants you to be as happy and polite as you have ever been. You know that you are supposed to respect your elders and you should respect your guardians, both your uncle and your aunt."

Shiva frowned and said, "But why shouldn't I be with you instead?

I want to be where ever you are."

"I will be in my brother's house and will see you often. But it is the will of God that you should stay with your uncle," Talah replied.

"But my uncle is mean; besides, if you go I will be alone. If I get sick nobody will take care of me, because no one will care. I won't have you to tell me stories, to hug me, or tell me you love me," Shiva protested in a very sad voice.

Tears gathered in Talah's eyes, which she tried to hide. After a moment she said, "He is your uncle and he is not mean."

"Didn't you see he was going to hit me?" Shiva asked angrily.

"Yes," she replied. "He was going to but he did not. Children are supposed to respect their elders and you were not being very respectful. Besides you will not be alone. You will be with your uncle and your cousins. And you are wrong darling. I will tell you stories anytime I come to visit. And I will take care of you if you get sick. I am not dying sweetheart, and I will take care of you if you need. But I hope that you never get sick enough to need my care or anyone else's."

"If you can come to tell me stories, then why don't you stay even if my uncle has custody of me?" Shiva asked.

"They don't want me to live in this house but I will be able to visit you as a guest. They can not kick me out if I come to see you; their sense of hospitality will prevent them from obstructing my visits." Shiva could not understand, though she was used to believing whatever her mother said. But Talah was right. The hospitality of Persians went back for thousands of years. People would stop by any time of the day and the host would not say a word, even if they did not like the guests. They believed that guests were presents from God and they were supposed to be respected and entertained.

Talah had to pack, so she asked Shiva to stay with her so she could talk to her. She had a couple of handwoven rugs, some dishes that were part of her dowry but most of them were broken, some jewels that were given to her at her wedding as gifts from her parents or relatives, and some pieces that were given to her by her husband. There were some clothes too, old and new. While packing she realized each one of those items came with a memory, which she told the story of for her daughter. She told her daughter the story of when she received these bangles and the story of when he bought her this dress.

Too soon everything was packed in a trunk and the two rugs were folded. Two of the servants who had worked for her while her husband was alive helped her to pack and volunteered to take her belongings to wherever she was going. They both were quietly crying about her departure, as though they could feel her heavy heart and her deep sorrow.

Soon, there was nothing left to do but kiss her beloved daughter and say goodbye before she left. She bent down and looked at her little girl and said, "Please promise me that you will be respectful to your guardians and be happy, for the sake of your father's soul and mine."

Shiva nodded tearfully and said, "I promise, *Maman*. I don't want to make you or my father's soul worried and I will respect my elders as you wish."

She kissed her again and said, "My sweet child, thank you for being such a brave and beautiful little girl, I am proud of you." She left with a load of sorrow and pain in her heart, and remembering the beautiful night she arrived at this house, she could not help but ask herself, *Why me?*

The two servants accompanying her in the narrow alley started to talk. They could not believe what they had seen.

"He is so wealthy; why is he so mean?" They were talking about her brother-in-law.

"Yes, why would it be so hard for him to have Talah in his house?" one servant asked.

The other replied, "Because she needs food and clothes."

"Well, she works all day and night like us. She could stay and be with her girl, and she would help them with the chores," the other servant said in an angry voice.

"He is afraid if she stays, that she would not let them do whatever they want with Shiva's money—that is the reason," replied the first.

Meanwhile, Talah was wondering herself if he did this out of greed or meanness. When they got to her brother's house, the servants left her with tears in their eyes. She started to help with the chores as she used to in her house. But her mind was focused on other things.

She could not wait for the day to end, but then the night was harder than the day. She could not find rest, tossing and turning until she fell into a fitful sleep, her mind filled with the scenes of her husband's death, the pain of it so strong that it woke her up.

It was close to sunrise and the time for praying. She could not help but cry as she prayed. She found herself again asking God, *why me*, which she believed was not appropriate. Time was lazy that day and waiting to see her daughter, the fruit of her love, made every minute far too long. She wanted the day to pass quickly so she could go and see her little girl in the evening. She could not eat much at lunch time. Her love for her daughter was immense, and nothing could make her feel better than seeing her daughter's beautiful face. She longed to see that sweet little face, those big brown eyes, and hold tightly the tiny frame of her little girl.

Finally it was evening, and she put on her veil, covered her face and ran out of her brother's house. She was going so fast that from a distance it looked like she was running. She got to her daughter's house breathless. The servants opened the door for her and she hurried in and called to Shiva.

Shiva appeared and with a squeal of delight rushed into her mother's arms. They held each other tightly, holding onto that moment which all mothers and their children experience daily without really appreciating how magnificent it is. But on this day, Talah and Shiva did notice its beauty. They appreciated the chance to hold each other, after what felt like forever. Then her sister-in-law appeared. Talah reluctantly opened her arms, which had been wrapped tightly around Shiva, and stood up to give her respect.

After the ordinary small talk she sat down, with her daughter close by. Talah could not tell Shiva the hard time she had had without her yesterday and last night, nor could she hold her tight in front of her sister-in-law. Her sister-in-law's behavior was not at all friendly, but cold and calculated. The servant brought tea and some cookies, which she politely took and started to sip on.

But the air was thick and there was nothing to say. Shiva too got quiet and just sat by her mother without saying anything. A few minutes later, Talah's sister-in-law said that they were supposed to go somewhere and their hosts were waiting for them. Talah got up, kissed her daughter goodbye, and apologized for intruding. Shiva asked eagerly, "Are you coming tomorrow?"

Her aunt answered quickly, "Oh no, your mother can come only on Monday and Wednesday afternoons." Talah felt a sharp pain in her heart. So she was wrong; she could not see her every day like she envisioned. She could see her daughter only two days, and if this day was any indication, then she would hardly have any time with her at all, she thought.

"Can she come to our house on Fridays?" she asked.

Her sister-in-law answered, "I do not know, but will ask my husband; if he gives permission she can."

Talah left with a heart full of pain. She was not allowed to be in her house to see her own daughter! Wow. How could she not be angry and how could she be expected to keep her faith at this monstrosity? She walked home slowly. There was no joy or excitement now. She had seen her beautiful daughter, and longed to stay with her, but she was doomed to be sad and away from her.

The way home seemed too long and the day was too hot with the black veil on her head and her face. "What did women do to deserve such a harsh way of living?" she asked herself." I have to be under this black robe from my head to my toes. I have to tolerate this heat and tolerate the pain of being away from my child because my husband died. I have to be thankful and to surrender and say nothing because I am a woman!"Tears poured out of her eyes and made her veil a little bit wet. When she got to her brother's place, she went inside a room and started to cry.

Her crying continued every night and her elations every week were only two—the short times she was allowed to spend with her daughter. She cherished every moment of it and once again grew sad when those moments were over.

Days and months passed. Soon it was more than a year. She gradually and surely went through depression without knowing. She did not sleep much and did not have much of an appetite or the will to do anything. There was not much to do either. She could not read and she could not work outside of the house. The house chores were done by the lady of the house. She was only a guest and had nothing of her own.

Finally all these concerns manifested in the form of a bad cold and she was so sick that nobody thought that she would survive. She felt that she was bad luck for her husband and that she was the cause of her husband's death. She blamed herself that he had gotten sick and died.

They called a doctor who was famous in Pasargad. He came to see what was wrong. He gave her some medicine and asked her of her life. She said she was a widow and told him that she was bad luck.

He said, "I am a widower too, but she did not die because I was bad luck. People die of a disease, not your luck or mine. We are alive and we have to live. Don't you agree?" he asked.

"Of course, but life is so hard for me."

"Really, can you tell me why?"

"I have a child who is away from me. I lost not only my husband but my daughter too." she said. "When he died, his brother claimed custody over her, and does not allow me to see her but two times a week," she explained.

"Oh, I see, that must be very hard for you."

"Oh, harder than you can imagine; you are not a mother to know or understand!" Then her face grew dark. "I wish I could just die and get it over with."

He answered kindly that he understood what she said. Then he continued, "If you die you never will see her face again. You are alive and you can see her now and then."

She said with a sigh, "Yes, but I only see her twice each week."

"Wonderful," he replied. "You must take care of yourself and get well. If you are sick or dead, you are no good for anyone, including your little girl. How old are you?" he asked.

"I am nineteen years old."

He shook his head and said, "So young and widowed!" He looked at her uncovered face and said, "You are young and beautiful. You need to be well and strong. Then you will be able to overcome all the troubles life may bring."

After he left she felt calm. Then she found herself thinking about him. He was tall and handsome, but his hair was turning gray. She could not determine what she felt; only that she thought his accent was strange.

The next day when the doctor arrived, he held her hand and took her pulse. He looked at her and smiled. "You are getting much better, I can tell."

Then he started to talk with her like a friend, like someone who cared. Talah was not used to conversing with strange men, in fact, women were often in completely different rooms than men in most gatherings. But he was her doctor so it could not be all that bad.

Gradually her fever vanished and her cold got better. The color returned to her glowing rose-colored cheeks. The doctor continued to come see her and talk with her. There was no sign of opposition from her brother, which surprised her. For a doctor to come to your house was very common while you were ill, but she was surprised that there was no objection now that she was well. Little did she know that the doctor had recognized her depression and had shared the possibility of its danger with her brother. He was coming to stop her from slipping into it again, and he was succeeding.

Soon she was up and well again. She also felt a deep respect and a growing amorous regard toward her physician. She found out that he had come with his father from a town she'd never been to. He was from Shiraz and had come to Pasargad with the governor.

"We love this small town, her people, and her orchards. We stayed here and made it our town," the doctor told her.

Gradually she felt a warm feeling grow in her heart when he came and talked. She wondered what his intentions were. She could see the sparkle of love in his eyes and could tell he was attracted to her. Soon she was delighted to find out that he had asked her brother permission to marry her. She felt very happy. Although Dr. Mamreza was much older, his knowledge and his kindness were enough for her to be proud to be his wife. He was the son of the most famous medical doctor in Pasargad. He had a grown-up son and two daughters from his late wife, who had died a few years before. His eldest son was studying medicine with him, as it was customary for boys to choose their fathers' professions.

What made this marriage so special was the fact that she knew her husband very well. She had talked and conversed with him long before they got engaged. There was no unknown for either of them. She loved listening to him and learning from his vast knowledge. He in turn admired her beauty, her joyful way of life, and her strong personality.

A New Season

The ceremony was simple but beautiful. Her days in her new house were very pleasant and rewarding. He was not only her husband but a patient teacher who taught her many things, like the property of each herb for curing ordinary ailments. She was becoming as happy as she was before. She felt her life, like nature, had survived through the tumultuous Fall and Winter. And now it was Springtime again.

She was so happy when she got pregnant again and her first son was born. They called him Babak. He was white-skinned with lighter hair and beautiful green eyes. He was smart and happy-natured. Their second son was born two years later and they named him Afshin. He was very animated, and his black hair and black eyes made him quite the contrast to Babak. Her stepson Sina and her stepdaughters were living with her also. Sina was a young polite man that Talah adored. Her stepdaughter Sara was a quiet and sweet girl, while Kobra, the younger one, was not so friendly. She was very upset over losing her mother at a young age and did not accept Talah as her mother. Talah could not make her feel better no matter how much she tried. But she did not complain about her. She had lost her parents herself and knew it was hard for a young person to lose one of her parents. She felt Kobra's pain and showed her only patience and care.

Her happiness was complete, especially since her late husband's brother changed his policy and let Shiva come to her house often. She did not know the cause of this change. Shiva was growing each day and her strong personality grew with her body. She wanted to be with her mother any chance she got, and it seemed that her uncle had to bow to her needs. Shiva and Sara became friends although Sara was a few years older than Shiva. Shiva was in her mother's house quite often now.

Talah did not have servants and extra money like in her first marriage, since Mamreza was a generous man and spent his money as soon as he had it. This gave Talah a chance to do the house chores, which gave her a good feeling she had not experienced before. Working hard and cooking for her young was a pleasure she could not ignore.

Soon five years had passed since those dark days. She was twenty-three and finally felt like spring was here to stay. She thought often that her life's winter had passed. It is springtime and I get to enjoy it. Nothing bothered her anymore, not her childrens' screams or even the hard work of cooking for five children.

She did not get upset with the hot weather under her veils either. She did not care about the differences between men and women. She was thankful that she was well and that she could be with her children.

Her husband's love gave her strength. He was wise because he could predict when she needed a boost in her personality and self-confidence. He told her that life is like the earth. It has mountains and it has deserts. You have to enjoy life when you can, nothing is forever you have to understand. Then he recited the following poem, which was her candle in the dark days which followed.

> *Oh you who feel a sadness; an unsettling pain*
> *Pulling yourself aside, letting your face disperse its rain*
> *Remember...*
> *Those who are gone, are gone.*
> *Those who came, have come.*
> *Whatever happened, has happened.*
>
> *Why hold this sadness?*
>
> *Its like in one swoop you want to tame the world's mountains and valleys*
> *To train them to lay flat,*
> *When mountains and valleys are by nature,*
> *Anything but flat.*[1]

So she was happy for what she had, and she soon forgot the horrible days of her past. Two years later Mamreza said, "I am getting old, our children are so young, and I am concerned about that. Shiva is getting to the age to get married. She is beautiful and wealthy. Sina is a young man who is handsome with the knowledge that makes him rich as well. What do you think if they get married and give us peace of mind? If I die Shiva will take care of our sons. And Sina, I know, will not wash his brothers off his hands."

Talah looked at him with amazement and said," I do not want to hear about your death, but I think your suggestion is a good one. Shiva is beautiful, and Sina is handsome. They both are from good families and both are well raised. You can talk to Sina and I will talk to Shiva. I think their marriage would be a wonderful thing for everyone."

He smiled and said, "I have talked to my son. He is anxious to have Shiva as his wife. You need to see if she is willing, then we will arrange their marriage."

Talah told Shiva when she came the next day, "If you would like to marry Sina, then we can go to your uncle for your hand."

Shiva loved her mother and the thought of being with her in the same house made her so excited that she jumped up and kissed her mother saying, "That way I can be here all the time!"

Talah was stunned. Was this the right way to get married? She felt that Shiva was still a child and that her motivation was to be with her mother rather than getting married. So she replied, "Shiva, you are thirteen years old. You have to get married with somebody and start your family. Sina is only twenty-one and just starting to be a doctor. He is handsome and good-natured. But you have to like him. You are marrying him for the rest of your life, long after I die. So you need to marry him for him, not to be close to me. Yes it would be great for us to be closer if you marry Sina, but that should not be the reason for your marriage. My dear Shiva, in our society most girls do not have the opportunity to talk to their future husband and see if he is a person that they want to spend the rest of their lives with. But from my experience with Mamreza, I know firsthand that it is such a pleasure to marry, knowing that you will have a wonderful time with your husband."

Shiva said, "So what should I do, Mother?"

"Well, you stay for lunch and dinner for a couple of days, and I will ask Sina to talk to you and you get to know each other before we ask your uncle."

Shiva shook her head and said, "I don't want to make you worry Mother, but I have lots of problems with my uncle lately. He does not want to let me come here because of Sina. Because you have a grown-up son, he says I should not be here all the time. I have to fight and cry every time I come here."

Talah now realized what had changed such that Shiva was in her house almost every day. It was Shiva's will to go where she wanted rather than her uncle's change of heart. She could feel the pain in her heart for her daughter who needed her mother at puberty, but who had to fight to see her a few hours each day.

She smiled and said, "Well my darling, you can fight a few more days and get to know Sina a little better, no? That should not be too hard, should it?"

Shiva's pink lips opened up into her very beautiful smile and said, "Yes, I can stay tomorrow night to have dinner with all of you."

That night, Talah told both her husband and her stepson what she had been talking to Shiva about and asked Sina to spend more time with her daughter the next afternoon, to see for himself if she was the wife he was envisioning for himself.

Sina agreed shyly and said, "Sure, I will be here."

For the next two weeks Shiva would stay a little later than usual, and Sina would stop his work a little earlier to talk to his future wife. They seemed to be fond of each other, and they both agreed that the marriage was to their liking. So one afternoon Talah went to her ex-brother-in-law's to ask her daughter's hand for her stepson. They could not find a better suitor for Shiva. Besides Sina's credentials, Shiva's uncle had realized that it was very hard to deal with a grown-up Shiva.

So they agreed to the marriage and this brought much joy to both Talah and Shiva.

Shiva's Wedding

The wedding was beautiful. The ceremony, like any other marriage in Persian culture, started with Shiva appearing with a white dress and a sheer green scarf on her head. She looked more exquisite than Venus, the goddess of beauty. She was sitting on a high chair so all the guests could see her. Gathered all around her, were many lady friends and family members. They were clapping and singing love songs and happy songs about the bride's beauty. Some were dancing in front of her and everyone was smiling. It was the most important day of Shiva's life, and they all were celebrating and congratulating her. Most of the ladies had removed the black veils from their heads and their colorful thin clothes with sparkling beads made the ceremony so beautiful. The servants and close family and friends passed trays of tea and cookies around and generally shared in the happiness of the ceremony.

Late in the evening they heard a man's voice saying, *"Allaaah Akbar!"* (God is great). This was a signal to the ladies that a man was approaching their sanctuary and they had to put on their veils. First Sina appeared, and sat by his bride. He was sitting in the middle of a crowd of women curious to see the groom. Everyone now covered in their dark veils, the cleric came in. The ladies opened a row for him to sit close to the bride. He started with a few verses from the Koran and asked Shiva if she was willing to marry Aboo Ali Sina. A lady behind her said she would like to get her uncle's permission. Her uncle, standing behind the crowd, said he was present and gave his permission. Then she asked her mother for permission and upon receiving it, she finally agreed. The cleric pronounced her married to Sina, and that beautiful summer night passed with so much joy and happiness for Talah and Shiva.

The days that followed were days of elation and happiness. Talah lived each day with relish and enjoyed every minute of her life as much as she could. Although she felt that her life had ups and downs like nature, she had weathered out the winter and it was again another spring for her to enjoy. Babak, Afshin, and Shiva were all beautiful flowers of her life, flourishing and happy. She was happy as she looked at their rosy cheeks, their laughter, and their play.

She was only twenty-six and in the prime of her life. Her life was a calm sea with sunrays of love warming the waves of her existence. She knew little of her future and she cared even less. Her wise husband, Mamreza *Hakim* (they called her husband *Hakim*, which meant he was wise or a medical doctor), had told her to be happy and strong, enjoying every day of her life, and to forget the past. So she believed that, and did not worry about the future; knowing that no matter what was wrong, everything would be all right and that she would always be okay.

Life is not Forever

The days of her past and her sad flashbacks had vanished and were now only a distant memory. Taking care of her young children and giving love to everyone with great patience made her highly respected in her society.

And two more years passed, beautiful years that would make the most enchanting painting in her mind forever. But she was so busy being happy that she did not notice her husband's grayish hair become silvery white. She did not see that his straight back was bending a little bit. She did not notice his look, which became more tired every day. But then, she saw him in bed one day. He was not feeling good and she knew that this was not a good sign.

Is it true that my beautiful Springtime has passed again? Am I about to come into the desolate time of Winter again? The chill of her last Winter shook her body and she went to her husband with tears in her eyes, pleading with him not to leave her alone.

Mamreza smiled and said, "My dear Talah. Life is not forever. We all will go one day and we can not fight nature and destiny. We have two beautiful children together. They need you. I want you to promise me to be strong if something happens to me. I have three other children who are not much younger than you but not as wise as you are. You need to give them courage to face the realities of life if I do in fact die soon."

Tears dropped from her pretty eyes like warm rain, as she asked, "Oh! Are you telling me that I will lose you too?"

"No, my dear, you will never lose me. I will be in your heart and in your soul. You have two beautiful sons who are my gifts to you; cherish them and be there for them. I was not able to store a large amount of money for you or the children, but I am sure they will be well off with their brother and sister's marriage. Shiva will take care of them since they are her brothers. Sina will work hard to do the same, and you, my darling, you must be there to give them guidance and strength."

Then his long white fingers rose to her face and dried the tears from her cheeks with affection. She tried to cover her fear and said, "What is wrong with you? Why are you not curing yourself?"

He smiled and said, "I have done whatever I could. There is nothing else anyone can do."

Shiva came in laughing. She was pregnant with her first child and was very happy that she was going to be a mother soon.

Mamreza smiled and said, "Look at her and your other children and be happy for them. One life goes; several lives will flourish. Life is to cherish and enjoy. Even when one dies, if you remember them as a fragrant flower, the scent will linger forever and ever." Then he quoted a poem from a famous Persian poet Sadi.

> *Oh Sadi! Immortality to the man who moves forth*
> *with goodness to his name*
> *While death visits him, even still living, with naught*
> *a good word to his fame.*[2]

The following days were long and hard again. Babak, her eight-year old, was asking her what was wrong with his father. Sina was trying to help and was deep in study to find a cure for his father. But he knew before any one else that there was no cure. Talah's guilt returned as she asked herself again if she was bad luck for her husbands. Sara, who was married now, was sitting by her father's bed most of the time with her little son Moji. Again, Talah found herself talking to the angel of death. *Are you coming back again to drink your wine? What is in people's tears that you like so much? Look at these innocent children whose lives are shattered because of your lust for your wine.*

Then one barren day of winter where the weather was so cold that every thing froze, she found her husband dead. And just like when a candle dies in the middle of night and everything becomes dark, Talah's life became dark too.

She knew for sure that she would go through another tough winter but she had no idea how tough it would be. The whole family was mourning the loss of a man whom they respected and loved. Then Talah started to notice an unusual closeness between Kobra, who was married then, and her brother Sina. Kobra was the loner in the family. She was neither very close to her father, like Sina, nor with any of her other siblings. Noticing that she was getting close to Sina, Talah felt a little better. She knew how much her husband had meant to Sina. Mamreza was his father, mother, teacher, and guidance. But she did not realize the devastating consequences that would turn Sina's life upside down, and hers too.

Talah's sorrow was deeper than anybody could imagine. Having gone through the same kind of loss before, she was suffering deeply. Only this time she was older and wiser. She had two children that she needed to attend to and she tried very hard to prevent their entire lives from being scarred by this significant loss. She felt guilty too. Why was she alive, while her husband was dead? But she also knew that no matter what, she could not return to the depression she once knew. The voice of her husband came to her mind over and over again anytime she started to give in to sorrow. "Be strong for our children the fruits of our love. They need you Talah, be strong for them." His voice was constantly in her ears and that gave her strength to face this awful hardship.

But being strong was not the norm for a woman in that culture. After the initial mourning, she started to manage the house chores as she did before her husband's death and tried very hard to make her children' lives as normal as possible. But her effort did not bear fruit. Kobra, who always was suspicious of her, accused Talah of not caring about her father. She also said that Talah had been waiting for this day to happen.

Talah was outraged by this accusation and said, "If I kill myself do you think your father will come back? Your brothers just lost their father like you did and the effect of losing their father at that age has a devastating effect on children. You should know about that. I am trying to minimize this by making life as normal for them as possible. I am also following your father's advice, who asked me to be strong for all of you. I am keeping my promise to him!"

She thought that would make a difference, but what little she knew about the effect of complicated childhood difficulties on one's personality. Kobra's bitterness went way back, before Talah was in the picture. When her mother died, her jealousy toward her brother Sina, her father's favorite, flourished. This jealousy extended to Talah when she arrived as her stepmother and continued even after she married and had her own life. But Talah did not have time to think that much about her jealous stepdaughter. Her sorrow and her work was more than enough, so she tried to ignore her and continued with her own effort to support her two children.

The following days were worse than she imagined. Sina, who was at first deep in his thoughts, looking sad and depressed, started to show a different personality. He became a different person all together. His behavior grew very aggressive and he started to use foul language whenever he had an argument with Shiva, which was quite frequently. Talah tried to talk to both Shiva and Sina to calm them down. Shiva did not know why he was so mean lately. Being pregnant, she needed lots of attention from her husband, which she did not get. She also was not used to this kind of aggressive behavior from her husband. Shiva felt that Sina did not love her anymore. Talah knew how close Sina and his father were. She tried to reason with Shiva, explaining that he was depressed and that she would have to tolerate his behavior until Sina came back to reality again.

Her advice worked for a couple of months, but Sina did not come out of his depression. He was bad tempered and did not show much interest in his life, his wife, or his unborn child. Only Kobra was there, whispering in his ear every day. What were they discussing was a mystery to both Talah and Shiva.

There was also another person around whom Talah detested. She was an old lady, a matchmaker, who would come to their house every day to talk to Shiva. She would listen to her complaints and advise her. Once the matchmaker told Shiva: "You know you are beautiful and wealthy. If you get a divorce from a man who does not deserve you, there are so many young men who would love to marry you."

Talah was present and she grew irritated and told her very coldly that she should mind her own business and not interfere with a married couple. "Divorce is the worse kind of thing in this society," she continued. "Shiva and Sina are having a new baby and with a little patience, everything will be okay."

Shiva shrugged and said," I do not know how much I can tolerate though. I have a husband who is getting mad at any slightest provocation and uses foul language to make me mad."

It was hard for Talah to convince her pregnant teenage daughter to be patient. Shiva was only sixteen years old and she regretted getting married. Her vision of life was the last three years of her life. Two years full of happiness and love. "What was changed now?" she used to ask her mother, "Sina obviously does not love me."

"But why was he so nice for the last two and half years?" Talah would ask her.

"I don't know Mother, maybe he was afraid of his father," Shiva would reason. Talah tried very hard to tell her that Sina needed help. It was not her that he did not love. It was his whole life he did not care for anymore. She could remember when she lost her first husband and the heavy burden of depression. She was not a doctor or psychologist, but she could see the same behavior in Sina. She could see that he ate little, did not do much work, and was sitting in a corner and was mad. She tried to talk to him with little success. He would get as furious when she tried to talk to him as he did with Shiva.

Several months passed and Sina only got worse. Then their baby, Ali, a beautiful boy, was born; a child that Talah envisioned making his parents' lives peaceful, but to her surprise his birth brought little change.

Shiva by now was determined and asked Sina to divorce her. He looked at her blankly and disappeared. A few hours later he returned looking very exhausted and said, "I will give you what you are wishing for but there is a condition."

Shiva was surprised at how calm he was and asked, "What is it?"

"I give you the divorce but I get this house and all its belongings. Everything left from my father is mine to keep."

Shiva looked at him and said, "But these are not mine to give you!"

He said, "Ask your mother, some are hers and some belong to her children."

Shiva asked, very surprised, "You mean our brothers?"

"Yes, but they belonged to my father and I want what belonged to my father after his death."

When Talah heard the news she was furious. "I can not take from the belongings of two orphans. They need some money to grow up. There is not much as it is."

But the problems still persisted. Shiva accused her mother of not loving her. "Do you want me to suffer, mother? Is this the love you have for me?"

"My dear child," she said, "I love you more than the whole world but I love your brothers too. They are too young. They need money to grow up. The gold we have in this house can be sold to cover a couple years of their lives. The handwoven rugs also can be used to cover a few more years. I can not leave with nothing to support them."

That night she made the same argument to Sina. "If you like, we will leave without anything, but you have to take custody of your brothers."

To her surprise Sina refused her proposal and said, "You will take care of them. You are their mother. But if Shiva wants a divorce she can have it if I have all my father belongings." This was so unlike Sina. If she had not known Sina for the last ten years, she would think that he was greedy and selfish.

She said, "This is not you, Sina, how can you be so indifferent to your brothers?" She saw Sina's eyes staring at the wall behind her and he did not seem to hear anything she said. She tried again, "You never were into money or materialism in this world. I always thought you were so much like your father. He gave his own comfort to make others happy—so why are you acting like this?" Suddenly, she realized that Sina was not there with her. There was a blank stare in his black eyes that scared her.

She went to her room and again tears rolled down her face. It was so much. She felt cold again. The marriage of her teenage daughter to her stepson was in shambles. She was scared of a future with no money and nowhere to go. She did not have anyone to lean on. She felt so tired and exhausted. *Oh Mamreza, you said this marriage would secure our children' future—look at it now. They are going to be penniless and have nowhere to go. Their own brother does not want them. He wants the small token you left but he does not want his own brothers. What happened to us? Why did you leave me? How can I fight all this senselessness?* His voice came to her mind:

*"Oh you who feel a sadness; an unsettling pain
Pulling yourself aside, letting your face disperse its rain*

Remember...

*Those who are gone, are gone.
Those who came, have come.
Whatever happened, has happened.*

Why hold this sadness?

*Its like in one swoop you want to tame
the world's mountains and valleys
Training them to lay flat,
When mountains and valleys are by nature,
Anything but flat.* [1]

She wiped the tears from her face and went to cook for the children. Shiva came to the kitchen and said, "Did you talk to Sina?"

"Yes," she replied. "His demands are the same but something is strange in him. He was staring at the wall and seemed to be unaware of what I was saying."

Shiva started to laugh hysterically and said, "See, I told you he is mad! You do not want to believe me mother! Why are you hesitant? If you are worried about Babak and Afshin, I will take care of them. I will provide for them until they can work on their own. Let's leave this house and be free of all the shouting and foul language Sina is pouring on us."

Talah looked at her and said, "What about your son? Who is going to take care of him?"

Shiva was startled for a moment then said, "I will take care of him, who else?"

Talah shook her head and said, "Have you talked to your husband about that?"

Shiva said, "If he does not care about anybody as you say, why should he care if I take the baby with me or not?"

Talah shook her head and said, "I do not know but you have to know that and decide if what you want is good for your son too."

Was Shiva aware of her rights as a mother? she wondered. Shiva was too young to understand the pain of being separated from her child but she soon found out the hard way.

As Talah had feared, Sina surprisingly demanded to have his child's custody. Unlike the Islamic custom, where the children under two stayed with their mother; he wanted his son to stay with him. Shiva's hope that Sina would give up his right to their child the same way he did with his brothers did not happen as she'd thought it would. He maintained that their son was staying with him. Was he hoping to change Shiva's mind with his demands or did he do it out of anger—nobody knew. Shiva was determined to leave her marriage at all costs and she did not yet know the price that she would pay.

Talah tried to remind her of the detrimental effect it would have on her child but Shiva replied, "I know Mother, I was there, remember! I am okay; he will be too."

"But you were five years old; he is only a few months old! I had to leave you, I had no choice, but you do not have to leave him. Please stay with him, it is the best choice for every one involved."

"How, *Maman*?" Shiva answered with an angry voice. "I stay and get shouted at. Hear all kinds of foul language, but do not say anything? Who do you think I am? A person made of iron who does not feel and does not get upset? I am tired of this life and I cannot continue anymore."

Talah could not say anymore. She understood her frustration but she was questioning her judgment. She also blamed Shiva's old lady friend, for some of Shiva's ill decisions.

Shiva's New Life

They left without packing. The day Shiva was divorced, Kobra was there to be sure they did not even pack their clothes. It was the agreement, she said. Shiva kissed her little baby goodbye with tears running down her face. Talah felt sick to her stomach and was wondering how many more problems she could endure.

> *In the breath of this moment, hold on, stay calm*
> *For all life's twists and turns, surprises will come*
> *Hold instead to yourself, stand confident, stand strong.*
>
> *Like a tumultuous ocean we get pulled around*
> *Struggling and twisting, being careful not to drown*
> *Instead surrender, then float,*
> *Before long these waves will bring you to level ground.*[3]

His voice came back to her ears. She smiled. His voice and his memory gave her unbelievable strength. And maybe this strength was the secret of her survival through these catastrophic times of her life.

The months which followed were calmer for Talah, whose children were close, but she worried for her grandson whom they saw every day. But the matchmaker did not stop coming to see them. From the day they moved, she had a suitor picked out for Shiva.

"He is a wonderful man who will appreciate you. He is a cleric and has devoted his life to God. But he also is very wealthy and handsome," she would say.

At first Shiva was worried about her child and told her she was not planning to marry at all. By Islamic law, she could not marry anyone for five months after her divorce, anyway. She was happy to be free and she also could go visit her son most of the time. But a few months after the divorce her son got sick. He was with his father and she was able to go to see him a few hours each day. The sickness lingered. She blamed Sina and Kobra for his sickness. But before she knew what was coming, she received the shock of her life. The angel of death had visited them again; her son did not recover from the sickness and unexpectedly died one day. Shiva's pain at losing her baby was too much. She was furious and depressed.

In the prime of her life and at only sixteen she was already divorced and now had lost part of her soul. "It is my luck" she would say. "When I was only a child I lost my father and was separated from my mother and now at sixteen I am a divorcee and have lost my beautiful son," she would say to Talah with tears in her eyes.

Talah wanted to tell her the second part was not all about bad luck. She wanted to tell her, "I warned you about your little son, but you did not want to listen." But she bit her tongue. She knew that blaming her would not change anything, so she tried to give her courage to stand tall above the waves of her life and ride them as she did herself. She then began to relay all the courageous words her husband whispered in her ears for ten years to hopefully help her face the troubles of her life.

In this breath of this moment, hold on, stay calm
For all life's twists and turns, surprises will come
Hold on instead to yourself, stand confident, stand strong.

Like a tumultuous ocean we get pulled around
Struggling and twisting, be careful not to drown
Instead surrender, then float,
Before long these waves will bring you to level ground.[3]

Gradually these encouraging words worked, and Shiva slowly came out of her distressed despondency. *Oh, your words are like magic that makes everyone feel better,* Talah told her dead husband that night. She wished she could do the same thing for Sina. Sina did not want to see or hear from her anymore. Sara told her that he did not feel too good and Talah, who loved Sina as her own son, wanted to help him but she could not. If only Mamreza were alive! He could do the magic. He was not only a physician but a powerful psychologist whose words were soothing and had a calming effect on every one. Yes, he was right; his memory for her was like the scent of a fragrant flower, which was lingering on her life forever. Then she was wondering if the angel of death was picking the best ones on purpose! *The most beautiful flowers are destroyed by you so you can drink the tears of innocent children*, she whispered. But soon she recalled her beautiful memories and fell asleep calmly.

And the matchmaker came back every day to tell more stories about the cleric. Pretty soon Shiva was falling in love with the cleric without even having laid eyes on him. She was ready to get married again.

Talah did not know much about this cleric. In her life she had to deal with her own family, some landlords, some businessmen, or educated men like her late husband. But a cleric! She was not sure about him, and told Shiva not to jump into a marriage where she did not know the man.

"From what I know of him I love him already," she replied sharply.

"But what do you know about the word of this witch who destroyed your marriage? How can you trust this immoral personality?"

Shiva got mad and told her that this was her decision, not Talah's and that the matchmaker was her friend. "If you think she is immoral because she encouraged me to divorce Sina, you are wrong. She is just a friend who could not see me suffering, unlike you!"

Talah did not say any more. But in her court she already assumed the matchmaker guilty of all charges. She deeply and passionately believed in morality. To her it was a sin to encourage someone to get a divorce, no matter the circumstances and she saw that the matchmaker did it without any shame or remorse. Talah thought that since she lacked the morality she easily could lie too, so she tried to argue her point with Shiva, but Shiva did not want to listen. Years later when she was telling her stories to her granddaughter, she still felt the same way.

She was right, though. Shiva married the man of her dreams. The man created by her matchmaker. She told her stories upon stories of what she wanted to hear. Shiva fell in love with an imaginary man created by her friend.

But her friend was paid by the real man, Shigh. She was doing her job as a matchmaker and was paid generously. She had made him magically have all the good qualities a man could have, when in fact all humans have some faults and nobody is perfect.

The ceremony was simple. Shiva was a divorcee and most people did not have an elaborate wedding after their first marriage. When she moved to her husband's house she realized that her mother was right. The house was empty—only an old rug covered a corner of one of the small rooms. He also was much older than they were told. His old age reflected on his face much more than it should. Talah sighed and tried to bite her tongue. She could not say a word.

"Shiva has been through so much in life already and I do not need to make her feel worse," Talah whispered to herself. She knew from her daughter's pale face that she was not feeling any better than her. How could she be okay when from day one, everything she was told was a lie? He was not rich and he was not handsome. He could have been when he was young, but with his shaven head and long thin and gray beard he looked much older than Mamreza in his deathbed! But even if Shiva did not need his money or care about his looks, then she would be happy if all the other characteristics she heard about her husband were true.

Time will teach us the lessons we do not accept from more experienced people. Shiva now could understand her mother's remarks about her so-called friend. She felt trapped but was hoping that his personality was not a fake! "Okay," she told herself. "He is not rich or young, but if he is kind and considerate I do not mind." She was scared to death. It was not easy to get divorced. And she went through so much pain and humiliation with her divorce from Sina that she did not wish to repeat her mistake. She knew now that in that male-dominated society it was not enough for a woman to have money of her own. She was scared of the unknown now. When she agreed to marry Shigh she was sure and happy, but seeing the obvious lies she wondered if it was a wise decision to get divorced in the first place! *If he acts like Sina, what can I do?* she thought, *but why should I worry about tomorrow? Let me make the most of today.* She tried to reassure herself, remembering her mother's advice.

Then time passed and soon she was pregnant again. This made her very happy. She was going to take care of this baby and she would not leave him/her, she often thought to herself. She found her new husband not like Sina, but not like her dream man either. He complained all the time. He was also hard to please. He knew a way to do everything. He would tell her how to cook, how to talk, and how to think. It was not easy living with him. But he always would talk smoothly and say, "I am much older than you, I know a lot more so listen to me, be a good Moslem wife." She would tell her mother, "He is difficult but at least he loves me." But she wondered often if he really loved her. He demanded that she stay busy and work all the time, something she was not accustomed to. "He is using my money for day-to-day expenses. He wants me to cook, clean, do the laundry, and take care of our children. Then he wants me to respect him as a master of the house, and to not raise any question regarding the expenses. He does not even let me have anybody help me with the household chores either," she continued to complain, even after her third child was born.

A New Proposal

In the meantime, Talah was living with her nephew Mamdali, along with Babak and Afshin. Since Mamdali was not married yet, she helped him with the house chores when she was not with Shiva. Mamdali had a friend named Roozbeh, who was also widowed with a few children of his own. He was a man in his thirties, a distant cousin and good-looking with a pleasant sense of humor. He would come to visit often and on these visits, he would tell her jokes and also laugh at her jokes.

A few months after Shiva's wedding, he came early in the morning after Mamdali left the house to attend his shop. Talah was surprised to see Roozbeh at that time of the day. She told him that Mamdali had already left. To her surprise, he came in regardless and said, "I know. Actually I came to talk to you."

"Me?" Talah asked.

"Yes, you."

They sat down in the main room, although it was very strange for a young man to be sitting in the same room as her without anyone else present. But he was family, she thought, and he might have some kind of problem where he needed her advice.

"So what can I do for you?" she asked in a motherly tone.

"You can marry me," he answered with a charming smile.

Talah was startled. Had she heard it right? Was he asking her to marry him? She laughed and said, "This is not a pretty joke, Roozbeh. Why are you here? And what do you want?"

"But I told you. I am here to be with you and I want you to marry me," he said, very seriously.

"Oh no, no," Talah replied. "You do not want to marry me, but if you like I can find the perfect wife for you."

Roozbeh said, "Would you really?"

"Of course," said Talah. "You are my cousin and I love you like

Mamdali."

Roozbeh looked in her eyes and said, "But cousins do get married and I am not Mamdali. If you are willing to find me a perfect match then it shows that you do not have any feelings for me!" he said sadly.

She felt herself flush at his words, and for the first time she saw Roozbeh as an attractive man instead of a brother. She tried to overcome her emotions and said, "But I can not possibly marry you. This is a crazy idea."

Roozbeh saw the flush on her face and said, "I accept your refusal if you tell me the reason why."

Droplets gathered in her eyes like dew on morning grass as she said. "I am bad luck! I will not marry anyone again because I do not want my husband to die! No I will not, especially with you. I am fond of you and you are too young!"

He looked at her with disbelief and then started to laugh uncontrollably. Talah felt herself relax and thought to herself, *I knew that he was joking.*

When Roozbeh finally stopped laughing he said, "This is so crazy! Couldn't you find a better excuse?"

Talah looked at him very seriously and said, "But this is not an excuse. It is a fact. I suspected that I was bad luck when my first husband died and when Mamreza died too, I understood that my suspicion was right."

"But you lived with them for eight and ten years. If you were bad luck why didn't they die right after marrying you?"

"But they died. They all die," Talah said hopelessly, as if she did not hear him.

Roozbeh spent another hour there trying to convince her that her belief was not true. He tried to tell her that her first husband's death was due to an epidemic and her second one's was due to old age and natural causes. But she did not accept any of his explanations.

He left that day, but came back again the next morning to ask her if she needed anything. Then, while there, he started to talk to her. He told her that he loved her dearly.

She answered, "No you do not. How can you love a widow with two young children and a grown-up daughter?"

He replied, "Your sons are a treasure; they are beautiful and smart. I am very happy to take care of them. You are a jewel yourself, I only do not understand why you have such low self-esteem."

Then he told her how he would continue to convince her to marry him and would wait until she changed her mind.

The following days, Talah found herself thinking more and more about Roozbeh. How handsome he was and how brilliant and happy he was. But the more she felt close to him the more she was determined to refuse him for the fear of losing him like the others. She knew firsthand how hard it was to lose a loved one, and she was scared of trying it again. She had been stricken twice and she was not about to let it happen again. But deep down inside she knew that she could not live with her nephew forever. *If he gets married we will have to leave*, she thought to herself.

The months that followed were an emotional storm for her. On the one hand she wanted to be happy and live each day fully, but on the other hand she was deeply superstitious. This paralyzed her and prevented her from enjoying her life. Instead of living for the enchantment of today she was looking back to her miseries and found her superstition, the idea that she was bad luck, to be the only truth.

But like a calm river flowing without hesitation, life went on and Talah saw more and more of Roozbeh. Sometimes he would bring his children to play with Babak and Afshin. He would come and talk to Mamdali every night and he became almost a permanent fixture in the household. And as time passed Talah's feelings for him grew, but the more she loved him the more she felt sure about not marrying him. She was trying very hard not to show her emotions. She hid her love for him and was determined to protect him from her bad luck!

One day Roozbeh came to the house in the morning and told her that she had no choice but to marry him.

"What do you mean I have no choice?" Talah asked.

"Well somebody has started a rumor that we are having an affair. And you know the law of the land, if we do not get married soon, they will flog us. It is supposed to be two hundred lashes and I do not think you can survive that!" he said hurriedly and very seriously.

"But we did not, and we are not having an affair," Talah said calmly, "How can they lash us when we did not touch each other?"

He shook his head and said, "But nobody knows that. The neighbors signed a petition that I come to this house everyday and you are here too, so they have concluded that we are having premarital relations, which bears the punishment of two hundred lashes. Besides, if we can tolerate the flogging what can we do with the gossip of it? Can we look anybody in the eye without shame? Can you imagine in this small town how people will react to our flogging?"

Talah could not believe this. She had heard of the flogging and stoning of adulterous men and women, but she always thought they had done something wrong. She never thought an innocent talk with a relative would cause public humiliation and flogging. How could they even think about this!

"Then why didn't my brother or Shigh mention any of this to me," Talah asked.

Roozbeh answered, "Well that is why we know. They told me to do something before you are publicly humiliated. Your brother is the mayor of the city and your son-in-law is a cleric. The cleric receiving the complaint told me to marry you before the rumor gets out of hand!"

Talah shook her head and said, "This is not the right way to get married!"

Roozbeh answered, "Then what is the right way, after we are flogged in public? I asked the informer cleric to come in half an hour to marry us. There will not be any shame or public disgrace." Then he smiled and said, "And I will be the luckiest man on earth. You know there is an old saying that your enemy will cause you to reach good fortune if God wants! These idiots wanted to harm you and I, but by getting married we both will be happy."

Talah looked at his joyous face and felt happy and proud for a moment. *He really loves me*, she thought to herself. Then the nagging doubts in her mind came back and she said, "Oh but what about your children?"

Roozbeh looked at her and said, "I have seen you with them – you will be a good mother for them. They love you too."

"I adore them," Talah replied, "but if I am bad luck and you die, they will lose their father too. It is not just your life you are playing with."

Roozbeh laughed and said, "Are you starting that nonsense again?"

The ring of the doorbell interrupted their conversation and a few minutes later a cleric was marrying her to Roozbeh. The only witnesses were their children. Her family welcomed their marriage, although they were a little puzzled as to why there was no prior discussion of their intention to marry.

She went to her new house and started a new life. Her husband's energy and optimistic way of living gave her more energy. The first time he held her in his arms the warm feeling of his love surrounded her heart and made her feel wonderfully happy.

My dear God, please let this Spring be a long one so my sons will have a kind father and his children a loving mother. These children are smiling and we are happy. It is a new day and new Springtime for all of us. Please do not change it overnight to a Cold Winter, she prayed every day.

Roozbeh was a good lover and a wonderful father. He was a blessing to be with. Every day after coming home from his shop he would tell stories to the children, which made them laugh, and kissed every one of them. Then he would tell Talah how wonderful it was to have her by him and how much he appreciated her. She felt like she was the luckiest person in the world. In many ways she was a fortunate individual. She was born into a well-bred family, and when married she had happy marriages unlike most women around her. Her husbands loved her madly, and she enjoyed her marriages completely. If only life were not so cruel and her husbands had survived!

Spring arrived that year with all its glorious splendor. Roses everywhere covered the gardens with beautiful red, and yellow blankets of love and the smell of orange blossom filled the air. Talah danced with the children in their courtyard with its tall walls hiding her from stranger's eyes. The sound of their laughter was music in her ears. Life is so wonderful she thought to herself. Her two sons were playing along with his three daughters and his two-year-old son was very fond of her. These innocent children were robbed of having both parents by cruel nature. But she could see that the love she bestowed on them was enough to make them happy and they were lighthearted and nourished. She loved those children and there was no difference between his and hers in her mind. She could see that this held true for Roozbeh too. He treated Babak and Afshin with the same affection and love as his own son and daughters.

What goes on in childrens' minds when they lose one of their parents, she wondered. Her own sons were sad for a couple of months after their father died and then they were fine. But now she could see that they were not just fine, they were as happy as the time their father was alive. She discovered that more than any thing else, children needed the love and attention of a father. Although it was a fact that Roozbeh was only stepfather to Babak and Afshin, he gave them the love and attention that they needed and consequently did not seem to worry about their loss.

Talah was illiterate. She could not read or write, otherwise she would have sung a hundred rapturous poems from various poets to describe her joyful life with her handsome new husband Roozbeh. Her luck was that she did not know much about the condition of the country in which she was living. Although her country was the source of vast amounts of resources, many people were living in deep poverty, bad health, and poor hygiene. There was no security, even in their own homes.

Talah was at home one day when some men with handkerchiefs on their faces forced themselves through the tall wall of her house. They were carrying rifles. The children got scared and started screaming. One of the men pointed his rifle to them and said, "Do not talk, do not scream."

The children rushed to her side and as she hurriedly covered herself with her *chador* she was frightened to death. Talah and the children watched these men as they stashed all their belongings in a big bag and then left.

Among the problems that plagued the country, one of the biggest ones was that the monarch and his numerous children and relatives had given the country's resources to the foreign powers. Education was restricted to only a few lucky descendents of the cleric, the prince, and the tribe's chiefs. Each province was a separate state and its governor ruled the region by using guns and robbing, torturing, or murdering people, not by election, as was desired by the revolutionists of that era. But Talah did not know all these problems, and she was just as happy not knowing. Yet as a member of her society, she did suffer dearly by being a victim of unjust law, by losing her lovers to deadly epidemics, and by being a victim of house robberies.

However, that year spring was magnificent and their new year's celebration had been glorious. The long string of new year ceremonies, starting at the beginning of spring, had passed and the last ceremony, which was to celebrate the fresh air and the green pastures on thirteenth of *Farvardin* (the first month of the Persian calendar) had arrived. Talah, like everyone else in the town, packed for the big nation-wide picnic that came every year. Talah, Roozbeh, their children, and all their extended families went to the orchard, which was full of almond and apple trees, that Mamreza had purchased for Babak and Afshin when he was alive; the only property they owned. The apple trees were full of pink blossoms and the almond trees already had some green almonds on them, which were sometimes eaten by the children. The pastures were lush and green with blankets of red anemones decorating on the grass. The sky was blue and clear and the day was pleasant. A big stream of water flowed from the mountain and passed through the length of the orchard, dividing it into two parts. Willow trees were planted across the stream and each one made a good shady place to sit under. *Heaven cannot be prettier than this orchard*, she thought.

While the children were played on the swings, the women organized the picnic by taking out the teapots and their cooked rice and soups. The men talked about different things under the shade of the biggest willow. The day was full of vibrant happiness for everyone. But no one in the blissful crowd could have known anything about what the future was about to bestow upon them next.

Another Epidemic

The next day Talah went out and saw their neighbor, who told her that her son was very sick. He had diarrhea and a high fever. She felt very bad. Something told her that there was a disaster coming to her small town. *Could it be typhoid?* she asked herself as she wished the woman's son a speedy recovery and good health. Her late husband had taught her about some of the most nasty diseases and their symptoms. She also remembered that he had told her that if it comes to a town nearly everyone gets it. She quickly became very disturbed and worried.

That day passed and then the next day Roozbeh had the same symptoms. Talah, who had suspected the typhoid to be the cause of the neighbor's son's illness, became even more upset. Every day that passed she sat by her husband's bed and looked at his rosy checks, which were more flushed by the high fever. She felt another storm coming to destroy her life again. "Why me?" she asked herself often. But she knew that she was not alone. There were so many other people in town who were losing their family members to the disease. In fact, every day there was funeral after funeral. The disease was spreading throughout the city. Every family had at least one sick person in their home.

Talah, who was desperately trying to take care of her sick husband, was also very worried about the children, which made her forget her misery and self-pity for a moment, as she was determined to save those children from the devastating diseases. Before every meal she would wash their hands with the *choback* or the natural soap, which they had, and she asked them not to drink any water but the water she would give them. She boiled water every day and put it in a jar called a *kozeh*, which was made of clay and would keep the water cool in the summer. This water was the only water that anyone in the household was allowed to drink.

During this time, she often remembered Mamreza *Hakim*, his teaching of hygiene and his advice to be strong for the children. A couple of weeks passed and Roozbeh became so thin that nobody recognized him. Even though he was feeling very ill, his smile was a permanent fixture on his thin face. He was the same. There was no complaining or anger in his voice. He looked like a candle burning, and his smile gave energy to people surrounding him. But like a candle, one day there was no more light. He was pronounced dead.

The heavy burdens of guilt and life's pressure once again fell on Talah's weary shoulders. She had lost a friend, a lover, and the light of her life. His funeral was not a big one like the usual ones in Pasargad. There were so many people sick and dying that people could not go to every one of them. So it gave Talah time to continue her rituals of boiling water and cooling it down. Of washing the childrens' hands before each meal and being a mourning widow in the ceremony that lasted seven days. She told herself, *another Winter to endure; what is going to be next?*

Feeling exhausted while trying to remain strong, little did she know of the shock she was going to get when the family gathered to see what to do with Roozbeh's properties. They found a letter that showed Roozbeh divorced her in a hurry the week before his death. This was a bigger shock than his death. *Why did he do it?* she asked herself over and over. Did he think that it was her bad luck that he got the disease? The more she thought, the more she was sure that her bad luck had to do with Roozbeh's decision. He did not mention anything about his decision to her, nor were there problems in their marriage, even after the divorce of which she was not aware. So why had he done it? She would not inherit anything of the money he left behind anyway, she did not even want any money since she knew his four children needed more than what he left them. They lost both their mother and now their father. He was afraid of death and wanted to prevent it by divorcing her. That was the only conclusion she could see.

Amazingly, the rejection she felt from the unexpected divorce was worse than the loss she felt before. The pain was so real and his rejection bore an inferno in her soul. This fire burned her deeply from inside. Once again she wondered about her rights as a woman in this society. *How could he divorce me without my knowledge?* she thought. *Lady, can't you see that as a woman your life and death, your wishes and desires do not count? Don't you see that you are the property of your husband as soon as you agree to marry him? There is no need to ask for a divorce since you are his property and he can throw you away if he wishes,* she told herself tearfully and in silent anguish of realizing the truth.

She had been through so much! She had seen so many cruelties in the law, against women. This was not much compared to what was happening to other women, but nevertheless, she had not expected that Roozbeh would do such a thing! She believed he was right to be afraid for his life, but still did not understand why he had done it. Then a nagging thought came back to her mind. She had not wanted to marry him for the same reason. Why had he not listened to her? She was in love with him and was afraid of losing him long before their marriage. He was not a superstitious man. So why did he finally act on it?

She saw his pale face with rosy cheeks come into her mind, saying, *I was suffering and remembered your suggestions and I wanted to live, that was all.* She wondered though, why he didn't get better after the divorce? *If I was bad luck then why did he die?*

Oh can't you see that you were wrong to believe in being bad luck? There is no relation between your bad luck and your husbands' death! His voice came into her mind with its beautiful laughter. Tears gathered around her green eyes and she felt a blistering feeling inside of her. She wanted to scream or run away to the deserts like the character, Majnoon.

She remembered the long winter nights in which Roozbeh would read Lily and Majnoon stories from a book of poems by Nezami, one of many Iranian poets. It was an Arabic legend that was talking about the love of a young man and a girl from two different tribes. They were studying in the same school and fell in love, but Lily's father did not agree to their marriage and forced his daughter to marry another man. This event had such a devastating effect on the young boy that he left his tribe and his parents and started running all over the mountains and deserts, writing and singing poems for Lily. His behavior to the people who were not in love was so strange that they called him Majnoon, which meant a mad man. Nezami translated this story into Persian poems. Now Talah felt the same burning desire to run away, and she wished she could sing or write poems like Majnoon. Would Majnoon change his behavior had Lily merely died? Was this fire inside him from the feeling of rejection or loss? She thought it might be both.

She had already experienced two other losses. She had loved both her other late husbands, but this one was worse. Not only did she lose her husband, but she also felt rejected and betrayed by him. Once again she was homeless and once again she wondered what to do next while sadness and depression overtook her.

Shiva, realizing her mother's state of mind, invited Talah and her sons to live with her. Talah had never liked her son-in-law very much, but she felt she did not have any other choice, so she went to live with her daughter.

That night, she felt so much pain in her heart that when she laid down, she was still silently crying and continued to cry until she fell asleep.

In her dream she was still sitting in the same room and was still crying. Suddenly she heard a familiar voice. She looked up and saw Mamreza *Hakim*, her second husband, who looked unhappy. It had been three years since his death and she remembered that in her dream. *He was dead; then why he was there?* she wondered, but still, she was curious as to why he was unhappy.

"Hello, my love, what is wrong? Why are you unhappy?" she asked.

"I am unhappy because you forgot your promise to me."

"Which one?"

"You promised to be strong for our children, but now you are drowning in self-pity and forgetting that our children need you now more than ever. Roozbeh was not just a husband for you, but another father to our children. They miss him dearly and they need more affection than ever. You are a grown-up woman. You should know that we can not change the world. There is health and there is sickness. There is also death and there is disease. They are too young to understand that our lives go through changes, as nature does. But all the hardship of Winter will pass and we will see the Spring again."

She said, "But I did not forget about them... I am taking care of them all the time and only cry in private. You can not blame me. Look at me. I lost three men that I loved dearly. How can I be happy and strong? How can it be another Spring? I see only the darkness of the night and there is no light anywhere nearby."

"That is where you are wrong!" he answered. "The children want to see you happy and joyful. You need to be truthful to them and be happy inside too. You did not see any light when you lost your first husband, but then you saw two more Springs in which each one was more beautiful than the first. How can you be sure there will be no more Spring in your life? You managed to prevent your children and his from the devastating disease which killed so many in just a few months. Can't you see that you are luckier than so many who lost several of their loved ones?"

"Yes of course I am. I think the hardest thing in life is to lose our children, and I am thankful that I was lucky enough to not lose any of them," she said with a sigh.

"Yes indeed. They survived because of you, be thankful for this and do not cry anymore." Then he recited a poem from Molavi, saying:

From the accidents of the world don't be afraid,
Whatever comes to you is not forever, don't be afraid,
Take advantage of these beautiful moments, don't be afraid,
Do not think of the past, or future hardships, and don't be afraid.[4]

She opened her eyes. There was a peaceful ray of light coming in from the windows. Their rooster was singing his wake-up song, which was accompanied by the Allah Akbar call to prayer coming from the nearby mosque.

Talah rubbed her eyes, got up, and looked around the room. "It was so real", she said quietly. Indeed the dream had felt very real to her. She could still see him standing in front of her, reciting the poem; she remembered it vividly. *But how could it be? I've never heard it before,* "From the accidents of the world."

"How do I remember it from hearing it in a dream!" she asked herself in disbelief. Nevertheless she believed that the dream was real. *The soul of Mamreza is watching me*, she thought, *and he wants to guide me through this terrible time*. But it had been quite some time since she had seen him in her dreams.

Maybe it was because the day before she had gone to the fortieth memorial day for Sina (in Iran, people have several memorial days after one's death, which include seventh day, fortieth day, and one year after death). She remembered him as a teenage boy when she had married his father. She had not seen him for some time; she had not even been allowed to visit him during his sick days. She had respected his wish, but she still considered him as her own son for so many years and she mourned him as if he was her own. Remembering all her history with Sina and his father was painful. Was that the reason she dreamed about him again? She remembered the dream again. *But why did he not talk of Sina, but talked instead of Babak and Afshin? And the poem he recited that I have never heard before, but can now recite from memory? No, he is watching me and wants me to be strong.*

She got up with a big sigh, and washed her hands and face to prepare for her morning prayer. After praying she felt much better. Her magician was back in her life and magically she felt better, determined to use every moment of her life as fully as possible, and to forget about all her trouble and sadness. But with all her effort to be strong and happy, life was not so easy for her. She did not like living with Shiva because of Shigh, her son-in-law. However it was the only place she had. She had nowhere else to go now after her brother's death and her nephew Mamdali's marriage.

Living with Shiva and Shigh made her see her daughter's problems under a microscope. It was hard for her to mind her own business and not say anything to offend Shiva or Shigh. But she could hear his constant verbal abuse, his constant complaining and his conclusive reasoning that always made Shiva the guilty party, no matter what was happening. She also saw Shiva's eyes red more often than not.

Shiva looked much older, bending to the demand of her hard-to-please husband and the ever-increasing needs of her three children. But she did not complain about anything. It was so strange for Talah to realize that her daughter was crying so much of the time but still hiding her true feelings from her mother. But she knew why. Shiva had chosen to marry Shigh against her better judgment and was too proud to admit her mistake. She also knew that having lost her first-born after her divorce from Sina, she had learned her lesson. Like most women in that society, she stayed in the marriage no matter how hard it was, for the sake of their children.

It was about this time that Talah got a suitor. An old widower with three children proposed to marry her. But there had been a specific event that had her make up her mind to remarry as soon as possible. Babak was drawing a picture in his book and was proud of it. But when Shigh saw it he became angry. Drawing a picture in Islam was considered a sin at that time, and a disgrace to God. He shouted and lectured Babak for a long time and told him that he was not welcome in his house if he wanted to commit such a discraceful behavior.

Babak, who was fourteen at this time, just looked at him and left the house. The daylight vanished and the night came with very heavy rain and cold, icy weather. Talah was very worried and asked several of her relatives to see if Babak had gone to their houses. Their answers were all negative and with each minute that passed, Talah was more and more worried to death. The day turned to darkness as moments passed with no mind to her. She was up and waiting all night for Babak, but he did not come back. She went outside several times shivered in the cold winds and wondered what her fourteen-year-old son was feeling.

"Where is he and what is happening to him?" she wondered. She went through her memory and could understand her son's anger. What had he learned in his short life? Losing his father, his older brother, and his stepfather in just six years was more than enough to send a healthy individual into a deep dark depression. But this fourteen-year-old beautiful child had endured all this pain without complaint. Babak was kind in nature and had an artistic personality. He was sensitive too. Talah could see a burst of anger showing here and there despite his happy charming personality. This burst of anger worried her. She tried her best to raise her children with love and care. But was she successful in healing their wounds?

For three days she did not know of Babak's whereabouts until Mamdali, her nephew, found him and brought him home. This was enough for Talah. She did not want the same incident to repeat itself so she started investigating her suitor. He was regarded as a kind and very liberal man. Nobody said anything bad about him. There was no news of complaints about him from his late wife either. In general he was well-respected and well-regarded in Pasargad. So she accepted his proposal and once again she married without being able to talk to or know her new husband. After two love infused relationships it was strange to her to marry a man she hardly knew. But now she was over it. Love was for when she was young.

Fourth Marriage

And she was fortunate to have even known love in that tight society more than once. This time she was not young and eager to get married like her first marriage. She was not in love for the knowledge and gentleness of her second husband, and this newcomer was not funny like Roozbeh. This marriage was a necessity for both of them. She needed a roof over her head and a father for her children and Ali needed a companion for his nights and mother for his children. She married Ali.

A few months later she was pregnant and she delivered a son at almost the same time her granddaughter was born. As she had envisioned, her husband was a gentle intellectual man. They lived in harmony for twelve years and brought to the world four sons. He was kind to Babak and Afshin and wanted their progress. They lost their first son, though at that time it was not uncommon to lose a child. Children died every day due to an illness of one kind or another. But it did not help the parents to know they were not alone. For Talah who had been through this road so many times, it was harder than ever. As a parent she expected her children to outlive her and could not understand it happening the other way around. Once again, sadness crept into her heart. Everywhere she looked she could see his little face and his beautiful smile.

But little did she know that this was nothing compared to what she had to endure later in her life. By then she had learned that the scorching fire of pain in her heart had to be ignored. She had other children to attend to, and her sadness and her tears were left for the time she was alone. And then the storm came that almost destroyed her. Shiva was pregnant with her sixth child when she went into labor, but the baby was in breech position and nobody could do anything. After two days of labor Shiva died. Talah, who was present, did not know what to do with herself. She had gone through so many losses but this one was different. This was even worse than when she lost her little son. Shiva was her child and her best friend. They were only thirteen years apart. They had been through so many stormy times together. They would sit and talk for hours and now she was gone.

She felt helpless again, thinking, *God, why could you not take me instead? Why should I go through this tornado of life so many times?* But seeing five pairs of blue eyes looking sadly at her made her realize that this hard-to-fight storm needed to pass her by. Not only did she have to take care of her three little boys, she had to do something for her five grandchildren. The eldest one, who was a tall handsome teenage boy, was very sensitive; losing his mother affected him in a way that made her worry. But Shiva's three younger daughters were too little to understand their loss. Time showed her worry was not without merit. Akbar, her eldest grandchild, died of an overdose a few years later after he ran away so many times, having made life difficult for everyone around him.

This was not her last loss either, although after the shock of losing her eldest daughter, she did not see anything harder to endure. She felt that she was too old and she would not survive until her three children grew up. And then here, again her husband got sick and died shortly thereafter. She was exhausted and homeless again. But time showed her that she was stronger than she thought; she had survived to see all of them get jobs, marry, and bear children. She sent a letter to her eldest son, Babak, who was working in another town, letting him know that her husband had passed away. He came and told her to pack and go with him. She realized that her time to be worried was over. Her son would provide for them and they would be okay. So she packed to go to a strange land and see a different life.

Book II
Babak

Babak

He was eight when his stormy life began. When his father became ill he was devastated. Then when he died he felt completely lost. He was very bright and smart. By the age of eight he could read complex things, and wrote with the most beautiful handwriting. He also loved his father's profession. He would talk to him for hours, asking him about the causes of different diseases and how to cure them. But when he died, there was a void in the young boy's life and a secret desire to become a doctor like his father.

The events following his father's death did not turn in his favor. His brother-in-law forced him to go to a religious school. After his mom remarried he told his step-father Ali about his wish to be a doctor. Ali tried, but unsuccessfully, to convince everyone to send Babak and Afshin abroad with money from the sale of their orchard. Shigh objected so fiercely that he had to stay in Pasargad and was forced to go to theology school. However, he was not very good at it, and left the school after a few years. When he reached the age of eighteen, Ali told him it was time for him to work and earn his own money.

He did not know where to go but Shiva was looking to hire someone to take care of her farmland. He took the job from his sister and went to live to the village where the farm was located. While he worked, and in his free time, he spent his time reading and thinking about his country's current affairs. The end of the First World War brought a wind of change to Persia. The monarchy of 250 years was deposed and a soldier named Reza Khan Pahlavi had come on the scene. His time as a war minister had proved his ability to mobilize people and to make progress. He was seeking the presidency and wanted Persia to become a republic, but the clergy was opposed to this idea and proposed that he become the new monarch. So when the houses of representatives at the time voted for him, he became a new monarch. His ambition fulfilled, he started to force his new ideas. For example, he implemented a mandatory draft of young Persian men into the armed forces, which was met with mixed feelings.

Also, at the same time, nobody knew the exact number of Persians in the population or their ages. There were no statistics to plan for the future. One of the first steps the new king took was to form an office of vital registration. This office was supposed to register vital data, such as birth dates, marriages, divorces, and deaths. For this purpose the government started to hire qualified people. This was done by taking an entrance exam. Babak registered for the exam and was accepted. He was sent to another town in Pars province called Kazeroon.

At that time it was unusual for one to work outside of his hometown, and his mother and sister were not happy about his decision. They tried to make him change his mind, but he told them that he did not want to work at the farm anymore, only to hear Shigh complain all the time, and because of this, he wanted to leave. They had no choice. His mother, seeing his determination, tried to give him a reason to stay, asking him to marry her nine-year-old orphan niece, who did not have much in the world, only a devoted mother who went anywhere she went and a small piece of farmland. But Babak refused, saying, "She is only a child, Mother! I will not marry a nine-year-old child." Afshin, who was there, told his mother that he liked Battol and wanted to marry her. Talah was pleased to hear that, since she liked her niece, and felt sorry for her.

But with no other reason to keep Babak in Pasargad, she had to accept her son's decision. And with that, Babak went to start his new life in Kazeroon.

Kazeroon

Life in that small city for a single man was not fun at first, but soon enough, life would bring a surprise for him. He started taking music lessons to play the tar, an old Persian instrument. If you understand the Islamic laws and how they prohibit music, you can understand the character of the few brave ones who tried to learn and play it. Mostly this was in hidden spaces, where only men attended. Even though under Pahlavi's new régime the environment became a little more open and religious prosecution was banned, the religious establishment still had plenty of power in the eyes of ordinary people. But everything that was not permissible by religion was still often done in private.

And so, drinking wine and playing the tar were the illicit activities that Babak enjoyed. Yet, even still, for a young man, there is a void that cannot find solace without a woman in his life. Babak was a handsome man. His golden hair and green eyes caught the attention of many women. His clean and perfumed body, his strong muscles, and his deference and respect for women made him the most eligible bachelor in the entire city. The problem was that all women, young and old, covered themselves from head to toe with the *chador*. For Babak, who had an eye for beauty, this was not easy.

When he read the love poems of famous poets like Sadi, Hafez, or Khayam, he could not help but wish for the same flame in his own life. But with all the women covered from head to toe, one could not tell if what he was looking at was an old lady, or a young and beautiful one. For women this part was easier, and although they were obliged to cover themselves at all times, they could let their eyes enjoy the scenery. Being able to look at the most handsome men in the markets or mosques was an advantage. They also had other accomplished women available to help them find their desired husband or a lover. These women were matchmakers who charged for their services. They were mostly at hand for arranging a marriage. But in rare situations, when a woman had enough money and courage, this convention could be discarded and they instead used the matchmaker to pursue a lover.

In the province of Pars, in the summer, most people chose to spend their time on the roofs of their houses to entertain or to sleep. These hot summers bore little humidity in the afternoons and often there was even a cool breeze, which made the hot weather tolerable. The roofs in most parts of Iran are flat and functioned as a big patio. People would cover them with hand-woven carpets and at bedtime, they would lay mattresses down to sleep on.

On one of those summer nights Babak came back from a long day at work. The roof had been cleaned and carpets had been spread upon it by Hossein, his butler. He sat down. Hossein brought him a tray with a bottle of red wine, a bowl of yogurt and crushed cucumber mix, freshly-baked bread along with an empty glass. Babak started with a glass of wine as was his habit and began to play his tar. Then, as he played, he heard a lovely song begin, sung by the most alluring voice he had ever heard. It was the voice of a woman singing the song he was playing. His heart started to beat harder. The singer made him feel something that he never experienced before. The first tidings of love crept into his heart. Who was this woman that was brave enough to sing to his music? And where did she learn the song or even how to sing? He wanted to play and play until sunrise so he could listen to this delectable voice forever. His notes ended and he started a new song. The mystery singer continued to sing to his new song as well. He played for hours, entranced by the singer's voice, drinking a little between his different songs.

Then the wine took over and gave him courage. He wanted to see the face of the singer who had stolen his heart so completely in such a short period of time. He put down his tar and started to think. *What should I do?* he asked himself. *Should I go and find her?* If he did what was he going to say to her, he wondered. *What if she is an old lady? But this was not a voice of an old lady. She is twenty or maybe thirty at most,* he thought.

After a long pause the wine gave him still more courage, and he stood up. With his legs shaking, he went toward the corner where he heard the voice. He looked at the next door neighbor's roof. There was nobody there. From where he heard the voice he could tell the woman was in that direction, but at a distance. There were the holes of a back room coming up like a big mushroom on the roof. Then he looked down and he was shocked at what he saw. The most beautiful woman he had ever seen, much prettier than old poems or any flower, was standing there, looking up like she was waiting to see him. Her long black hair spread around her exposed white marble shoulders, and her smile showed her perfect white teeth.

He looked at her admiringly and then politely said hello. He then apologized for looking down and said, "I could not help it. I just wanted so much to see who the owner of such a pretty voice was."

Laughter filled the air and as it reached him, his heart beat even harder. "Oh, that is quite all right," she answered. "No need for apology, Master!"

He was surprised hearing that word! Usually it was customary for the servants to call their employer "master." But the house next to his belonged to a very wealthy merchant who was away on business trips all the time. In fact, Babak had not ever met him because he had been away since he had moved into this house. This beautiful lady had to be either his daughter or his wife. Her clothes and jewelry did not seem to be of a servant. So why did she call him master? And why was she standing there looking at him, knowing that he could see her without anything covering her?

His heart was beating so hard that he could hear it. And he did not know what to say next. He put his right hand on his chest and said, "So nice to meet you, madam, I am Babak."

Her laughter spread around, rising into the air again as she said, "The pleasure is all mine, sir. My name is Roodabeh."

He repeated it softly to himself, "Roodabeh..."

Then he spoke louder, "It is a beautiful name, more than appropriate for a lady so pretty," he replied. Then he said quickly, without waiting for her answer, "I don't want to bother you any more madam. Please, take care."

She sighed and said goodbye.

That night he felt like he had a very high fever and could not sleep. He never had seen a lady as beautiful as Roodabeh, nor had he heard any woman sing like her. He was used to women that were covered all over, and furthermore, they were not supposed to let any man hear their voices. But Roodabeh was different. She was not just beautiful, and with a extraordinary voice, but she was also a courageous woman. Oh, he wished so much that she was the neighbor's daughter and that he could propose; ask the merchant for her hand. Babak smiled when his thoughts reached to the point of asking the neighbor he had never met to give him his daughter's hand. Then he felt saddened by the idea that her father may refuse his proposal. All night he could think of nothing but the image of beautiful Roodabeh in his mind.

He knew a matchmaker who had tried to arrange marriage for him a couple of times. He thought that he could ask her to do the trick. She could find out who she was and whether or not she was married, he thought to himself. The next day he was very busy at the office, but when he went home and started playing his tar, his flame came back. Roodabeh's voice accompanied his music and the same scenario ensued. This scene was repeated many nights, and the more he heard her voice, the more he talked to her from the roof down to the back room, the more he fell in love. Their conversations were affectionate yet brief. He did not dare to talk too much for fear that her parents would find out and he could not see her anymore. She told him she learned all the songs he was playing from her tutor. She could recite the poems he liked and anytime he recited a poem she would answer him with another one.

He was incredibly impressed with her knowledge of poetry, art, and music. In a time where most women were illiterate or barely could read, Roodabeh was exceptional. She reminded him of the Persian women described in Shahnameh, an epic book written entirely in poetry a few hundred years ago. In this book the poet portrayed the Persian woman as a human being who could rule, advise, and even fight like men! This book was hidden from most ladies in Babak's time. They did not want women to read about Gordafarin, a woman who fought an invader while wearing men's clothes and stalled him until the Persian army reached them. Or Manijeh, who fell in love with Bijan, an Iranian fighter and not only invited him secretly to her family's home, but also fell in love with him regardless of her father's objections and severe punishments. Babak smiled when he remembered those stories. Yes, Roodabeh is like one of those ladies, her name came from that book and her father let her learn, not only reading and writing, but also music. Oh, it would be such a miracle if he could actually marry this girl, he thought to himself.

His mother and many matchmakers had tried unsuccessfully to convince Babak to get married, but he always refused since most of these candidates were too young, nine to twelve years old in fact. He wanted a wife who was open-minded, literate, who could read and understand Persian music and poetry. This did not seem possible until he met Roodabeh. He could not imagine finding a woman who knew any kind of art in a world where his brother-in-law prevented him from drawing a human face or going abroad to study medicine. He still was very bitter about his education.

But love is so powerful, and he was so happy and in love that he did not let his past bitterness shade this present happiness. He wanted Roodabeh so badly, and he often wondered why she did not come to the roof of her house, which was only a few steps from his roof. That way he could see her closer. But in the closed society of that time he could understand perfectly that it would probably be very dangerous to ask that of her. Roodabeh seemed very brave and probably she knew her situation better than he. If she could come to the roof she would; was it not her who sang to his songs and was it not her who called him master, signaling to him, that he could look at her from those holes as much as he wanted? Oh, for sure she would come to the roof if she could. He felt warm and excited from the thought of having Roodabeh close to him.

The Matchmaker

Every night he thought of Roodabeh until he fell asleep, and every night he dreamed of being with her, until one Friday morning, when the matchmaker came. Babak was an early riser and although it was Friday and he did not have to go to work, he woke up early, glanced at the roof next door and then inside the back room. When he saw no sign of Roodabeh he went downstairs, ate the breakfast Hossein brought him, and started reading. Reading was his hobby since childhood. He got all his knowledge from the books he read daily, but in these amorous days he read love poems to recite to his beloved at night. Hossein came in and said with a wink, "Soghra Khanoom is here to see you."

She was the matchmaker he had been waiting for. In fact, in the past few days he asked Hossein if he had seen her or not, and he said he had not.

"Oh, let her in please, and bring some tea," he told Hossein. He felt warmness overtake his body, like a teenager going on his first date.

Soghra Khanoom came in and after they exchanged a few words about the weather, she asked him boldly, "So, what do you think of Roodabeh?"

Stunned at her directness, he asked, "Roodabeh? What about her?"

Soghra Khanoom smiled, then winked, and said "She is madly in love with you."

Babak was thrilled to hear this, but calmly asked, "How do you know?"

She replied without hesitation, "Roodabeh herself told me that. How about you? Are you attracted to her too?"

Babak could tell from the warmness in his face that his face was red. Yes, his emotion had betrayed him and he could not deny it. "Yes," he said, "I am thinking about her day and night, I can not stop thinking about those beautiful eyes and that long black hair of hers." He stopped. Had he gone too far? What if this was a trap? He was not supposed to tell anybody that he saw Roodabeh unveiled!

Soghra did not seem to notice his desperate look. She said with another wink, "Would you like to see her in private?" Babak inhaled a deep relaxing breath. He could tell for sure that she was not an enemy. She wanted to bring his love closer to him.

So he answered eagerly. "Yes of course I would love to see her in private, but how?"

Soghra Khanoom gathered her *chador* around herself, got up, and said, "On Wednesday night, around eight, go to your neighbor's house. There will be nobody to bother you that night. Look around and make sure nobody is in the alley to see you. If nobody is in sight, go in. The door will be open and you do not need to knock." Babak was so excited that he could not do anything but say okay.

He gave her some money as a tip. And with that, she disappeared into the street.

Babak was puzzled. For days he had been waiting for Soghra Khanoom to come see him. Not to ask her to arrange to see Roodabeh in private and hear she was in love with him, but to ask Soghra to arrange his marriage to her. When she started talking about Roodabeh he was thinking that she was another candidate, but one who he would love to marry. So why had she left in such a hurry? He had so many questions to ask of her. He wanted to let her know that Roodabeh was the best woman for him. *Well*, he thought, *I will tell Roodabeh myself. I will tell her how much I love her and how much I want to marry her.*

He continued with his book of poems, and each love poem he read reminded him of his love for Roodabeh and of her beauty. He grabbed Hafez's book, the mystic fortune teller who supposedly told lovers if they would get their desire fulfilled or not. He opened the book and read delightfully his Hafizian fate:

> *Lips beaded with perspiration, she is intoxicated, her hair spread wild,*
> *She came to my bed and sat close, in the dead of the night.*
> *Her head bent close to my ear, and with the song of soul she said,*
> *Oh poor lover of mine, has sleep captured your eyes?*
> *A lover whom such a wine touches the mouth in midnights light*
> *Is unfaithful to love if he does not worship this elixir's might.*[5]

He closed the book as the memory of Roodabeh's beautiful hair once again entered his mind. He smiled at the thought of seeing her in her house on their first date. But Wednesday was so far away. He wanted to see her then and there. But unfortunately, he could do nothing but wait.

The poems were not helpful either. With each one he longed for Roodabeh more and more. There was a knock on the door. One of his friends came in and asked if he would like to go play cards with him. He was delighted. He always loved playing cards but on that day, which seemed the longest day of his life, hot with the fever of love and lust, playing cards was a way to escape the pain of feeling so lost without her.

The day passed and when night came he left his friends early, unlike their usual playing times, at 7:30 p.m.. They could not make him stay no matter how much they insisted. He wanted to go home and play for his love till dawn.

He wanted to tell her he could not wait to see her and ask her to let him see her sooner. He got home and quickly went to the roof. Started playing the best love song he could remember, but did not hear any voice from his beloved's house. He was frightened. What was happening? Did her parents find out? He was asking himself questions that he did not have any answers to. At times he was happy that he could see her soon, on Wednesday. But then doubt entered his mind, the idea that maybe this was the reason she was not singing anymore that night.

Finally he summoned his butler. "Hossein, do you know what is going on in our neighbor's house?"

"Yes sir, I heard that the master of the house came back from a long trip. There have been many people going in and out since early morning." A sigh of relief came from Babak's mouth. *Oh, that is why she is not singing tonight. Her father is home and she does not want to make him mad*, he thought to himself. But he could not help wonder that if this was the case, how could she see him in private on Wednesday? Maybe she wants to introduce him to her father, he thought, but he rejected that theory when he remembered that the matchmaker wanted him to be careful that nobody would see him. If he was going to propose then it could not be a secret thing!

He remembered the Shahnameh again and its stories. In so many of the Shahnameh stories the girls would meet with their lovers secretly in their own houses, then they would get married. Babak loved this ending and fell asleep with lucid dreams of marrying Roodabeh. The days that followed were not such pleasant times for him. Every day he went home eagerly to catch a glimpse of his loved one or hear her voice. But the more he played the more disappointed he was. There was no sign of her or her voice. The back room was empty with no movement in it whatsoever. For the next several days in Babak's mind hours seemed like days and days seemed like months.

Finally Wednesday night arrived. Babak's heart was beating harder than ever as the clock got closer and closer to eight o'clock. He wore his best suit. Fastened his newest tie. He used his favorite cologne. He did not know if he was supposed to be happy or not. He was eager to see her but he was frightened that he may not be able to see her after all. At 8:00 p.m. he went outside. There was nobody in sight and he pushed open the door of the house next to his.

As Shoghra had promised, it was open. He looked around and when he was sure that he was alone in the narrow alley, he went in. As soon as he stepped in, a lady came and said "Please come in."

He passed through the courtyard and went up a few steps, then went into a beautiful big room covered with lavish Persian rugs, and color-coordinated furniture placed tastefully around the room. There were also two intricate wooden coffee tables that were covered with silver dishes presumably full of cookies. The room told him of the marvelous taste of its owner.

The same servant who guided him in returned with a tray carrying a cup of tea, as is the custom in Persian homes when a guest arrives. He was wondering who he was going to meet. His love or her parents? He was sipping his tea when he heard a lithe footstep. He put down his tea hurriedly and waited nervously. Then there she was, by the door stood the woman of his dreams. She was wearing a green dress made of a thin, sheer material. He stood up to greet her and even before saying hello, started with a poem:

> *The sheer green of your dress, lovely maiden faced fairy*
> *Induces this very grass to bend down and turn in shame.*[6]

Laughter filled the room and Roodabeh came in. "Oh, you are so romantic and charming, master!"

He felt that he was shaking inside. 'Master' also was a code name for women to tell men that they were available as well. But he had never heard a girl tell any man that he was her master unless she was his servant. Then again, the girls he knew were so young and maybe that was why they never said anything like this to him. But was she really telling him she was available, he wondered. He bent down and took her hand in his and kissed it as she stood in front of him.

She was so impressed with his polite behavior and the romantic gesture, that she said, "My dear, you make me wonder how ladies let you remain single!"

"Please, sit down." she said, gesturing at the chair behind him. He obliged. She choose the sofa next to his chair. Then she became quiet; her brown eyes landing on his face found his green eyes eagerly looking back at her. He took a deep breath and said:

> Your honey tinted eyes peeking from behind
>   those lush eyelashes,
> To me looks like the henna colored deer grazing
> In a field of black roses.[7]

Smiling, she replied:

> I don't know what color your eyes are.
> I only know they are the color of beauty
> Sometimes the color of the ocean
> Sometimes the tint of the sky
> I don't know what color your eyes are...
> Sometimes the color of forests and jungles
> Sometimes green grasses of spring.
> I don't know what color your eyes are,
> I only know they are the color of beauty.[8]

The servant reappeared with two cups of red wine. They each took one and continued their conversation, with him telling her how much he loved her and how miserable he had been the past few days that he could not see her. She assured him that she would see him on a daily basis and told him she was in love with him too.

But she neglected to mention why she had avoided him during the last five days. Obviously the owner of the house had been in town but that night there was no sign of him or anyone else but the quiet servant who occasionally came in and out to serve them. He was soon drunk with wine and lust. He could not think logically how could she afford to entertain him so bravely in a closed society where even talking between a man and a woman was taboo.

Then she asked him if he would play for her.

He agreed and the servant went to his house and brought his tar. He started to play. She sang to his slow languid love songs and danced to his happier songs. And when she danced, he was moved with excitement. She was a woman with so many talents. He had such a deep respect for her talents and as he admired her he also wanted her passionately. They had so much fun and enjoyed each other's company so much that he forgot about time, and everything else. But when the big clock started to ring midnight, he put down his tar, got up, and putting his right hand on his chest he said, "I have to leave my darling. Although I wish I could spend all the time in the world with you, it is getting too late and with your permission I will take my leave."

She did not seem happy to hear this and as she wiped her face with the green silk handkerchief to clean the sweat caused by the movements from her last dance, she said with an airy voice that went straight through his heart.

"Darling isn't it such a beautiful night?
Among wine, sweet things and candlelight
In the scope of all this, how can you leave
Even if it is midnight?"

His arms opening he drew her in, close to his heart
Stroking her hair he told her the evening was indeed like great art
Then said, "Your face is so pretty, more so than candle light,
And wine and sweets are lovely, but those lips are in my sight
If you will grant me a kiss good night,
I will be happy, and my dreams will take flight."

And closer she went to him like a ship pushed by waves
Her eyes staring into his, begging wordlessly for him to stay
As the wine pulsed blood into her cheeks, her heart pulsed rapidly
The forbidden nature of this union
Manifested in his careful embrace of her body
As she clung to him desperately like the fence holds onto ivy

And as his lips reached hers they each slowly searched
The meeting of their faces was fire unearthed

Warming their bodies from within to without
This forbidden desire burning them both inside and out
His cautiousness matched in opposite respect
By her wild and dauntless lack of regard for things circumspect.

He pushed her away and said in a respectful way,
"I have to leave now but when can I see you? What day?"

Breathlessly she answered, her smile betraying her heart
"You can come any day you want, just let it be soon
make the time go quickly, I don't want us to be apart.
You can come any day you want, just let it be with care
Make sure that when you come, no one knows that you are here."

He looked at her with confusion, looked intensely and said,
"What are you talking about? Are you out of your mind?
How can I come any day and have no one know this lie?
People are nosey, sooner or later they will discover.
Do you understand? They will come after both you and I.
They will come after us and there will be no cover to offer."

She put a finger on his lips and said in a whisper, "I understand."
"You work during the day, but come in the night.
We will drink together, get drunk and together be light

He kissed her again, and then said good night.

He took his tar and departed with a heavy heart, back to his own house, so close and yet so far away from her. He lay in his bed that night thinking hard. She was beautiful and full of surprises, she was warm and he could not find any one as intelligent or as talented and enticing. Oh, he was such a lucky man to be able to hold her in his arms. But it would be so much better if he could hold her forever. He wanted to sleep with her without shame or fear. He knew for sure that he had to marry her if he wanted her forever.

But where were her mother or her father?

That was the strange thing about her. No mention of them. But what could he do to become their favorite? Finally sleep found its way into his eyes and he was so tired that he could not even dream.

Truth Revealed

The next day he was so busy that he hardly noticed the day pass. That evening he waited till it got dark, then he went to his neighbor's house and again, when he was sure there was nobody around he knocked. The door opened quickly and he went in. They began sharing time together every night when it got dark. Their talks were pleasant and her entertainment constantly interesting. But every time he tried to talk about a long-term relationship, she diverted the conversation or ignored it all together. They carried on this way until one day he received an order from his boss to take a business trip for a few days, and had to leave that evening. He went home at lunch time and asked his loyal butler Hossein to find Soghra Khanoom. He wanted to send his love the message that he was going to leave a few days. Hossein went and came back with the matchmaker.

"Hello, dear master, how are you?" she asked.

"I am okay, and how about you?"

"Thank you sir, I am okay as well." Then she winked at him and said, "How do you find Roodabeh?"

"Oh, she is marvelous," he replied.

"Yes, she told me you are fond of her, but she is a little disappointed," Soghra Khanoom replied.

He asked why, surprised to hear that from Soghra Khanoom.

"Oh, she wants more in this relationship, you know?" she replied pointedly, making her meaning clear.

Babak said with smile, "Oh, yes I know, I want more too, that is why I want you to arrange the marriage, you will be paid generously if that goes through. I love her so much and—"

He was interrupted by her startled voice. "What marriage? A woman can not marry two men, sir; it is only men that can have more than one wife!"

He was stunned. "What are you talking about?" he shouted.

She said, "Oh sir, you do not know? You really do not know?"

"What do I not know?!" he shouted again.

Soghra Khanoom sat down and said, "I am sorry, I am talking about Roodabeh. She has been married for years to Tajer."

It felt like a big heavy object hitting him directly in his heart. He sat down and put his head between his hands. He felt a sharp pain on his temple that continued through his head and quickly covered half of his head. For a while he could not say a thing. The sharp pain was distracting and his mind was unable to find any words to reflect his feelings. Soghra Khanoom was looking at him with sympathy. She was blaming herself for his misery, but consoled herself with the fact that they were neighbors and in love even before she came to him. Besides how could she know that he did not know that Roodabeh was married?

They sat there in silence for several minutes. Finally he was able to talk. "If she is married then what does she want from me? I have been in her house every night for the past few weeks and did not see anyone there! What kind of husband is he?"

Soghra Khanoom shook her head and said "The kind of husband who leaves his beautiful young wife for months and goes on trips. She is in love with you and that is all she needs. What does a woman want from her love, sir? She married an older man when she was too young to understand better. And now she is alone for months at a time with unfulfilled needs. Don't you understand?"

He answered with a sad voice, "Yes, I understand her husband has to be an absolute jerk not to know her needs. But that is not a comfort to me is it? You know the laws in this country and the consequences of this kind of action. We both could be stoned to death."

"Oh sir but if you are in love that is not to be feared. Have you not heard?"

> *One who is in love does not fear life*
> *Does not fear death, does not fear prison*
> *They become like a wolf starving in a desert*
> *Who isn't even scared of the call of the shepherd.*[9]

Then she started to talk smoothly and said, "Besides, why should you be fearful? With the new laws there have been no stonings."

He replied, "It is true that nobody has been stoned to death for a long time. Nevertheless, what about God, heaven, and hell?"

She said, "But sir, I did not know you cared for heaven or hell. You drink, play music and cards. Each one of them can take you to hell! Why does this instance scared you?"

"This is different," he answered. "Adultery is the worst kind of sin. I should be scared. With drinking wine or playing music I disobey my God—he will understand. But if I commit adultery he cannot forgive me; I need forgiveness from her husband."

She sighed, "What is the difference between adultery and polygamy, sir? In every culture and any faith they both are bad. Of course the people who do them deserved to be hated. If our God is just they are both bad, don't you see?"

Babak said, "I am not married or polygamous; why should I care?"

"Well sir, what I am trying to show you is what a just God we have. Don't you think that having relations with a lonely woman is like going to a second wife?"

Babak could not think clearly and the woman was a master of deception. It was time for him to leave. He decided to deal with the problem at another time and said, "I called you to tell her I am going away for a few days. It might not matter now since I do not know what will I do and which way to go."

She answered, "Yes sir I understand. You need to think about what you have found. Take a few days and ask your heart and be wise. I will do whatever you advise."

He became calmer and took a few bills to give her and said, "Thanks for coming. I will take your advice."

He left the town with a heavy heart. He was wondering about right and wrong. On the one hand there was love and pleasure. On the other hand he had his faith and beliefs. His mind was ordering him to forget love and lust. His heart begged him to fight his common sense until it left him alone. He remembered his time at the theological school. The long nights of thought and the conclusions he had reached about God.

He could see the Koran verse that said, *God is great and will forgive when you have faith.* He believed in God and Islam, but he had given up on being a true Moslem for some time. From the days of studying theology he knew that he was not strong enough to be a devoted Moslem. He chose not to lie or steal. He chose not to kill or bribe.

Music was an art, playing cards was to have fun. Drinking wine did not hurt anybody, so why did there have to be so much fuss? But adultery was always one of the worst sins, the one that he had always wanted to avoid, and now he had to decide how strong his faith was. He should ignore his heart and not look at somebody's wife!

The road to his destination was long and rough but his thoughts were rougher than that deserted road. It was late at night when they got to the village of his assignment. He was tired and exhausted, both physically and emotionally. The host prepared a bed for him to sleep; he had a long day ahead of him. He thought it would be as other nights in which he could fall asleep as soon as he put his head down. He wanted to have a long restful sleep. With such a bumpy road and a heart full of pain he was exhausted.

However, to his surprise there was no sleep to be had. His mind kept pulling him between his love and his faith. He was a Moslem and Islamic principles had lived in his mind since he was a child. There has always been a strong emphasis in the Moslem population to fight their sensuality. They always seem to find themselves choosing between their temptation and their faith. Babak was not that devoted, though. He was young and had a long time ahead of him. He believed strongly that he would not go to hell if he drank wine, or if he played music for his own pleasure, if he could have a chance to ask forgiveness before his death.

Then he saw Roodabeh in his mind. That beautiful face, those brown eyes and long hair spreading on her bare white shoulders, oh, her hair looked like black water running on a white bed. He thought, is there anyone as beautiful as her? No, he had not ever seen a woman like her. He remembered every minute he had spent in the last few weeks with her. That heavenly voice and those fanciful dances of hers, *oh my God why did you make her my neighbor and why should I fall in love with the lady of my dreams to only find out she is married?* But he knew for sure if he had obeyed God's orders and did not play music he would not have heard her voice and consequently gotten into this mess. He also knew he was not supposed to look at other people's houses or look at the neighbor's wife or daughters. *Yes, indeed,* he told himself, *it is for sure my fault! God knows best and to prevent this kind of disaster I need to be in control of my soul.* He remembered his teacher's voice in the theology school. "Fight temptation and control your soul.

Satan is waiting to make you give in to temptation and make sure that you will be punished severely. *Indeed he punished me in the most peculiar way*, he thought.

Then another thought came to his mind. The same idle thoughts that prevented him from becoming a cleric a few years before. The same kind of rage he felt when he was prevented from going to school abroad to study medicine. The same questions which came to his mind when his brother-in-law punished him for drawing the face of a human being. Why? Why is our religion so hard to follow? Why should it prevent you from any kind of fun imaginable? What is wrong with playing music or drinking a glass of wine?

His answer came from the Persian poems of mystic divinity:

Go drink wine,
Burn the pulpit, put the Kaaba in fire.
If you do not do anything inhumane,
God will forgive and you will find heaven.[10]

This poem was his way of dealing with guilt. His God was just. He could break God's laws and commit sins as long as he did not hurt any human beings.

But now Khayam's idle poem came to his mind:

Put my lip to the lip of a goblet, drinking greedily the wine
To find that ethereal mystery, the secret of long life,
And to my lip came the lip of the goblet, bringing me wine
With a whisper it said
Those who have died do not return to tell us of the divine.[11]

Then there was Roodabeh again and her beautiful smile. This love that made him more drunk than any wine he had ever encountered. He could not forget her smile. Nor could he go without her for a long time. *What should I do?* he asked himself. The night was long and his mind tired.

He whispered another poem to himself:

Love arrived to my heart.
And from the other side wisdom flew.
I thanked God a hundred times,
That this stranger my heart no longer knew.[12]

And yes, he was madly in love and there was no way he could listen to his wisdom. But the battle was not over. His brain would not sleep until he was convinced that this love was dangerous and he was better off leaving. *How can you love a woman who is so cheap? How can you risk your good name to be with a woman who does not know the meaning of fidelity?* Then yet another poem came to his mind.

> *"Fidelity in women is like the flower's scent. If a beautiful flower is without a scent,*
> *It is attractive while it is fresh.*
> *You won't want it when it wilts, while you keep the wilted flower with a scent.*
> *The wilted flower will be used to make perfume if it has a scent.*
> *Then you use it wherever you want.*
> *The perfume will spread the air*
>   *which will remind you of the flower with a scent.*[13]

Roodabeh is beautiful but she still remains an infidel. Like a beautiful flower with thistles. His thoughts changed again as he told himself, *oh yes, she is beautiful and an infidel, but to whom is she an infidel? To her husband or to me is she an infidel? She loves me, I can tell. She is not loyal to her husband who is away all the time! Can we blame a woman who wants a companion? But why is she married if she is not happy? Why should she live with a man who does not make her happy?*

And with this, the voices of his sisters came to his mind.

"I was not happy but what could I do?" he could hear one sister telling him.

"I got a divorce, see what I had to pay? Because I was a woman, what could I say?" he heard another sister telling him from somewhere far away.

He knew if Islam was hard to follow for men, it was worse for women. They did not care to drink, or play tar, or music. All they wanted was a loyal husband to be their own and not to share with anyone else. And if they were not happy in their marriage they had no choice but to stay. Then he saw the light in the sky and he found that the night had gone, and that it had brought the day. He washed his hands and face then got ready to pray.

He could not help but to wish to be with Roodabeh in his prayer. That day was as tough and hot as yesterday. He was there to register and give birth certificates to the villagers. It was the beginning of modernization, but this was hard to tell the villagers. Babak and his assistants went through dirt alleys and raw brick houses. They saw the babies, old men, and ladies. But there was no sign of young men. They all knew the reason. The country needed law and order, military and armed forces. Reza Shah was doing this by drafting the young men in three forces. The illiterate villagers were listening to their clerics and were scared and thought that their young men would be killed. The military was what villagers dreaded.

They searched but could not find the missing men. Regardless of obvious lies they started to issue the villagers birth certificates. Babak asked all his friends to issue what fit. They registered all the villagers, from old men and babies to ladies, with the last names listed as "Liars." He was mean and he was mad. He did not sleep again that night. Love was scorching him from within. The villagers' illiteracies and stupidities made him feel even worse. The assignment was done in a few days, and they all went back home to rest. And now, back at home, he still did not know what he must do.

His mind was in constant battle with his heart and he continually wondered which way to go. He was tired and exhausted so as soon as he got home he fell into a deep sleep for a few hours.

When he woke up he felt worse than ever. Now that he was back home, he felt his love so close by. His heart started to beat very hard when it began to get dark. There was a strong urge pushing him hard to go on the roof and play his tar. Fortunately right then a friend stopped by and asked him to go play cards. He went with his friend trying to avoid the insistent command of his heart. They played till dawn despite his desperate desire to sleep and contemplate his forbidden love. The play continued all that Friday and when it was midnight every one was tired. When he got home, his bed was spread on the roof ready for him to retire. His sleep was deep after all those nights of sleeplessness.

His dreams that night were ardent and beautiful. He was in an orchard. Trees were in full bloom. The roses were loaded with pink, white, and red blossoms, and there she was, Roodabeh in the most beautiful white dress, dancing for him. There was nobody in sight except him and Roodabeh. Flowers were everywhere, and beautiful singing birds. He thought he was in heaven but then he felt a warmness on his skin and opened his eyes.

The sun was out and the streaming of its rays had warmed his face. He got up and went downstairs. His breakfast was ready so he took a few bites and drank a cup of tea, then got ready to go to work. Although he was as handsome as ever and seemed calm, inside he was a wreck. He could not get rid of the opposing feelings he had for the delectably beautiful girl he was in love with.

The moments of that day felt like a year to him. He did not know why he felt so reckless and why things were so slow to him. But that lazy day passed too like any other day and he went home as disturbed as ever. After dinner and drinking a glass of wine he could no longer avoid going to the roof to play his tar. He started playing one of the Persian sad songs and then sang quietly to himself.

> *Oh god the evening in darkness dankly descends.*
> *And no doctor, nor nurse to help is present.*
> *Every time night comes my pain increases*
> *This burning love I hold, transcends, releases*
> *Faster and more wild than ever is my fever*
> *This night more than any other, pain delivers.*[14]

All of the sudden he heard a voice, her voice, singing the same song as he heard the first time she sang. But the voice was not from down the back room but closer than he could imagine.

He started trembling, like a tree. His young face became pale and could see, on the roof under the stars he could not believe his eyes.

Roodabeh stood there beautiful and lovely.

He wanted to tell her all about his lonely nights, his wandering mind. He wanted to share with her his thought and his internal fights. But he remembered his God and told himself this is a forbidden love.

If I become weak I will be disgraced. He did not want to be weak or despicable. He told himself this. Then stood up and covered his crippling feelings.

She said, "Hello, handsome man of my adoration. You are well, without any pain, I hope. Without you the world had no peace. There was no climate in the orchard of life… I was miserable and alone; did not know where you were and what you had done."

"Hello, lady. I do not think it is right to be here so late at night. You are a married woman and at a single man's house. What do you think? What people will say if they find out?"

She told him, "Here under this sky; there is nobody but you and I!

Are you afraid that the stars will tell our stories?

Or that this beautiful breeze will take our secret and spread it all over the city?

Darling the stars are not spies,

And the breeze does not know how to give failing reports,

In the silence of the night there are no clergies and no courts.

There are no prisons nor any guards.

Do not scare me about people's talk.

A man who is not brave in his ways,

He will be far from enjoying any of his days.

You are red fire, where is your heat?

You look like fresh running water, why are you still?

You are young, where is your youth?

Nothing is lovelier than a smile spreading your lips.

Frowning does not become your face.

And why are you frowning? Am I not your love?

Maybe you are upset that I came.

Or is it possible that you found someone better than I?

Found someone whose kisses are hotter than mine."

He was apprehensive; he knew of the consequences. He felt like he was at the edge of a cliff, and closed his eyes, afraid to fall from the edge of his faith. He answered her in an angry and trembling voice, "Oh you felicitous copy of fairy, I know not if you are human or pixie, it is an understatement to say you are equal in beauty to jasmine and lilies.

I have not found anyone, and I need you as much as plants need rain, but I have to leave this relationship; there is nothing to gain!

The consequence of our relationship is death or severe pain,

You can not be mine as you are a married woman.

I realize this with immeasurable pain.

Go now and let me wallow in my tortuous agony.

I do not want to commit a sin.

Don't you know how God punishes sinners in hell?

He punishes eminently with severe malady."

Roodabeh gazed at his face, fixated on his lips, as he talked of these things, looked at him like an artist admiring a finely sculpted face.

She felt her heart like a bird in its cage,
Flapping its wings and wanting to rise.
So she pushed back on her chest, where lived her heart,
To prevent the rise of this bird tearing her apart.
She sat down, looked at the stars,
Like dew around narcissus, tears gathered in her eyes,

And told him, "Although I can not have you, I cannot have any comfort without you. If my love is a sin to you, then why are you so kind? Damn you!

Do not speak so much ill of our love,
And do not abstain from this liaison.

You say that I am a married woman, but this statement is false; how can I be married if I do not have a man?

Do not scare me with God's punishments; he already punished me when he made me a woman.

You call our love a sin but you refuse to see my marriage as a sin.
I was nine when I was sold, this story should be illuminated; told.
In other parts of the world, this is not acceptable,
and seems unnecessarily cold.
He bought me from my father in the form of marriage of course,
Then without asking me, took me as his spouse,
And all these years I have been a prisoner in a palace-like house,
All Moslem women are in prison of course,
But at least some have love and a warm loving domain,
While he is away for month and months,
I live in his foreign terrain.
He is busy seeing foreign lands, bringing money, things for the house,
But he is not lonely, as I am, he has slaves and temporary wives.
And he is not committing sins although he has me as his wife!
I was content with the circumstances since that was my life.
I learned music and how to sing. I read books and learned to be alive,
Then I heard your tar, and you bending down to see me,
I saw a man who was kind and polite with a face of divinity.
Your beauty and your cordiality,
with your enchanting tar combined,
Were enough to kill any existing faith of mine.

And without intention, I fell deeply in love for the very first time.
You came into my world with all the good things one can have.
Smelling sweetly, I lost myself in your handsome chiseled face
Telling me sweet poems; here with your voice exists no disgrace.
I thought you knew who I was.
What you did and said then drowned me in a sea,
This sea I called love but now for all its tumult and logic
I can no longer see."

He heard all this and saw her tears. His heart melted and kneeled down in front of her. His ardor had grown stronger, and wisdom told him again, *either choose me or her.*

The fight between love and wisdom arose over her.
Finally it was his wisdom that was defeated.
And love stayed as his wisdom fled.
But before it was gone said, *Go and have her.*
I hope God will give you mercy and take you away from her.
I hope he keeps you safe from the harm that will surely be caused by her.
But he was not listening to his mind any longer.

He put his hand on her black hair and stroked it as his thumb erased the traces of her tears from her face. She smiled and said "Are you ready for sin?"

He answered chidingly. "According to you this is not a sin."

And like a drunk groping for water in the middle of the night, she leaned into him. When she put her lips on his and started to kiss, it was not a mere kiss but a burning fire. Unconscious of their surroundings, they fell into each other's arms. Their consummation was more magical than either had even dreamed possible. And then, like a drunk, he felt weak and fell into a deep sleep. When he opened his eyes, it was sunrise. And with the warmth of the sun on his face, he felt his heart expand and grow full.

Feeling ethereal, Babak experienced a new dawning in his heart. He felt blessed and light, everything was beautiful in his eyes. When he looked around, he found himself alone, she was no longer in his arms.

But the aroma of her perfume lingered and told him she had not been gone long. *So it wasn't a dream,* he whispered softly. He did not want to leave his bed having last seen her there, instead, he laid quietly, relishing the memory of her.

But it was time to get up and do ordinary chores of the day. He got up and went to work, and happily, today, nothing felt like work. Nothing bothered him on this day. His joy was contagious. He told jokes and worked hard all day. But he could not wait until the day was over.

Finally, the day passed and as it left, it brought the night behind it. The story repeated that night and then soon, every night.

Darkness Descends

These nights, she did not appear on his roof. Instead, he would go and sleep on her roof. They had a sign. He would throw gravel to her roof. If there was nobody around she would rise and he could see her. Then he would jump to her roof. Most of the time she was alone and they would spend time together, taking pleasure in each other's company.

Conversing and sipping their wine, they both felt like they were in heaven with each other, and could not imagine life without one other. He would tell her:

> *The fire of your love can not touch another's as long as mine exists*
> *And why would you leave a candle in the mosque when at home it would be missed?*
> *To the moon of your face I swear to you even in your lack of faith*
> *That anything oppressive or unfaithfulness you deliver, in my heart still feels like faith.*[15]

He was madly in love and could not see anything but her. He forgot about the fear of God and the guilt of committing this sin. Instead they found heaven in each other. The summer passed and with the arrival of winter he was forced to go to her house not from the roof but by her door.

Then years passed and gradually people started to notice. Whispers about the sin they were committing spread. But they did not notice or hear the whispers of people nor the danger that was growing close. The constant absence of Roodabeh's husband afforded them more than enough time to enjoy their forbidden love. As spring drew to a close and the weather grew hot people once again started to think about sleeping on their roofs. This was greatly welcomed by Roodabeh and Babak.

It was a beautiful spring. Roses were blooming in abundance. They felt happier than ever. The fever of spring was in their veins and the bliss of love in their hearts. Without knowledge of their future, they were living a sinful but joyful life. Until that dark night that took all the joy from their lives.

On this fateful night, as had become their code, he threw gravel towards her roof, but did not see anyone. So he started his dinner then played his tar but did not hear any song from his love. So he started to drink a glass of wine. The lack of response made him nervous so he drank more wine to calm himself down a little. Soon he was almost drunk and became very eager to see his lover. He threw more gravel to the neighbor's roof, and when he did not hear Roodabeh's voice he went ahead and looked on the roof. Somebody was lying down where Roodabeh usually slept. He threw a small gravel to that bed. And what he saw was like a tornado on his life. He felt stunned, like getting hit by a bolt of lightning. The person in the bed got up and looked at him like he was a mad cow. This was not his lover but instead a strong man looking at him as though he wanted to kill him. He sat down right away and crawled down the stairs.

His heart was pumping hard blood and all the hair on his body stood up straight. He was shaken and did not know what to do. He could see the trouble and shame ahead of him. It was going to be all over the town that he had made love to a woman that was not his own. He felt guilty and scared. He did not know what to do and which way to escape. He was very worried; what had he done? What would happen to his lover? How to protect her from harm? These questions came to his mind but he did not have any answer other than to tell himself that he must be over-reacting. *Maybe*, he comforted himself, *maybe Tajer does not know why I threw the gravel. Maybe he just thinks I was a kid playing a joke. Maybe she can make him calm, tell him that it was nothing to be worried about or to be concerned with.*

But the night was hot and his thoughts were bothersome. He could imagine people whispering about him on the streets, telling each other that he was a bad person, that he was someone who commits adultery.

Meanwhile, in Roodabeh's house there was a big fight. Tajer was not only angry, he was furious with his wife. He had been suspicious for some time. He had heard the rumor that his wife was in love with the young man next door with the green eyes.

He would not have believed the rumor if he had not seen the changes in his young wife. When she had been married to him at the age of nine, she had been scared to come to his house, and over the years had usually not ever given much of a damn about his moods. Rather than care for him, she would instead seem withdrawn and sad all the time. But now all of the sudden she became alive. She became happy and vibrant; she also became pleasant and calm. The more he complained the less she was upset. With this calm and mature behavior anyone would be pleased, as he was only home a few days a month. If this suspicion had not been eating his brain, he could have lived in peace. But it was strong and pestering.

The rumors in town grew stronger in the spring when he came back from his next trip. They told him details and as a result, one night he prevented his wife from sleeping on the roof. Instead, he slept in her bed and before long sure enough, he saw the neighbor's head, peeking over the edge expectantly. When he saw this, he quickly went down to his wife's bed and started to pull her out of her bed by the hair. She had been asleep and could not believe her husband was behaving in such a wild way. He started to scream and kick her, acting like a madman. Terrified, she found her veil and managed to run away. Alone in the street she decided it was time to end her marriage. As she traversed the narrow streets alone, she could not stop crying. She knew the situation. He would kill her if he could. She fled towards the safety of her sister's house.

Her husband, infuriated, began to curse. He was missing the last dynasty. If it were that time, then he would have been allowed to kill them both without shame. But the green-eyed man was one of the government's agents. If he killed his wife's lover, he would be surely punished by death. Although he was still allowed to kill his wife, she had unfortunately managed to escape him. If only he had killed her that night! He was sorry he had not done this at once. When he could not find her anywhere in his house he became worried that she had gone to the neighbor's house! He could not sleep all night. When he woke, he sent the maid to her sister's house, and realized she was there.

He went to his sister-in-law's to ask Roodabeh to come back to his house. But Roodabeh refused. She knew if she went she would be killed without a doubt. Since he could not kill her, he decided on divorce. The divorce took only a few minutes and then he was free, since for a man it was easy to divorce his wife. Roodabeh, now age twenty-four, became ecstatic. She had been so scared that night. Her body was still aching from his kicks, her head still hurting from him pulling her hair. But now she could see no obstacle to a happy life with her beloved Babak. She had to let him know what was happening and ask him to set up the date for their wedding. She wanted to find her matchmaker Soghra Khanoom to send a message to Babak but decided to wait a few days until the rumors died down.

Separation and Pain

When Babak woke, it was light outside. He got up and as usual went to do his prayer. He did not know what to say. He asked his God to forgive him and asked Him to keep his lover safe. He did not have an appetite so instead he drank a cup of tea, which was all the breakfast he could handle. The day was hot and hard to work in. His mind was so scattered that he could not get much done. Was it his paranoia or were people looking at him strangely? A coworker asked him what was wrong. He answered curtly that he was simply a little tired.

He could not bear not knowing what had happened. But he was so ashamed of his part in it that he was scared to ask anyone to get the news. A few days had passed and he was worse than on day one. Finally he asked Hossein to see what news he could find. When he came back, Hossein told him that a few nights ago there had been a fight at the neighbor's house and that his wife had fled. He was happy that she was safe but wondered why she did not let him know where she had fled to.

After a few more days, which were even longer and harder, he could not bear life without news from his beloved. While he was worrying about her he got more bad news from Pasargad. His sister was dead and he had to go to her funeral.

His time in Pasargad was full of pain as he found himself remembering his sister's face. Her beautiful eyes were fixed in his mind. He could not believe that she was dead; she was far too young to have already passed so soon. Already exhausted when he got there, when he saw his mother's sadness, the pain and exhaustion overwhelmed him. He was in deep mourning, and as he held her children he felt his heart break. His sister had been so kind, so close to him that he could not bear the loss of her. He stayed there for a month, and when he finally headed back he was mournful and grief-stricken.

His brother Afshin had been living in Pasargad but got a job in Kazeroon. So he took his pregnant wife and traveled back to Kazeroon with his brother. Babak had so much on his mind — he had lost his sister and was still worried sick about his beautiful Roodabeh. But when he got back he decided to move from his house so that he could have room for his brother and his sister-in-law. Besides there were so many memories of his time with Roodabeh there that it was best to change his surroundings, he thought.

But neither the new house nor his brother being close gave him any comfort. He could not erase the memory of all those nights with Roodabeh and the bothersome way she had vanished. But he did not want to ask anyone about her so as not to disgrace her name. In small towns where everyone knew each other, a single man's inquiry about a married woman was enough to start a rumor. Regardless of if it was true or false, it would be enough to ruin and disgrace her. So instead he filled his days with work and his nights with playing cards and drinking wine. Sometimes he would play his tar and only sad songs would emerge:

> *In this moment that I feel the sadness of my separation from you*
> *I feel entering my mind the memory and feeling of you.*
> *And entering further that specific night when with me you sat,*
> *And said how without me, that you cared nothing for the world*
> *Now this separation is sitting between us*
> *The link of our hearts has been broken between us*
> *Slave to my pain*
> *Do not try to tell my heart anything of faith*
> *Belief, I do not have.*[16]

Roodabeh waited a few days and then sent Soghra to his house. But she came back and told her, "There is the wet bed, but the baby is not there."

"What do you mean?" she asked, terrified.

"Well, he has gone to Pasargad and nobody knows for how long!" the matchmaker replied.

Roodabeh did not say anything, but she was disappointed. Why had he left her alone in this town? Didn't he realize that it was his love that had gotten her beaten and then divorced? Was it possible that his love was not really love but lust? In her sister's house she could not last long since now that she was a divorced woman she was severely looked down upon. Her name was infused with rumors, and stories that she was unfaithful. Her family felt deeply ashamed and looked at her the same way. It was not just loneliness she had to bear but also all the whispering about her disgrace. Four months had passed since her divorce; she celebrated her freedom with little remorse. But her family was putting pressure on her to get married for the sake of her family's good name.

Her ex-husband was spreading the story of her unfaithfulness and he told as many as he could that he would have killed her but that he preferred to divorce her. Her family was trying to deny this. If she remarried quickly their word would seem true against his. This rumor made the men in town tell tales about her beauty and some regarded her quite lustfully. There were several men who proposed. This fact made her family put more pressure upon her. Roodabeh did not want to start another loveless marriage. She had experienced the most wonderful time in love and wanted the joy and passion she had had with Babak.

So she found her matchmaker again and sent her to see if Babak was back. Soghra went and when she discovered that he moved, found the new address and went there to see him. But when she did, Battol, Babak's sister-in-law, answered the door. Without hesitation Soghra thought she was his wife. The news had a devastating effect on Roodabeh. She was jealous and terribly upset. *All men are the same*, she thought.

Under pressure she agreed to get some information about the men who wanted to marry her. To her surprise all of them were married and she would be their second or third wife. *If I have to have rival wives then why would I not get married to the one I love?* she thought to herself. *I have to find him again and be with him. He probably married because his family wanted him to, just like I had to marry Tajer, and now am being forced to marry one of these men with other wives.* So she asked Soghra to find Babak alone and ask him to propose.

One day, as Babak was walking out of his office, he heard a lady say, "Hello, sir." As he recognized Soghra's voice, he felt his heart lurch. Soghra was his connection to his lover and he was as excited to hear her voice as if he had heard his lover speak herself.

"Hello, Soghra Khanoom! It has been a long time since we last spoke." He greeted her with a warm smile.

"Yes sir, I came to your house but you were away to Pasargad," she replied.

Babak said, "Oh yes my sister passed away and I had to leave in a hurry."

"I am so sorry, why did she die? From natural causes I hope," Soghra replied sympathetically.

Babak looked around, he did not want people to see him with a woman in the streets. It was late afternoon and he knew nobody was in the office since he had been the last to leave. He turned around. "Follow me into the office. I would like very much to talk to you in private. My office is empty and we can talk there." In the office he said, "How is Roodabeh? I am very worried about her."

Soghra explained that she was divorced but fine.

He explained all the time he had spent worrying and spoke of his sadness in the absence of her presence. "I am nothing without her."

Soghra smiled. " She feels the same but she needs to be sure that you really love her. Now that she is divorced you can marry her and have her forever."

Babak smiled, he felt a light in his chest. After all these days he felt he was alive. "Oh my god, I would love to marry her. Tell her I am ready and anxious," Babak said.

Then Soghra said, "Somebody has said that you have a woman in your house and Roodabeh thinks that she is your wife."

"Oh no, that is my sister-in-law. I do not want to marry multiple wives." Babak explained.

He generously tipped Soghra two toman (one-tenth of his monthly salary), and she hurried back to Roodabeh and told her that she had seen Babak and that he was still in love. "He said he would love to marry you and said he's been sick and tired from not hearing from you. He is single and I was wrong. She is his sister-in-law; his brother is staying with him for a while. He was away for his sister who had recently passed away."

Roodabeh was happy to hear all this. Especially since she was under so much pressure to marry a man named Golam. He was a friend of her family's and already had two wives. He was rich and did not seem to mind the nasty rumors her ex-husband spread, that Roodabeh was a cheater and that this was the reason for their separation. She could not understand this man with two wives—why should he want to marry a cheater as his third wife? She knew if there were no suitor then she would not be put under such pressure.

After a long pause she told Soghra, "Go find Babak and ask him to send his sister-in-law to our house to propose. I need to get married as fast as possible."

Soghra told her "But I do not think he can. With his sister dead you need to be patient.'

Roodabeh told her, "But I don't have time! They are pushing me to marry soon to absolve them of the rumors instead of living in constant shame."

"But my dear lady, you know to get the best fruits you need to wait. Every one can pick up fruits which are not ripe but to have a ripe sweet fruit you need to wait until it is time. You are well aware that there is no comparison between Babak and Golam!" Soghra explained.

Roodabeh replied curtly, "If he loves me then there is a way."

Soghra went and found Babak the next morning.

"Dear master, Roodabeh is impatient. She wants you to marry her this month and you have to send your family to her family so she knows that you are serious."

"I love Roodabeh, but I can not obey her demand. My sister just died and we can not break the custom. Traditionally we have to wait a year after somebody dies for anything like a marriage, especially if she was young and dear. My mother has been waiting to see my wedding for a long time, but if I get married now she will not be here. Beside why is she in such a hurry? I love her and soon enough there will be time to cherish each other for the rest of our lives."

"Well," Soghra explained, "she is under pressure to remarry again. They are ashamed of her divorce, they do not want her be single anymore."

"Is she living for herself or for that family of hers?"

"Well sir, unfortunately families are important. You love her and are lonely and hurting but still you do not want to marry her for the death of your sister," Soghra said.

He paused and then said, "Yes, you are right but what can be done? I can not marry at this time and honestly if there is a rumor in this town that we were lovers and that was the reason for her divorce, I do not think jumping into marriage is good since it will stress that the rumors are true. In a few months people will forget all these rumors and I will be set. To tell the truth, even if my sister were not dead, I would not marry her when there are so many rumors spread. I will marry her in a few months, though—that is my condition." His argument was valid and Soghra could not say any more than what she had already said.

When she took the news to Roodabeh, she was upset. She could not understand his logic. She did not believe the story that his sister was dead. She believed instead that he did not want to marry her and that this was an excuse to avoid the commitment. She got so mad that she decided to take a trip. She got a ticket on the caravan to get away from town. The news got to Babak, and he took this as a sign to find a way back into her heart. He bought a ticket to the same caravan. When she found out that Babak was going, she canceled her ticket and her trip entirely. Living with an abusive man all her life, she could not comprehend true love. She had cheated on her husband and loved this man, but she could not trust even the man she loved. She did not believe what he said or the deepness of his love.

But Babak had other problems in his life to deal with. After Roodabeh canceled her trip and refused to talk to him, his sister-in-law went through a hard labor which took several days. This reminded him of the painful memory of his sister's death. Whenever childbirth was not natural, there was the danger of death for both mother and the child, like what had happened to Shiva. He was busy trying to help the doctors, and did what he could do to help his family. When his nephew was finally born he heard the news that his stepfather had just died and his mother and his three brothers were left alone. He had to go back to Pasargad to arrange for their move to Kazeroon, since they did not have anybody else to care for them. He knew that if he did not do something, his mother would be lost without his help.

Golam's House

For Roodabeh his absence was proof that he was lying and that he did not care about her. Meanwhile, pressure from her family increased and finally she gave up. She could not live forever in somebody else's house. There was no means of working or earning money for women at that time. Even with all the troubles in her marriage, she still had had enough to eat and wear when she was married. She had her own house and some freedom to do what she liked in it. But now she was the black sheep of the family. She was considered a disgrace to them, and no one had any sympathy for her situation. All they wanted to do was to wash this dark spot from their hands.

A few years before, this kind of accusation could have been punished by a severe death penalty by the close relatives of the accused as an honor killing. Roodabeh's family did not kill her, but could not help but show their disappointment in her actions. They tried to believe that she really did not have an affair, but that she was only accused of a crime she did not commit. To end all the gossip, they believed that the best action for her was to remarry as soon as it was possible.

Finally she agreed to marry Golam the merchant, her family's friend, who had two other wives. She did not care about marriage or love anymore, as much as she cared about her survival. She chose Golam since she knew would be an absent husband. Merchants often had to travel to far away lands and each of their trips would take months or sometime years. Another factor which was attractive about Golam was his wealth. Again most merchants were very wealthy and it was an honor to be married to such a rich person. This was the main reason Roodabeh's family wanted her to marry Golam. Her marriage ceremony was simple and when she finally arrived at her new husband's house she was greeted by three women. One of them was her new sister-in-law and the other two were her rival wives. Roodabeh had seen her sister-in-law before and during her marriage ceremony.

But she was surprised to see her rival wives welcoming her. They were very warm and friendly. She had no way of knowing the friendship they would soon develop.

The first few days she spent with her new husband. She asked him why he remarried so many times? His answer was simple. "I did not see my brides in person and then I did not like what I saw after I married them." So he married a second and then a third wife. Roodabeh did not know if she was what her husband was looking for or not but she did not care that much. She did not have any feeling or passion for him whatsoever. Soon life was dull again just like it had been before she met Babak, except now she felt such vivid pain when she remembered him.

> *Oh my god how beautiful were those green eyes of his,*
> *How sweet were those lips of his,*
> *Those long white fingers were making such magic on that tar of his,*
> *How can I survive without the burning love of his.*[17]

She would think about him and cry whenever she was alone. When her husband left for his long trips she felt relieved and thought, *I can cry more now without being scared of him ever finding out my deep sadness and depression.* The ladies in the house were trying so hard to please her, but this was still a mystery to her. Why did her two rival wives try so hard? A few days after her husband left she was alone in her room, so she grabbed her harp and started to play and sing one of Molavi's poems.

> *I wish to see the rose garden so, let me see your face,*
> *I wish to taste sugar so, please open your lips,*
> *I heard from the air the song of your drums again,*
> *I wish to see my kings forearms, so I came back again,*
> *Told me "go and don't hurt me any more" with your love-airs.*
> *I wish to hear "don't hurt me any more" with your love-airs again,*
> *Oh pleasant wind which is coming from the pasture of love,*
> *I wish to hear good news from the basil so please come to me,*
> *God knows that without you the city for me will be like a jail.*
> *I wish to be vagrant in the mountains or deserts,*
> *I am depressed from all these complaining people,*
> *I wish to see those tumults: and the drunken roars again.*
> *On the one hand a glass of wine, in other hand the hair of my love.*
> *I wish to see your beautiful dance again.*

*Yesterday a wise man was searching the city, with the lamp and said,
I wish to see a human being since I am fed up with these demons
and beasts.
I told him I searched and did not find one.
He replied, I wish to find what is scarce,
Although I sing better than nightingales,
I have a seal on my lips because of people's jealousy,
I wish to scream again.
He is hidden from everyone's eyes, but all eyes are his,
I wish to see that obvious art that is hidden from all those eyes
        but his again.*[18]

Tears ran down her face as she remembered the times she would sing to the music of Babak's tar, but when she looked up she was startled to see three pairs of eyes staring at her in awe. The door to her room was open and her sister-in-law and her rival wives stood at the door, peering in at her. She quickly tried to wipe her tears away from her face. Her heart was pumping very hard and her face lost all its color from fear. But she saw smiles and friendly admiration in their eyes, which calmed her down. Then she heard the voice of one of her co-wives.

"Oh you sing so magnificently." Then the other one said, "Indeed, you also play the harp wonderfully and beautifully as well."

"Why did you stop?" her sister-in-law asked, as she pretended to not see her tears. Roodabeh had doubts about these friendly faces. She did not know them and as a result did not trust them either. But she tried to overcome her doubts and said, "Please, come in, why are you all standing by the door?"

The women came in and one said, "We did not want to disturb you, only we heard that enchanting voice of yours and came to hear it a little better."

"Thanks." She tried to smile but it was so hard.

"Please continue singing," another woman said.

"Oh no", she replied. "I can't possibly."

"Why not?" her sister-in-law asked her. Roodabeh's eyes filled with tears; oh it was so hard to pretend to be happy. She thought she could be alone and cry as her heart desired, but now she felt that she did not even have that right.

"Oh, do not hide your feelings; we are your friends," her sister-in-law told her.

"Yes, we know how you are feeling and are here to help," said another lady. Roodabeh was speechless and did not know what to do. After so many days and nights of suppressing her sad feelings she could not hold her tears any more. Tears poured from her face but she told herself not to be fooled; how could they understand her feelings when her own mother and sister did not even want to know?

"Oh, being in love is so hard," said her sister-in-law. She felt a shock jolt her spine and her inner fear came back. *They are here to get me! But no matter how unhappy I am I should not let another disgrace attack me. I went through so much and now I have to tolerate these women's sarcastic remarks too?* she asked herself.

"Yes I know because I was there," continued her sister-in-law with a loud laugh.

"You were?" Roodabeh asked.

"Yes dear, we all were there or are there, you are not alone."

Nasrin, the second wife, laughed bitterly, "Look at us; we are in our prime. We need men but we are alone! Where are our husbands? Who are they sleeping with? We do not know. What we do know is that they are free to be with any woman their hearts desire. How many days and nights can we sit at home and wonder what to do next? We the merchant's wives are not ordinary women you know!" She said it sarcastically.

Roodabeh looked at them suspiciously, "So, you all have lovers?"

"Yes, we do," giggled the sister-in-law, Zahra. "Nasrin and I do."

Kobra, the eldest woman said, "Nobody likes me since I am not as pretty as they are, so I help them and through this feel that I am getting my revenge!"

"But who knows how you look under a veil," asked Roodabeh.

"Oh honey, you can fool men with your *hejab* for marriage, but they want to see you before they become your lover believe me! You can't tell me your green-eyed lover did not see you before he fell in love with you," Kobra continued.

Roodabeh ignored her remarks. "You said you are getting your revenge! But tell me, on who?"

"Of course, our husbands! I was so much in love with him when I married him but the first night I was here, he looked at me and said, 'They told me you were not good looking, but I did not know you were so ugly.' He has always been very mean to me. He used to constantly pressure me to get more money from my father for him. Then after my father died and I inherited a large amount of money, he used it to become a very rich merchant. This is when he married Nasrin. At first I was jealous and hated her. But soon I found out that she is also miserable like I was. Now by helping her to have fun with her lover, I feel better, that is my revenge."

"But he does not know – if he is not aware of it how can it be bothersome to him?" Roodabeh asked curiously.

"Oh he knows, but he does not have any proof. We make sure that nobody except us and our lovers and our matchmakers know about our affairs," Nasrin said.

"How does he know then?"

"Well, Nasrin is refusing him since she found her lover. He could not see the reason for some time, then he figured it out but he told me that he does not want to make her happy by divorcing her so he married you," Zahra answered.

"How about your husband?" Roodabeh asked Zahra.

"He works for my brother, who forced me to marry him since he is his best and most trusted friend. I did not want him from the beginning, but when I finally found my lover, I decided it was okay."

Up to that day Roodabeh thought she was the only cheater in this world, but now that she saw that she was not alone, could she really believe it? She was still not sure. But she knew that being in this house was not as bad as she had imagined it would be. *It is even better than my sister's house*, she told herself.

In the days that followed she found out that everything she had heard was true. Maybe the women in that house wanted to add her to their camp more than anything else. The only one in their gathering who did not seem interested in any wrong-doing was Kobra, who kept quiet for her revenge and for the sake of her friendship with the other women. She also was kind and smart. She was not fussy about her appearance, convinced since her childhood that she was ugly. She had a small figure, and was thin and short with straight black hair. Her face was full of brown spots, some quite large. She never used any makeup on her tiny face. So as the days passed, Roodabeh's friendship with the three women grew stronger each day. And every day they gathered around her wanting her to play her harp and sing.

Do not ask how am I feeling away from my beautiful idol.
Do not ask me what happened to his love for me,
From the earth to sky see the light of his face,
Do not ask me how tall was he or how was his face.
Please see the jewel of my tears from separation of my love
Do not ask about the purity and waves of that sea,
Do not put your foot in my blood of sadness,
Do not ask me about melancholy or bleariness,
You see the sadness of my heart do not say anything
Do not ask about that jovial, disturbed love of mine.[19]

When Babak got to Pasargad, he found his three brothers, eight, six, and four, were all alone with his mother.

His mother was relatively calm but penniless. Babak suggested that they move to Kazeroon with him. She accepted without any argument. As they travelled back, his thoughts drifted to his love. *Oh my God, I have a big family to support now. Will she be okay with this?* he wondered. But he was unaware of the vicissitudes of time and Roodabeh's new marriage. His mother was with him and he thought, as soon as he got to Kazeroon, he would tell her how much he was in love. With two dead in the family it was hard to talk about a marriage. But he could not lose his chances with the woman he loved. While riding on the hot desert he repeated the poems he read from Molavi:

Snatch that beautiful idol's eyes, hair, and her face.
First my rest, second my tolerance, and third my concerns,
My resolution and my tolerance and concern
were stolen by three things
One was her beauty, second her countenance and third her features
Beauty and countenance and her features into the world spread out
Causing first trouble then nuisance and finally great revolt
This trouble and nuisance and riot of mine are from our separation.
The first is constant, the second unlimited and the third is everywhere
Constant, unlimited and everywhere to her love I have succumbed
First strange, second in love and finally disgraced
I became strange, fell in love and became disgraced,

First screaming then wailing and third great melancholy
My groaning, moaning, and disturbances are from the fact that she is first pretty, second agile, and third delicate.[20]

His thoughts were interrupted by the noises around him; it was dark and they were going to rest for the night.

"Is it safe to sleep in this desert?" his mother asked.

"Yes," Babak replied proudly. "It had not been possible before Reza Shah. These roads have always been full of robbers that were waiting for prey but now nobody dares to bother anyone. There are police stations everywhere and they protect passengers like us." Babak was right. Some called Reza Shah a dictator, but he brought calm and security to the country. The country had finally started to show some progress after almost two centuries of idleness and backwardness. He had shut down the small tribal authorities and made a strong central government, which was the dream of all intellectuals at the time. Furthermore, he ended the unwritten caste that only privileged children could get governmental jobs. Now, anyone with some literacy was able to get a job with the government and although the top-ranking jobs were still reserved for the previous privileged princes and clerics' sons because of their higher education and influences, normal people, Babak amongst them, were able to acquire a job with the government and a chance to succeed with ability, rather than through a relative's influence. Also, the introduction of modern schools in every town made it possible for all children, rich or poor, to be literate.

But all of this progress was not embraced by everyone. As the head of a constitutional monarchy, Reza Shah had a lot of power, but he still could not implement the changes he foresaw for the country acknowledging the other divisions. Since the powerful landlords and clerics did not see it to be within their best interests to join hands with him, he had to force his reform on them, which made him seem like a dictator in some people's eyes and a hero to others. But to Babak he remained a hero.

They spread their hand-woven carpets on the desert and their mattresses and blankets on top of them. Everyone soon fell asleep except Babak, whose mind was still distracted. The night was clear and cool. The sky was deep blue with thousands of stars like a sea full of shiny flowers. He looked around him at everyone deep in their sleep. But his heart was uneasy, and for him, sleep was nowhere within reach.

His thoughts floated back to the poems that lived in his heart and he started to recite them:

> *You are not in love, so it is alright for you to sleep.*
> *Since her love and the feeling of sadness is mine.*
> *So it is alright for you to sleep*
> *I am torn apart from the sunshine of her love*
> *For you who do not have this lust in your heart.*
> *It is alright to sleep.*
> *I am like water wandering around to find her union*
> *You do not have that worry, and do not want to know where she is so you can sleep*
> *I am falling in love and do not know what it is going to do to me*
> *You are free of all the sadness of love*
> *So you can sleep.*
> *I am deprived of my talents and my mind*
> *You have your talent and your mind intact*
> *So you can sleep.*[21]

It was almost light when he finally fell asleep and soon he too awakened to continue the journey. When they reached Kazeroon, they settled into the same house where Afshin, his wife, and their new baby were living, now along with his mother, and his three half-brothers. There was so much to do and even as he had to go back to his office to handle the piles of undone papers, his mind was still with his love. He was worried because he still did not know how to reach her or talk to her. His message to Roodabeh just before his departure had not been answered. So as soon as he got to the city he asked Hossein to find Soghra again and to tell her to come to his office late in the afternoon. His house was too crowded and he would not be able to see Soghra without explaining who she was and what she wanted.

He began to stay late every day in the hope of hearing some news from Soghra. Without knowing why, he was depressed and disturbed. It had been seven months since that dark night when he threw the stones at Roodabeh's bed. And in the last five months he had not been able to see her at all. Meanwhile there was so much happening in his life. Did he sense trouble then? Or were his depressed feelings the result of the recent events of his young sister and stepfather's deaths? He had only recently lost two people whom he had loved dearly. He thought of his stepfather who was like a father to him. Most of his childhood had been spent in his house. He was the one who wanted to send him abroad to study medicine if only his stupid brother-in-law had not interfered! His thoughts danced into his childhood and his stepfather's face reappeared in his mind, smiling. "Oh I miss them both," he whispered. There was a knock on the door and a black veiled woman entered. Her voice shook him again.

"Hello master! I was told to come here late; is it safe to talk now?" He jumped up and answered her greeting warmly.

"Yes of course it is."

The woman took off her black veil from her face and breathed deeply. Her face was smiling and her wrinkled skin shining.

"What can I do for you sir?"

Babak looked at her in disbelief. She should know why he sent for her so why did she ask this? *Oh*, the thought crossed his mind, *she is a messenger and a matchmaker, she needs to be paid for their services.* He took a five toman from his pocket and gave it to her. The old woman accepted it happily and thanked him, saying humbly, "May God grant you a long life to live, sir."

Still no news! She looked at him and repeated her first question again, "What can I do for you sir?" Babak felt dizzy and told himself it is not an issue of money; she has bad news and does not want to share it with me. *Oh my God didn't you punish me enough? What can it be?* He was afraid to ask the question that, he was so eager to know the answer to. There was a heavy silence between them. The old woman wondering why was she there and the young man afraid to ask about his love.

After a long pause he asked, "I was wondering how our friend is. Why did I not get an answer to my message?"

"Oh sir, you were away, and she was forced to remarry again. She got married only two weeks ago to Golam Khan," Soghra answered hesitantly.

He felt dizzy and shocked. "The same Golam Khan who is the richest man in town?" he asked.

"Yes sir, the Golam Khan."

There was another heavy pause. "But I thought he already was married," Babak said, trying to be calm while a flood of pain surged through every cell of his body.

"Yes sir, he has two other wives. He is very rich but stingy. He proposed to Roodabeh's father and brother-in-law himself. All the matchmakers are so mad that they could not benefit from his marriage," she continued, trying to relay to him she did not have any part in the marriage. But Babak was so deeply submerged in his own thoughts and pain that he did not hear anything she said. He remembered the poem from Iraj again and began to recite it:

> *Fidelity in women is like the flower's scent.*
> *If a beautiful flower is with out a scent*
> *It is attractive while it is fresh.*
> *You won't want it when it wilts, while you keep the wilted flower with a scent.*
> *The wilted flower will be used to make perfume if it has a scent.*
> *Then you use it wherever you went.*
> *The perfume will spread the air which will be reminding you*
>   *of the flower with a scent.*[22]

Soghra, who was confused by the poem, asked him, "What are you saying, sir?"

"Oh never mind," Babak answered. "I am thinking that her love for me was a big lie. Her true love is money and prestige. How foolish was I to think that she could love me?"

Soghra shook her head in disbelief and said, "Oh, no sir you can not assume that. She talked to me on numerous occasions and I heard from her how much she loved you. I do not believe that her love was a lie even for a moment"

"Oh really, then how do you explain her recent marriage? While she was married she loved me but just when I was feeling less guilty for loving her and thought there was a chance to have her as my wife she remarried again," he said with an angry voice.

Soghra shook her head as if she were a philosopher talking to an illiterate person and said, "Well sir, with all due respect, you are a man and can not understand the woman's world. We are the property of men. We can not decide for ourselves what we should do. Look at how the society calls us! I was Ali's daughter before my marriage, then I became Taghi's wife and when he died, although my son was only five years old, I became Akbar's mother. See, people never referred to me by my name but my relationship to my male relatives. We are not allowed to argue with our elders. We are supposed to bow and submit to our men. You can not expect any girl or woman to try and oppose a marriage against her father's wish–"

Babak interrupted her and said, "Yes, that is true when she is only twelve years old, but this cannot be the case for a twenty-four-year-old divorced woman like Roodabeh, who is also educated!"

"Oh sir! An old and poor fool like me can be more independent than a rich and educated woman like Roodabeh. I am a matchmaker and make my living so no man can tell me where to go or what am I supposed to do. A female servant in Roodabeh's house also can marry anyone she likes since the money she earns comes from her work, but not for Roodabeh. She can not work as a tailor, a matchmaker, or a servant. So regardless of her education she is not able to work. She is not rich either, her father is and he is the one who pulls all the strings. And aside from her helplessness she did not get any support from you either. You refused to propose to her when she asked you to."

"Yes, but I tried to take a trip with her to tell her how much I loved her. She refused to take her trip or talk to me. Then she goes and marries this man with two other wives just because he is rich? Come on, Soghra Khanoom, she obviously did not care about me or she would have listened to what I was going to say."

"Well, the problem is that when you tried to talk to her, she was angry and then when she calmed down you were away. She could not resist her family's pressure any longer. She called me several times and asked me to talk to you and beg you to go to her father and ask for her hand, but you were away. Her conclusion about your love was the same as yours about her love. So she caved in. She was in a very bad situation. All the rumors and all the accusations had been spread through town. If she did not listen to her father or even hinted about her love she could be killed by her father or brothers. See, you do not put yourself in her shoes, you only can accuse her."

Babak sighed deeply, "Well nothing can be done now. I hope she is happy in her new marriage." He got up, signaling to Soghra that he wanted to end their conversation. While she gathered her *chador* and covered her face she said, "I will let her know of your concerns." She disappeared in the narrow alley and left Babak with his uneasy feelings.

She married two weeks ago; this is right when I felt disturbed and very unhappy, he thought. *Is there a connection in our minds? Is this why was I so troubled even though I did not know anything about her new marriage? Why all these two weeks was I not able to sleep?* Then his mind started to blame him for falling in love with an infidel. Nothing had changed. He was still standing the same place as he stood more than three years ago. He was still in love with a married woman. Only a brief moment of hope had lightened his mind. The hope he shattered by following tradition and worrying about what people would think. He held his head between his palms and with pain remembered Rumi, who said:

> *Go put your head on the pillow and leave me alone*
> *I am ruined, a night-prowler, and addicted, leave me alone*
> *I am awash with a wave of passion. All days and nights alone*
> *You can forgive me, or you can persecute me alone*
> *I am alone with my tears, standing in the corner of sadness*
> *You can make a hundred miles with my tears alone*
> *In the king of beauties one can not find faith*
> *Your skin is yellow with her love.*
> *Be patient, have faith*
> *This pain has no cure but death,*
> *So how can I tell you to cure my pain?* [23]

He was too tired to think any longer, so he got up and walked home calmly even as torment plagued his mind. At home, his brothers needed his attention and the little one, Aria, was there to play with.

Late at night when all the children were asleep he hugged his tar and played, singing quietly to himself:

> *Oh you are ending the relationship, please don't,*
> *By anger you are making me pay too much, please don't,*
> *You are taking away my joy and happiness, please don't,*
> *You are adding pain to my heart. Please don't,*
> *You are giving me a cup full of sadness instead of wine. Please don't,*
> *You are adding blood in the clear running water of mine.*

A New Turn

At Roodabeh's new house she still was missing Babak desperately. She sang with her harp and cried whenever she was alone. Her sister-in-law and her rival wives were eager to hear her love stories. They asked her if Babak was really the beautiful idol they had heard he was. They wanted to know all the details of their love affair and why they became separated.

Roodabeh now knew all their secrets and began to trust them. She told them her inner thoughts, which she had not dared to share with anybody, her deep affection for Babak and her disappointment that he did not love her enough to marry her. "He is just like any other man," she said. "He just wanted to have a good time, that was all."

"But how do you know that?" her sister-in-law, Zahra asked. "Besides, if he had proposed, do you think your family would have let you marry him? I think he was right in the idea that jumping into marriage was not a good one since it would stress that the rumors were true."

Nasrin continued, "Yes, see, we are trapped in these old spider web customs of ours. You see so many books full of beautiful poems, all written by men for their lovers. It is okay for them to spread the word of their love. But if a family hears that their daughter loves a man they kill her, or worse, they force her to marry her first suitor. It is considered a shame for a family to acknowledge that their daughter is in love.

"Also, they look at how much money he has rather than what kind of person he is. If I may be so bold, I would imagine your family would not choose Babak over Golam," Nasrin said.

There was a rush of blood to her face and she replied angrily. "Why, simply because he is younger, more handsome, and single?"

Loud laughter exploded from all three as Nasrin said. "Yes, exactly. He is all that, but he is not rich."

Roodabeh answered, "But he has prestige, a high-salary job…"

Nasrin interrupted her and said, "Oh honey, but they do not measure by these things, they measure only by how big his house is or how much land he has. Even if he does not spend a penny of his money, he is considered rich if he has a house or other properties. And for most families that should be enough to make you happy. If you want my advice just accept your situation and use it the best way you can. Why don't you reconnect with your lover and make yourself happy again? This way everyone will be happy. You and Babak will be happy seeing each other, and also, your family can be happy that you have a rich husband who will provide for you."

Roodabeh couldn't help but feel a tiny sliver of hope, now that her new friends were asking her to pursue her dream and try to see Babak again. *Oh, is it even possible?* she asked herself.

A warm feeling spread throughout her body as she contemplated the thought of seeing her dear lover again. After all these trials and tribulations, she had gradually accepted her situation and was happy with the memory of him. Now there was a glimpse of possibility, and the hope of seeing Babak again was thrilling even as it was dangerous. What if her husband found out? What about her family—what would they do to her? What about Babak? Would he even be willing to see her again? How could she reach him? How could she learn of his thoughts and feelings? There was only one person that could answer her questions, and that was Soghra Khanoom.

Some months ago, Soghra Khanoom had come to Golam's house to visit Roodabeh, bringing with her a bag full of fine materials for sale. Since women were not allowed to go to the market, poor women like Soghra brought these materials to rich families so their women could choose material, for their clothes. Then they would give it to their tailor, usually another woman, to sew it for them.

Soghra had asked how she was then, and if she was happy with her new marriage. "Yes," she had answered, she was fine. The old woman's presence was a startling reminder of the wonderful time she had with Babak, and seeing her, she badly wanted to ask if he knew about her marriage. But she kept quiet since her husband was in the house and did not dare even whisper his name for fear of being heard. Then all too soon, without mentioning Babak at all, Soghra left their house.

Now thinking back, she wondered. *Oh, she had come at once,* Roodabeh thought. *Perhaps she had come to give me a message from him? Why didn't I ask her then?*

Roodabeh sighed painfully. *I do not know how, and I do not know what is he doing these days. How empty life is, without him.* She sighed and then took her harp and started to sing:

> *Where is the one who makes me drunk without any wine?*
> *Where is the one that I swear only on his life?*
> *Where is the one who took my soul and my heart?*
> *Where is the one who broke my promises and my repentances?*
> *Where is the one whom every one is screaming from his desire?*
> *Where is the one whose sorrow took me out of this life?*
> *His place is in my soul and if he is not here it is so strange,*
> *Where is the one who is asking me to give him my life?* [25]

But even with time, Roodabeh's sadness did not disappear. She was in constant pain. Not even talking about her wonderful past with her new friends, that used to calm her, was helpful. She constantly wanted to hide in a corner and cry. Now the women asked her who her contact with Babak was, and when they found out, they sent a servant to find her.

And then, one gray afternoon when the sky was dark and Roodabeh's heart was tight, Soghra came in.

But the strange thing was that she did not have her veil or her head scarf on. The same held true for the woman servant who went to invite her. Soghra excitedly told them how they were taking off all the veils and *chadors* from women's heads and faces. All the women in the house gathered around, staring at her as if they were looking at a ghost. The servant, who was shaken, said in a whisper, "She is right, they took mine too." All the women fell silent at the thought.

Kobra broke the silence and asked, "Who does such horrible things?"

"Oh soldiers, our young men," Soghra said proudly.

"But this is against religion," Kobra said, shocked.

Soghra laughed and said, "Oh honey, I do not think either our king or these young soldiers believe that."

Nasrin, who could not hide her excitement, said, "Tell us who ordered these soldiers to do this? Is there something we are not aware of?"

Soghra replied sarcastically, "Don't you have a radio? Have not you heard?"

"No, we do not have a radio," answered one of the women.

"Our husbands do not provide us with one," said Nasrin.

"Oh, no wonder," she replied thoughtfully. "His stinginess is well known." Then she continued. "To answer your questions, yesterday the Shah ordered the soldiers in all the cities and towns to stop women and take off their veils, *chadors,* and scarves everywhere they go. All of the government officials are supposed to attend meetings with their wives, mothers, and daughters without the *hejab*. The Shah himself will do that tomorrow morning. All the men are supposed to wear the same clothes that western men are wearing all over the world."

Everyone was silent. The younger women were excited and happy, but the older ones seemed sad.

Zahra, who was not pleased with Soghra's remark about her brother's stinginess, broke the silence and asked, "Soghra, so did you get all this news from your radio?"

Soghra looked at her and said, "No honey, an old poor fool like me cannot afford a radio. But I go to rich people's houses and they tell me the news."

"What are the clerics saying about all this?" Nasrin asked, eager to know more.

Soghra answered, "Nothing, they do not dare to say a word. Have not you heard of the tribal heads that disobeyed the Shah's order? They all vanished. The clerics are scared for their lives too. Besides the soldiers are standing in front of each mosque and on every corner! You know, the intellectuals are saying it is going to be a new era. We will be living better lives and women will be free from not only the *chador,* but also from all the inhumane treatment we get."

"Does that mean polygamy will be gone also?" Kobra asked.

"I do not know if that is on the agenda. The Shah is more focused on the clerics and tribal heads than anything. Clerics can choose either to remain clerics or can opt to become government agents, but they can not be both. Already so many of them have chosen the latter. The most ardent supporters of the Shah are the former clerics or their sons. There is also an order to ban some of the religious ceremonies in which people hurt themselves, like *Ghemeh Zani*. Even though these ceremonies took root so long ago, during the Safavid dynasty, this new Shah is banning them. People are saying that since everything he has done so far has made our lives better, this has to be good too."

Soghra was talking from her point of view. A poor woman with no support, having had to make her own living, she had become an atheist long ago, from having seen injustice everywhere. She had been talking to the few intellectuals who knew their great country's history, and her consequent sleepiness through the past two centuries. Yes, Persia had not only been asleep for a couple of centuries, she also had been submerged in the spider web of superstition. The lack of systematic education created a large illiterate mass. The clerics, who had once been the leaders of sciences and new discoveries, became greedy and saw the illiterate superstitious mass as something to use to their advantage. So they promoted this ignorance. The intellectuals on the other hand, had been trying hard for years to change this course of events. They knew of their great past, and were aware of the rest of the world's progress. They were trying to shift this nonsense. So as a result, they supported the new Shah. An iron-willed man who stood tall, he actually was able to implement all these changes, everything the intellectuals wanted, without yielding to anyone. But to many others he was regarded as an evil man because he forced these changes down their throats.

This was most true for those whose power and prestige were threatened by his actions. The tribal leaders whose power was replaced by governmental offices, the bandits who could not steal people's life savings anymore, and the clerics, whose *maktab* (religious schools) were replaced by the modern schools, were all opposed to the new changes. Yes, they would not forgive the man who was making all these waves in only one decade. But like water passing through a creek, slowly but surely the great country of Persia awakened once again, and began to move rapidly towards progress.

There in that gathering too, were mixed feelings about these recent events, to the point that for a while everyone forgot the purpose of Soghra's visit. There was contemplative pause, as everyone took in the gravity of this change. Then began a heated discussion about the current happenings.

Some agreed with Soghra that this was a window to a better future, while others disagreed, saying that this was going to be the end of world and the beginning of sinful earth, which was promised for so many years.

Nasrin sighed and said, "We were not allowed to leave our house for shopping purposes. Now that going out without *hejab* is mandatory, our husbands probably will imprison us forever. We will not be allowed to go to our family gatherings or go to the bath houses either." That was a good point, which provoked another heated and deep discussion for hours. Roodabeh told them about the Iraj poem that was written against *hejab*, and as an answer, he had received a challenge from another poet of his time just a decade ago ordering him to take his wife out without *hejab* so people could follow him. Now Shah was doing what was considered a dirty word against Iraj.

Finally Soghra got up and said, "Well, I have to go, but did you need anything else?"

The four women looked at each other; in the midst of their excitement about the new agenda in town they had forgotten their main purpose for summoning the old and fiery woman. Nasrin winked at the other women and they all left the room to let Roodabeh talk to her messenger of love.

"Sit down please," Roodabeh asked the older women. Soghra sat down again with wide open eyes. She did not know the reason for her summon. Roodabeh saw her inquiring face and said...

> *How is my beautiful, sweet love?*
> *How is the light of my eyes?*
> *How is that strange amorous glance?*
> *How is that imposter lock of hair?*
> *How is that strange beautiful face?*
> *How is that splendor in the garden of rose?*
> *How is that splendid poem of hair?*
> *Which is covering his beautiful face?*
> *Ask the doctor of the lovers*
> *How are the lovesick narcissuses of his?* [26]

Soghra looked at her, feeling her emotions and said, "If you are asking me about Babak, he is fine but he is hurting over your new marriage. He talked to me couple of weeks after your marriage, excited about the prospect of having a joint life with you. But I had to tell him the sad story of your marriage. I am afraid he did not take it easily! He is very upset."

Tears gathered around her eyes and with a sad desperate sigh she told the older women that she had not had any choice. "He did not propose and my family pressured me. I had to obey!'

"Yes, I know, dear, but I am afraid he does not," Soghra answered sympathetically.

"Why not? Does he not realize the situation of women in this town?" Roodabeh replied, letting tears pour freely down her face.

"You do not understand," Soghra replied. "Babak is pure and honest. In his world there is no room for tricks or lies. He had a hard time last time to convince himself that his love for you was not a sin! Now he is hurt by your marriage, convinced that money is more important to you than love. To him you married a wealthy man, of which he is not."

"Yes, but you can convince him that he is wrong. Tell him about my tears and my sadness. Tell him that I was forced to marry while he was away.

Please convince him of my love,
Convince him to come to my house and embrace my love.
Go, my friend, go and pull my love to my house,
Bring for a moment that runaway idol to my house.
Tell him all the sweet songs, tell him florid excuses,
Pull that beautiful face toward my house,
If he gives you an appointment that he will be here,
All is a trick he is cheating you with promise.
His reason is so warm, that he can fasten the fire,
Like a magician he can close the air
Please my friend, go and pull my love to my house." [27]

Soghra looked at her tearful face and said, "I will try my best, but cannot promise much."

Then she got up and looked around to gather her veil and *chador*, but remembered that they had been taken by the soldiers when she was coming in. It was strange for her to be without them. Although she was fond of the new king she could not help but feel slightly naked in the street without her *hejab*. She took the coins Roodabeh handed her and left the house.

Roodabeh sighed, then went to her harp and as she started to sing, the women gathered around her to hear her gorgeous voice cry:

Where are you, my light in the fog?
Where are you my lovely king?
Where are you, for every universe has become drunk by your amour!
Where are you, comfort of my heart?

Where are you, just for a moment come out to see
For all the prisoners of your love, your heart, your face
Are staggeringly drunk from the wine of your space![28]

The Ceremony (Kashfeh Hejab)

That day was a big day for Babak. He was happy to see *hejab* be prohibited by law. That day he tried very hard and convinced his mother to wear a long dress. A big hat was placed on her head instead of the familiar *chador*, and then they went to the ceremony, with Afshin and his young wife, wearing the same kind of outfit as their mother. Both women were shy and felt strange without their *hejab*. This was true of every woman in the ceremony. All the women, old or young, felt naked, and although they were still covered from head to toe, only now instead of black robes they had long dresses and hats. Habit is a strange thing. Most young women were happy and welcomed the changes, but they still felt naked, for they were quite used to having been covered by the black robe since the age of eight or nine.

This ceremony was so much different than any of the other ceremonies he had ever attended. Really, the presence of women made it so much better. His thoughts wandered to history and he started to ask himself, when had Persian women become secluded from society? At the time of Achaemenes, pictures showed the queen with a crown on her head. In Sasanid's era, a couple of women had even become king. Even now in remote villages no woman covers her face or even all her hair. *Their clothes are colorful and beautiful,* he thought, *they converse freely with men, and there is no seclusion of the sexes. But in cities we see such different pictures. The women are hidden in houses, covered from head to toe with black robes if they come out in the street. Is this going to be different? Are they going to be able to participate in all aspects of society now?*

His thoughts were interrupted abruptly, by the sight of a woman passing by in the crowd. He could not see her face but her long black hair was visible under her big hat. His heart started to pound; he felt weak all of the sudden. *Can it be her?* he asked himself. He could not calm himself down for the thought of seeing a glimpse of her face. He was not listening to his inner voice, which told him that it was impossible for Roodabeh to be in that crowd. She was a merchant's wife, with no relation to this governmental ceremony. But his sensitive side told him that Roodabeh was not like any other woman; she breaks the law, she does what she wants. She is a liberal woman and this ceremony is to celebrate women's freedom and the country's first step toward modernization. He felt hot and dizzy at the same time. He had to try to see that woman's face and see for himself if it was Roodabeh. This inner anxiety also told him that he was still very much in love with Roodabeh and was dying to see her, even if from a distance.

The turmoil became even worse when he was finally able to see the woman's face at the tail end of the ceremony. She was beautiful, but she was not Roodabeh. The woman smiled at him when their eyes met. It was flattering to get a smile from such a beautiful woman; he bowed but felt a sharp pain deep inside his heart. After the ceremony he asked Afshin if he could take his wife and their mother back home. After he was assured that they did not need him, he went back to his office to work. Lately he was getting away from his inner thoughts and his sad feelings by working harder and longer hours or by playing cards with his friends during the weekend.

The Return of Passion

Later that day, as Babak was at the office trying to do some work, he found he was too disturbed to do anything. *There were not too many people visiting the office either; they are afraid of losing their chadors*, he thought.

He opened a drawer where he had left his unfinished work, but suddenly, he heard a familiar voice.

"Hello, sir."

He looked up. The woman with the red braided hair did not look much like the old Soghra Khanoom he had known, but she had the same voice. *She looks so much younger, though she could look better if she combed her braided hair*, he thought to himself. He felt a little bit calmer. *I have somebody to talk to now*, he thought, rationalizing his sudden happiness.

"Oh hello, Soghra Khanoom! I did not recognize you in your new outfit, you look so much younger," he said.

Soghra Khanoom smiled and said, "Oh thank you, sir. People are telling me I will burn in hell if I come out in the street this way. But I need to make my living, you know! Besides, I cannot afford to lose a scarf or *chador* each day. I lost two already," she absentmindedly complained.

He called the waiter and asked for two cups of tea, then said, "It is a new era, why should you spend so much on those robes, when you look so good without them?"

She smiled, obviously pleased with his compliment, and said, "Oh sir, it has been a long time since I have gotten any compliment on how I look; thank you, you've made my day."

"I really mean it," Babak replied.

"How are you sir? Have you found anyone to keep you company?"

Babak's heart started to beat faster again; for a few minutes he had forgotten his feverish desire to see Roodabeh, but hearing Soghra Khanoom's comment brought back the old memories and his terrible inner disquietude.

He said, "No, I am scared of the disloyal ways of women."

"Really sir, or are you still in love and can not replace her?" she asked, hoping to hear the answer she was seeking.

Babak smiled and thought, *how does she know my inner thoughts? She is an illiterate, poor woman, but she can read my mind, gives me the answer a philosopher would give, and advise me like a professional psychologist,* Babak wondered to himself.

She interrupted his thoughts again, asking him, "Is that true sir?"

"Yes unfortunately, I can not get her out of my mind."

Soghra Khanoom smiled and said, "Why unfortunately? When your lover feels the same way?" He felt a rush of blood to his face, so she had been sent by her again! She continued, not noticing the young man's change of color. "I was in Roodabeh's house today, and she begged me to bring you to her. She has lost so much weight sir, you would not recognize her. She is crying all the time, remembering the times you had with her."

"But I do not believe that. If she was so miserable then why did she ruin our future by getting married?" Babak answered coldly.

"I asked her the same question and her answer was that she had no other choice. She did not believe you would marry her, as she was a divorcee and you were a single man. Her family was also strongly pressuring her to clear their name by getting married. As I said before sir, you do not know how weak we are and how little we can do in our lives." She continued, "Anyway, nothing has changed. You are still in love and so is she. There is nothing to prevent you from seeing her if you wish. You can tell her how you feel too. It will be good for you two to see each other and clear things up, even if you do not wish to continue your relationship with her."

She stopped. She did not want to hear no from him. If only she could make him see Roodabeh once, it would be enough; she had done her job.

Babak was quiet for a few seconds and then said, "A lot has changed though. But I guess it would not be harmful to see her once more." He could not resist the temptation. He wanted her and he wanted her badly. Her love, to him, was so deep. He had held that burning feeling inside long after he had left that city, so he could not say no.

Soghra Khanoom, who was very happy, asked him, "When would you like to arrange the meeting?"

He wanted to say tonight, but remembered that he was invited to a neighbor's house for supper. So he said, "Tomorrow night would be good."

She smiled widely and said okay. Then she gave him the address to Roodabeh's house and asked, "What time sir, so I can tell her?"

"Eight o'clock would be perfect; I will eat my dinner and then join her," he replied.

He went home that day whistling. Those in the house noticed that he was happier than usual. His butler smiled, he had not heard him whistling since he had come back from Pasargad. He did not know the reason, but he knew that his master was not sad anymore.

After dinner, when he returned home, it was late and he went to bed. He suddenly felt so much calmer than he had in recent nights. He felt lighter and more relaxed. He knew the reason. His long lost love wanted him back. But should he go? What good would come out of this relationship? His wisdom started to chastise him again: *she is a married woman and you know by entertaining this you will commit a great sin.* His heart saddened at the thought of not going. His sensitive side argued: *you already are sinful; it does not make any difference anymore.* Then he remembered a poem:

I wish my mother died or I was not born,
I've had bad luck since I was born.
Everyone is freeing the slaves,
I was free but became a slave.
The love of my idol, the love of my idol,
Made me a slave,
With hundreds of tricks she made me weary of everyone's.
I became poor, disabled, tired, and vagrant
I do not know, what is the remedy of my pain?
I went to the doctor to cure my pain.
Maybe she could give me a remedy to destroy the pain.
I became drunk when she gave me a glass of wine,
I was praying day and night as a devoted person,
I became drunk every night since my heart filled with love's pain.[29]

He fell asleep with the opposite thought. The next day started normally, except the clock seemed to become lazy and time passed slower than usual. He still had difficulty deciding what to do about the situation; which way should he go; what path should he choose?

But that night, he felt much better than he had in several months. What was the reason for that calm? He began to whisper another poem:

> *She is both my pain and my cure,*
> *Just like my intellect which is perplexed,*
> *Love is confused and dazzled.*[30]

After dinner he left the house and walked through the narrow alleys to find his way to her house. The big gate was wide open. He was not sure if this was the right house, but as soon as he stepped in front of the door a young woman appeared and invited him in. He went inside and turned left to the big courtyard with a small building on the right and a door to another courtyard. This must be *birooni*, (the outside courtyard and house) he thought.

He had never seen this kind of house, and had only read about them in books. Since the Ghajar dynasty, these kinds of houses, in which there were two houses—one inside the other—had been built throughout the different cities of Iran, but only by princes and wealthy men. The outer courtyard was for the men to receive their guests and the male servants. The door was open and people would come and go all the time. The inner courtyards were built to keep the women out of sight. They were there to cook and clean and take care of their children; and when they needed anything, they would tell their husbands, who would send the servants to buy the required food or grains.

But that dark night, nobody was there. A big jail, Babak thought. The young woman smiled and greeted him. Then she guided him to the inner house or the *darooni*. The woman did not look like a servant. Her clothes was made of the most expensive materials. He wondered why a rich woman like her was guiding him. Finally, she stopped in front of one of the rooms and told him, please go in.

Babak entered a well-decorated beautiful room with a door in the other side of the room. He was alone, but he was breathless. *Where is she?* he asked himself, remembering the first time he had ever laid eyes on her, thinking that he had found the woman of his dreams. *How foolish was I to let this all slip through my fingers?* he started to think, but then a dreamy voice shook him and he turned towards it.

There, sitting at her harp and more beautifully than ever, was Roodabeh, with her long black hair on her beautiful bare shoulders. She had a sheer blue dress on, which made her exquisite body even more beautiful than he had remembered it. With her harp flowing music beneath her hands, she was singing:

Beautiful spring has arrived,
My young lovely blossom has arrived.
You came happy, come, my king,
You are my cypress, my rose bush, and my king.

Glow, glow, my moon. Stay alive forever,
For hunting me in the world's coppice,
Because you are a jewel that is scarce,
The sea is boiling from the dream of seeing your face.

In this strange town, how are you?
In this trip, how are you?
Get up, get up, and let's be comfortable in my house.

You are the light of my moon,
You are my joy and my life,
Boil up my deliberation,
So my grapes become my wine.

Oh my love, my deceit, the trap of my heart,
Do not leave my house, I'll give you my life,
I'll give you my heart,
Oh my beautiful idol who burned my heart,
Stay, stay, and see my smoking heart.[31]

When she finally stopped singing, she put her harp down, and looked into his eyes. He was stunned. All the while, he had feigned indifference; he had wanted to complain about all the problems he went through, and the suffering her bad decision had brought for him. Now that he saw her in that beautiful blue dress, he could not even speak.

Now she was only his love, who he had been so eager to see. No trace of bitterness was left in him after hearing her heavenly voice and the intense emotion behind it. As he looked at her tenderly, he began to say:

Oh my soul, my soul, you are my sin and my faith,

Please change to a gem this unworthy stone.

Change my curse to faith, and my body to a soul,
Cure my pain, oh my cure and my pain.

Since you are found of me, then glow, and glow,
Sing and say, that I am yours and you are mine.[32]

Before he could finish his poem, he saw tears falling from her face and he noticed how thin her face was, much thinner than when he saw her last. He was shaken, but opened his arms and let Roodabeh put her head on his shoulder and cry.

"I did not have any hope of ever seeing you again," Roodabeh told him. They shared with each other the bad times they had been through—the difficult nights and tearful days.

It was late when he left her house; he promised to come back and see her again the next night.

The next night came and went. He was amazed at how she could see him in that house.

"Aren't your rival wives in this house?" he asked.

"Yes, they are, and the lady that greets you is my sister-in-law," was her reply. He could not believe what he was hearing. "See, our husbands are away and have their lives; so we are helping each other to have our own lives."

Babak could understand the dilemma, and said, "If only polygamy could be outlawed."

"Is it possible?" asked Roodabeh.

"There is no telling. Anything is possible at this point."

She smiled and said, "If that happens, I will not be his wife since he has two other wives."

"Are they like you?" Babak asked.

She laughed and said, "Only the first one is faithful and in love with him, if that is what you want to know."

"Then how can you bring me in this house?"

"Well, this is her revenge, since he was not faithful to her," Roodabeh answered.

They continued talking for hours without getting tired. She wanted to know all about the changes that their country was going through.

He knew plenty about all subjects of life. More than anything, they both shared a passion for the poems and music that they played together. It was so unfortunate that they were not a couple and that they never could be.

And as life slowly passed, they continued their secret relationship. He knew when her husband would be in town and when to visit or not. They were extra careful that nobody would see or know of their relationship. The only problem was his mother, who kept telling him that he should start his life and get married. He always had an excuse one way or another.

But as time passed, he wanted to have children of his own. His brothers were growing up and so were his nieces and his nephews. But he would not be unfaithful to his wife, and if he was in Kazeroon, it would be impossible to resist Roodabeh.

He contemplated the problem often. A few years passed this way and one day his mother told him that since his nieces were grown up and of marriageable age, she preferred to go back to Pasargad, so they could find suitable husbands.

"They are still too young," he answered. "But if you are homesick it is okay, I will send money for you and the children."

With his family away he started to push for promotion. He did almost everything the department head did, except he was his assistant. When he asked for the promotion, he finally got what he wanted. He was appointed as head of the department of registration and records for the city of Bandar Kangan. This was what he had wanted for a long time to become—the department head. With his vast knowledge and his organizational skills he deserved much more than his current job. But receiving the promotion brought him sad feelings. He had so many friends in this city and he still had deep feelings for Roodabeh, who he continued to see regularly.

But it was time for change. On one side was his ambition of getting ahead and on the other side was his forbidden love. She could not pack and go with him and he could not forget his dreams and ambitions. He also had to obey his superiors. His job was in Kangan, not Kazeroon, even if his love was in Kazeroon.

The night before he left he went to see her for the last time. He told her about his new assignment and with his tar started to play and sing:

I am leaving your city and have not seen you enough!
I did not pick any fruits from your trees.
I did not have a deep sleep under the shade of your branches.
I could not get in your orchard since I was feared by your guards.
I went to ruined places in search of treasures.
Like a snake I went into caves.
I passed by good and bad like a shadow.
I am not clean nor defiled now,
But obliterated in you.
I am glad that I had the antidote of yours,
Since as all the others,
I too, tasted the same poison of yours.[33]

The message was loud and clear for Roodabeh: he did not get much in this relationship and he was leaving with lots of doubts and regrets. She did not blame him but greatly mourned the loss of him. The night was full of sadness and tears. They departed with heavy hearts and the feeling of emptiness.

And as he left town he whispered to himself:

I left my soul to my love and left!
Who has done what I did? I left!
I cut my hope, put my trust in God and left!
Since I did not see my place,
Suddenly one night I left!
If she had love for me or not,
I abandoned everything and left!
I said goodbye to all whom
Were kind or unkind to me and left!
Oh I dropped my love,
With disappointment and regret then left.[34]

Life in Kangan

When he arrived in Kangan he could not believe what he saw—a place worse than anywhere he had ever seen. The weather was hot and humid. There was nothing in this town. There was nobody to talk to, only his loyal butler Hossein. Even the fruit that is always present in Persian homes were missing in that town. The only things they had there was sand, fish, and heat. The natives were all illiterate and very poor.

He had one employee, a young and hard-working man, with whom he became good friends. He soon met with the other three government officials who were in charge of different departments. He started talking with them about the long and hot nights of that remote city. As they talked, they started to become friends.

"We have to do something to be able to survive," he said.

"What can we do?" one man replied.

"Well, we can get together and play music!" Babak replied.

"But who plays?" asked Farhad, one of his new friends.

"Well, I can play tar," Babak answered.

Soon he realized that all three of his newfound friends had some kind of talent. They started to gather nightly, rotating houses as they used their own talents to entertain themselves. But deep inside Babak was not happy. He missed his friends and his beautiful Roodabeh. So he decided to get married.

For this purpose he traveled to Shiraz. Babak, always stayed at his cousin's place when he went to Shiraz. They were the daughters of an aunt who lived in Shiraz and had not moved to Pasargad with Babak's father and grandfather. One of them was married and had two children from a good-natured man who had a shop in Bazar-Vakil. The second one was a good-looking middle-aged woman who was very capable in many ways. She sewed beautiful clothes, cut hair, and cooked very delicious foods. Babak admired her and often told her of his appreciation of her art.

In the trip for which he went to Shiraz in search of a companion, he was confronted with the same obstacle that he had encountered for the past fifteen years of his life. He could not find any girl he could get to know before marriage; what made the matter harder was the simple fact that he could not trust any recommendation he got from his friends. He would get a recommendation from this friend and would ask another one: what did he think? The second friend would tell him all the reasons he should not marry this girl but would recommend another girl. This would continue and as he listened to all the negative remarks, he did not know who to trust!

Meanwhile Ziba, his single cousin, was giving him all the attention he could possibly need. And one day, knowing why he came to Shiraz, she said to him, "Why should we not marry each other?"

Babak, who was startled by her sudden proposal, answered, "But Ziba, we are cousins."

"Isn't customary to say that cousins' marriage is written in the sky?" Ziba replied.

Babak paused a little and said, "Modern medicine says it is wrong to marry your cousin, since some diseases are inherited through family, and it is not good to marry your close relatives."

Ziba started laughing and said, "Then all over Iran people should have all kind of diseases since lots of people marry their first cousins."

Babak frowned and said, "Yes, that is true; if they do not have any problem that means they did not have any malfunctioning genes in their family tree."

Ziba, who did not want Babak to feel bad, changed her tone and said, "We do not have any known problems in our family, either." That was true, but the fact that she was much older than him (ten years) was bothersome. For centuries men in Persia were accustomed to marrying younger women, not older. There was a legend also that marrying older women would make you grow old fast, but Babak was not superstitious, so he told himself there was no proof behind this claim.

Ziba broke the silence and asked him, "What are you thinking?" She was fond of him and was determined to have him against all odds.

Babak looked at her; she was a pretty and capable woman. She was kind and smart, but he was not in love with her. In fact he had never thought of marrying her until she proposed. "Anyway," he replied, "you know there is the issue of age difference, too."

Ziba knew the culture; it was true that most men married younger girls, but to get Babak to marry her she had to use his weakness.

"You know I agree with you on both accounts, but we still have to get married."

Babak frowned again and asked, "Have to? Why?"

Ziba dropped her head down and said, "Yes, we do. Your travels to our house, your overnight stays have caused people to think we have some kind of relationship, and I am becoming disgraced in the eyes of society and do not like it. I only tried to be a good hostess when my cousin came to my house. It is not fair to be seen so scandalously."

Babak looked at her and saw that there was real pain in her face. He wondered to himself, she was a beautiful lady; why had she not gotten married when she was younger? When Roodabeh asked him to marry her for the same reason, he had not since he did not want people to know that he had had a relationship with a married woman. And now another woman was asking him to marry her. The difference was that this time, he had not had any relationship whatsoever with Ziba. He could tell her, 'No, I am not interested,' and leave. Nobody would give him any problem, but for no valid reason, she would be blamed and disgraced without having the power to change anything. *It must be so hard to be a woman in this society,* he thought.

His thoughts were interrupted by her voice, now pleading. "Please consider it; I do not know what to tell people with all the rumors around. If you marry me, everyone will stop gossiping."

"But my dear Ziba Khanoom, I am not in love with you. We are not lovers and I do not know if we can live together in harmony. What happens if we marry and do not like each other?"

Ziba looked at him in despair and said, "We can get married temporarily. I know I will be more than happy to live with you in any condition, but if you do not find me to be up to your satisfaction, the law gives you freedom!"

Babak, realizing that she was not going to accept no for an answer, replied, "I do not believe in having more than one wife if you are referring to that. If I marry you and we have problems, we will get divorced."

"No problem," Ziba said happily, "even a few months living with you would be a pleasure for me."

Babak was startled again. *Is she madly in love with me, or is she desperate?* he asked himself. Then he looked at his older cousin and said, "Are you sure what are you telling me? I am repeating what I said: this is not a good reason to marry someone."

Ziba looked at him philosophically and said, "You know, every day thousands of couples get married, and most of them do not even see each other's faces before the day they get married. They marry for family fortune, name, or just to get married. And all the women in our society have no rights regarding whether or not to stay in their marriages. Every man can divorce his wife, and her opinion does not count. They can also remarry and leave the first wife in jealousy and despair. There is no guarantee that either of them will be happy forever. Some are and many others are not. But I know what I want. You are handsome, smart, hard-working, and kind. You are any woman's dream and, better than that, you do not believe in polygamy. In marrying you I would have my dream come true and get back my good name. If I could not make you happy you have every right to divorce me, and I admire your honesty in telling me your condition now. For you I will be whatever you want and hope to be able to make you happy."

Babak could not say much—in fact he was tired of being alone. Whatever it was, he did not have anything to lose. He was too lonely to go to Kangan alone. She was pretty and smart. Even though she was around forty, she would still be able to produce children for him and they could have a happy family. He knew her and was sure that regardless of her age, she had so much to offer. So, he accepted her proposal and they were married that same week in a small but beautiful ceremony.

They packed immediately and left for Kangan. She was good for him in almost every aspect of his life, her cooking was excellent, and she never argued with him. She was everything a man could ever want in a wife. Even though there was neither a barber or a tailor in the small town, he did not have to worry about his clothes or his hair. She was an expert at cutting his hair, and was better at it than any barber he had ever been to. She also sewed new suits, with the skill of which no other tailor could match. She was perfect in many ways, except that after several months of marriage there was no sign of pregnancy.

Babak, who was amazed at her love and devotion, became sad at the nagging desire to have a baby in his life, especially since for such a long time he had his brothers, and nieces, and his little nephew nearby. But in Kangan he missed all of them. He wanted to hear the laughter of the children and their curious faces when he told them the history of Persia. And now in that sandy deserted town he felt depressed. *She is a good wife,* he told himself. *I am not alone anymore.* But could he be content with the rest of his life this way, he wondered.

A couple of years passed and except for the lack of a child and Ziba's strange and superstitious ways, nothing else was bothersome. Ziba was older than him and was insecure. Therefore, she grabbed onto a rope that eventually would choke her. Her superstitious mind pushed her towards a dark and rough path, she was using magic to make him love her. She would use sorcery with all kinds of potions, which she would add to the food. Either the food tasted bad, or even a couple of times he saw the ready-made potion that was about to be added to his food. He told her in so many ways that these so-called love potions were harmful to people's health and that she should avoid them.

He was afraid of the bacteria and microbes that could be in the potion mixture, and he was not wrong in this thinking. Some magicians used dirt from the old graves and mixed it with other ingredients to make the potion, but the more he explained the potential harm of her sorcery and potions, the less she listened.

But after about three years, there was a light of hope in both of their lives. She was pregnant and happy. He was thrilled and told himself, *thank goodness, with a child in our lives Ziba will feel more secure and will stop making all those crazy potions of hers.*

And after long days and nights of waiting impatiently, their son was born. He was the most beautiful child he had ever seen. He was a big child with lots of black hair, big black eyes with long eyelashes, and beautiful white skin. He was a joy to have. Their happiness seemed endless; he felt content and relaxed; only he did not know what life had in store for him. He named the child Sina after his older brother, and he bestowed all the love he had in his heart to him.

When Sina became one year old, Babak applied for a transfer from Kangan. He did not think his son should grow up in such a place, without relatives nearby. He also felt bad for Ziba, who was home taking care of Sina, and except for her sewing, did not have anything else to do and nobody to talk to except his butler, Hossein. But transferring from Kangan was hard as nobody wanted to replace him in that remote place! Furthermore, he wanted to move to Pasargad, so he had to wait until there was an opening there.

But soon there was a big storm that swept all of Persia. The fire of World War II reached Persia and burned it altogether. There was a need to send troops and supplies to Russia, and the Iranian plateau was the best bridge between west and Russia to avoid German armies. There was a problem though. Iran (Persia) had declared her neutrality to avoid the devastating affects of war. Her ruler, the Shah, did not want to take any part in the war. He was too busy building the country's infrastructure after decades of bad management and abuse. Iran, for the last two centuries, had become weak and this had become the site of two superpowers struggling to take over her: the British, who had arrived at the beginning of Safavid dynasty and as a result had guided Persian kings toward destruction, and Russia, who was trying very hard to gain as much power in Persia as the British.

The Persian kings, politicians, and even the people became only puppets that helped them with or without their knowledge. The Russian revolution gave Iran little chance at survival, because first, one of these two super powers was busy in her own affairs, and then the other one had control of vast sources of oil and wanted stability and security in this country, which hosted their most valuable resources.

Reza Shah's determination and will was the answer to their prayers, or their own creation as his enemies declared. He wanted to improve the lives of himself and his fellow citizens. The British wanted a secure environment to be able to send their oil to the world market. So, they helped him at the beginning in his fight against big landlords that were governing different parts of the country and preventing ordinary people from making any progress. One can argue that if they had been progressive individuals, then the country would not need a leader like Reza Shah. Each of them could have improved the lives of the people in their region, like the European landlords and the owners of industrial factories had done for their people. Unfortunately, the landlords in Iran thought only of themselves and their immediate families. You could not hear anything good about them. There were no hospitals, schools, or factories built by them. In their courts were abuses and injustices. When Reza Shah attacked these establishments, he made it his right to confiscate their property or, in most cases, they gave him more than half of their land. This behavior later became an excuse for his opponents to call him a cruel dictator. But to ordinary people who saw their country's improvement, it was a small price to pay.

Soon the British realized that to a strong nationalist like Reza Shah, there was no difference between them and any other nation. He wanted the best for his country and accepted help from anyone that helped him to reach his goal. His first disgust with the British had been when he went to the oil-rich providence of Khozestan. He was amazed to see how much oil was sent abroad by British ships and how poor the people were in this rich province! Could anything be done for them? How just was that? To take one's country's resources yet not even employ the citizens of the land that has given you this wealth was despicable to him. Most Persian intellectuals and politicians knew how tricky the British were. The Persians had seen the British take the knowledge of eastern culture and natural resources, but also felt them looking down at the same people, trying to tell them how they knew that they deserved a better life than them! The history of Persia for the last two hundred years had been full of tricks and deceitful behavior from the British government.

The Shah could not trust her country's northern neighbor either. The great country of Persia was ill and needed immediate attention. She needed advisors to work for her and her people. Who could they trust? The Germans came forward and were among those who lent their hands. Reza Shah hired several German advisors to build bridges, roads, and trains. The projects were almost complete when World War II broke out, and the German advisors preferred to stay in Persia and complete their jobs rather than return home to face a devastating war. Little did Reza Shah know of the events that waited for him at the end of war. He claimed neutrality since he knew very well that his country was not strong enough to withstand any war, and that becoming involved in the war would only prolong her illnesses.

But the Allies (especially the British, who were worried about the close relationship between the Persians and Germans) pushed to conquer the defenseless land of Persia. Their excuse was that since there were German advisors in Iran, they needed to step in and aid in expelling them from the country. Reza Shah, who knew his own weakness and did not want to get involved in the war, obeyed their demands and expelled all German advisors. But this was not enough. If they did not conquer Iran how could they take supplies and reinforcements to the Soviet Union?

And here the storm came in from two directions at once; from the north, the Soviet Union soldiers, and from the Persian Gulf, the British with their new friends, the Americans, they all poured into Persia. The newly established army, which only fought its own internal enemies and was not well equipped, could not withstand three different armies with the most sophisticated weapons in the world. Reza Shah went to the House of Representatives and resigned. If there was anyone who was guilty in his country, he reasoned, it was he. He was the most powerful man in his country and he was ready to take his punishment, whatever it might be. His crown prince swore in front of the parliament to be the new king. The army was dissolved and the country went through chaos.

The Allied troops went through Iran in two different directions toward Tehran. They took whatever they could take. They used the train without paying for it. Used all the supplies they could find even while there was hunger all over the country. The problems of a lack of food combined with the poorness of the population caused the robbers to go back to what they were doing before Reza Shah's reign.

Babak, who became very depressed at seeing his country go through such turmoil just when he thought it was going in the right direction, decided to take a vacation and go to Shiraz. He packed everything, because he did not want to go back to that hot little harbor of the Persian Gulf. When they arrived in Shiraz, Ziba was so happy. She saw her sister and her other relatives. Sina was like a beautiful flower that attracted the attention of anyone passing by. His beautiful black eyes on his white skin made people stop and stare at him. Then he would smile at them, which made his little face light up with the most beautiful smile. He was like a sunray in those dark days of war.

Babak was nationalist by nature. Islam was his religion, but Iran was his love and passion. And now that his country had been attacked and his hero abducted, he felt terrible and listened to the news every day on his small radio. Sina's smile was the only comfort he had through these days of concern for his country.

Sina was generous with his laughter, and gave his father what he needed anytime he looked at him. He will be a physician like his uncle and his grandfather, he always thought. His own forgotten dreams and ambitions were all centered around his two-year-old son.

Babak's heart was full of love and he was generous with his love to others around him. He had taken care of his orphan nieces and his three brothers. And even though he had his own family to take care of, he still sent enough money for his mother and brothers in Pasargad. But with the arrival of Sina in his life he experienced a different kind of love and devotion. He wanted his son to become a great person. To beat all his own obstacles and become what had been impossible for him to be. But time was planning a different path for him—a path that he had gone through several times as a child, and now that he felt great and in control, he had no idea how soon he would have to endure the same pain he felt so long ago.

While in Shiraz, he went to the office to see if he could find a position in Pasargad. Meanwhile, Ziba's relatives were trying very hard to make sure they felt at home and had a good time in their house.

That day it was a bright spring morning. The roses were in full bloom with their heavenly aroma. They were invited to go to one of the orchards in Shiraz where the apple trees were in full bloom. When they got there, the orchard was magnificent with all kind of blossoms. The day started very pleasantly; they were sitting under a big willow tree. As they sat sipping on their tea and eating fruit, they told each other jokes that made everyone laugh. Babak's jokes were the funniest and their laughter filled the orchard like music. Children were running everywhere and the mixed sounds filled the air like any fun picnic.

But Ziba was not laughing; in fact she was not even smiling. Her face pale and her eyes worried, Babak noticed her right away. She had Sina in her arms. He was still smiling but his face was paler than ever.

"What is wrong?" Babak asked, his voice full of worry.

"I am afraid that Sina does not feel good," she replied. "He is vomiting and I think we should leave immediately."

"Of course," said Babak.

Quickly, everyone started to pack. They had to leave in their own carriage, which would take hours to get to Shiraz. Time was lazy and the minutes seemed like hours to everyone. Sina's condition did not get any better, but only worsened. Both Babak's and Ziba's hearts beat violently with concern. They loved their beautiful happy boy more than themselves and now they were racing against time, hoping to make it to the hospital in enough time to save him.

As Babak sat next to Ziba, who was holding their baby Sina, his hand stayed on his forehead, praying all the way. He was praying for forgiveness from the almighty God. He was praying for God to give them enough time to get to the doctor before it was too late. Ziba was praying too, with tears running down her cheeks. Her arms wrapped around Sina, holding him so close to her chest as if she wanted him to know the affection she had for him; as if she could take the pain away by holding him tight.

The two-hour journey finally finished, they arrived at the hospital and were greeted by one of the few doctors. The doctor examined him and prescribed some medicine for two days; and thankfully they felt calmer, assured that Sina was going to get better. They had been afraid that they would not have enough time to get to the hospital, that they would lose Sina, but in those days of war and chaos, there was not much difference between the hospital and that remote orchard where his sickness began.

For Ziba, Sina's illness was worse than anything else. Ever since she had fallen in love with Babak she had developed an unknown fear. It may have stemmed from insecurity, for she was in desperate love and had never imagined that she would get what she had wished for. But amazingly, she had convinced him to marry her. The conditions and arguments that Babak had made before their marriage (although they were very honest and straightforward) were the main cause of all her fears.

He was young and handsome, a funny and hard-working individual with a wide open heart, who enticed all kinds of people to love him. And this idol was her husband; they had lived happily for six years now. But only in the past two years, with the arrival of Sina, did she feel content and secure. She could see a change in him that she had not seen before Sina's birth. He was happier, and with more energy and affection. She did not feel threatened anymore by the way women admired her husband's polite behavior. At the same time, she had not seen as much of his occasional bursts of anger, which came out once in a while when he was tired. The anger and shouting were so unlike his usual kind and caring nature, that she took these angry moments as proof that he did not love her—an idea that frightened her to death. But since she had become pregnant with Sina, for the past two years he was always kind, and she was secure enough not to get frightened of a little of his shouting. She was happy and could see he was too.

And now her love, her life, and her total well-being was hanging on a very thin string of hope. She desperately wanted to believe that Sina would be well soon, and that they would continue their happy life together again. But a whisper in her heart was telling her otherwise. She tried not to think or say anything negative about Sina's illness, but her heart was beating harder and she felt like a butterfly was inside, trying to fly away. And as the moments came and went slowly, with their hopes and dreams hanging on this tiny string, the day came where there he was—Sina's beautiful white face topped with thick black hair and beautiful long eyelashes, laying still on his bed. His pretty big eyes were closed and his tiny elegant body was motionless. The candle of their life had melted and finally turned off.

As Ziba screamed and cried so hard that everyone could hear and see her pain, Babak's tears fell on his cheeks quietly and steadily. They had both lost someone dear to them and they both were suffering from the same wound. Could they comfort each other and overcome this tornado in their life? The answer was unknown to both. Ziba, who was in the midst of her life change, both physically because of her age and emotionally, not only mourned for her lost son but also had to deal with her old forgotten friend, her insecure fear of the future. The butterfly in her heart did not fly away with Sina's death, but instead, stayed with her.

Meanwhile, Babak was deep in his own sorrow and disbelief. *Why Sina? Did he die because of my sins?* he asked himself. *Oh yes, you did everything that was forbidden to you to do. You drink wine, play tar, and had an affair with a married woman; you needed your punishment and God gave it to you, his stern wisdom would come and tell him. But why should my sins burn him? I am the guilty party. Sina did not do anything. He was just a beautiful happy baby. Why should he die for my sins?* Then there was a voice coming to him that said, these are things that happen. *God is not punishing you at all. This is only to test your faith. You have to be patient and endure the harshness of life.*

"There must be some reason beyond it," he thought, then heard his mother's voice in his mind telling him. "God knows better. Be patient, my son." But it was so hard for Babak to be calm. He had been through so much in his life. Losing his father at the age of eight and then losing Roozbeh a few years later were both big blows to his life, and both events resulted in too much sorrow for one little boy to handle. And yet he still grew up to become a loving human being, with all the affection any good man can have, and without any bitterness. But even later as a young man he went through so much loss. The combined losses of his sister and then a few years later her son, were very hard. And then he found the joy in caring for his little brothers and nieces, but only after a long struggle between his love and his faith, to which he eventually lost his most cherished love. *But then, did God not bring you Ziba, who gave you comfort and content in your life?* he thought to himself. Yes, of course she did, but the biggest joy of his life had been Sina, who he lost to this same God's will.

It hurt so much not seeing his face; a face as white and as delicate as the petals of jasmine. He missed his child's sweet smile and in remembering it, he felt the deep scorch of pain in his heart. Within days he noticed all his golden hair changing to gray.

A New Life

Then he got a letter from his office, which said he was reassigned to Pasargad! This was what he had been waiting for, for the past two years and now that he had it in his hands there was no sign of happiness to overcome his despair. He told Ziba of his new assignment and she smiled; her sadness did not disappear, but a ray of hope crept into her heart. She told him, "Good, you might feel better if you are near your family and relatives." He looked at her and thought, *yes, I will be with my nieces and nephews. My brothers will be close by and so will my mother, whose soothing words will give me reason to be alive.*

That day he went out to do some last-minute shopping. Suddenly, a young man with torn clothes caught his eye. He was covering his eyes with his arms and was walking close to a wall of the building on the street side. He was shivering, which gave the impression that he had been cold for a long time. But the strange thing to Babak was that the boy had a very familiar face. *Who does he remind me of?* he asked himself. He thought a little and looked at him again. The young man was obviously trying to hide himself somehow and turned his head the other way. It then dawned on him. Could it be Kavoos? He looked at him closer, surprised. Yes, he could be, in fact he had the same height and walked the same way. *Oh my God, is that what he is doing these days?*

The young man was his brother—the oldest of the three and the black sheep of the family. He had been running away from school all the time when they were in Kazeroon and the letters from his mother indicated the same pattern of behavior on his part when Babak had been stationed in Kangan. He felt sadness wash over his heart. He looked at his butler, who was with him and asked, "Do you know that boy?"

Hossein looked at the boy and said, "A beggar, I think."

"Yes, he looks like a beggar, that's for sure, but he is also my brother! Go and tell him to come with me. He does not have good clothes on so he needs some clothes first." They then went to the bazaar while the two men followed him, Babak in his clean-tailored suit, while his butler and his half-naked brother followed him.

He stopped in front of a tailor shop and gave the guy enough money to make three suits for the young man shivering from the cool spring breeze, then asked if he had one suit ready-made. The tailor had one but had to fit it to suit his size. Babak bought a ready-made one. Then he told Hossein to take Kavoos to a bath house and while he was getting clean, to come back and take the suit to him and take him home.

As they parted, Babak felt sorry for his brother. What was wrong with him? Had losing his father been such a big blow to his head that it made him behave abnormally? But he and Afshin lost their father when they were almost the same age and grew up okay. His other two brothers, who were younger than Kavoos, were very bright and studious. Then there had to be something else wrong with him. But in those days there was no psychologist around to answer any of these questions, nor was there an accurate or magical medicine to make a young child or adult suffering from ADD or depression or any other kind of mental illness feel better.

It was obvious that he was unable to accept any responsibility whatsoever, and it was shown over and over that he did not stay put and would disappear into thin air only to be found on the streets of Shiraz, shivering in the cold morning breeze. But the incident, made Babak think of all who were dependent on him. His wife and mother, his brothers who were starting to finish high school, and Kavoos, who obviously needed him badly, someone who even at age twenty had the mind of a ten-year-old boy!

That night, depressed from his big loss and the bad news of war and his brother's condition, he grabbed his tar and started playing with a voice that told the sorrow of his loss:

> *Oh the owner of this beautiful orchard, aren't you sad?*
> *Autumn has arrived, autumn has arrived*
> *From each branches of trees find green leaves, green leaves,*
> *Oh gardener, listen, listen to the loud voices of the trees.*
> *Which from all sides are in mourning, without tongues,*
>   *without tongues.*
> *You never will see any tearful eyes nor dry lips,*

Yellowish cheeks without reasons, without reasons.
So the sad alm is walking in my heart
And asks with sorrow, where is the garden of roses?
Where is the garden of roses?
Where are the lilies, narcissus, tulips, or jasmines?
Where is green grass? Where are judas-trees, judas-trees?
All the trees, all the trees,
Are in mourning as they stand in black robes,
Without leaves, without leaves
Oh my dear delicate flower where did you go?
Answer me please, answer me please.
Did you fall inside a well or fly far and high?
Toward the expansive and reaching
Big blue sky, big blue sky. [35]

Return to Pasargad

The following days they packed their belongings, and this time Ziba was busy too, since she had so much: furniture, antique dishes, and rugs she wanted to pack. They were moving to his birthplace, the place where he had yearned to return for so many years now. And Ziba knew that this would be their permanent place. So she packed everything she could; her house was going to be magnificent, she thought, and a weak smile appeared on her lips, only to vanish right away into tearful eyes as she remembered her little son on his deathbed.

With all her sorrow she knew she had to be strong and do her duty. Her husband needed her now more than ever. She paused and asked herself, *but will he? He is going to be with his family and a lot could happen!* The butterfly in her heart returned again and any positive thoughts vanished quickly in the loud flapping of butterfly wings that spread that unknown fear. *What is wrong with me?* she thought. *My son is dead now. What else is going to happen? Is there anything that can even match today's sorrow?*

"Why am I so scared?" she whispered to herself as she packed. "What is this fear that is shaking me day and night?"

Those days they both were trying to stay as busy as possible with ordinary work, in order to forget their heavy hearts and the painful memory of their little boy's illness and death.

Finally, the big day arrived. Babak rented a truck with a driver to take them to Pasargad. Everything was packed. Babak, Ziba, and Kavoos sat by the driver while Hossein sat in the back. A few hours passed and when they were in the middle of a deserted road the truck stopped. There were big stones in front of the truck, which made them feel like they were lost; maybe they had taken a wrong turn? There were enough stones to prevent the tires from moving forward. What was going on, everyone asked themselves without any clear answer.

The driver got out; there was no sign of anyone on the dusty road. The other passengers got out too. They were thinking of the solution when they heard a deep voice. "Please raise your hands above your heads." Babak looked toward the voice and saw an armed man, whose face was covered, aiming a gun at him. He obeyed and then he saw several other armed men appearing from all directions. "Bandits," he whispered to himself.

There was no need to wonder any more. The bandits were there to steal all their belongings. The truck was emptied. They ordered Ziba to take all her jewelry off and give it to them. They even took off the driver's, butler's and Kavoos' coats. They ordered Kavoos to give them his watch too—the new watch that Babak had bought for him the day before.

All this time Babak was ordered to stay aside; they saw his watch and his tailored suit too, but strangely enough, they did not ask him to hand any of these things over. Did they know him? If so, were they one of the Pasargad tribes who had been robbing people in the old régime? Or did they think that since they were robbing him of all his belongings, why should they bother with his jacket and his watch? Whatever it was, he did not understand the reason why they took his butler's and his brother's jackets but not his.

Then with the furniture, clothes, and antique dishes all packed, the bandits left the scene an hour later with half of the armed men, while, the rest of them were busy pouring more stones in the back of their truck so that it could not move in any direction. When they were assured the family would not be able to leave for another hour or two, they left in the direction of the turning mountain. Babak and the other men started to move the heavy stones away from the car. And only after two hours of hard work they were able to open enough space in the dirt road so the truck could move forward.

They all got into the truck with dust all over them and the driver started the truck. "Oh my God, we lost everything!" said Ziba with tears in her eyes.

She was just finally recovering from the shock and the deep fear they had all felt when confronted by the gunmen.

"No, we did not, we all are okay. They could have killed us all," the driver replied.

"Yes, we should be thankful that we were not shot. Money can be replaced," added Babak. And in reality he was not worried too much. He was only sad. Sad to see that the security they all felt under their powerful ruler had once again been shattered. Sad to see his beloved country under attack, but personally, he had lost a son whom he had valued more than any amount of money in the world.

Then he grew angry. "Damn British! Why don't they leave us alone? As soon as we start to achieve the minimum standard of living that any human being deserves they have to come and destroy it!" he shouted.

Ziba looked at him, her eyes full of tears and said, "But those men were not British! They were speaking Persian."

"Oh yes, they were speaking our language all right, but they were probably not Persian; they were most likely local Turks who went back to what they have been doing since they came from Mongolia with Chengiz Khan. But their rifles were made in Britain."

"What do you mean?" Ziba asked, fascinated. She was still very distracted; this was the second time in a month that she had lost important things that she loved. She wanted to keep her mind off of these things and nothing was more soothing than hearing her beloved husband tell her about her country's stormy history.

Babak began to explain, "Well, they are nomadic people who came with Chengiz Khan, either from Mongolia or along the way, some sources believe. Their original profession was hunting and then later on, fighting. In the war against Iran they conquered each city by killing hundreds and confiscating their belongings. They have settled in different parts of the country. They kept their nomadic life structures. They have their own chiefs, who are the most educated and rich in the country. Our last two dynasties came from these tribes. Other sources think that the Arab caliphs bought the Turkish poor boys and made them their soldiers. These boys were young, brave, and loyal to the caliphs. So they rose to upper levels of the army, and as soon as the Arab empire got weak, they made their own dynasty that covered the whole land of the Persian empire, except Iraq and Saudi Arabia, which was left for the caliph. They send him some taxes to keep him happy.

"That was the time in which most Persian scholars made inventions and wrote so many books in Persian and Arabic in the field of medicine, astronomy, and chemistry. Persian poetry flourished and we saw many great Persian poets emerge from that era.

"However, this theory does not explain why Turkish tribes are scattered all over Iran's plateau, So, the first theory seems to be closer to reality. Anyway, they speak both Persian and Turkish languages perfectly well. They are not bad people, either, they just have a different culture. They believe in the rule of the jungle. The more powerful you are, the less chance you have of being killed, and that to survive they needed to kill or steal."

Ziba, who was listening intently up to this point, became impatient and said angrily, "Do you justify what they have done to us?"

Babak answered. "No, of course not. But that is how the law of the jungle is. Their forces were more than us, so they took all that we had. The jungle's law does not mean it is human or right; it only means that everyone has to take care of themselves, like animals do."

Kavoos interrupted and asked, "What about the British, then? If these men were following the law of the jungle and their own culture, then why did you say, 'Damn British'?"

"Well, because the British follow a humanitarian way of life for themselves, but exercise the laws of jungle for us. Since they got here, our political climate has been in chaos. We have not introduced any new scientist, great artist, or beautiful poet to the world since they arrived. All the architectural monuments of the Safavid era have been forgotten. They encourage tribal chiefs to fight each other so they can sell more weapons, but they are truly looking at us like they look at animals. But more than anything, right now I am referring to the abduction of Reza Shah, the only man that made these roads safe for us."
36

Here Babak stopped, looked at his younger brother and said, "Do you want more reasons?"

"But I read in the newspaper that the Allies had to come here because they needed to help the Russians."

Babak paused a little and said, "Of course, but why didn't they ask us to help them, rather than pouring into the country unwanted? And not only this, but in the process they have also taken many of our resources. Do they have a right to do this, ruining everything we have built for the past twenty years?"

"Well, I also read that they will be paying us back for our troubles," countered Kavoos, "Are they lying to us, then?"

Babak answered with a tired voice. "I do not know if they will pay us or not, but I think they could help Russians in a better way than abducting a sovereign country's king and causing a resultant famine. They do not need all these troops here. If it was just to help Russians, then what are Russians doing with their armies in Iran? They want to justify these actions, but they cannot fool us. They are stealing millions of dollars of our oil, and they want to change our government by forcing us to replace our old stable government with this new weak one." Here he stopped, becoming again absorbed in his own thoughts.

The driver broke the silence and asked, "What do you think of the new king? After all, he is Reza Shah's son."

Babak replied, "Unfortunately, he is not as powerful as his father. If he were, these roads would not be susceptible to the robbers' forces."

"Did people think the last Shah was a bad dictator?" Kavoos asked.

"Of course they did. Groups like these powerful tribal chiefs and the clerics were upset that the Shah ruined their ability to continue abusing the people for their own self interests. The many powerful princes of the old regime also detested him."

Kavoos, who was still curious, then asked, "What about his wealth? They are saying that he had so many pieces of farmland when he left. They say that he was after the money for himself."

Babak shook his head. "Even if he was, he gathered his wealth from the rich and powerful, not the middle class and poor. But to me, that was not the case; he was working for a better Iran. Before his reign we had only handful of schools all over Iran. Today, every major city has a school, plus the medical university in Tehran. We have all these roads that we did not have before, and we had sixteen years of good security. Our relationship with the world community was good. We all have lived in harmony and thousands got jobs and a better life. I think it was his leadership that gave us this more secure life. Of course, he was not the only one who made all this progress happen, but his leadership was the key point."[37]

They arrived tired and hungry. Their clothes were full of dust. Some of them had clothes that had been torn trying to open the road to move the car. Kavoos and Hossein were cold from losing their jackets to the bandits. When they finally got home and ate, the food tasted incredibly good to them. Although the whole ordeal still seemed like a bad dream, they could not imagine its impact on their lives.

Babak, a generous man who has given all his adult life, now had to receive from others. There was a question of where to live and without money he could not rent the house that they had planned on. Babak's cousin, Moji invited them to stay at his house until they were able to buy or rent another house. He had no choice but to accept his offer. Their house, like any other Pasargad house, was built with two rows of detached rooms. Babak and Ziba were assigned to one of these rooms. While Babak had been in Kangan, Talah and the boys occupied another room in Moji's house and Afshin and his family also were living in one of the rooms. Now with Babak's arrival, all rooms were occupied and in each room lived one family, where they all shared the kitchen and the only bathroom.

Since Babak had started his life in Pasargad, he was content being with his family again. The war had taken a toll on him though; he could not understand the unjust behavior of people who took advantage of the situation to become rich. Much to his disapproval, his brother Afshin was among them, selling grain mixed with dirt to increase his profits. Soon he was rich enough to move out of Moji's house.

The sadness of losing his son still was with him, and there was no hope of replacing him. Since Ziba went through her change of life when Sina was only one year old, she could not bear anymore children. What was worse for Babak was that Ziba's insecurity was back, and so was her sorcery.

Life in Pasargad was very hard for Ziba. Living in a house with several other family members was not easy. Her physical and emotional well-being also was not good. The loss of her son took her into a dark alley of depression and her menopause only made it worse. One day, she was preparing the food and had a love potion ready to add to it, but had to get something from the yard when Babak came home and saw the potion. His anger was extreme and it caused a big fight.

The next day she left Pasargad. She did not see much future in her marriage and with the tumult of menopause she no longer had the desire to hold on. Six months later they were divorced. So after almost eight years Babak was forty and single again!

Several months after the divorce his mother sold her only property, an old house she had inherited from her father. She gave the money to Babak to buy a house for himself. He did; the big house next to Afshin was for sale and they bought it. Babak, Parham, and Samad

Grey Hair and a New Marriage

One night they all were gathered around the small *manghal* in their living room. Afshin and his family were there too. Afshin looked at his older brother and said, "Don't you think it is time for you to get married?"

Babak looked at him and said jokingly, "Sure, it is past the time to get married." Indeed, it was. Afshin had two sons and a daughter by then; the oldest one was ten years old. But Babak was still single and childless.

Afshin said, "I am serious. How about Mamdali's daughter?"

"She is too young," he replied.

"No, she is sixteen years old and very beautiful," said his mother.

Mamdali was considered the black sheep of the family, for after he had been widowed, he had remarried his servant. But nobody was debating his first daughter's credentials. From both her father's and her mother's side; she was from the "perfect family." She used to come to his house often and he could never understand why she was stressing so much to cover her face all the time. He remembered her visits as a child and she was indeed very pretty. After the war and with new regime, the anti-hejab law was banished and women were free to wear what they liked so most of them went back to *chador*. There were few who did not cover their faces, but the rest did in the midsized towns.

In the bigger cities, there were so many women who refused to go back to the old times and were going out without any scarf or cover on their heads. But Laiya, the young girl his brother was proposing he marry, was one who had always been very careful that nobody see her face.

Afshin interrupted these thoughts, asking again, "So, what do you think?"

"I do not know; give me some time," he replied. Since his divorce he had been very lonely. In the evenings he would play his tar, playing only sad songs. His time was spent with friends, playing cards or drinking and playing tar. But he was lonely and tired of it. His three nieces were all married. His brothers were grown up. Samad was finishing high school. Parham was in law school and almost at the time to get married, but he was the only one with no children and alone. Yes, he had to get married, he thought. *If everyone gets married without knowing each other, why shouldn't I?*

The next day was Friday and all his nieces and nephews were invited by his mother to his new house. Laiya was invited too as usual. At the dinner, since he could not see anything but her lovely big brown eyes, he decided to play a trick on her. He took the dish everyone liked and went behind Laiya and held the dish in front of her without a word. She turned to see who was offering her the dish and her face showed under her black *chador*. She was the most beautiful girl he had ever seen. She laughed while turning her head quickly so her face did not get exposed to a man for too long. Then he said with a smile:

All the beautiful ladies like to show their faces.
Are you ugly? Is that why you are covering your face?[38]

Then he continued that:

A fair-faced lady will not bear to be hidden,
If you close the door she will stick her head out of windows.[39]

Laiya did not say a word. She knew her older second cousin. She had talked to his wife and knew most of his good and bad behaviors, but she had never thought of marrying him.

Babak had a long night ahead of him that night. All the memories of his past twenty years were passing in front of his eyes. His love affair and its painful separation, his marriage, and the painful loss of his son. Should he marry a girl twenty-two years younger than himself? He was wondering, but her smiling face and her beautiful eyes gave him hope. There were a couple of problems though. He thought her father was stupid. He also did not like the way she was covering herself. He was a civil servant and there were so many other civil servants who came from other parts of the country with a much more modern way of life. He wanted a wife who was modern, not old-fashioned. *Could Laiya play that role?* he wondered. *But she is very young. Young people are more eager to embrace changes*, he thought. In the days that followed, his mother continued to pressure him to make a decision regarding Laiya, and finally he said yes, he would marry her, in the hopes of a happy future.

The next day his mother told Laiya's father about the proposed marriage and he agreed with no objections. The wedding was supposed to be very informal and small. He had just bought his house and after losing all his belongings a year before, and combined with the divorce, he did not have extra money to spend on an elaborate wedding.

"No problem," Mamdali told them. "We can have the wedding in Moji's house then."

It did not cross Babak's mind that his agreement did not mean Laiya's agreement. Laiya was summoned to Moji's house, thinking she was going to join them as usual for their family get together. When she got there she realized that her father was there too. Fatemeh looked at her and said, "This dress is not suitable for the ceremony," and went to her closet and found a green dress, which is customary for the brides to wear in the wedding ceremonies in Pasargad. Laiya did not understand the fuss and did not know what ceremony she was talking about. She changed her clothes to Fatemeh's green dress and they guided her hurriedly to a room with a mirror and an elaborate table set up for a wedding.

"Whose wedding is that?" she asked, surprised.

Her three friends looked at her and replied, "Yours! Don't you know that?"

"No, I— "

Her words were interrupted as her great-aunt appeared and asked her to sit at the table. She obeyed wondering who was going to be her husband. There was no time to think though. Nobody had talked to her about the possibility of marriage. There was one young eligible bachelor in this family. *Could it be Parham?* she asked herself. Parham was single and she thought she might be marrying him.

Her thoughts were interrupted by the cleric who announced the groom's name. It was Babak! Was she happy about it? She later claimed that she was not!

Laiya

Laiya was born in Pasargad. Her father was a calm businessman who had a bakery to make cookies. Her first big shock came when her mother suddenly fell ill due to kidney disease. Her mother was taken to a hospital in Shiraz where she soon died. Her husband buried her in that city and came back to Pasargad, which was odd behavior. Usually the body of the deceased would be buried in town so the relatives would be able to visit the grave. But he was not like the other people.

When he came back to Pasargad, he hired a nanny for the children: Laiya, eight, and her brothers, who were six and four. They also had a two-year-old sister. It was so sad for Laiya, the oldest one. She dreamed one night that her mother came and asked her to go with her. She held her hand and went to a beautiful place. There was a door that opened to a garden full of fragrant flowers. When Laiya saw the garden through the big iron gate, she remembered that her mother was not alive. She looked at her mother, who looked exactly like she saw her last and screamed, "You are dead; I am not coming with you!"

Her mother looked at her and said, "Okay. You do not deserve it." She woke up with tears in her eyes. What was that dream, she thought. Maybe it was her wish to be with her mother even while she was scared of being dead.

This fear stayed with her all her life. Later, when she had children, she was still scared of the dark. She would ask her sons or her daughters to accompany her when she needed to go out to the yard at night. This got even worse in her old age—she was scared to be alone at home even one moment. Her mother's death was a big enough shock to be unhappy in her life, but life was not going to let her go with just one loss.

One awful afternoon after her mother's death, when the air was hot and the sun had a burning way about it, she went to their small courtyard. There, in the middle of the courtyard, was their pool. The pool was calm and Zohreh, her little sister, was floating on the water. Suddenly, she felt horrible. She knew that two-year olds could not swim with closed eyes. She started screaming, feeling sick to her stomach. Parham, her father's cousin, ran into the yard. He had heard her shouting from the alley. He saw the little girl and pulled her out of the water. Looking at her cold, breathless body he said, not noticing Laiya, "Oh my God, they killed her! How could they not see her come out and not realize she was missing for such a long time!"

Laiya started crying and she did not remember anything after that moment, even though she always remembered very vividly up to the time she saw her sister on the water and when her cousin pulled Zohreh out. After that, she tried hard not to think about the episode.

So her father found another nanny to be with them when he was out. This one was trying hard to fill their mother's place. She would hold them, giving them as much love as she could. Her name was Danah, but nobody called her by her name. She was called *Naneh* Ali, since her son from her former husband was named Ali. Laiya and her brothers felt comfortable with her. But she wanted not the children' love, but their father's. She was moved by him the first time she saw him and as the time passed, she fell madly in love with him, although she knew it was very unlikely if not impossible to marry Mamdali, who was not only from a good family, but also owned his own bakery shop plus other properties he inherited from his parents.

Who am I? she would tell herself, *just a servant and inferior to his class, so be wise and listen to me, before you get ruined, please forget his love*, a voice would come to her mind and bring tears to her eyes. But she told herself again and again that if you want something badly, you will get it.

Right about this time Mamdali asked his aunt Talah to find him a wife. She knew a girl and gave him her description, as was customary to do in those days. Mamdali told her to seek her hand from her father. The endeavor was successful and the wedding date was set. Danah, who had been hoping to find her master's heart by being extra nice to his children, felt terrible. She wanted to be the lady of that house, not a servant to her master's new wife. She could not help the burning desire she felt when she saw Mamdali. She wanted him so badly and she tried getting his attention by different techniques. But with her short small figure and all those holes on her face, reminders from the last bout of small pox that hit the population, she was less than attractive. More than that, she was a servant from a lower class and she was a widow with a child. She knew that she had to be a master of deception to be able to become the lady of the house. She also knew for sure that his family would not agree to his marriage with her, and that he was not even particularly fond of her, except when he saw her with the children.

What could she do, she asked herself. Well, use the children for sure. She started by telling them wicked stepmother stories and the fact that the stepmothers were so terrible that they hated their stepchildren. Then gradually she told them that their father was going to get married. The children were scared badly. So this was the end of their relationship with their father? What could they do to prevent the wicked stepmother from ruining their lives, they asked. She told them, "Maybe if your father knew how much you hated his decision he would not get married!"

Meanwhile, she told Mamdali that she knew his new bride. Mamdali, who was curious, asked her how she knew her.

"Oh, we both had small pox. And the poor girl lost one of her eyes," she answered carelessly. Then she looked at him with pity, "Oh master, I did not think you would choose such an ugly woman as her!" she looked at him for a second longer, and then she left the room.

Mamdali, who was as nervous as any new groom would be, and who was wondering if he could love this new wife as much as he did his beautiful late wife, became depressed. He was deep in thought when he heard his daughter Laiya crying.

He bent down, asking, "Why are you crying?"

"Oh because you are going to marry that ugly woman and forget about us!"

Mamdali looked at her in amazement and said, "But you have not seen her; how do you know that she is ugly?"

"Oh, I know. I heard from the neighbors."

Mamdali tried to control his increasing doubts and asked again, "Why do you think I will forget about you? My marriage is partly for you, so you will have a mother to take care of you."

Laiya answered sharply, "But she will not be our mother; she will be our wicked stepmother. She will hate us, and she will make you hate us too."

He tried to calm her down, but he was unsuccessful, so he called Danah. She came in and held Laiya in her arms, telling her beautiful words and how much she loved her. She then sat down and told her to lie down in her lap. She started to swing her back and forth like she was only two years old. Laiya was calm now. Her words were soothing and her arms full of love and security. Soon she fell asleep and Danah carried her to bed as Mamdali watched the affection and love she bestowed upon his daughter. He knew how his children felt since he himself had lost his mother when he was very young. He never knew how to show his affection to the children and had been touched for some time now at how Danah gave them so much love.

That night he did not sleep too well. A thousand thoughts passed through his head. How could he tell his aunt that he did not want to marry the girl she had found for him? But if he did that what should he do? He needed someone to take care of his children and to be his friend. *Danah is good with the children but can I marry her? Society will not be happy with that decision though*, he told himself. He did not know how much it would affect him and his family in the years to come, but in the darkness of that night he knew that the best mother for his children was only her. But how to break the news to his aunt? He was not sure.

That night was long and sleep was scarce in his eyes. His mind was chasing the past memories, good or bad. His first wedding, his beautiful wife, her blue eyes, and her painful death all appeared in his memory and just as quickly, vanished.

He fell asleep a little while after midnight and after a very short sleep woke up. He had to go to his bakery. Danah saw him as he was leaving the house and could tell he was not himself. She smiled; she could see that her magic was working; the seed of doubt had been sown in his and his children's hearts. If she could continue, she could have her love, a secure life, and be happy forever.

Oh God, is it possible? Can I have a happy life after all this time? Please help me God, she would say to herself. She started the day again by gathering the children and telling them wicked stepmother stories, and later in the afternoon she asked the boys to go to their father and beg him not to get married, repeating the drama Laiya played the night before. The boys were able to sow more doubts in Mamdali's mind, and all the while, Danah played her role as a good and kind mother to them.

After the children went to bed, he called her in to see him, and asked more about his bride to be.

"Oh dear sir, you are my soul; you should know by now. I want you to be happy; I have loved you completely since the day I met you. You are my master and I will do anything that you want me to do. But I can not be a liar, sir. She is very ugly, not to mention bad-tempered. I can not imagine the children having even one day of happiness with her," she answered, trying to appear as feminine as she could.

She continued, telling him that she considered him superior to her, that he was her master, and that she would never steer him wrong. At the same time she continued to reiterate, as a matter of fact, that his bride-to-be was not only ugly, but bad-tempered. And that his children would never be happy with her.

As she talked, she absentmindedly let her *chador* slide from her head, and her small but pretty body was revealed in front of his eyes. She had a thin sheer dress on, which showed her figure perfectly. Surprised, he thought to himself, *she has a pretty body!* He had not laid an eye on any woman since his beloved wife had died. He had been through so much pain trying to juggle his work and his three children's demands. Losing Zohreh was a terrible shock to him and he also blamed himself for it.

Seeing Danah with his children gave him a comfort he had not felt before her. And in the darkness of that night he felt something else. He felt he wanted that woman whose words were so soothing, and whose loving relationship with his children was so moving.

He left the room before he took action on this new desire. He was deeply religious and did not want to do anything sinful. But lying in bed, he could not stop thinking about her. He did think about the possibility of marrying her for the sake of his children, but he had not thought before that point that she was attractive. But now, after so many months of being alone with no woman in his life, he felt like a young boy again with all sorts of delightfully lustful thoughts. He knew for sure it was best to marry a woman that he knew than to marry someone he had never seen before in his life.

The next day he smiled warmly at Danah and with a deep affectionate look said, "Good morning." Their eyes met and now they mutually felt the burning fire of desire inside their hearts. He quickly turned his head and left the house. Danah knew that she had won him, and felt so happy. She would be the lady of the house after all.

Mamdali went to his aunt that day and told her, "I do not want to marry this girl. I have heard that she is ugly and has a bad temper."

She asked him, "Who told you these lies?" He refused to tell her, which made his aunt angry. She knew for sure that it was a lie. She knew the girl's family; they were very calm and polite. She was very pretty too—not ugly at all. She also felt terrible; how could she tell them that her nephew was breaking his promise and that he did not wish to marry their daughter after all? She thought that it was so shameful. They were both upset. He was under the assumption that his aunt did not tell him the truth. Talah on the other hand, did not appreciate being assumed a liar and was embarrassed to break the agreement of the marriage.

They fast grew angry at each other, and he quickly left, as it was his habit to do at the first sign of conflict. She had no choice but to send someone to the bride's house to give them the bad news. "The groom has cold feet," she said. "I'd like to see what I can do. But right now, he is under some assumptions that are not true."

That night, when he got home, he had made up his mind and asked Danah to be his wife. They got married that same night quietly, and suddenly. Danah's joy was boundless. She felt that she was the luckiest woman on earth. She hugged the children and gave them the news. She was their stepmother. The boys were still young and very fond of her. But Laiya, who was nine now, remembered all the stories she had heard about stepmothers and was convinced that all the stepmothers were wicked and hated their stepchildren.

The next day was the most beautiful day Danah had ever seen; she woke up finding herself lying in her master's bed as his wife. Something she only imagined distantly had become reality! *There is a God after all*, she told herself as she kissed her new husband with affection and love.

What was a fortune for Danah brought terrible misfortune for Laiya. She had this belief that all stepmothers were wicked and that they hated their stepchildren. It made no difference to her if her stepmother was someone she did not know, or the woman she knew as her nanny, and even if she was so kind. In the stories Danah told them, always the women were kind to the children until she became the stepmother. Well, it must be true for Danah too, she thought. She was also jealous. Her father used to talk to her when he returned from his work, asking her about her day and what she did today. This made her feel that her father loved her a lot. But after his marriage, he did not ask her anymore. She felt ignored and was sure that Danah had done something to make her father ignore her.

The problem got worse when people started to hear the news. There were three friends in her neighborhood who usually played with her. They laughed when they heard the news.

"No one marries a servant," they told her.

Later, her friend's mother and grandmother saw her and started to talk. "Is it true that your father married Danah?"

"Yes," Laiya answered politely.

She started to laugh and said, "Oh my God, what did he do to you and your brothers? What can a servant teach a child?"

Then her mother continued, "When people find out this news, they will not want to marry his daughter either."

They were talking like he was not her father and she was not there. She felt so bad that she decided to go home and cry. But before she could get there, the story was repeated. Another neighbor saw her in the alley and asked the same question. She started on the same path and said many things that implied that her father was a stupid man to marry a servant.

Another neighbor arrived and said, "She is low class, but your mother was from the upper class of landlords. How could he replace that high-status woman with a servant?!"

She wanted to run away and hide. Everyone she saw that day had some bad thing to say about Danah. Her main fault was that she was a lower class and poor. Their neighbors were not upper-class either. One was teaching the Koran in her home and held a *maktab* (religious school); the other was sewing women's clothes; a third had a small shop and could hardly make ends meet for his family of seven. The only family in their neighborhood whose mother and late wife were from the prominent family of landlords was Mamdali. He had several orchards, two houses, and properties he had inherited from his mother and his late wife. His big bakery was impressive, and he was very active as the head of religious ceremonies. He belonged to the top classes of society, classes of landlords, and entrepreneurs with ties to the religious class.

When Laiya finally got home, she went to one of the rooms and started to cry. She felt so bad. Her worries that she lost her father's love and that her nanny's love had turned to hate since she married her father, like in the stories, all felt very real. But now she knew that she might not find a husband from any good families, and that her father was stupid. And that he had betrayed her mother too! As the day passed, she tried to play as usual and see her neighbors, but the story happened again. Grown-ups kept talking to her and telling her what a shame it was to have Danah as a stepmother! The more she heard, the more resentful and bitter she became toward Danah. This stayed with her the rest of her life, and even forty years later when her father died, she did not think she had a good father though her half-sisters thought very differently.

For her father there was a different picture. He married a woman who did what he wanted her to: she took care of the house and the children. He was away all day and would only get home at night when the children were in bed or were ready to go to bed. He could not understand the turmoil that was inside the heart of his oldest daughter.

He did not notice the people's comments either. He did not care much for cheap talk. He was married to a woman he had chosen and it was his business. He had never lived by the norms. He just lived within the religious rules and regulations. Marrying to a lower class woman was not forbidden in his religion. But in that society it was not normal and he was considered stupid. This affected his children in ways that he did not realize. His first wife's children were ashamed of having him as a father and his children from Danah were subjected to all kind of abusive and disrespectful behavior. Was he aware of any of this, Laiya often wondered. She did not know, but even if he knew she saw that he did not care. Did he not bury her mother in a faraway place? She wished so much that she could visit her mother's grave and be able to talk to her and cry like others did. But her father was different, stupidly different, she thought.

As the days passed, she grew into a beautiful young woman. In the next six years she got two half-sisters from her father's new marriage. Her neighborhood friends got married one after another. She would go to her father's aunt often since her granddaughters were almost the same age as she was. The elder one was married, but was living with her grandmother and her sisters. Her uncles were living with them too. That was a fun place for her. There she could forget all about her stupid father and her stepmother. They would talk together and share their pain and happiness with each other.

Aunt Talah was still upset with Mamdali, not like the others for his marriage to a lower-class woman, but for telling her to propose his marriage to another family and then backing out of it at the last minute. His action humiliated and shamed her. She never forgave his behavior.

As the years passed, Laiya grew up with the belief of that her father was a stupid man that did not care about her. This anger combined with her genetic weakness, and her childhood's tragic events took her into a depression that she suffered for years to come. But more than anything, her sudden marriage was a surprise she never forgot. Her marriage gave her prestige and a comfortable life. Her husband did not ask much from her except to live differently. He drank a cup or two of wine and played his tar every evening. Things that were forbidden in her mind, she was sure that she would burn in hell for listening to the music and being present in the presence of a drunken man. She kept her thoughts to herself though, until she got older.

Her husband was opposed to the religious ceremonies that she was accustomed to. He did not like to go to the mosque and prevented her from going too. During religious holidays she would stay at home while everyone in town went to the mosque. Babak did not force anything, he just told her what he did and did not like and she obeyed him, since to her, a woman had to listen to her husband. But this was not without resentment. He asked her not to cover her face or wear a *chador* in the parties they attended or gave. This was hard for her since it was against her beliefs. They both did their daily prayer and deeply believed in their religion, but their interpretations of the religious laws were different. She told him it was not right to drink or play musical instruments. He replied, "I am following our great poet Hafiz and believe that there are things much worse than drinking."

Drink wine,
Burn the pulpit, and put fire in Cahaba,
Sit in the winery,
And drink forever but do not hurt anyone! [10]

Laiya, whose education consisted of going to *maktab*, which taught them only the readings of the Koran, was not intellectual enough to understand the deep meaning of this poem or any of the other poems her husband recited. The differences between their ideologies made life hard for both of them. Yet, he loved Laiya dearly and his love for her only increased when their first child was born. He was determined to make his marriage a happy one, so he stopped his drinking habits and shortly after that, his musical instrument went into hiding. This way his young wife might be a happier spirit, though he often thought of the life he could have had if his wife were like the wife of his best friend, Safa. Safa had married a beautiful, educated woman named Mina, who was much like Roodabeh, modern and intellectual, though unlike Roodabeh, Mina was faithful. But even as he thought of this, he knew he had made his choices, and was committed to this life that he had chosen.

Laiya was happy to see her first-born daughter, Nosha, who was so beautiful that the whole family and even sometimes the people in town talked about her. She felt like she had a new toy and would hold and kiss her as if she were a precious and rare doll.

But her heavy feelings of unhappiness did not leave her. She thought that she was born to be constantly hurt and losing her mother so early was proof that this was true. She did not care about her father and told everyone so. Yet, when her husband mentioned that her father was stupid for some of the things he did, she would get mad and scream at the top of her lungs, saying things like 'Why are you insulting me!?' She did not even seem to notice that he had given up his love for music to make her happy, or that he stopped drinking his daily glass of wine within their first two years of marriage.

Babak soon realized that his young wife was suffering from some unknown disease, but he did not know what it was. So he started living his days the way he liked, more or less. Being away from home was a good remedy to avoid the constant and unnecessary fights. He soon bought an orchard that was next to his house from the money he got from the sale of land his father had bought him when he was a child. Then he started building it, little by little, spending all of his free time in the orchard.

Soon his second daughter Nooshin was born, and he told his wife that this was enough. He told her that a small family is better than a big one, so he had her get on birth control, and for this Laiya was furious. Even though she had two daughters, she was not happy. She had never wanted to have daughters; she wanted a son and without any more children, she would not be able to have one. But he stressed that he was more interested in having a small family and did not care for any more children—daughters or sons.

He adored his daughters and was famous throughout the town for his love for them. But after another bad stroke of luck, in which Laiya lost her brother, she became so depressed that she would get angry at the smallest thing, and would cry for hours. But worse than that were the pains in her abdomen. She went to a doctor and apparently the doctor realized she needed another child to get better and told her to stop the birth control. Soon she was better and then their son was born, to a great rejoicing on her part.

But even the arrival of her next two sons, one after another, did not make her happy. She was in her own world all the time. Her attention was always only on the youngest child while she was nursing, and she fought with the rest of them about everything imaginable. Babak, who had fallen in love with his young wife, and who had tried for years unsuccessfully to make her happy, had his children to love now. He bestowed all his love on them and soon he found himself defending his young wife's behavior with his children. "She is not well," he would tell them. "Please bear with her."

Book III
Nosha

Nosha

Nosha did not remember much about the first four years of her life, but she did remember vividly being five years old, and the darling of her whole household as the first child of her parents.

Her mother, the twenty-one-year-old daughter of a businessman, was very beautiful but also always sad looking. Nosha did not know the word 'depression'; it was only years later that she understood how her mother had suffered and what the disease really was. Her father, on the other hand, was very happy and kind. What she remembered most about him through her life was the beautiful poetry that he recited to his children.

Nosha's parents were not the only adults in her household. The oldest person in her family was her paternal grandmother, a very strong woman who lived with them. Even though she looked old to Nosha, she was always happy. Like Nosha's father, her grandmother was always telling jokes when friends or family were gathered around. She also stayed busy all the time, doing something around the house or going to see her friends.

Nosha adored her grandmother, because she was very kind and loving and would take Nosha to visit friends, a wonderful adventure even though there were no children to play with. Nosha did not mind the lack of playmates, since listening to the talk of others was always entertaining enough.

Two other people lived in Nosha's house with her family. The first was a tall, strong, black woman, who cleaned, cooked, and looked after the children when no one else was at home. This woman they called *Naneh* (like nanny in English). *Naneh* worked hard, lifting heavy things and cleaning everywhere. But *Naneh* also sang, and danced, and laughed all the time, and generally was happy despite her hard jobs.

Naneh was paid a monthly salary, plus food and given clothes on occasion. Her home was next to Nosha's, and was tiny in comparison.

Naneh had a daughter and two sons. After cooking and serving food for Nosha's family, *Naneh* would take her food home and eat with her own family.

Also present in the household was the gardener, named Oujan. He was a strong, tall man with hands rough from pulling weeds all day, attending to the orange trees, and taking care of the flowers that Babak ordered for him to plant. Nosha loved to walk in the orchard, so much that Oujan always called Nosha 'the gardener's daughter'. She liked his gentle teasing, since she knew he considered her as one of his own, to protect and to nourish and to revere.

Asghar (the butler), was a waiter in a restaurant near the office where Babak worked. In the evenings, when the restaurant was closed, Asghar would come to Nosha's house to help with the shopping, to fertilize the palm trees, or to pick dates as they ripened.

While he worked, Asghar would talk constantly. To the children, Asghar would tell stories or jokes. He always talked to Babak about politics and the news. Asghar always had the most current events and news on his mind and would spend long periods of time discussing the events of the day with Babak.

The servants, Oujan, *Naneh*, and Asghar, all had been given nicknames by Babak, and as far as Nosha was concerned the servants were all part of the family. *Naneh* was called *Kalontar*, a police officer, since her voice was loud and demanding. Asghar was called *Morshed*, after the religious leader of the mystic dervishes, one of many branches of Islam. His constant discussions were what earned him the nickname. Oujan was named *Darkhor*, which means one who eats doors, because of his healthy appetite. The children adopted these names when they called them, and guests would laugh, amused, when they visited.

Watching Asghar, *Naneh* and Oujan, Nosha realized at a very young age that to be happy, one does not need to have much money. While some of her mother's friends were wealthy but always upset, *Naneh* was poor but happy. Oujan also did not have much money, but happily lived among the treasures of the garden and his children. Nosha, a child who listened and watched, saw that one can be happy with only a few material things and can likewise be miserable in the

The House

The house was on a two-acre lot, with most of the property taken up by an orchard of cypress trees. There were four doors in the walls that surrounded the compound. Two of them were small, old, wind-gnawed doors; one could not understand why they were there. The other two doors were heavy and gate-sized. Each of the large doors had a metal ring attached to it. The family most often went in and out through the south-side door, which was located in a very narrow alley made up of other high walls, and the doors of other houses. The houses in Pasargad always had tall walls surrounding their inner courtyards, as tall as three meters or taller, which was for the security of the household and for privacy from the world surrounding them.

The other large door opened onto a garage-like space, which was called a *dalan*. Next to the *dalan* was the courtyard. The courtyard was covered with stone and concrete on one side and tall, wild, fragrant rose, pomegranate, and orange trees on the other. A small pool was located between green orange trees and the ornamental jasmine tree that bloomed fragrant white flowers every year. Years later, Nosha discovered a nearly identical structure on the streets of Paris and she thought to herself, *no wonder I liked that courtyard so much!*

One day when she was in college, Nosha had returned home to find a concrete above-the-ground pool sitting where her beloved jasmine tree had stood.

"What is this ugly thing?" she asked.

Naneh sighed, "You should have been here to see how much trouble it was to build it."

Oujan chimed in, explaining how the pool was built, how many men it had taken, and how loud the normally quiet garden had been. Both he and *Naneh* seemed to agree with her that it was ugly and unnecessary.

"But why did they build it in the first place?" Nosha demanded.

"It had to be done!" Nosha's mother explained; she was convinced that a pool was a status symbol, and had fretted until the thing was built. "Everybody has one like this!"

That was her mother's way of life—looking to see what other people possessed, and then wanting the same things regardless of what she had and how beautiful her own property was already.

The east building in the compound consisted of three rooms, a hallway, and a kitchen. The two larger rooms were connected by the smaller room, with the walkway running past all three and into the kitchen. The rooms were a little above the ground, so there were three steps down to the courtyard.

The room closest to the *dalan* was a guest room, and contained a beautiful carpet and expensive furniture, which was so large that it made the small space seem much smaller. The other large room was the family's living area. Like almost everyone in the city, Nosha's family slept on pallets at night in the same room where they ate their meals and relaxed together. If anyone found the family room too crowded, on most of the days of winter there were metal chairs in the courtyard and the orchard to sit on and converse. Only during rare bad weather and rainy days did Nosha feel truly constricted with her family in that one room.

The third, smaller room in the east building was the pantry; in it were big clay containers full of rice, flour, dates, oil, and other non-perishable foods. They were purchased on a per-year basis and each day Laiya or Talah would get the food out of the pantry and give it to *Naneh* to cook. Meat was purchased daily from the market, if it was not the hunting season. *Naneh* also cooked fresh bread every morning, then went to the store to purchase the meat if it was needed.

The east building had plenty of sunshine in the winter months, which made it the ideal place during the day and into the night. Their small *manghal* warmed the room at nights and on rainy days. Most of the time, though, no more heat was necessary. After the sun had poured through the three arched windows all day, the room was very warm and comfortable even during the winter.

The west building had two rooms, and where the east building was designed to keep the heat in, its western counterpart was designed to keep the heat out. There were holes in the ceiling overhead and no door to the outside, except for the front room. The front room had a door to a back room, the courtyard, and a long hallway. Half of this hallway's wall was against the larger kitchen and the other half had no wall at all, only poles holding up the ceiling. In the summer months, the west building was cool and made the hot days tolerable. No sunshine entered either of the two rooms, and the breeze creeping in from the hallway made them the ideal place to rest in the warm days of summers at a time that there was no electricity for fans, and air conditioners were almost unheard of.

Nosha never understood the function of the two kitchens. Was the purpose to make this kitchen cooler also? She never asked *Naneh* if the east kitchen was cooler than the west ones; the woman seemed happy to prepare the food in the east-side kitchen in the winter and west-side in the summer.

Grandma Talah

With her perfumed clothes and smile all her own, their grandmother Talah was the life of every party. Her jokes made people laugh and her spirit gave them hope. She had gone through so much in life and still was so joyful. Nosha often regarded the old woman as an amazing inspiration.

Only when she was talking about her beloved daughter Shiva, who died while giving birth, did Talah look sad. Instead of speaking Shiva's name, though Talah always said *Naneh Mordeh*, and for a long time Nosha thought that her late aunt's name was *Naneh Mordeh*.

Nosha remembered vividly learning otherwise one day, as her grandmother talked of her long departed daughter. Nosha innocently had asked, "How old was *Naneh Mordeh* when she died?"

Her mother looked up, angry, and told her daughter, "Shut up and do not talk to your grandmother like that!"

Nosha was stunned. She looked at her grandmother, to see if Talah would take her side. She did not know what she said that made her mother so mad, but Nosha knew that, as always, her grandmother would come to her rescue. This time, however, Talah only sat quietly, looking at a distant past and could not see Nosha's inquiring eyes.

Nosha looked at her mother with amazement and asked, "Why? What did I say?"

"You should not call anyone *Naneh Mordeh*," was the cold reply.

"What? Isn't that her name?" Nosha begged, completely confused.

"No, her real name was Shiva."

"But grandma always says... says..." she was scared to repeat it.

Her mother, beginning to understand, explained with a calmer tone, "Your grandmother calls her late daughter *Naneh Mordeh* because she wishes that she had died herself instead. *Naneh Mordeh* means her dead mother."

Nosha was stunned, and looked back and forth between her mother and grandmother, not knowing what to say.

"She was only twenty-four when she died," her grandmother whispered. Talah's voice sounded as though she were reliving that day and experiencing again all the pain that Shiva's death had caused. In Talah's breaking voice, all the years of missing her only daughter and first child, the reminder of her first love, were as plain as a bare wall. Her pain was understandable, and her loss too.

Talah's story was long and full of ups and downs. The story never followed any simple or straightforward path; it was full of flashbacks to now and to then. Good memories and horrible ones all mixed together with different time periods. Talah seemed constantly to relive her greatest contentments only to experience over and over again her deepest despairs.

Nosha knew that her Grandmother Talah was a remarkable individual, who knew the ups and downs of life better than almost anyone else did. Talah also knew how to live with joy despite the fact that life ends for everyone eventually.

Talah would talk about her own death as though she were planning a party. She had a suitcase full of expensive cloth materials, a white sheet of cotton cloth brought from Mecca and several other things. Sometimes, Talah would take the objects out and show then to her granddaughter.

"This white cloth is what I will be buried in," she would say, holding the fabric up and inspecting it for flaws and imperfections. There were none. Nosha always felt a strange chill when she thought about how she would one day see Talah cold and lifeless, wrapped in her precious cloth.

One night, Talah began to tell Nosha stories about her late husband, Nosha's grandfather. The only complaint Talah had about him and their ten years of marriage was that he did not pay attention to money and he spent it as soon as he got it.

They both must have been beautiful, Nosha thought. Both her father and her uncle were very handsome, with her uncle slightly taller and a little slimmer than her father. Nosha's uncle had black hair, and dark black eyes set on the white background of his skin. Her father was shorter, an average height for Persian men, but had a very light, almost blond hair and green eyes, with skin so white that it was strange in their little town where most people had a dark complexion. It was a trait that ran in Nosha's family. Her grandmother had green eyes and so did she and her cousins.

Green and blue eyes were not terribly uncommon for people in the town, but dirty blond hair and skin as white as her father's were very rare. Nosha often wondered where her father had gotten his light complexion. She could not tell the color of her grandmother's hair since Talah used henna and other dyes to keep her gray hairs from showing. All of Nosha's aunts had the same color hair, since they all used henna too.

Nosha reasoned that her father might have gotten his looks from his father. Her grandfather and great-grandfather were foreigners to the people in the small town when they arrived in Pasargad. Nosha's grandfather was known to be from Shiraz, the capital city of Pars province.

"So, how did you meet my grandfather?" Nosha asked.

Grandmother smiled as though it had been only yesterday when she met him.

"I was sick and he came to see me for my cold. He was nice and handsome. He talked with a beautiful accent, which was new to me. He came back to visit me again until my fever went away. Then we got married and your father and uncle were born. So life was going like a beautiful stream; although we had our difficulties we were happy. Yes, happy."

Nosha looked at her grandmother; Talah seemed distant, far away from the present and immersed in both the past that was pleasant and good, and another past that was tragic and painful. Talah's life was an ocean full of stormy days followed by calm ones. Nosha could see from her expressions whether her grandmother was telling her stories about her stormy life or the calmer days. When she was talking about her grandfather, she could tell it was the tale of her good times. Still, she probed Talah's memory.

"But my grandpa was a physician; he should have earned enough money!" Nosha asked.

"Yes, of course," grandmother answered cheerfully. "But people do not get sick all the time. He spent any money he earned the day he earned it so there was no money left for the rainy days, and with the bad economy of that time, people did not go to the doctor unless they really were sick!"

"Did you get to know your first husband before you got married?"

Nosha asked.

Talah chuckled, "Oh no, the girls were supposed to cover themselves from head to toe at that time. Only after Reza Shah forced women to abandon the black *chadors* did any female past puberty leave her house without a *chador*. So while a man might see his wife before the wedding these days, when I was first married you were lucky if you saw your husband before the ceremony was over. Even in my time, some people tried to change things. Some men refused to get married until they saw their bride."

"You mean every girl at those times had to cover themselves from head to toes like the cleric's families?" Nosha asked.

"Oh yes honey, everyone."

"Even the villagers? They have beautiful clothes and they do not cover themselves from head to toe."

"No, they always wore the traditional clothes. Only in the cities was the black *chador* the norm."

Nosha was confused more now. For sometimes she noticed that the Persian women were wearing three different kinds of outfits. Her father's friends all from other cities were wearing westernized clothes; the married ones wore heavy makeup too. They got their ideas about fashion from many magazines with colorful pages and news about fashion. Nosha, her sister, and her mother wore western clothes too, but Nosha's mother did not wear any makeup. The women in Pasargad wore mostly westernized clothes, but added a *chador* when they went out into the streets or when a man who was not a close relative was in their houses. The *chador's* color and thickness varied according to the beliefs, age, and affluence of the woman wearing them. Finally, in more traditional families, all the women wore a black *chador* that covered their bodies and most of their heads. Some went even further and covered their faces with the fabric, by pulling the *chador* and holding it up with their hands.

The younger generations, and less traditional women wore very light *chadors* made of sheer materials. These garments were wrapped loosely over the head, covering only part of their hair, and then draped over the shoulders. Many women chose exotically colored *chadors* and the often-translucent materials, which made them even more mysterious and beautiful still.

Then there were the villagers, who had their own customs that varied from region to region. Their clothes were long and colorful. Their scarves were made of sheer white materials that were drawn tightly around the head and fastened with a golden pin. But the village women left part of their hair out too.

Nosha loved those colorful clothes and once borrowed one set from one of her classmates. She took a picture while wearing the outfit and admired the color and the strange fit. But Nosha soon realized although the villagers' clothes were more beautiful than her own, they were not as comfortable.

"Well, if I had to wear *chador*, I would rather wear the villagers' clothes than the black *chador* of the more traditional families of Pasargad," she told her grandmother.

One afternoon in the summer when, the air was so hot that no one wanted to go outside, Nosha heard Talah telling her mother another piece of her life story, and since she loved to watch and listen, Nosha sat down by them to hear it.

"He would buy a whole load of watermelons, cut them, and set them out around the pool, asking me and the children to choose which one we would like to eat!"

Nosha realized that her grandmother was talking about her grandfather again.

"The whole load of watermelon!" Talah repeated, for emphasis.

"How many were there?" Nosha asked.

"Twenty or more!" the old woman answered.

"But could you all eat so many watermelons?"

"No, not really. That is why I am telling you he spent his money without thinking, and then we had problems later on," came Talah's response.

"Did you feel poor then?" Nosha wondered.

Talah nodded with a smile, "Sometimes I did. I remember one day when I wanted to cook the bread but realized that I did not have any flour. I told Mamreza about it. He said, that unfortunately he did not have any money left but that I could go to his father and ask for some; for they surely had plenty, and that we would give it back when he got some more money.

"I agreed to go to ask his father for flour. Your grandfather asked me to lock the door behind me so nobody would bother him since he did not want to see anybody that day. Our door, like the one we have now, was a big wooden door with a metal ring, which we had to use with a big metal lock to lock it, and it was an obvious way to tell people that nobody was home.

"I knew my husband. He would get very depressed when he did not have much money. So, I granted his wish and went to my father-in-law to borrow flour. When I got there and explained the reason I was there, his father got the flour and tried to weigh it. However, suddenly something strange happened. The scale leg broke. He looked at me and said, 'Go and tell my son that there was a sign from God telling me that I should not give him anything anymore, and that the almighty God has cut any of my resources from him.' I thought he was joking, but when I looked at him, I saw he was dead serious.

"'How could he do it?' I asked myself. I had two children of my own plus my two stepdaughters and a stepson with nothing to eat. He had so much money, but not only did he not give us any flour, but he was also refusing to lend it to us! I left his house with a heavy heart, knowing the reason why he was so filthy rich. I wondered how one could be so cruel, and I was mad at Mamreza for being so careless. I was sure that we would have to fast that day, since we did not have any money to buy flour or meat or rice, and we had eaten the last of our reserves the day before.

"For the first time in my life I felt very poor and without any place to turn. So I went home to complain to my husband. When I opened the door and told him what happened in his father's house, he shook his head and said with a smile, 'He might be right.'

"I wanted to scream at him, not only because he was not mad at his father for refusing us a little flour, but also for being so calm and amused, while his children were hungry. Even though most of the time I admired your grandfather's unselfishness and kindness, that day I was frustrated. Well, you should know him by now, I told myself. Obviously, with no expectations of his father, our state of affairs did not bother him as much as it did me.

"As I stood before him, I was bewildered. When that man did not have money to spend, he would get easily depressed, so why was he chuckling?

"I told him furiously, 'Fine! Then what should I do with the hungry mouths of our children?' He handed me a bag of 150 *shahi*, enough to pay for our whole month of groceries!

"I was even angrier. 'How could you do this to me? Sending me to your father while you had so much at home?' I screamed at him.

"He replied with his usual calm poise and said, 'The almighty God sent this to you; I did not have it at the time of your departure.'

"I looked at him stupidly. How could God send him this money?

"Memreza saw my confusion and said, 'When you left, I heard somebody ringing the doorbell very loudly for a long time. I went behind the door and heard a man begging me to open the door. I felt bad and answered that I was home but he had to wait until my wife came back. He told me about his wife, who was a patient of mine and needed her prescription to be filled. I prepared the prescription and slid it under the door. He slipped this money to me the same way and departed. After he left, I realized that he had given me more than I usually charge. I guess he was so happy to find me after ringing the door and kicking it so hard!'

"Mamreza ended his story with a smile. I was amazed, and I did not mind that the man gave more money than he should have; knowing my husband, the man or his wife had probably not paid at all the last time they were here. Because of the bad economy, most of the time people were too poor to pay, or it was not the harvest time; at these times, my husband would tell them: pay me next time, and often forgot about it. His passion was to cure the people's sickness; the money was its fringe benefit.

"I looked at my husband, still awed by the mysterious ways in which God works. Obviously, the man did not see that big lock on the door, or he would not have rung the doorbell. On top of that, my husband had not come with me that day, and thus did not miss his patient. I shook my head, but everything still seemed miraculous.

"While thanking God for his kindness, I felt a sudden surge of love for my husband. My husband was calm and kind. He possessed no anger, or bad feelings, just a calming spirit and a warm disposition. I still could not believe my father-in-law's behavior, and felt mad at the old man still, even though we would not have to worry about food for some time. But for that one moment, I was content simply to love my gentle husband."

Grandma Talah smiled at the memory, and then closed her eyes for her afternoon nap.

After the long hot days in Pasargad summer, the nights were cool and pleasant. The town was set between two tall stretches of mountain, which made the nights as cool as the days were hot. Nosha's house especially was cooler because of the orchard and the trees. Outside, under the stars, they had two sets of beds; each set contained four wooden beds that were connected together by a hatch. In the summer nights these wooden beds were covered with Persian carpets, and then at bedtime were stacked with four folded mattresses. On one set, Nosha and her grandmother would sleep, while the other set belonged to her parents and her sister. Later, when her brother was born, her sister joined them too.

Her grandmother would tell her stories when they laid down and that night she was talking about her first husband.

"He was an easygoing man, and he was home most of the time talking and being with me. His absence from home was only when he went to the village to manage his property, which was only a few days per month."

"You mean he did not go to work everyday like my father?"

"Oh no, those days there were no offices like your father's."

"If he was not working from the office like my father and he was not like grandfather, to see his patients from his house, where did he get his money from?"

"He was a landlord, darling. Just like any other landlord, he paid for the seeds, the equipment, and the land of course was his. The peasants did the work for him and got one fourth of the income. He was very devoted to his family and when I got pregnant, he could not have been happier. I was happy too, I felt like a princess. I was young and in love with a man who adored me. I did not want anything more. I was happy, very happy." She fell asleep, whispering.

When laying down in bed Nosha could see thousands of little stars in the deep blue sky above her. This was her favorite time, and she would count them as she fell into a deep contented sleep. The summer nights were a good time for stories. There was no TV or any other activities. The kerosene lights were not much light for reading, so she would ask her grandmother to tell her stories. And those nights in which her father was away on hunting trips, she and her mother and sister were a captive audience for her grandmother's life stories.

"He told me one day, 'What if my son (Bo-ali Sina from a previous marriage, named after the famous Persian physician, but we called him Sina) married your daughter?' I told him it was a wonderful idea.

"So came a beautiful wedding. I was so happy and so was Mamreza. The bride was only twelve years old and—"

"Twelve?" Nosha interrupted. "How did she get married at that age?" She was scared to find out that in less than six years she could be eligible to marry.

"Yes, at those times girls were getting married at much a younger age. Only since Pahlavi's era has the marriage age been raised to sixteen," her grandma replied. This was not that much comfort to Nosha, though. She could still not imagine getting married at only sixteen.

How and when did her grandfather die, Nosha wondered, so she asked her grandma that night when they were lying down in bed.

"I do not know; he died quickly after a few days of being sick. It was my fault, I thought at the time. He was the second husband who was dying in front of my eyes. I was bad luck; I was *kaleh khor*." She said this very firmly, like she still believed it.

"How can you say that?" Nosha asked. "You are a very kind, gentle and warm woman. Don't ever say that!" Nosha demanded.

She laughed at her granddaughter's emotion, kissed her, and said, "Thank you darling, but I can not accept your demand."

"Why?" Nosha asked.

"Because I was bad luck! How can you explain that I married four times and lost all my husbands?"

"Four!" Nosha exclaimed. She nodded. Nosha frowned and started to think. Maybe she was right! Not one or two but four!

She smiled at her and said, "Well you see it too—that I was bad luck."

Nosha could see the tears in her eyes for a moment and then she said, "But this was not the end. The days that followed my husband's death were very hard, since Sina and Shiva's marriage broke down and Sina did not show he had any interest in the marriage. But he did not agree to the divorce either. The Islamic law did not leave any right for women to get divorced. It does give them a little financial incentive if their husband wants to divorce them whether they want it or not."

"What? That is not fair" Nosha said angrily.

Her grandma replied with her usual calm voice, "No, God is great and he knows better than us."

"Let me understand. If I grow up and get married, then I have to live with my husband as long as I live! And furthermore, I cannot leave him even if I do not like him. Is that true?" Her mother nodded yes. Nosha continued, "But if my husband wants to divorce me, he can any time, even if I do not want the divorce, right?"

Her grandma and mother said yes at the same time. If he pays the *mehrie* money (the agreed money Moslem men put in the marriage contract on the wedding day) he can do whatever he likes.

Nosha shook her head and asked, "And you are telling me that God is great?"

"Yes, of course," her grandmother answered.

"But you and *Baba* always taught me that God is just. I do not see any justice in this rule."

"Well," grandma answered, "maybe it is just because almost no woman wants a divorce anyway. The men have to pay if they divorce their wives, and since most of the times they cannot afford it, they do not go through with it either. I do not know any divorced couples around here, do you?"

Nosha was not satisfied and said "No, but Shiva wanted the divorce didn't she?"

"Yes she did, and we all paid dearly for it!"

"What do you mean?"

"Well," as I said before, "Sina would not agree to the divorce unless I agreed to give him all of his father's belongings (the property which was inherited by Babak and Afshin)."

"Did you agree?"

"Not at first, but the problem continued and Shiva was crying every day. One day she told me, 'You left me when I was so young to grow up without a mother, and then you made me marry Sina and go through these difficult times. Now is the time to show me your love. Let me know for the first time that you love me. We are all in hell anyway. It is not right for my brothers to go through all these fights either.'

"I looked at her beautiful eyes; she was crying. I could not take it. I loved her so much, and yes, she was right. They took her away from me when she needed me, and at age fifteen, she thought she was in a hell I created for her. But that was the law and I had to obey it."

"What do you mean it was the law?'

"Well honey, there is a law that if a man dies, his children would be fostered by their paternal grandfather, uncle, or an older brother, if they have one," she answered.

"What about the mother?" Nosha asked.

"Mothers do not have any rights," her mother snapped.

"Well," her grandmother explained, "No woman can afford to raise a child by herself; it is hard both ways," she said, ignoring Laiya's remarks.

So Nosha asked with a worried voice, "So you did it?"

"Well, I agreed to most of Sina's demands. Shiva got her divorce, but the baby died and Sina followed him a few years later."

"How?" Nosha asked again.

"Oh there was yet another epidemic and he died then. But from what people were telling me, he was in a very bad shape emotionally, even before the epidemic. He sold some of his properties and left the rest to Kobra, one of his siblings. Only one of the orchards, which Mamreza bought in the name of Babak and Afshin while he was alive, was left for us. That is the orchard that your father sold to buy this orchard." She pointed to the backyard orchard.

"Do you mean he purposely left everything to Kobra?"

"Oh yes, and she paid for being so greedy too. See, nobody should take the property of an orphan child; it is written in the Koran—they who do so will be punished. We all had to pay. Shiva and Sina paid by losing their child. I had to go through tough times, and Kobra, who I think was the reason and the force for Sina's demand at the time of divorce, also paid."

"What was Kobra's reason for being mean?" Nosha asked.

"Well, this is my guess: she was greedy. With greed, she could not see what she was doing to the family who were so close to her. She did not care about her young brothers, and she did not see what she was doing to Sina. She encouraged him without seeing his sickness. She asked him to make the divorce demands. That is why she got everything. Sina was alone and depressed. Kobra was using him to get herself rich. But God is great. Her punishment was very severe. She died poor, with lots of pain and alone!" she sighed.

"How," Nosha asked curiously.

"She got married to a husband who was as greedy as she was and mean as a devil. He pretended to be nice; he lived off her property, sold one property after another, and spent the money until Kobra did not have a penny. Then he started to show his true face. He showed his meanness. He was bad-mouthing her, beating her, and not giving her enough to eat. And finally, after all this torture, she became sick. Her husband's first reaction was to become meaner and complain about her sickness. Then one day he carried her out of his house and left her on the street. Can you imagine what she went through? She gave all her belongings and her life to a man who refused to care for her when she needed him the most."

"What about her relatives? Did not she have any?" Nosha asked.

"Which relatives?" Grandma continued. "The brothers who she robbed of their own money? Sina was long dead. Babak and Afshin were too young and needy themselves. Sara, her sister, did not have much, besides she was not too fond of Kobra. She still was bitter about her behavior when Sina was sick and the way Kobra tricked him. So they were not on good terms when the news came that she was left alone on the street. Sara, however, was kind and forgiving, so she took her in, but Kobra died a few months later with a heavy heart and the bitter reminder of her love for her husband. I do not know if she knew that all this misfortune came from her greed and unkind heart at the time she died."

"Did she have any children?"

"Yes, Mrs. Kazemi is her daughter," she replied.

Nosha knew who she was. During the New Year celebration and rituals, she had met her. One problem with the holidays was that if one of the family members is the oldest, all the close and distant relatives will visit your house, and such was true with Nosha's family. Because of her grandmother and her father, many distant relatives visited them. And of course, the many friends of her father too. She had dreamy memories of their New Year celebrations. She knew, though, that she did not like those strangers who called themselves her relatives but who she saw only once a year, trying to kiss her. One of them was Mrs. Kazemi.

She was a black-eyed, black-haired, middle-aged lady, with very bad taste in clothes. She came to their house once a year and claimed to be her aunt. Her father agreed with the claim and so did her mom, but she could not accept her as her aunt since she never came to her house. Even though she saw Shiva's daughter's often in their gatherings, there were never any sign of Mrs. Kazemi. Were her father or grandmother still angry about Kobra's behavior, or was it Mrs. Kazemi's father who put such a distance in their relationship? She could guess that her grandma was very bitter of Kobra, and her father often remembered the cruel behavior of Mrs. Kazemi's father. He used to call him the most selfish man on the earth, someone with the mentality of criminals. Years later, Nosha realized what he was saying had truth in it. Mrs. Kazemi's son committed a crime that was unheard of in Pasargad!

Nosha broke the silence and asked "Did you like Sara?"

"Oh yes, she was the sweetest girl I have ever seen. She was kind and lovely."

"What happened to her?"

"She died too. See, I was bad luck and I think I was punished by God, in having such a long life to witness so many people who I loved dying in front of my eyes!"

Nosha was feeling guilty again about asking a question that made her grandmother upset. So, she tried to change the subject to take her mind off of this bad luck business and asked, "Did she have any children?"

"Yes, Moji is her son." He was Nosha's Aunt Fatemeh's husband.

Ironically, her grandmother had managed to create yet another marriage. This one was between her step-grandson and her granddaughter. Moji was the kindest person anyone had ever seen. He was a quiet person who got along with everybody. According to her mother, Aunt Fatemeh had a perfect marriage. She was happy, and you could see it.

Nosha started to think about these strange circumstances. Sina married Shiva, but they got divorced, then she married an older man and had five children. Later Sina's nephew married Shiva's oldest daughter and they lived happily ever after. Was it a coincidence? Would Shiva have agreed to the marriage if she were alive? Nosha did not know.

That night, the sky was clear and the stars were more beautiful than ever. The jasmine tree's perfume spread through the air and she was feeling wonderful despite the sad story she had just heard. Strange! She had two aunts. One was assertive and revolutionary. She refused to be abused by her husband and suffered the consequences. Nosha admired her and could see how brave she was. As her grandmother said, Nosha did not know any divorced woman in their city, and she also heard her mom frequently say that women had to take crap from men since they needed them.

There was also a truism that every young girl knew of. It was a whisper in the girls' ears by their mothers at their weddings. "You go to your husband with a white dress to part from him with a white cloth at the time of your death."

Nosha was witness to lots of troubled marriages, which neither men nor women could break. Why didn't her maternal uncle divorce his wife when she came to their house crying? He must have been stopped by the family's pressure (until years later when the law was changed and his wife agreed to the divorce).

She could see obviously that her mother was not happy in her marriage and yet she was telling them she had to stay!

But her aunt was very different from her mother. Her mother was playing the victim. She did things she did not like, and she wanted everybody to know it. But Nosha could not see that much of a reason for her mother to feel like such a victim. She was telling them she was controlled by their father even as she was the most controlling person in the household herself. She was the one who always complained, and she was the one who wanted to change their father.

Nosha asked herself, *What about my other aunt? The deceiving creature that was greedy and insensitive. Who could she be like?* Her grandfather had not been greedy and was certainly not deceiving! But her uncle Afshin was, according to her father. Yet, there were more and more differences between Shiva and Kobra. And it was not Kobra's deceiving character. She was a victim, too, and had been deceived herself! *She must have been very stupid*, Nosha thought. *How stupid can you be to leave all your belongings to your husband who was so cruel? Giving your money to men meant suicide!*

She did not have to give anything to her husband, either, by law.

The prophet Mohammad, who had a rich wife, made sure to add this protection for the wives who had money of their own. So how had Shiva been so brave as to leave her marriage? And Kobra so stupid to give all her belongings to the man who left her on the bare street while sick and weak?

Nosha did not want to be like Kobra; she did not want to be calculating or stupid. She fell asleep before she could find any answer to the conflicting characteristics of her uncles and aunts.

One cold winter night, her father and his guests were playing cards in the guest room, and the women were all sitting around the *manghal* in the middle of the living room. Her grandmother started talking about *Naneh Mordeh* again.

She had been survived by four children; all were beautiful. There were three sisters, Aunt Fatemeh, Aunt Ozra and Aunt Atiyeh. They all had green or blue eyes, but the oldest was the most beautiful one. Grandma was telling her how she looked exactly like her mother.

Their brother Hossein was a tall handsome man. He had also a white complexion with green eyes and black hair. They all were extremely religious and very close to each other. Hossein was not religious though and had a Marxist attitude. He had married Nosha's cousin Privash. She was the only daughter of her uncle Afshin, and she was only six years older than Nosha. Babak was not too fond of that marriage and he did not hide his displeasure.

Babak always told everyone when Nosha and her sister were present that any marriage that has more than four years of age difference is bound to be hard. Nosha was happy to hear that and felt secure knowing that she did not have to marry anyone in her teenage years since no teenage boy could marry that young!

"So how was her second marriage? And why you did not approve of it? Did she have happy times?" Nosha had these questions in her mind every time grandma was talking about Shiva.

"Well," she said, "her husband was smart but sneaky. He was pretending to be religious and was very old-fashioned. He also needed Shiva for financial support, but did not like that Shiva was trying to help me and her brothers. He was not too kind to my sons and that hurt me very much."

She was quiet; it seemed to Nosha that she was re-living the past again, and still was trying to make sense of the insensibility of the situation.

"But grandma, I think it was so hard for Shiva to live with Uncle Sina—you said it yourself. Besides Uncle Sina was not survived by anyone and you love my aunts and uncle Hossein very much, don't you?"

Grandma looked at Nosha with pride and said, "Yes of course, you are a very smart girl. I should not complain. Whatever God wants is what happens and I should thank him for all his blessings."

"Yes, Grandma, but we get hurt if somebody does not treat us well. Tell me, what did you do next? Did you get married again?" Nosha asked.

"Well, seeing two husbands die in front of my eyes convinced me that I was bad luck and should not curse another man's life!"

"But that is nonsense!" Nosha shrieked.

"Oh yes, that was what he said" Grandma replied.

"Who?" Nosha asked, riveted.

Grandma replied in a dreamy voice, "Roozbeh, my third husband."

Nosha exclaimed, "So you did get married again!"

"Not at first. Not until he told me with a very emotional gesture that he would never leave me and he would wait until I changed my mind.

"So finally I accepted his proposal. I became convinced that this time I would be happy forever, or at least as long as I lived. And so it happened that I married for the third time to a man I knew and loved for a long time before my marriage. I was so happy that I felt like I was flying in the clouds and thought that there was nobody as happy as me. He was kind and full of love. We had very good times and enjoyed it truly. Those days were brighter than any happy days I had ever seen. We were like two lovebirds who did not see anything but each other and the beautiful moments we had together. It is the most wonderful thing to share your life with someone who loves you and respects you. It was like a dream, and like a dream, it was short-lived. It was a spring of my life that ended abruptly with the arrival of another epidemic. Once again, everywhere you went you would see sick people and the funerals of the dead ones. And soon I saw what I was afraid of all along. Roozbeh was sick and my heart was beating like crazy. I was going mad. No, it is not going to happen again. No, not this time, I was praying day and night to God. Please God, forgive my sins and let my husband live. I wanted to get sick instead of him. I was crying in secret and caring for him with all that I had. He was sick but still kind. He even tried to make me feel better by telling jokes. I could not imagine life without him! But how could I help him?

"It was not a good time for anybody. There were funerals after funerals and two days after Sina's funeral, it happened. What I had dreaded most. Roozbeh smiled while his hand was in my hand and said I love you. Then I saw his beautiful eyes close and his hands got cold. I knew it was the end. I screamed and cried. But it was another end to another man's life. As I had suspected, I was bad luck.

"A few days later I got shocking news. He had divorced me before his death. He thought if he divorced me he would survive, but he did not." Here, Grandmother stopped.

She was quiet and Nosha started to think too. Really, why did he divorce his wife with out telling her? "So what happened next?"

"I was upset and I was hurt. I missed him so much, but I thought to myself, if I was bad luck why did he die regardless of the divorce? We stayed with Shiva. Soon I got a marriage proposal from a widowed man. I agreed since I needed somebody to take care of me financially and did not feel okay about staying with Shiva."

"Was that my Uncle Parham's father?" Nosha asked.

"Yes," she replied. Her eyes were sleepy. *Naneh* appeared with the folded mattresses, which signaled to them that it was time to go to bed. The mattresses were spread out on the carpet of the living room floor next to each other, then *Naneh* brought out the small *manghal* to keep the room warm. And they all went to bed.

As she laid there, Nosha thought over her grandmother's stories. She knew that grandma had three sons from her fourth marriage; one of them was living in Pasargad while the other two were living in Tehran. Then she went back to her grandmothers confusion, and the strange way Roozbeh had divorced her. There had to be a reason for it, she was convinced! As she laid next to her sleeping grandmother, she thought about Roozbeh, wondering about his strange behavior until she fell asleep.

The next morning, as Grandma was forcing a raw egg and a glass of milk down her throat, she told her, "I know why Roozbeh divorced you before he died, and it was not because he was scared of death. He was a very open-minded man; he would not have married you if he wasn't."

Grandma said with a big grin, "So why did he do it?"

"He did it for you, and he succeeded, don't you see? He wanted you to see for yourself that you had nothing to do with his death! If he was dying because you were his wife, then he should get better, should he not? Well, he didn't, and probably he knew that too. He did not think he would survive his sickness, but he wanted you to live and get married again. He loved you and did not want you to live with sorrow and guilt! You did, too. Don't you see?"

She looked at her beloved granddaughter and said, "Well maybe. You have a point that he loved me, but right now it is getting late and you should go to school. So hurry up and go."

Nosha walked out of their big door and into the narrow lanes, as Oujan followed her with her books and school bag. She was in elementary school and loved hanging out with her beautiful cousin Parivash during break time. She and her friends seemed so much older than her. But she loved her beautiful blue eyes, her pale skin, and the long black eyelashes she had. She reminded her of beauty of certain flowers, especially morning glories. She was in sixth grade and engaged. Actually she was legally married, but they were waiting for her to finish elementary school before they lived together.

Parivash was just a child and did not know anything about marriage. Nosha did not remember her wedding. She had a very faint memory of the time her aunts gathered in their house with her grandmother and were talking about Parivash, and then next thing she knew, Parivash was married. As was customary when the cleric asked her if she was ready to get married, she hesitated, and to respect the elders in her family, she said that she needed to know if her father, mother, uncle, and aunt agreed to the marriage; only then could she say yes to the question. Parivash did so and then asked her uncle Babak's permission too. Babak's answer was shocking to many who witnessed the wedding.

"Oh, my dear niece," he replied. "Nobody asked me when my opinion could make a difference. So why ask now?" His wife would say how this was just a custom and you were supposed to say, of course I agree. But knowing her father, Nosha knew he did not agree with the marriage and could not tell a lie either. Her father always stressed telling the truth and hated anyone who did not.

Whenever she listened to her father and his complaints about his brother Afshin, she could not resist the temptation to compare them to two well-known men in the country's history. Another Babak that they knew of was a hero who was trying to make an Iran independent state after the Arab invasion and by contrast there was also a man named Afshin who was an Iranian army officer. Unlike Babak, he did not care that much about Iran, but wanted fame and power for himself, and became a paid army officer for the Arab *Khalif*. His tactic for capturing Babak was very sneaky, and although he succeeded, he became a hated person in their long and rich history. Likewise, Nosha's father's name was Babak and he was kind, without tricks, and helpful to people. He was loved by so many, yet Nosha never heard anybody say any good things about her uncle Afshin.

How could it be? Two brothers from the same parents yet they were so very different. Afshin was rich but stingy. Babak was hardworking but shared what he had with his family and friends. He was a very clean person; Nosha never saw anybody as clean in their small town. His suits and his shirts were always clean and ironed. His many ties matched his shirts. He used the most perfect cologne sprays. You could always tell he was coming by the sweet aromas emitting from him. He even used to rub cologne on his feet before wearing his socks. If you were living in Pasargad and saw how people were living, you would easily notice the cleanliness her father was stressing.

Nosha remembered one afternoon in her uncle's house. All her cousins, who numbered more than twenty, were shaking the mulberry tree to get to the ripe fresh raspberries. Then they picked the fallen raspberries from the ground and ate them. Nosha was there and so was her sister who joined the crowd. Just then, their father walked up and saw them. He was furious. He took them home and told them to wash their mouths.

Not knowing what to do about the mulberries they had eaten, he washed their mouths with permanganate, a disinfecting agent. He did not dare to force them to drink it, knowing that it probably would make them sick!

"Why are you so worried?" Nosha asked. "Everyone was eating the fruit and they did not get sick."

"The microbes," he said. "There is this awful disease that lives in the soil; when it gets into your lungs it makes you sick. The house with the tree belonged to a lady who had tuberculosis, and the possibility of the tuberculosis microbe being in that soil is very high."

It made sense. When they went to school, the health officials came to vaccinate them. The tuberculosis tests were positive for most of the students. Disease prevention and hygiene were not a priority in Pasargad. Nosha and her siblings did not know too many locals, except their father's immediate family, who came to their house and visited them often. Her parents had so many friends, though none from Pasargad. Most of them were government officials coming from other parts of the country.

Soon it was cold again. Nosha had just come back from school. It was raining and she could not go to the orchard or the courtyard. Everyone was in the living room. Her father was playing backgammon with her uncle Parham. The rest of them were gathering around the stove to keep warm. She finished her homework and was bored. So she went and sat next to her Grandmother, asking her, "How old were you when your first husband died?"

"Oh, it is a long story, "she said.

"Tell me about it."

"I was just eighteen when that troublesome epidemic hit the city. People were getting sick everywhere you went, but there was no help and no cure. And it was in those terrible times that I lost my first love, my prince, my beloved husband." She grimaced, as if she was once again experiencing the pain she gone through years ago.

Nosha was quiet, and could not imagine how she survived after losing somebody so dear to her. She could see the pain in her voice and on her kind face.

Oh my dear grandma, you are a beautiful creature who is happy regardless of any problems that arise, Nosha thought. She really was marvelous. Nosha could not understand or appreciate her as much as she deserved though. She was too young to understand. The problems she had experienced throughout in her life were enormous. But how incredibly she had come out, as delicate and lovely as ever!

"It must have been very hard," Nosha said with affection.

"Oh yes, it was hard, but not as hard as when the memorial ceremony was done. I was still experiencing the shock of losing the love of my life when my in-laws informed me of what they had in store for me. They told me to leave my house, all the belongings, and my child! I did not care that much about the money, but leaving Shiva and being away from her was the hardest thing I went through."

"Why did they do such a cruel thing?"

"Well, when greed comes, humanity goes out the door. They wanted to enjoy the money she had, and I was in their way. See, my husband was a rich man with only one child. Everything he had belonged to Shiva. So her paternal uncle took control and told me to leave."

"Why? And why didn't you get anything from all that money," Nosha asked.

"It is the law. When a husband dies the wife only gets one-eighth of the aerial property."

"What is aerial property?"

"If the property has trees that bear fruit, then wife gets one-eighth of the fruit trees."

"But what if the property does not have fruits or trees?" Nosha asked.

"Well, that was my case. I just got a small amount of money he agreed to give me at the time of my marriage, which did not last too long."

"Were you able to visit Shiva at least?" Nosha asked.

"Yes, I could not wait for my visitation time, but it was only a couple of times per week. They were not able to stop us from seeing each other you know. Even if they could stop me, they could not stop her. She had a very strong will, even when she was a child."

She stopped and told her it was time to go to bed.

That night, she went to bed again wondering about her grandmother's time. *Strange law*, she told herself. *I will never let that happen to me. I will be a doctor or a teacher when I grew up. It must have been a different time when grandma was young. All our teachers at school are wearing makeup; they do not have any head coverings and they are working. I know that the money they earn is theirs, and they can do whatever they want to do with it. But that custody law was bad. It is not enough to have money of your own. If the husband's family can get the custody of a child, what was the use of having money?* Nosha asked herself, but she made a promise to do something about it when she got married.

The question of her brave aunt's happiness was nagging her, so she asked grandma about it again.

"Oh honey, we reap whatever we sow, and yes, we all paid for what Shiva did."

"What do you mean," Nosha asked.

"Well, Shiva got a husband who did not scream and shout like Sina did. But he was complaining all the time. Different people have different faults. To me, it was much easier to deal with Sina if you had a little patience than with Sheikh, since he was controlling everything. He was controlling her money, her moves, and even my sons' future and occupations. He sent your father to *maktab* to become a cleric like himself. Shiva was getting pregnant every two years and soon she had five children and was pregnant with the sixth one. She was exhausted taking care of all those children and tolerating a nagging husband but she was taking it anyway. It was her choice, so no matter what she got and how unhappy she was, she did not complain about it."

"Then what happened?" Nosha asked.

Grandma said with a sigh, "Well it was her sixth pregnancy that killed her. She had a very difficult childbirth and with no doctor on site to take care of her, both the mother and child died."

She was quiet, and Nosha could see that she was again staring at a distant past by the mist in her eyes. No wonder she became sad whenever she talked about Shiva. Nosha felt guilty for making her sad by reminding her of that dreadful day in which her beloved daughter passed away. For a while, Nosha was quiet too.

She did not know what to say to a woman who saw so many losses in her life and was still living a full and happy life with little attention to the painful memories of her past. She admired her so much, because could not imagine tolerating even one loss of her own.

Father's Orchard

That morning, the orange blossoms were in full bloom, spreading their sweet perfume out into the air. The roses were covered with red, pink, orange, and yellow fragrant blooms. The jasmine trees were covered with their star-like flowers. Nosha was running through orchard and feeling fantastic. It was Friday and she did not need to go to school, so she was enjoying the magnificent showdown of nature in her backyard orchard. No wonder that people called this orchard heaven on earth! Every corner of it was designed to be entertaining.

She passed the back trail beyond the house wall and turned right into the main road, which divided the orchard into two levels. The white and blue irises made her stop. There were a couple of hyacinths still in bloom. She loved their aroma and bent to pick one up.

Then she continued her journey until she got to the middle of that long gravel road. With all the flowers and the heavenly aroma, she was imagining that she was a famous princess who was walking in her beautiful palace! She heard the kind and warm voice of her father just before reaching the wide street that was witness to their many family gatherings in the evenings.

Her father's voice startled her at first and brought her back to real life. She could not see him but his voice was so near. As he called her, she answered him "yes!" And went toward the voice, turning left into the second main street of the orchard. Sitting in the middle of a bunch of citrus saplings, he was grafting orange branches to them. There were two wide rows of saplings.

Every year there were many branches of strong citrus called *bakrain*, rooted in those two rows, and her father or Morshed grafted them with porange bark. The orchard was multipurposed. The saplings were sold every fall to the locals who wanted to start their new orchards of orange trees. Then their oranges, lemons, sour oranges, sweet lemon fruits, and some dates also were sold to the market. The other rare fruits, such us grapes, plums, prunes, apples, and persimmons, were grown only for their own consumption. The flowers and exotic trees were for beauty and entertainment. She did not know it then, but her father loved flowers as much as he loved entertaining his friends. He made every corner of the orchard beautiful so he could spend his time with his friends or relatives in a heavenly environment. It did not matter to him that he had spent more money on the flowers, which did not bring any benefit, than on the fruit trees, which brought him income. Years later, she realized that her heaven was created by her father's good taste and that not all orchards were so beautiful. Several of her cousins and even one of her brothers owned orchards later, none of which were as lovely as the one she had been raised in.

"What are you doing, dear?" Her father asked while stripping the green bark from the fresh branch of an orange.

"Nothing," she answered. "I was just wandering." Then she sat down by him wondering how it was that he worked so hard, yet had time to take care of them and have so many friends. He was a director in one of the government's offices in Pasargad. In fact, he had the highest rank anybody had in that small town. He could climb the ladder higher if he left Pasargad, which he refused to do. He would work seven hours a day from 7 am to 2 p.m., six days a week, except Thursday when they worked until noon. The workload was forty hours per week, but there in the afternoons, he was free. This is the time he would be busy with the orchard. Grafting, rooting, ordering fertilizer, inspecting trees, and telling the gardener which ones needed pruning and which ones needed more fertilizer. Dealing with the sale of the saplings and the fruits were all parts of his job.

"You work so hard," Nosha told him. He smiled and said:

> *Go to work and do not ask*
> *What is work?*
> *Since the everlasting investments*
> *Are the result of your hard work.*[40]

He was reciting one of the Persian poems to her.

"Yes," she said. "It seems that you are used to working so hard!"

He smiled again and said, "Yes my dear, since I lost my father." He continued with a poem from Sadi the Persian famous poet.

> *I know the pain one goes through when one becomes an orphan.*

Since I was very young, I lost my father and became an orphan.[41]

"Where did you work?" she asked.

"My sister's house," he replied. "The problem was that no matter how hard I was working it never was enough for him."

"Who?" she asked.

He looked at her with affection and said, "You want to hear my life story?"

"Of course," she answered.

"Okay," he continued. "We were living with my sister when I was twelve. She was kind and nice, but her husband was something else. He was a cruel and uncompromising individual. He always was asking us to do this or that, and he never was satisfied no matter how hard we tried. He did not pay attention to our needs either. When I was older, I used to go to mosque and sleep overnight so I did not have to see him, or have him order me around. But there was a problem with that arrangement when it was cold since the mosque did not have a heater. I did not have any blankets either, so most of those nights I could not sleep because I was shivering and longing for a warm bed to sleep in."

"What about your mother and your stepfather? Were they mean too?" she interrupted.

"No, no, they were not. In fact, my stepfather was much nicer than my brother-in-law. But when I was sleeping in the mosque my mother was not married yet and was still living with my sister."

"What did he do to make you so mad? How could you prefer to sleep on a cold floor than sleep in your own bed?"

"Well, I loved to draw. Once he saw me drawing a face. He started screaming his lungs out and told me that I would get a lot of trouble with God and that I had to make that picture come to life when I died. And of course you can not do such a thing since it is only God who could do such a thing," he continued.

"But he said that I would for sure will go to hell. I said to him, 'Okay I will go to hell' and asked why was he so upset. His answer was that since I was in his house he would go to hell too. And he had to stop me from doing such an awful thing!

"That was one of the coldest nights I remember, but I did not want to stay in his house anymore. I went and slept in the corner of the cold and musty mosque. I was suffering from all his demands, screams, and the guilty feelings he induced in me.

"I was also going to maktab, and learned reading, writing, mathematics, literature, and the Arabic language. I was done with that old school. My new stepfather knew how much I wanted to become a doctor as my father had been, so one day while everyone was present he said, 'Let's sell the orchard that Afshin and Babak have and give them the money to go study abroad. Babak likes to study medicine and Afshin can study something that he finds interesting.' In those days, most of the young men from prominent families went abroad to study science, math, medicine, etc.

"There were not any institutions left in which our famous scientists, mathematicians, or medical doctors, like Aboo Ali Sina, Zakaria Razi, etc., had studied. For the last 150 years, Iran had been getting poorer and had been going backward instead of forward. While the world was exploring new ideas and new technologies, our teachers were telling us not to draw any pictures since God would punish us, or instructing us on how to wash our hands or face before prayers."

He became quiet. Nosha could see pain cross over his face.

"Why," she asked.

"Stupid rulers!" he answered. "Ever since the Ghajar dynasty came to power, the superstitions became the norm. We lost a chunk of our lands and all our resources to foreign powers. So the Ghajar dynasty could survive. Only in the beginning of the 1900s did they start sending a handful of students abroad to study. My step-father knew about these students and thought that we might be able to go too."

"So why did you not go?" Nosha asked.

He told her with a sigh, "My brother-in-law did not let that happen. He became furious and told him that he wanted to make us atheists. 'We do not need nonbelievers in our society!' He was crazy. My stepfather was a mild and old man. He did not want to get involved in a fight that he could not win. Having five children from his late wife and three with my mother, he did not have enough to support his own big family and did not have any power to sell our belongings to let us go study abroad either. He did what he could do and was disappointed with my brother-in-law's reaction. He just gave him a very meaningful smile at the suggestion that we would become atheists. Then I was sent to theology school."

"Did you study theology there to become a cleric?" Nosha was curious now. She knew her father had some friends who were clerics. And on New Year's Day, they would come to see him. And at these occasions, the women in the house were supposed to hide themselves somewhere so that they were not seen. But she did not know her father had gone to school with them.

"I was a classmate of *Hagi* Acbari and *Hagi* Mohmoodi," he answered. Those two individuals were the highest ranking clerics in their town. Nosha wanted to know why her father did not become a cleric. But at the same time, she was thanking God that he had not. She could not be hiding in a corner of their house all the time.

"I was eighteen when I decided being a cleric was not something I could do. We had very hard and bad tempered teachers, and the materials were so hard that I quit.

"At that age, I was very strong in my opinions. By then, my brother-in-law was too old to take care of the farm, so he asked me to go to the village and take care of the farm's management. For the first time I would get a small amount of money for my expenses there as a salary. So I agreed to this arrangement happily."

Nosha could feel his pain as he talked about being raised for all those years by a tough, hard-to-please man. She also could see how childhood affected one's behavior in the later years. Sometimes he was very hard to be around and inflexible, while other times he was a very good-natured man. He was loved by so many and was very popular person in their city. But life had also taught him that he could not be nice all the time. He was kind to many, except those who were mean to him or did something to hurt him; then he never forgave them for it. However, Nosha thought the effects of their tough childhood life was harder on her uncle Afshin than her father. Afshin had the same resentment toward his enemies, except that he wanted to seek revenge rather than compromise and did not care if he hurt some innocents in the process either.

He continued after a moment of silence. "At that time in our country there were lots of changes. We did not know at the time, but there was a strong man rising from the army and he became the war minister. A couple of years later he became king and started to build the country's infrastructure. We did not have any governmental buildings. Every region was governed by the local khans, who were very cruel, and anarchy was everywhere. There was no medicine, no hygiene, and no school as you see it today. The local khans routinely robbed people in the daylight and the victims did not have anybody to whom to complain.

"How could they?" Nosha asked. "Could people not fight back?"

"No, honey, are you kidding?"

"So did you like the farm work, and is that how you know so much about agriculture?"

"Oh yes, to your first question, but no to the second one; see, I like to read, and despite the past 150 years, we have a very rich culture. Our books tell a lot about any subject you want to know about. I know about medicine, agriculture, and literature just by reading." It was true; one of his favorite activities was reading when he was home.

"Then what happened?" Nosha asked.

"Well, that man Reza Shah started to build, and while building the country, he needed people to build it. They told everyone to apply if they had enough education to do the task and if we could pass the test, we could work for them. I applied for the job, not knowing if I could get it or not. I was on the farm one day when my nephew came to bring me some supplies, and when he was leaving, he said, 'Oh by the way uncle, there was an envelope that got delivered to our house which has your name on it!' I asked him why he hadn't brought it with him, and he replied 'Well, Mom said I should let you know, but Dad said he did not think it was important!'

"I told him to wait a minute. I packed as fast as I could and went home with him. On the way, I remember that could not wait to see the package. The distance from the farm to my sister's house seemed so long that day. I was wondering if it was my imagination or if we were going slower than usual. My heart was beating so hard when I opened the envelope and yes, I was hired as a government official in a city called Kazeroon."

The sun went down and a cold breeze began to stir, which made them a little cold. He got up and said, "Okay my angel, go inside before you catch cold."

"But what happened next?" Nosha insisted.

"I will tell you tonight." He kept his promise later that night.

"When my sister and my mother heard the news, they were very upset. I left Pasargad to start my new life in a strange city that I lived in for more than ten years of my life."

Here he stopped talking and Nosha could see that he was thinking about something, a piece of memory perhaps. Then she remembered her homework, opened her bag, and started to do her homework sitting close to the only kerosene light in the room.

That night in bed, she remembered a piece of her father's story. Batool had only been nine years old, a child at the time, when she was married to her uncle Afshin. Nosha was only seven and could not imagine getting married in two years or even five years, like her cousin Parivash. Then she heard a distinct laughter in her mind, one that always made those around it laugh too. It was from her Aunt Batool As soon as she put foot in their house she would laugh and they always knew who it was. Batool always laughed; there was no reason for her to laugh, but she did it anyway.

Her arrival at their house always was announced by her laughter. Nosha's mother did not like her that much. She also was very jealous of her. "Oh, God gave her everything," she would say. "She is lucky, that is why she is laughing so much." But was it true? Batool lost her father when she was very young and she got married when she was only nine. Her husband, ten years older than her, was Afshin, a man who was difficult to handle to almost everyone! How could he be the nicest husband in the world, as one would think, the way her mother often talked?

Years later, she realized that it was not her uncle who was a good husband but Batool who was a happy spirit. Some people are born with a good balance of emotional chemistry, which made them people who saw the good in life, even despite tragic events. She thought again of her grandmother. Had she not gone through so much in her life, and yet still had so much joy to give to those around her? Likewise, Aunt Batool had lost her father, and was married off when she was very young. Even so, she quickly learned to tolerate her husband's personality and anger. At the same time, she had some money coming to her from her farmland. It was enough for her stingy husband to be nicer to her than he might be otherwise. Also, her mother, a thin woman who worked all day long in her house, was living with them. Nosha suspected that the presence of Batool's mother was the reason her mother thought that Batool was luckier than she was. But she refused to see her happy personality and the obedience she had learned to have from when she was a child.

Mothers at that time taught their daughters to obey their husbands like he was their God. Maybe that is why my mother cannot handle it! Nosha told herself. Her mother had died when she was only eight so who could have taught her to obey her husband? Batool had four children. Her oldest son was twelve years older than Nosha was. He was a teacher, and her second child, Parivash, Nosha's schoolmate, was married. Her third child was two years older than her. Nosha fell asleep trying to find out the secret of her Aunt Batool's happiness.

Then one day, like any other day, she came home from school, to find strangers walking around the three small rooms they had. "What are they doing?" she asked her mother.

"They are going to bring *bargh* to our house," came the reply. Nosha tried to understand what that meant. She did not know the meaning of *bargh*, which was used only to denote lightning, along with thunder (*raed va bargh*) and in her young mind, electricity was the lightning associated with thunder. She wanted to know how they could bring something that was happening only in the sky to her house.

But she did not need to wait too long. Soon the room was lighted with an electrical bulb that was ten times brighter than their kerosene lamp. She was amazed and happy at the fact that she no longer had to bend to do her homework in the cramped corner in which the kerosene lamp stood. She could now go freely anywhere in the room to do her homework. She felt very excited; her toys were her books and being able to read even at night under a good light pleased her greatly.

Nosha become obsessed with finding the secret of Batool's happiness, who always laughed, and was quite a contrast to her mother, who was never happy. Her mother's stories were all about the sad memory of her mother's death or the horrible story of catching the body of her little sister in the pool of their house, but what the hardest for Nosha to hear was the fact that she had not wanted to marry her father. This always pained Nosha—the fact that her mother did not like her father.

"Why did you agree to marry him then?" Nosha asked her once.

"I was forced to get married," she would say.

"Did you object to the marriage?"

"No, of course I didn't. I knew that was my father's wish, so I did not dare to object to it."

It was very hard for Nosha to understand how one comes to obey another person so blindly. She accepted the marriage without objecting, but she claimed that she was forced to do it! How was it possible that she was forced, if she had not objected? But Nosha could see clearly that her parents were not happy. There were constant terrible fights in their house. She could not see whose fault it was, but she did know that she did not like to see them fighting.

At these times, she would run to the orchard, and stay there, pretending she was a princess, until she felt better and could wash the sad feeling out of her mind. Then she would stop by Oujan and talk to him. She would watch his interaction with his family when they were in their house. They would all gather together, with jokes and smiles on their faces. She always wondered why these poor people seemed so much happier than her mother. They did not have much. Their only income was the small salary her father provided them. *Well*, she thought, *maybe it is easier to be poor; maybe that was the way for someone to always be happy*, she thought to herself. Oujan, his family, and *Naneh* were her reasons. But then she would think of her grandmother and her aunt Batool and she decided that anyone could be happy, rich or poor.

A few years later she found out that her mother was right in a strange way. Children were taught to respect their parents so much, especially their fathers, that they would not dare say no to them even if they were not happy with their fathers' decisions.

Her aunt Olya (her mother's half-sister) finished elementary school and was ready to go to junior high school. Laiya objected to it. To her, if she went to junior high school she would become immoral and that would be bad for their family. Nosha could not understand this! Was it not good to get an education? So you could better your life? Then how come her mother believed that if her sister went to school that she would become immoral? Nosha's teachers were all good human beings. They all wore pretty makeup and were all very beautiful. They were not teaching anything immoral!

She thought Olya would be furious about this decision. But to her surprise, she moved to their house and was happy that her older sister told her not to go to school! *Why is she so happy?* Nosha wondered. Later she found the answer lay in her socio-economic background.

Nosha came home from school and after changing her clothes went to find her grandmother who was involved in killing a line of ants that were going up into one of the rooms. Nosha recited a poem that she had learned at school.

> *Do not hurt an ant that is carrying its food,*
> *Do not disturb its life since it is alive and likes its life,*
> *Do not be cruel and steel-hearted,*
> *Do not let an ant become sad and heavy-hearted.*[42]

Her grandmother looked at her with amusement and said, "But they are hurting us what can we do? They crawl into our food, go into our rooms, and if we do not kill them they will eat us alive!"

"But they do not eat us! They just want to have their food," Nosha tried to answer.

But her grandmother continued, saying, "Can you imagine if they crawl onto your body? You will feel itching all over your body, inside and out."

Nosha looked at her with confusion, and wondered if that was the case, then why did the poet write such a poem, as she watched her grandmother killing the little ants. For a moment her young mind went into the kindness that the Persian poems taught her, but she saw clearly at least for the ants, that she couldn't prevent her grandmother from killing them by reciting the poem. *I should follow these poems myself, maybe, and stop trying to teach these grown-ups what I learn,* she thought But she could see how this was especially true with her mother and grandmother; her father on the other hand knew so many of them by heart that she did not feel the need to tell him anything! And she never saw him killing ants or hurting anybody anyway!

She wandered away that day to hear the stories of her grandmoth-

Nosha and Her Aunt Olya

Nosha had not known her aunt Olya a year ago. When she started school, she used to go and play with her beautiful cousin Parivash, who was tall with pale skin. Her beautiful blue eyes under her black long lashes made people stop and look at her. She was always smiling, and was always so kind, just like her mother, Batool. Nosha loved her cousin and wanted to be with her every chance she had. Parivash's friends, who were all sixth graders, thought that Nosha was beautiful and liked her, and she enjoyed their attention.

But then this chubby, badly dressed kid who was in fifth grade brought her friends one day and told them that Nosha was her niece. Nosha, who did not know her that well, only remembered her from their New Year's times, when she would go to see her grandfather with her mother and siblings once a year. He would give them each a big banknote on the first day of spring the Persian New Year. Those were the times that she remembered seeing this chubby girl with her curly black hair. Yes, she knew that she was her mother's relative. But that day, she did not want to be associated with her. In her eyes, she was ugly and badly dressed. She denied knowing her at all, and refused to go with her.

Nosha was accustomed to attention bestowed upon her from strangers and relatives. In that school, so many children wanted to be her friend. She did not know the reason though. Was it because of her father's good name or her unusual beauty in Pasargad? In the crowd of dark-skinned, black-eyed, black-haired children, she was the only one with blonde hair and light eyes. Even her beautiful cousin Parivash had dark brown hair. All this attention failed to replace her need to receive attention from her own mother, though, which she always missed.

It was almost the end of school year when she got two surprises. The first was the marriage of her cousin Parivash, and the second was seeing Olya move into their house. She could not believe it, but that chubby kid whose invitation she had refused was now sitting at the stairs near the door talking to her mother when Nosha got home. She went closer and politely said hi. Her mother looked angry. And without waiting for an explanation, she asked, "This is my sister Olya; why did you tell everyone that you did not know her?"

Sister! Nosha thought. This was the first time her mother had introduced her to this kid as her sister! She had seen her, all right, but her mother had never mentioned that she was her sister. It was so strange, though. If she was her sister, then why did she never come to their house? Why, when her father's brothers were in their house practically every day? She even saw her cousins from her father's side almost every week. Her mother's brothers also came to their house often. But not Olya! She opened her mouth to say something, but her mother was involved, talking to her so-called sister, so Nosha sighed and wandered into their orchard.

So when the school reopened that year, Nosha found herself with a new family member in their house, this new Aunt Olya. Her mother decided to take her in so that she would not become immoral, which she claimed she would become, if she continued going to school. Olya accepted this with no resistance and came to stay with them. She was a very warm and affectionate girl who respected Laiya a lot. She always called her 'my dearest sister'. She obviously was proud to live in her sister's house. She told Nosha and her sister bedtime stories, and generally was warm and affectionate with them.

Nosha now liked her a lot and apologized one day, telling her how she had not known then that she was her aunt, the day she had refused her invitation.

Olya laughed and said, "I know you did not see me that much before." Then she told her of one of her teachers that had been very mean and called her bad names.

"Why?" Nosha asked.

"Well, she thinks since she is from a family of landlords she is better than everyone. She has always been mean to the children from the lower class," she answered.

This was strange for Nosha but she had heard the rumors about Olya's mother. Had Laiya not told them so many times that Olya's mother was a servant? So was that why she was happy not to go to school? She did not have to hear her mean teachers, and she could enjoy feeling better than others because of Babak's status in Pasargad, Nosha thought. But this discovery was not that satisfying. She wondered why her father's status did not make her mother happy. Why did she not enjoy all the flowers in the orchard? Why did she not walk along its lovely paths, to hear the nightingale's singing or to breathe in the fragrant smell of roses?

"Well, did you not see your father's anger the other day?" her mother asked her when she asked about her sadness. Then bitterly, she continued, "Oh, I am a prisoner in this house!"

But was that true? Their fight the other day was not that Laiya wanted to go somewhere and Babak did not let her. The fight was related to Laiya's constant power struggle in the house. Babak was very concerned about the people who served him. He wanted to make sure that they were well fed. He would pour food for Oujan and *Naneh* before he started eating. That day he was pouring food for them as usual. Laiya started complaining that he was giving too much to them. Babak explained that since they worked hard, they needed more food. This caused Laiya to start screaming and complaining, and eventually Babak burst into a rage and threw all the food, whatever was left, into the garden. It was an awful day for Nosha and her siblings. Laiya started to cry and fell down with her hands on her heart. Babak rushed to give her some medicine and the act seemed to repeat every few days. The fights were usually about things that Babak liked to do, such as giving gifts to his friends or his nieces and nephews or giving food or money to the servants. Laiya would complain about why he gave so much. Or, why he was bringing guests. Why was he playing cards.

It was not long after Olya came to their house that they got bad news. Laiya's younger brother was not well. She had two brothers who were both teachers. The younger one was teaching at a remote village near Shiraz. Laiya's youngest sister, Zahra, came and stayed with them while her father and her stepmother left Pasargad to tend for her brother. Zahra was also a chubby girl and had a yellowish skin complexion. She did not seem very bright to Nosha; although she was two years older than her, she still did not know any of the alphabet. Nosha was not allowed to go out of her house without an adult. But Zahra just wandered the alleys and streets whenever she wished. And one day she pulled her *chador* over her head and left the house. When she came back, she told them that when she went to her house she saw that someone had cleaned their courtyard and covered the whole courtyard with carpets.

Laiya looked at her and said, "Oh my God, my brother is dead!" Then she started to wail and hit herself, crying. Nosha and the other children could not make a connection between the courtyard covered with carpets and their uncle being dead. They looked at her sadly and then they all started to cry as well. Laiya continued crying, not paying any attention to the children. Nosha was sure that her mom was making a mistake. She wanted someone to come and let them know that it was just a misunderstanding.

Nosha loved her uncle who always brought her toys from Shiraz. He was tall and slim with a dark complexion. Unlike her other uncle, who was very handsome, this one was not but he was much kinder. He was only twenty-two years old. How could he be dead? She kept telling herself, *this is my mom's imagination, he cannot be dead*. She had not seen anyone die in her life.

She did not know about the customs either. It was customary to prepare a big place for the day after a funeral. Men would go to the mosque while women would go to the home of the deceased to comfort the family. In the summertime, for funerals, people would clean their courtyards and cover them with carpets and pillows so people could sit down. In the winter, they had to designate several rooms for people who came for the comforting. The younger the deceased was, and the higher his socioeconomic status, the more visitors came.

They cried for hours. It was getting dark and the children were so tired that did not know what to do. At the point where Nosha could not cry anymore, because she had a stuffy nose and could not breathe, her father came in. He saw them sitting down on the ground with red eyes and tears all over their little faces.

He bent down to hold his daughter's hands and asked, "What is the matter?" Nosha told him about the carpeted courtyard. He said, "So what? He died, but you need to sleep." He washed their faces and took them to their beds. Did he know in advance about the incident? Probably, he did. Maybe he was hiding it from their mother. But now she knew it too. Nosha was so tired that night that she fell asleep instantly.

For the next few days, her mother was not home. Nosha and her sister were not allowed to go where their mother was. Her aunts were gone, too. When she came back, she looked very sad. This sadness did not vanish with time. She cried a lot and talked about her brother.

Olya still was living with them and people started to notice her. Her first suitor was one of Babak's employees. He was a young man, but her father objected and did not like him. Her second suitor was her own father's employee. This time, Laiya objected to it since he was not from a good family! He left her father after they objected to his proposal. Then a young, tall, and good-looking guy with dark skin came to work in his bakery. He was a distant cousin of Laiya's father. He looked smart and was very funny. They liked him although he was poor, but it was enough for them that he was from a prominent family in Pasargad. His father had passed away when he was very young and his mother was remarried.

Olya moved back home. And soon they fell in love. He proposed, and was welcomed by Babak and Laiya. Her father was not sure, though. But Olya started to cry when she heard that her father was not sure and Laiya pushed her father to accept their marriage. Olya was only fifteen when she got married. The groom's mother objected to the marriage because of Olya's mother! But he did not pay attention. They got married in a small ceremony in which Olya and her brother and sisters were present, but none of his many family members attended.

High School and Nosha

Before she knew it, she was eleven and finished with elementary school. She had dreaded this day. Already at age eleven she was as tall as her mother and there were proposals coming from many men in the city. She was afraid of being forced to get married. Unlike all the other girls in town who dreamed about their marriage from a very young age, Nosha wanted something else. She had inherited the love of reading from her father. Her father was subscribing all the available magazines. And with Pahlavi's rule, all these magazines were promoting modernity and education. She wanted to become a doctor or a writer. She certainly did not want to be like all these women who were stupid and talked behind their husbands' backs constantly.

But could she become a doctor, though? Had her aunt Olya not told her friends when she stopped going to school that her sister had prevented her from continuing her education and that it would be the same for Nosha?

Nosha knew first-hand that it was true. In Pasargad, she could not even find one boy who went to college—forget about a girl becoming a doctor. Most girls were done with school when they finished elementary school if they were lucky. Parivash and Olya were direct examples.

Her heart grew sad at these thoughts, and she promised herself that she would try her best to achieve her goals. She knew that now was at the crossroad of either pursuing her dream or becoming a slave of tradition. She knew very well that she did not have a strong personality. She was very sensitive and shy. She could not even ask her parents for little things she needed. Pursuing her dream would be harder than anything in that town, she thought. *What if they prevent me from going to school?* She loved school, and each summer she would wait impatiently to go back. When her father bought her new books, she would hold them as if they were the most expensive jewels, and would sleep in happy anticipation the night before school opened.

When she was in fifth grade, her life and happy school days were shattered by an illness. She had fevers and chills almost every day. Most of that year she was home sleeping in her bed. All three doctors in town came and saw her. They did not know what was wrong. Her father tried his best to make her feel better and was grasping for anything that might cure these mysterious fevers. She would get better, go to school, and the next day she would have a fever again.

Nosha carried bad memories of those times with her as one of the sore points in her childhood. She remembered the pain that ached all over her body, and how it hurt so much that it was so hard not to scream. But she did not, since there was no one to answer even her groans when her father was not home. Once she told her mother how much she was hurting all over her body, and was angrily told, "Oh stop this nonsense; I have so much pain all the times and do not complain." Nosha stopped saying a word about her chills and her body aches. If her mother was suffering from so much pain that it was worse than her fever of 104 degrees, then she had to be in hell and Nosha felt bad about complaining. After several months of having fever and staying home, the doctors recognized the cause of her illness. She had malaria. The diagnosis proved to be true and after she was treated for it, she got better and was able to go to school again.

She loved her house and the orchard, but she preferred to be away from it during the day. By age eleven, she was tired of hearing all the sad stories of her mother's life. She also did not want to hear about her immanent marriage. She could see and hear her aunt Olya admit one day that Laiya started all those fights. Yes, Nosha's father was spending lots of his free time entertaining his friends, playing cards, or giving gifts to his nieces or nephews, but this was his personality. He was kind to the servants, his friends, and his children. Why could not Laiya accept his personality and live happily? Nosha could not find the answer, but she preferred to be away when her father was home alone with her mother. Their fights were intolerable for her to deal with.

꽃

And finally, the day she was dreading arrived. She finished elementary school and she knew there was a long and winding road of trouble ahead of her.

The next six years of her life were so stormy. Her mother told her that her father had prohibited her from going to school. The world became dark for her and she started to cry, the only way she knew how to express her feelings.

Her goal was so high, but she felt like she could not even pass the first step. In her town there were two high schools. One was for boys where almost all the high-school-age males went (a six year program which was combination of junior high and high school). The other one was the female high school (this one was called high school while it was in fact junior high), in which only a few lucky ones, the way Nosha saw it, attended. It was so strange to Nosha that her modern father, who had forbidden them to go to the mosque and had never liked any of the superstitions ways, would impede her from achieving her dream! In reality, why should Babak, who was so upset when her brother-in-law did not let him go pursue his higher education, want to prevent his daughter from going to (junior) high school? Nosha was shy and never asked her father why. Years later she realized that it might have been a lie. The idea probably had come from her mother, but she told her it was her father's idea knowing that she loved her father very much and would not dare question it. But her father did not say anything to change the decision. Was it because he had come to believe that women did not want to advance in their lives? Or was he so easily influenced that even his young superstitious wife could persuade him of this fallacy? He certainly had not said a word when Laiya was trying to convince him about the danger of school to Olya's personality! And with his own daughter, should he promote destroying her morals? Nosha was searching in her little head to separate the facts from fiction.

There were horrible stories where her mother told them about the cruelty of her father. And now she was being told that her modern father did not want her to go to school. Nosha believed her. Years later, when Laiya was swearing that she sometimes had not had anything to eat when Nosha was young, Nosha realized that there was something disturbed about her mother. Things did not add up. She knew how much food had been cooked in their house, and she witnessed so many days that her mother filled several plates of food and sent them to some needy people in their neighborhood. If she was hungry, why did she not eat from one of those plates? Who would prevent her from going to the orchard and picking the fruit that sweetly ripened in the orchard each season? Who would prevent her from eating the cookies she always baked?

It was then that she started to doubt all the terrible stories her mother told her in the past and in the future. Her relationship with her mother changed dramatically. There were fierce fights between them. On one occasion, Laiya was cutting a piece of meat. Nosha was sitting by her, close to the *manghal*, which was placed in the middle of the room, and all the children were sitting around it. Nosha said something that was not to her mother's liking. She raised her hand with the knife still in it and went to hit Nosha with it. Nosha, seeing the knife, pulled herself away and blocked it with her hand. Of course, her hand was cut and blood spread everywhere. Laiya started screaming, "Oh my God!" Did she realize this time that she was abusing her children or was she afraid of people finding out her problem? Nosha wondered to herself. Her hand was washed and *Naneh* went and brought a doctor.

"Nosha has cut herself and we want to know what we can do?" Laiya told the doctor. Babak was on a hunting trip and when he came back, he just saw the bandage.

"Did you hurt yourself again?" he asked her and Nosha simply answered, "Yes."

Even as a child, Nosha constantly read all the magazines that Babak brought home. She was reading so much that Babak decided to keep the magazines at his office so she would not have a chance to read. He thought she could do better in school if she did not have so much to distract her. The magazines also were for grown-ups, not for pre-teens, he believed. But a few months after he stopped the magazine's delivery to his house he received a letter from one of the magazines that stated that Nosha had entered a contest and had won, so they were sending two years of free subscription to her. He was amazed. She was only eleven yet she had won a contest?

When he got home, he asked her about the contest and she replied that the contest was about books and their writers. There were fifty books, for which she wrote their writers' names.

"Which books were they?" Babak asked.

"They were mostly books from around the globe, which were translated into Persian," she answered.

Babak felt deeply that she was not just any normal eleven-year-old. She was much more mature and she deserved to have what she enjoyed. From that day on, he asked that the magazines be delivered to his house.

Yet Nosha continued to cry every day. This did not remain hidden from Babak's eyes. One day he looked at her and said, "Do you know how dirty that school is?"

Nosha looked at him with red eyes and asked, "Which school?"

"The high school downtown; it is the worst possible place for children to be."

Nosha said quietly, "But I want to study; I do not care about where the school is."

"Well in that case, why not do home study?"

Nosha suddenly felt a little better. A ray of hope shined down on her. The next day she got all the books she needed to do the home study. But who would teach her? Her father was busy working at his office, taking care of orchards, and taking his frequent hunting trips. Her mother barely could read! So the sadness inched into her chest again. There were a couple of female teachers at the local high school, but they did not do any tutoring. There was a poor girl who came to their house and knit sweaters for pay. She had finished the middle school and had enough time to teach, so Babak asked her to teach Nosha for a couple of hours a day.

"What subject?" she asked.

Nosha was good in most of the subjects, but was intimidated by English, one of the required courses which she did not know anything about. She told her that she needed help in English. So she tried to teach her what she knew, but unfortunately, she did not know how to teach.

Then there was another problem. She had a cousin named Hamid, who was two years older than her. He had been giving her some English lessons before this new teacher began working with Nosha, but one day he abruptly stopped his tutoring. When her new teacher started tutoring Nosha, he started telling Nosha that her teacher did not know much about English and she was teaching her wrong. Nosha was a smart girl; she knew the reason behind Hamid's bad-talk was jealousy. But deep inside she also knew she did not learn much from her new teacher. She wished that Hamid had not quit and she could continue to learn from him.

So she told her father that this teacher was not teaching her much and she could not learn from her. Her other cousin Aria, who was teaching at the local high school, volunteered to teach her. He was tall and very handsome, and was rumored to be one of her suitors. That rumor was enough for Nosha to refuse his offer. She had been hearing this rumor since she was maybe five or six.

She remembered the day very well. It was spring and per tradition, on the thirteenth day of spring, she went with her entire family to picnic. A big orchard full of almond and apple trees was selected for their big picnic. They were gathered under several big maple trees, which were big enough to give them their much needed shade in the summer. It was impossible to stay under the sun for more than a few minutes during Pasargad's summer. The first thing they did in those picnics was to make a couple of swings with the strong ropes they had with them, using the strong maple branches. This way all the children would stay busy with the swings and would not bother them.

Nosha got into one of the swings and started to swing. Aria, twelve years her senior, stood behind the swing and started to push her. The weather was pleasant. The orange blossoms filled the air with their perfume. Aria was pushing the swing so hard that it made Nosha feel like she was flying, which gave her a sense of euphoria. All of the sudden she heard the servants, who were standing nearby, watching them. They all started to sing the song that was well known in the wedding ceremonies, with smiles on their faces like it was Nosha's wedding. But Nosha was not smiling. She got angry. She did not want to swing anymore. So she tried to get out of the swing. If Aria had not noticed, probably she would have had a bloody face or some sort of serious injury. Aria held the swing and told her, "You should have told me to stop the swing before jumping out." Nosha did not answer him. She ran away and went where the grown-ups were sitting.

From that day on, she always tried not to sit close to her older cousin, though this was the opposite of Aria's actions. He always was trying to sit as close to her as he could. And now Nosha knew that he was the one who prevented Hamid from teaching her. If Nosha were like any of her friends, she would have been pleased with the possibility of Aria's offer. He was the most handsome man in town and fun to be around. He had inherited his mother's joyous attitude.

He was not only happy himself, but made everyone around him laugh with his jokes and his uplifting behavior. Maybe that was the reason Laiya liked him so much. Aria could make her laugh. Nosha was quite frightened by the fact that her mother liked Aria, because she was scared to death of being married off at an early age. Fortunately, Babak did not like the rumors and frowned whenever he heard about Aria's desire to marry his daughter.

So, with no teacher to teach her and the foreign language which frightened her so, she was back to crying again. Fortunately, the school moved to a new neighborhood, and she was sent back to school. It was such a happy day for her when she went back to school and saw her friends, and more importantly, was able to study!

But so many of her friends were missing in her classroom, and she knew they were married or were staying home waiting for a suitor. She was studying hard, which paid off, and she was announced the first in her class. Now she felt wonderful and did not see anything keeping her from her goals of a higher education.

Her second year in middle school was a little bit shaky for her. There was a plan to transfer the middle school to another place, since it was currently at a rental property. When her mother heard about it, she told her that if that happened, she would not be able to go to school any longer, since the new school was going to be far away. Nosha was so frightened that she went to her principal, Mrs. Nera. This woman was the only lady in their small town with a higher education, and the reason was that she was born and raised in Tehran, but was in Pasargad because of her husband, who was the head of the education department. Her principal did not see her frightened face or her terrible feelings, though. She laughed and told another teacher sitting by her that she thought the reason her mother had told her this was that Nosha was going to get married soon.

Did Mrs. Nera know something she did not know? Mrs. Nera, like so many other government officials, was a friend of her parents and visited their house often.

It was not strange for her to think she was going to get married. There were three prominent men wishing to have her hand in marriage. The first was a tall handsome town doctor, who had been her father's best friend for the last few years and who spent most of his free time with Babak. The second was the city judge, who was a tall but ugly individual, and third an engineer from Shiraz.

Why do all these grown-up men want my love? I am only thirteen years old, and they all are more than thirty! she would ask herself. But was her father not twenty years her mother's senior? Hadn't her cousin gotten married to a man nineteen years older than her? *Look around and see if you can find a woman who is not younger than her husband*, she thought. *What should I do?* she was wondering. *Were all these rumors right? Did these men want to marry her? If so, why was her mother not pushing her?* These thoughts went through her little head and she could not find any answer to any of her questions. She went home that day feeling terrible.

And as the days came and went, the school moved to the new location, which was now a ten-minute walk from her house instead of the three minutes she was accustomed to. She continued to go to the new school without any objection from her father. It was strange since her mother had told her earlier, "Your father will not let you go to school if the school moves to a new location." Why did she scare her like this?

That school year coincided with major changes in the socioeconomic picture of Persia. The Shah was proposing to divide the lands among those who worked the land, destroying the land system as it had existed until that day. The two houses of representatives did not approve the desired law, so he proposed the referendum. During those days, the magazines and newspapers were filled with stories about the proposed land reform. This was very popular with the intellectuals. Being a neighbor to the Soviet Union, Persia was bombarded with leftist propaganda, and most intellectuals who wanted a reform in the socioeconomic status of the mass population felt that the landlords were not helping. The fact was that neither the landlords nor clerics wanted this reform. They would lose their income and their influence.

Yet the Shah was proposing to buy the lands from the landlords and sell them to the peasants who worked on the land but got only a fraction of what was produced. There was no other way to improve their lives since more often than not, the landlords prevented them from any activity in which they could become independent.

The land reform was not the only question on the referendum. The referendum was based on several proposals: land reform, and the establishment of literacy, health, and advanced development armies. Young soldiers were assigned to go to the distant villages and, according to their education, work in these three new invented armies to improve life in their developing country.

There were more than sixty-five thousand villagers who had no school or any teachers. The Shah felt that young soldiers could go to these remote places during the two years of their drafting to teach the children after a few months of military and educational training. But the new armies and the land reform were not the only issues in the referendum; there were other things within it that Nosha did not understand.

But what she could see was the movement in the society. Everyone went to the polls to vote and strangely enough, the women were asked to vote. The land reform and all the other reforms proposed were all too good for the intellectuals to reject them. For the poor and uneducated peasants, there was a reward of owning the land they worked for so many years, so they welcomed the reform. The other groups in the country, too, did not see any problem with the peasants owning their own land and the children getting an education, and new roads being build by their young engineers instead of going to war and being killed—they also joined the crowd.

So in one day, millions of people went to the polls and voted on what later was called the White Revolution, and won, in spite of the religious establishment that outlawed the referendum by ordering the devotees to reject the proposed land reform, stating that the lands owned by the landlords were religiously prohibited from being sold against their will.

After the referendum was passed, the land reform began. There was opposition from both landlords and the clerics, and Nosha read in the newspapers about a protest in Qom, "the city of religious establishment," by someone named Khomeini, in which a few people were killed. The report was not clear enough to say why they were killed. Then there was another piece of news, in which one of the engineers who went to one of the villages to divide the land was killed. The reason and the killers were named clearly this time. Locally in one of the villages, a young man who was one of the property owner's sons, killed several of his peasants with a gun, and was arrested.

One thing in the White Revolution pleased Nosha, and that was the promise of a better life for women. In the referendum, the women were allowed to vote for or against the referendum. Nosha was talking to a boy her age in a family gathering and she said on the seventeenth of *Dey* (December) women got rid of their veil and on seventh of *Bahman* (February), they gained the right to vote. He said, "There is no law for women's vote yet."

"There will be soon," Nosha replied, and for sure, one of the White Revolution's laws was the right of women to vote.

In the days that followed gradually the excitement calmed down. There was no more talk between her friends and classmates or the teachers about how much land their family had lost, and there was no new news in the papers and magazines about the land reforms, but there were many articles about the new branches of the White Revolution. Soon the first group of young soldiers went to the villages to teach, and had the opportunity to be hired by government if they wished as elementary school teachers after their two-year draft. Ironically, most of these young men were landlords who went back to these villages to teach their peasants' children how to read and write. They still had some pieces of their land there. They also started to use the money from the sale of their lands to invest in other things, including, but not limited to, their children's higher education.

Meanwhile Aria, Afshin's son, was fiercely building an orchard on a piece of land his father had given him. He also had a dream of building a big beautiful building in this orchard. One day he brought a building plan and explained to Laiya and Nosha where each room was going to be located and how many rooms were supposed to be in the building. *This plan is too big for Pasargad!* Nosha thought that day. But his father, Afshin, was rich, and Aria was living with his parents and could use all of his salary to build his dream house. Besides that, there was a rumor that Aria, like his father, loaned his money with high interest to people, which made him richer. This was true—with the lack of lending banks, most often the borrower could not repay the money but only the interest.

One day, there was a discussion between Babak and Laiya, which was overheard by Nosha.

He said, "So with all the differences between you and your brother, Aria wants to know: what should he do?"

"I said there is nothing he can do; he should continue his life away from us!" Nosha could understand the conversation to some degree.

Apparently, Aria was talking about his life and his dream of marrying her and was disturbed about the brothers' problems. So she was not surprised when Aria came to their house to say goodbye. He said he was transferring to Tehran so he could pursue his dream of being a physician.

Did he really want to study medicine or is he saying that because my father suggested it before becoming a teacher? Nosha asked herself. Then with a sigh of relief she thought, *well, at least its one less suitor!*

The Loss of Talah

That year Nosha experienced her first great loss in life. Her grandmother, who she adored, moved out of their house and into her uncle's house. She would go and visit her there almost every day. The steps of passing time were beginning to show on her face now. She was not as joyful as she used to be, she was suffering from high blood pressure and had recently had a stroke, which prevented her from talking clearly. For Nosha, who had admired her all her life, she remained an idol. She did not even think that she was ready to die. Before her stroke, she remembered so many times her grandma was talking about her own death, but at those times Nosha thought that those were just a reminder of what they had to do in case she died—not her actual death.

But one day when she went to visit her, she found her old grandmother lying down. She looked like she was sleeping, breathing with no other movement. She was told that her grandma had had another stroke and that she was in a coma. Nosha did not mind seeing her in a coma, for at least she was breathing and Nosha held onto the hope that one day she would wake up and smile again. But two days later, a woman who Nosha detested came to her uncle's house and started chatting with the grown-ups.

Her name was Razi, and she was one of her parents' cousins, but Nosha did not like her because she saw her telling her mother things that made her upset and more depressed. That day, she left in a hurry but came back ten minutes later. Nosha had to go to school so she left her grandmother. When she came back, she was startled to hear the news that her grandmother passed away.

But what really surprised her was what she heard later. Apparently, Razi had come and told all the women that they could not sit and wait until Talah woke up, but that they had to ask God whether she should live or die. If she were supposed to live she would wake up; otherwise, she would die.

The way that they asked God was the source of trouble for Nosha. There was a tomb in Pasargad that the locals believed was one of the Prophet Mohammad's grandsons. There were many such tombs all over Persia. The bigger the town the prettier the tomb was, as well as the building over it. Most had a dome on the top that was covered with ceramic tiles. In the bigger cities, these tiles were more ornate, and in a few of them, the dome was covered with gold. Inside the domes were the tombs, which were surrounded by an iron cage with a lock on it. People would throw their money inside, hoping for their wishes to be granted, and the lock was there to prevent thieves from stealing this money. Babak always believed they were not really Prophet Mohammad's grandsons, and he told his children, "It is wrong to go to these places and ask a dead man to grant your wishes, especially since we do not know for sure who they are." He never went to the *Emamzadeh* in Pasargad and did not let his children visit there while they were young, unlike many others in town.

So, when Razi visited, she told the women gathered around her that if they poured water on the lock in *Emamzadeh* and gave that water to Talah, she would be either cured or die quickly. They all agreed that was good advice and she left to get the water. Since Talah was unconscious, they poured the water in her mouth by force. When sure enough, she died, they became excited, amazed that Razi's trick worked so fast. But when Nosha found out, she was outraged. She could not believe the degree of their stupidity! She was only thirteen years old but knew that the lock in question was touched by hundreds of people every day. And she knew that not all those hands were clean. Understanding what had happened only made her more upset, especially at her mother.

"You killed her! That lock is exposed to all all kind of germs. Even if you gave that water to a strong, healthy young man, the least damage would be his sickness!" she screamed at her mother.

Laiya just looked at her young daughter and said nothing. Nosha looked back at her mother in disbelief. What was she thinking?

But her mother had not been the only one that approved of Razi's proposal. All her aunts approved of it too. They were happy that God had answered their prayer so fast and that she was not suffering any longer. Nosha was glad that her grandmother was not suffering any longer as well, but the act of giving dirty water from a few-hundred-years-old lock that so many people, sick or healthy, had touched, was stupid to her.

She looked at her mother, feeling bad for accusing her of murdering her grandma, but Laiya was only quiet; this was her way. Sometimes she was not bothered with anything you said to her, and sometimes she would complain for nothing and create a big fight; then she would scream and cry until she fainted. Nosha loved her as any child loves their mother, even though she did not get any attention or love from her. She did not remember her mother ever kissing or hugging her, and could not help but wish that she would, like she did her two young sons, Navid and Nozar.

Nosha loved her two little beautiful brothers. Navid, with his lush green eyes and his golden hair, was the darling of anyone who saw him. He was so bright that most people were amazed by his comments and actions as early as age two or three. He was also so hyperactive that he could not sit still for very long at all. He used anything he saw as his toys, and his favorites were the plates, which he would use as a car steering wheel and run around the yard as if he were driving a car. And one-year-old Nozar, with his light blue eyes and golden hair and his incredibly beautiful smile. She would spend most of her free time playing with them, which pleased her mother and kept her from bothering Nosha so much.

The end of junior high was near; they were taking the last of their exams. But Nosha was very disturbed. *What am I going to do now?* she asked herself.

She had reached the highest educational level any girl could have in that city, a city that was only the size of country of Lebanon! *What is this entire struggle really for?* she wondered, trying to keep her heart strong. But it was difficult not to be worried about the future ahead.

She was about to finish her junior high school and unless she moved out of her city she would not be able to pursue her education any longer. But there was no way of moving away. Her father was retired and tending to his orchards which was enough to cover the expenses of his five children and the elaborate parties he enjoyed so much. She knew that it would be impossible.

One day a classmate named Javaher noticed her depression and asked, "Why are you so unhappy?"

She said, "Well this is the end of my dream, I want to study more and I can not."

Her friend replied, "Why not?"

She said in a sad voice "Well there is no more school here you know, and I do not think my parents will send me anywhere else to pursue my education."

Javaher replied laughing, "Wow you are lucky. What if we change our parents. They want me to become a doctor or something. Can you imagine me studying like that?!"

Nosha could understand her friend. Javaher was the daughter of a landlord who was living in the villages where their farms were, but they left her in Pasargad to go to school. However, she resented going to school and studying. Her grades were the lowest in their class and was very upset that her father did not agree for her to get married.

The thought crossed her mind that she did wish she was their daughter, how much easier it would be for her to become a doctor. But she was not and she needed to do something about it. So she called all her classmates together and suggested that they go to the office of education and training to see the director.

"What for?" Javaher asked.

"To ask him to open a high school for us," Nosha replied.

"Not me," Javaher replied. "I am happy that I do not need to come to school next year!"

Altogether, Nosha was able to gather seven girls who agreed to go with her. After their final exams they all went to the education department and asked to see Mr. Sahel, the director of education. As Mr. Sahel accepted them in, he looked at Nosha, asking, "What can I do for you?" He was one of Babak's friends and wondered what was she doing in his office.

"We are here to ask you a big favor sir; we would like to have a high school for girls. We do not think it is fair that the boys in town have a high school and we do not."

Mr. Sahel looked at Nosha with amusement and said "How many are you? Eight? I can not open a high school for just eight students!"

Nosha, feeling very disappointed said, "But sir, we can be more, not all the students came with me. There are at least twelve of us."

But Mr. Sahel shook his head and said, "Bring me twenty students and I will open one for you."

They all left the education department very disappointed. She well knew that there were only twelve ninth graders in her class altogether and that many of them really did prefer the married life that was expected of them.

The next three years were the hardest for Nosha. Her father agreed to hire two tutors for her two hours a week, each. There were a few educated men who started teaching them when she was in the second year of junior high which included the hard subjects of English, Math, Physics and chemistry. She asked for Math and English teacher for her first year. But studying everything else on her own was very hard.

She would try to spend time in their backyard orchard studying, but was constantly drawn in her teenage imagination the temptation of going back into the house to talk to people who were there, or instead sitting and reading the magazines and newspapers. It was so hard to discipline herself to study.

Soon she realized that Physics and Chemistry were much harder than English, so she started to visit her old junior high school so she could ask questions of Mr. Abdi, who was teaching chemistry there. The school officials were fond of her and let her come and go freely and Mr. Abdi answered any questions she had during his breaks. However, soon she realized that there is a rumor circulating that Mr. Abdi was in love with her. Frightened at the possibility of scandal, she quit going to school. But without asking question she could not understand her Physics and Chemistry problems. Then she realized that she could not even take her exams in their local high school; instead she had to travel to another city to take the final tests. Babak told her not to worry, that he would take her, and they went to Shiraz to take her final exams. It was a good time for her there since they stayed in her best friend Mahnaz's house.

When she started her sophomore year, her English teacher moved from Pasargad and she decided to hire a tutor for Physics. But because of the rumors she decided not to ask Mr. Abdi but another young man named Moheb who was teaching Physics in the boys high school. He was a tall but not so good looking man. But after only a few months of tutoring, Nosha felt that Mr. Moheb had a crush on her. She tried very hard not to be alone with him. She would desperately beg her sister or her brothers to stay in the room while he was teaching. But that did not work, for they would get tired of sitting still listening to him talk of subjects that they had no interest in. Then inevitably one day when her siblings were not in the room, he suddenly asked her to marry him. She was stunned. She did not know what to say.

She paused a moment and then said, "Look, I am going to the right and you want me to change my path entirely and go left. I have told you that I would like to become a medical doctor and I do not want to get married at this point in my life." At this, Mr. Moheb looked at her with disappointment and said, "OK, thanks."

But from that day on he was not into teaching that much. He would refuse to go forward, instead telling her to solve the problems while he was there. This would take so much time that at this slow pace they hardly finished even half of the book.

But she had no other choice, since Mr. Abdi had also moved out of Pasargad and Mr. Moheb was the only one who could teach her. Then, in her senior year her math teacher moved from Pasargad, the Mayor's wife introduced her to Mohammad. He was a medical student that came to Pasargad to teach part time. In the two days he was in Pasargad he would come in the evenings and teach her English, but unlike her past teachers, he told her to speak instead of reading the grammar and doing exercises. His tutoring was fun and they talked about everything. He told her what was expected of her to be able to get into the university that she wanted. She concentrated so hard to study and was determined to not only get her high school diploma but to also enter the university.

Meanwhile, she was very bothered by all the proposals from different young men in the city, and one particular that her mother was pushing her to accept. But fortunately, with her father's help she was able to deter these proposals and then finally, the big day arrived. The entrance tests were being administered at each university, millions of student were taking the test and only a select few would be accepted.

Since she did not want to risk her chance at being accepted, she registered at Tehran University, Pahlavi University and Tabriz University. Her father made the long trips to Tehran and Tabriz with her. They had so much fun together. He was always smiling, and was good person to take a trip with. The tests however, were not multiple choices that year and with her bad hand writing she knew she would not get accepted. She was so disappointed after each exam. The last test was in Shiraz, to which her whole family accompanied her. To make matters worse, her mother fell ill and in the summer month of vacation her father decided to rent a house for two months in Shiraz to live in until her exam there was over and her mother was treated for her ailments. With her disappointment in the other exams she was very anxious about taking this last one, but was not so hopeful of passing it.

They arrived in Shiraz two weeks before the test and she began to attend an English class. When coming home every day, she heard a lovely man's voice calling, "Fariborz: please call me at 3324."

She never looked up but she strongly suspected that the man with warm voice wanted her to call him, otherwise why should he repeat the number to the same person every day? *Is he not getting tired of standing in front of our house every day giving his number?* she asked herself.

Finally the big day arrived and she sat on a chair to look at the papers which would make or break her faith. But to her surprise, the questions seemed so easy and she checked one after the other. Finally the day was done and she was relived. This time she had higher hopes about being accepted, but still would not let herself hope too much. *Well*, she thought, *I have done everything I could do. I will just have to wait and see.*

Love and Wonder

That day she was sitting in her room, deep in her thoughts. Her high school exams were done and she had taken the main college exam; now she was waiting for the results. Was it possible that she would be the first girl from her hometown to go to college, she wondered to herself. *There are millions of students taking the entrance test and one out of hundred would get in*, she thought. It was a vague dream in fact to get into the universities, for anyone, much less a girl with her background. She had only home studied, yet she was competing with students that came from the country's best schools. Those students also went to the after-school program, which was intended to prepare them for the test. Anxious and worried about the odds, she tried to stay calm.

Was it really the right choice not to get married? she found herself wondering. She had focused all of her effort on one thing and that was to get into the university and study medicine. But at that moment, she was not so sure. She was not sure if she could reach her goal, and she had not even considered the alternatives.

Right then, she was startled by a strange noise. Something dropped in the middle of the room. Her window was open and she realized it came from that direction. She took the object; it was a piece of stone that was covered by a piece of paper. She was wondering why someone should throw a stone into her room. Then she thought it must be a strong muscle to be able to throw this from such a distance, as she opened the paper.

Her room was on the second floor beside the alley in which the entrance door opened, and it was way below the house itself. When she opened the wrapper around the stone, she realized that it was a letter. It was written in a very nice handwriting and the sender was very polite.

My name is Siyavash. I am a medical student. I am entering my fifth year, this coming year.

Then he gave his telephone number and asked her to call. But the number was very familiar to her. It was the same number as the one she constantly heard the young man repeat every time she went out. She was curious to see who the sender of this strange letter was.

Then she paused a little. She was not used to anything like this! The young men in Pasargad never tried to talk to her like this. Most of her suitors came to her house as a guest of her father's and they talked and shook hands, but they never gave her a letter! This was rather unusual and funny.

She went to the window and glanced down. There he was, a tall handsome man who smiled and waved his hand. His black eyes contrasted beautifully with the white complexion of his skin, and he had a healthy glow of color in his face. His straight black hair fell gracefully against his forehead as his pretty lips stretched into an easy smile.

He is so handsome, she thought as their eyes met. He looked at her for a moment and then asked if she would call him. She nodded her head with a smile. He smiled back and waved again. She sat down with a strange feeling. She felt her heart was beating harder and she was wondering why. She was almost eighteen, and yet she had never felt anything like this. *He is going to be a doctor, the same path I have wished to take since I was a little girl. He has such charisma; why have I not seen him until today? But I know this telephone number and his voice. It is the same as the man who was giving his number to Fariborz.*

But she also knew that she did not look around like most of her friends. She was always trying so hard to be a good girl in their tight society. She knew that people were talkative when a girl looked around or talked to a strange man she did not know. Nosha was not afraid of talking to men; she certainly had talked to so many of them in their gatherings. But she never looked around or paid attention on the street when young men tried to talk to her. She wanted to be modern, but in a way that even her conservative society would accept her. But perhaps there was a first time for everything.

Then she read the letter again and was wondered how she could call him. There was no phone in the house, and to call him she would need to go and use the public phone! Should she do that? Ordinarily, she would not do such a thing, but Siyavash was not like anybody else. There was an urge to talk to him and know more about him. She looked down again, and he was gone. He might be waiting for her phone call, she thought. She ran out of the house and went to the corner where the public phone was located. She called the number and heard his warm voice answer. Yes, he was waiting for her. He knew that from her room she could see his tall building, and if he went to the roof, she would be able to see him. He also asked her name and told her she was the most beautiful girl he had seen.

"Thanks," she replied laughing. "There are so many girls more beautiful than me."

"Not to me," he replied. She had to make their conversation short since there was someone waiting for the phone. She went home wishing that they were living in Pasargad and she was in her own house; then she could talk to him all the time. She told herself, *no, you could not; everyone would know then*. In fact, the phones in Pasargad were different. People had to call the operator and ask the operator to connect them to the number they were calling instead of dialing it themselves. She shook her shoulder and said "Probably I would not be able to even look at him if we were in Pasargad."

They met every day from a distance. She would stand inside her house with the door open, looking outside, waiting for him to come. He came with his beautiful smile and stood on the other side of the alley, but when they wanted to talk she would call or he wrote letters, which got more personal each day. She wrote too. Those days were happy days; she felt a different feeling, very new to her.

So she waited every day to see him from her window or from the door. Sometimes he was there smiling at her, but at other times he was not, obviously doing his ordinary chores. But he would come, she knew, every day. And every day for hours, he was standing in front of that crowded alley to see her. She felt important when she saw him standing in the heat of the summer just to catch a glance of her. His letters too, were warm and simple, and she loved and cherished every letter and saved each one like a treasure.

One day she was standing at the door, her golden hair dancing in the summer breeze waiting for her prince to come. He appeared with his usual smile and a couple of shopping bags in his hand, but he was not alone. There was a beautiful woman accompanying him. She looked a lot like him. The same white skin and beautiful black eyes. She must be his sister, she thought. They were talking and laughing when they passed her. But he turned several times looking at her with his smile. She had seen two of his brothers and his father from her window. He had told her about all his siblings. Five out of seven brothers were medical doctors; all five were specialists, and Siyavash was the sixth one going to have a medical career. His father was an army general and his sister was married to her cousin, who was a colonel in the army. That was not all though, all his extended family were very educated and existed at the top levels of society.

This was bothersome for her though. Because although her family was well off and very prominent in her town, they lacked the higher education that his family had. In a society in which class played a big part, she felt inferior to him and felt her family was an unfit match to his. These thoughts made her a little bit cautious, and she was trying hard to control her emotions. She loved to see him and talk with him. She read his letters and felt honored, but she did not see that much of a future in the relationship. She often wondered why he was attracted to her! She was a girl from a small town who could not even leave her house alone, with a very old-fashioned mother and very primitive extended family. He, on the other hand, had everything a young man could have: a beautiful face, a smart mind, a bright future, and a good family. For the first time in her life, she felt she was not the princess so many men were dying to marry. She was not good enough for him; she was convinced.

The next day she received a letter from him. He told her the woman who was with him was indeed his sister, who had told him, 'She is very beautiful, especially her hair.' *I did not mention that her heart is more beautiful than her face*, he wrote.

His sister thinks I am beautiful, she thought with a smile, *so is it possible that they will accept me?* She still was skeptical; it was one thing to admire one's beauty and quite another to accept someone as your own family.

The next day Siyavash gave her a book called *Lonely Patricia*. The book originally was written in English and translated to Persian. It was the story of a lonely girl who did not want to get involved, but her neighbors were gossiping that she could not find anyone. So she decided to teach them a lesson. She told her nosy neighbors that she had a date at a very famous restaurant, but to her dismay, she found out that they were following her to see her date. So she was forced to go to the restaurant and, out of desperation, sat at a table that was occupied with a handsome man. She did not know the man, but she whispered to him, 'please pretend that you know me and that you are my date'. Her neighbors left after seeing her with the young man and she explained to the stranger how she hated their gossip. She went home, but the young man, who was a lord and very wealthy, fell in love with her and started to send flowers, continuing until they got married.

It was an intriguing story but was very much like her situation. All her doubts about his family education and high status were distant worries now. Did Siyavash sense her reluctance or doubts? She did not know, but the book was the best gift he could have given her. She wrote to him: *Like Patricia, I am lonely and like her, I have found my Prince Charming.*

At this time, Siyavash wanted so much to see her in another place than that narrow alley, somewhere they could talk or walk together. It was a hard demand for Nosha, since she had never been allowed to leave her house alone from when she was small child. Someone accompanied her at all times. She also wanted to see him closer than the distance they had in the alley. She wanted to be able to converse with him in person and see him while they talked, too. Calling from the public phone was very hard for her and talking from the street was nearly impossible. So when he asked her to meet him at the medical school the next evening, she said she would try to be there.

Trying to find an excuse to leave the house, she told her father that she wanted to go to the bookstore to buy some books and that she would take her younger sister Nooshin with her. So that day, after her father asked what kind of books she wanted, with some hesitation he said, "Okay, you can go, but Nader will go with you." She was furious. Nooshin knew about Siyavash, but she did not want Nader to know. If her father knew that she was writing to a strange man and had called him, it would be the end of the world for her.

She had always had a deep respect for her father. He was the only one who stood up and refused to arrange her marriage at an early age. He was the one who for the past three years had carried the burden of paying her tutors to teach her privately and furthermore, took her to different cities to take the tests. All these were unusual in her family and in her town. So to pay him back, she was determined to be what he and her society wanted of her. She wanted the same thing also.

She wanted to keep her tradition even while she was excelling in her life. But nature has its way and all this time, none of her suitors had caught her eye—whether they were pretty or ugly, rich or poor—and now that she was fond of a man, he was not someone her family knew, and even she was not sure of his intentions.

It would be so easy if she could fall in love with one of her suitors or one of her father's many friends. But that did not happen, and now that she wanted to go on her first date, she had her brother forced on her. He was seven years younger than her, and it was so offensive to her that her father wanted him to go with them as a chaperone. *Is he my watcher now?* she thought indignantly. But there was no way out of it.

She promised Siyavash to meet him at his school and she was determined to see him, but she also knew that she could not talk to him the way she wanted to. Of course, there was a way to bribe Nader, but she was too honest even to think about such a thing. She went to the bookstore close to the medical school, bought a few books, and then asked her brother to wander around. They entered the medical school at the time she was supposed to and there he was, her prince, patiently waiting for her. Nader, who played with his nephew Fariborz and knew him, also said hello to him. He answered without his usual smile. Obviously, he had not expected her to be with her siblings.

They walked and as Siyavash leaned on the fence that was around the school pool, she saw that he was deep in thought. She felt sad; *See, he does not understand! Can you imagine having him with the family you have?* she asked herself. Since she had always read so much, since she was a little girl, she saw a different culture through those magazines than her little town culture. Even her father's friends were not as religious as her relatives in Pasargad. But she could understand her father's concerns, since even those magazines were full of stories of young girls falling in love, only to find out that their love was a sham and they were only playing to trick them to have fun, rather than a true love.

She told herself, *I am going to that prison of mine and he is here in this free town. He can have any girl he wishes to have and I have to get used to the fact that this is too farfetched of an idea to become any sort of reality.*

She went home disturbed, and wrote an apologetic letter to Siyavash. His answer was soothing and was full of good advice:

Oh my beautiful sweetheart, I was disappointed not to be alone with you, but I do not want to see you with a sad face. Of course, you get upset when you see them treat you like a child, but remember one thing, that you must love your life and yourself more than anything else. If you are not there, there is nothing nor anyone, including me. So love your life and be happy; things will change.

Love,
Siyavash

Her heart was filled with love and admiration for a man she only was seeing from a distance. She had read the love poems when the lovers were separated and she felt the same feeling in her heart.

As the summer drew to end and she knew they had to leave Shiraz soon; she became sad at the realization that she would be lonely again without seeing his face. Around this time, there was bad news. Her mother, who had been complaining of pain in her abdomen for several years, was admitted to the hospital. She was getting a hysterectomy and Nosha volunteered to stay with her. That day she got another letter from Siyavash, who wrote:

To my beautiful Nosha,

I am thinking about you day and night. I see your green eyes and golden hair which will be going to that faraway land of yours. I see you much like an exotic flower, delicate and lovely through every stage. Are you going to be there in spring too? In that case, I see you like those orange blossoms which scent the air on the top of the trees. I love you and will wait for you. Will you?

Love,
Siyavash

She felt so lucky; anytime she had doubts about his love, his soothing letters changed her doubts to a lovely blossoming hope for the future.

The Operation

She and her father stood behind the operating-room door for more than three hours. They did not know why the operation took so long, but finally it was done. During that long time behind the operating room, she managed to divert her mind from the long waiting to the lovely letter she had received that day. She wanted so much to see him after the operation was done. But she was in the hospital, not home. When they brought her mother to her room, she and her father were waiting there. Two of her doctors were also there waiting for her to regain consciousness. Nosha was standing nearby, looking at her mother. Then she opened her eyes and found herself lying down on the other bed in the room and the two doctors hovering over her.

She did not know why she was there.

"What is going on?" she asked.

"Nothing," said one of the doctors, laughing. "You fainted."

She was amazed. "But why?" she asked.

Nobody answered her. They became busy taking care of her mother, who had regained consciousness. Her mother was okay and her doctors were happy. They left and after she talked to her mother for a short while, she also left the room. She had to find a phone to call Siyavash. If she did not have time to respond to the love letter he'd sent, the least she could do was to call him.

When she volunteered to be with her mother, she knew she would see less of Siyavash, but at least on the other hand she could call him more often since she could use the phone in the hospital, which was not as crowded.

She went down, dialed his number, and asked to talk to Siyavash. The voice on the other end of the line told her it was him. She said hello, but soon realized that this was not Siyavash's voice. Then she got mad; this was the second time that she had tried to call him and instead other men in the house played a practical joke on her. The first time she just talked and the other person did not say much and since she was talking in the crowded street, she was fooled. Siyavash told her later that she had talked to someone else the day before. Furious, she told the person on the other side of the phone, "You are not Siyavash. I am tired of being treated this way and I am not going to call this number again!"

Then she hung up the phone, not waiting for an answer.

It had been such a long day, waiting at the operating room door, fainting, and now this. She went back to her mother's room. There were a couple of people talking with her father. He was worried about her fainting and they were telling him that it was not wise to keep a young girl in the hospital. So he told her to go home, and she did, anxious to see Siyavash. However, she accidentally left the book he had given her with all his letters at the hospital. No worry, she was going back, she thought, so she did not need to take it—a mistake that she regretted later.

For some reason, she did not see him in the alley later that day either. Disappointed at not talking or seeing him, she went to bed for the night.

The next day her sister came to her with a pale face and said, "Nosha! *Baba* knows everything!"

"What do you mean?" she asked.

"He knows about your relationship with Siyavash and talked to me about it. He told me to ask you, if you wanted to have relationship with a man, why don't you accept the marriage proposal of Jahan? Siyavash is a medical student but there are many doctors who wish to marry you. And then he asked me why you are so blind that you can't see that he is lying and is trying to use you?"

Nosha felt so bad. She had not wanted for this to happen. "How does he know? What happened?"

Her sister shook her head and said, "I do not know, but he has read all Siyavash's letters." It was strange! Her father never went through her personal belongings. But she was horribly ashamed and sad. Obviously, she could not do much now. Was her father right? Was Siyavash playing with her feelings? She did not know but it was strange to her that her father did not understand that it was not marriage that she was after. She just liked Siyavash, period. Whether was he going to marry her or not was beside the point. She had not been attracted to anyone up to this point and it was something she could not control.

Jahan was a good person and her mother's favorite, but she did not think that was going to work and her father agreed with her then. So why did he bring him into the picture now? She decided that the best thing was to end her relationship with Siyavash.

A few hours later, to her surprise, she realized that Nader was following her around to watch her. He boasted about it. She tried to go to the public phone the next morning when her brother was asleep. She called Siyavash and told him about her father and the fact that she was very restricted and could not call him anymore; then she quickly said goodbye, afraid that her brother may find her gone, and went back home.

That afternoon some people came from Pasargad to visit them. After letting them in, she was closing the door when she heard Siyavash's voice asking, "Please take my letter." She closed the door, frightened that everyone else had heard it too. But then a letter slipped in from under the door. She looked at their guests. They were not looking at her, so she took the letter and went to her room.

> *My darling, I am so disturbed about your father. I wish I could do something to make you feel better. We need some time to sort this out, but I am wondering why you did not burn my letters so we would not be in this situation. I love you and I did not do anything for you to break up with me. Can we do something about it?*
>
> *Love always,*
> *Siyavash*

She did not know what to do anymore. It was hard for her to tell him she could not call or write anymore. She did not want to disappoint her father, but she could not fight her heart either.

She tried to sneak out again to call him.

"Listen, you did not do anything, but I am under strict supervision and am leaving shortly. What do we get from this relationship?" she asked.

"Well, we can write to each other when you leave..."

She said, "It is impossible for me to send a letter out; I am always inside the house and with this incident everyone is watching me."

He said, "Then I will send you letters and will not expect an answer until you can write."

She was wondering what to do. She asked her sister, "He wants to write me a letter; can I ask him to send it to you, since father is not suspicious of you?"

She said, "No, if I get any letters from him I will tell *Baba* about it."

She did not know what to do. She wanted to explain the situation to him but she needed time to talk. *What if I go to Mahnaz's house and he called me there? But Nader will know that I called.* She knew Nader was always over there and would certainly see her and tell her father.

She decided to go to the public telephone booth once more and told him, "If you can ask one of your relatives to call and say she is Nasrin and ask for me, then I can talk to you." Then Nosha gave him her friend's number and the time to call.

She went to her friend's house and as they were talking, the phone rang. Mahnaz answered but then quickly got angry and told the person on the other end, "You must tell me the truth, who you are and who do you want to talk to?"

Nosha did not hear the other end. But after she put the phone down, she told her, "Can you come to my room?"

She followed her. She looked at Nosha for a moment, then asked point blank, "Do you know Siyavash?"

Nosha, who was very private and did not say anything about her relationship with Siyavash, told her yes. Apparently, she was his classmate, and they knew each other.

Mahnaz said, "He asked for Nasrin, and since I knew his voice, I got mad and thought he was trying to play with me."

Oh God, he had made a mistake. Instead of asking his nieces to play a fake Nasrin, as Nosha had wanted, he called and asked for Nasrin.

"Why didn't you tell me?" Mahnaz asked. Yes, of course, she could help, but Nosha was very tired. She really did not want to hide anything from her father and continuing this relationship, she kept sinking deeper into lies and deception. Obviously, Siyavash was not better than her in that respect.

She asked Mahnaz about Siyavash.

She said, "Well, he has a couple of nicknames, one of which girls in our class call him since he is the tallest person in our classes."

"But what do you know of his personality?"

"I do not know," she answered. "The boys want to play with our feelings sometimes, but I can not judge him based on other men's bad behaviors."

Mahnaz was basically repeating the same rhythm as her father. She paused a little, what choices did she have? One was to continue her deception and lies; she could ask Mahnaz to help her send his letters back and forth. Or she could just forget about this relationship and continue her life. She would be sad and miserable, but at least she would not be lying to anyone. She chose the latter and told Mahnaz to tell him she could no longer call him and that it would not be possible to write or receive any letter from him either. Then she left.

A few days later when her mother came back home from the hospital, they left Shiraz and the long alley behind. She went home with many memories from that narrow alley in Shiraz, her favorite city. With a heavy heart, she realized that he was not even in the alley so she could look at him for the last time. In fact, for past few days after her talk with Mahnaz, he was not there anymore at all.

When they arrived in Pasargad, she felt sad seeing the dusty streets of her hometown. She could see the thick dust covering the trees. At home, she was in a much worse state of mind than the day she found that letter-wrapped stone in her room. She was sad and wandering around the house, without any hope or aspiration. She missed seeing him so much. The last two months had been the best time of her life. But she did not realize then how much of an impact he'd had on her total being. Oh, how much she wanted to see him or to receive his letters. Why had she not asked Mahnaz to get his letters and send them to her? She would've done that. Mahnaz was a few years older than her and had told her she had a boyfriend since she was in high school. Why she was so shy about sharing her feelings with even her best friend? But she could not do anything now. She had left without even a goodbye. It was so easy then, but she did not imagine how difficult living in Pasargad would be without any news from him.

The following days were lazy and summer was so hot. Her heart was heavy and the waiting intolerable. She had little to do to keep herself busy, and she whispered Moshiri's famous poems to herself often:

> *Without you I passed that alley again under moonlight,*
> *All my body became an eye to find you in my sight,*
> *My desire rose in my body like a boiling wine,*

I became the same crazy amorous, not fine,
In the hidden room of my heart,
The beautiful memory of yours started to shine,
The perfume of your reminiscence laughed.[43]

Every day she would rush to the door to receive the newspaper in the hope of seeing the results of her *konkoor*. She was not so hopeful of acceptance. She could not believe she might be part of the top one percent of smart students who entered college. Even so, she was anxious to see the results.

One night she was lying in her outside bed, and looking at the clear blue sky with tons of stars; the jasmine's sweet scent in the air. The weather was pleasant and a cool breeze brushed against her face, making it much cooler than it was. She thought, *how much I used to love nights like this, what is happening to me?* She knew the answer though, something was changed. Her house and her beloved orchard looked like prison to her now. She wanted to fly and go to Shiraz to see him. Oh, how much she wished to be a bird who could fly! Her thoughts wandered around her future, which did not look so promising. All her friends either were married or were in the teaching training program designated to train them to become teachers. They had their path paved for them and she was the only one who rejected all her suitors and refused to choose their path in the hope of getting a higher education, and now she was not so sure.

Thinking and fighting her sadness, she fell asleep. In her sleep, she had a beautiful dream. She was standing in the medical school in Shiraz, the same school she visited when she was going to her date with Siyavash. Siyavash was there with his usual smile. "Did you get admitted?" he asked.

"Yes I did," she replied.

"Congratulations; it is a great accomplishment!" he exclaimed.

Her heart was beating so hard that she was breathless in her sleep but she felt wonderful, just like when she saw him below her small window and gazed at him to memorize every part of his face. She woke up with the smell of jasmine petals very close to her nose. She raised her head and saw a pile of jasmines on her pillow. Her father had done it again, she thought.

Every summer morning he would go to the orchard and handpick jasmine flowers; then he would return and put them on her pillow before leaving the house. Without touching her or saying a word, he would tell her thousands of love songs by the perfume of those jasmine flowers, she thought. She knew her father was the best father in town and that he loved her dearly. Any sacrifice she made for him was nothing compared to what he did for her.

Her thought went to her dream; she was not a spiritual creature, but she had realized for some time that her dreams usually turned to reality. Was this one coming true too? Was she going to be accepted not to any other university but Pahlavi University, where Siyavash was studying? She was still very skeptical. Even if she were going to college, she would not be able to get in the top and toughest university in Persia. But that day she felt revived and a more than a little hopeful about her future.

The flowers reminded her of the unspoken problem between her and her father. The question started to pound in her head: why her father probed in her belongings? She still had that book with his letters inside. Unlike what Siyavash asked her to do, she did not burn them. They held the best memories of her life and she was not going to destroy them.

At breakfast, she asked her mother about the day her father found her letters. "Well, that was a bad day for me!" she replied, feeling sorry for herself, as usual. "While I was just recovering from my surgery the front desk called to say that someone was looking for you. Your father went down and as soon as he got there he saw that Fariborz had jumped on his bike and left. He came back puzzled and told me there was something going on! He grabbed your bag and opened the book, and you know, he read all those letters. He was wondering where you met him. 'She is not going anywhere, we hardly let her out of our sight!' Then he thought that maybe it was through Nooshin who goes to school."

The mystery was solved. It was Fariborz who had told her he was Siyavash when she called, and when she said she wouldn't call that house anymore, he must have gotten frightened that his uncle would get mad at him, so he went to the hospital to talk to her, which made the problem much worse. That also explained why her sister was so reluctant to help her, since without a reason she was blamed for what Nosha did! She was more anxious to see the results of *konkoor* than ever now. But that day's paper and next few days' papers had nothing to see. She whispered to herself:

> *I am sad and seeing you is my cure,*
> *Life is my prison without a glimpse of your face.*
> *My mouth closed like a pistachio's,*
> *No talk of the secret which needs to be told.*[44]

The fifth day she looked at the paper. She almost had a fit.

The *konkoor's* results were in it. As she opened it, her hands were shaking. The names were organized alphabetically and the first name she saw was Siyavash's last name, Afras. There were two names in there with that last name, Afshin, who was accepted to almost all the universities in Persia with top grades. And the second one was Siyamak, who was accepted to a couple of the universities, probably because he knew where he wanted to go and chose those instead of all of them. Are they his relatives? she wondered.

Then she started looking in the M section for the name of one of her friends in Shiraz. She did not dare to look at P yet. She was afraid and wanted to postpone her disappointment. But her shaking body and her anxiety overcame her fear and she started looking for her name. Then tears of joy ran from her eyes, and a scream of joy escaped her mouth.

"Yes!" she shrieked, "I made it!" She had in fact been accepted to the medical school of Pahlavi University!

"It is a great accomplishment," she shouted loudly and then stopped, standing in wonder, remembering the words from her dream, her thoughts returned to him again. Would she see him again? She did not know.

Medical School

Every day after her classes, she went to medical school building to eat lunch. There were cafeterias located in three places on the campus, Eram Dormitory, the medical school, and the engineering school. Since her dormitory was closer to the medical school, she chose that cafeteria to go to for lunch and dinner every day. She was so overwhelmed with the volume of her summer English courses that she did not have time to think about anything else. Her six-week English class that summer was very hard; it went for eight straight hours every day with tough quizzes each and every week.

Since the university was an international university, all the subjects were taught in English, so it was critical to know English before starting the main course work. For Nosha, who had home studied, English was the last subject to worry about, so the English course was very hard. But she had worked so hard to reach this goal that she was not going to let this obstacle take her in a different direction. She was determined to stay there until she finished her education. There were so many stories about very smart students who got into Pahlavi University, but failed to meet the requirements and were consequently kicked out. She later saw this happen to several of her friends over the next few years.

Siyavash was very sad and hurt when Mahnaz delivered the message that Nosha had sent him. *Why didn't she tell me herself?* he thought. And then, when Nosha and her family finally left, and the door to the rental house they lived in was closed, he felt a heavy feeling in his heart. She was gone now, and he would not see her pretty face again, even from a distance.

But a month later, school started again and this year he was assigned to Sadi Hospital. His work there was hard and long. The hospital was free to the general population and the demand for medical care was high. From all over the province of Pars, people who could not afford to go to the private hospitals (or the more expensive public ones) would come there. Every time you went in or out of the hospital doors, you could see the whole sidewalk covered with sick people sitting and waiting for their turn. It was hard going in and out of the hospital because of these people. With his white uniform, when he had a break, he preferred not to cross among all those people, because inevitably, they would gather around him and beg him to let them in sooner. He would turn left instead and cross through the gate to the medical school next to the hospital and use that door instead.

That day, too, he took his usual detour through medical school. He was about to walk out through the gate when he saw a familiar figure getting into a taxi. He felt a jolt in his heart. The figure was Nosha's, with the same slender body and fine golden hair. He rushed out to see if it was really her, but the taxi left and he could only catch a glimpse of her profile. But there was no doubt in his mind that the girl he had seen was Nosha. When he went home, although he was very tired after twenty-four hours of no sleep, he went to his father's room to look for something. He knew his father kept all the newspapers that had his sons' name on them, from when they took *konkoor*. This year's paper was among them too since his brother Siyamak had been accepted. When he found it he rushed through each page until he saw her name. Yes, she is here, he told himself, but a sadness overwhelmed his heart. Then why had she not called him? The answer was obvious—it was the same reason that she had not said goodbye. But she called me her prince charming once, he recalled. I can win her heart back again. She is not hours away from me in a city of which, according to her, she could not write or call anyone from. He fell asleep while thinking of the fact of her so close by.

The next day he went to the medical school cafeteria again and got his lunch, stalling as he waited to see her. The cafeteria was full of students and it was not easy to find anyone if you did not know where to look. When he was done with his lunch, the more he stalled and looked around, the less he was able to find her golden hair. He finally got tired and started to leave the cafeteria, when finally, he saw her again reaching the glass doors in front of cafeteria. He rushed and reached the door before she got there, then opened the door for her. She was so deep in thought that did not notice him and said thanks, but when she turned to see the polite man who had opened the door for her, her face lit up, delighted, and said, "Oh! Hello!"

"Hello to you, long time no see!"

She was breathless, but tried to cover her excitement and said, "Well, it seems a long time, but really it is only been a month."

"For me it has been more than a year," he said, looking at her and laughing.

Her face warmed and a flood of blood rushed to her cheeks. He noticed this and told himself, she does have feelings for me—otherwise, why would she be blushing at my remarks?

As they crossed the street together he asked, "Where are you going?"

She looked at him smiling beautifully. "To my classes," she replied.

"Oh, yes. Congratulations on your acceptance by the way, it is a great accomplishment!" he told her, looking at her admiringly.

Melting under his deep black eyes, she looked down to avoid giving herself away, and said, "Thanks."

"How are your classes, by the way?"

"Hard," she answered.

"Do you need help? I can help if you like."

"That is wonderful of you, but I do not want to affect your schoolwork," she replied, still looking down.

"No, do not worry, I will help you when I have time."

"OK, that would be great," she said, and she smiled shyly.

An empty taxi stopped in front of them. She shook his hand and got into the taxi. As she left, he found himself alone, but happy. Now that he had found her again, he was sure that he was not going to let her leave him anymore.

When he got home, his brother was leaving the house for his class. "What time are you done today?"

"At five, why?" he replied.

"Oh, nothing," he said.

He went back and stood in front of the medical school around 5:15; his estimate was that she would be going there to eat after her classes. And sure enough, there she was at 5:20. He started walking toward the cafeteria, pretending he was going there to eat.

She saw him and said, "Hello, Siyavash."

He turned and said, 'Oh, it is you darling. How are you?"

"Pretty good, thanks," she said shyly.

They went to the cafeteria together and got dinner. As they sat down at a table and started to talk, she told him that she had an exam the next morning and that she would be going back to the library to study.

"I can come with you to help, but only on one condition."

"What?" she asked.

"Well, since I have to be in the hospital tomorrow all day and night and can not see you, I would like to invite you for Friday's lunch."

She started laughing. "You want to help me and in return I should accept your lunch invitation?"

"Yes, why are you laughing now?"

"Well if you do me a favor, I should do you a favor in return."

He interrupted her and said, "Well, having lunch with me would be the best favor you could give me."

"Really," she asked, then said, "In that case, it will be a pleasure to have lunch with you."

Finishing dinner, they headed for the library. The school shuttle stopped and they both got in. As they sat beside each other he said, "It is so great that you are free now."

She said, "Yes, indeed it is great." But inside her head, she questioned her decision of accepting his help. Just being with him or talking with him infected her with a voice that was screaming against studying and instead invited her to a lazy night of walking and conversation. That day she had found herself thinking about him earlier in her classes, her mind wandering around his image like a bee attracted to honey; she'd had to constantly divert her mind to be able to concentrate and understand the lectures.

They arrived at the library, which was packed with freshmen who were taking the English courses. She found the girls staring at Siyavash with admiration from every table they passed. Then she looked at him and found his eyes fixed on her face with affection. She felt the blush raise to her cheeks again. They found an empty table in a corner that was not too crowded. She opened her books, not sure if she would be able to concentrate. But to her surprise, she realized that it was easier than she thought. Her vocabulary was so poor that she usually had to find the meaning of 80 percent of the words on each page, and for every lesson she had to spend hours just looking up the words in the dictionary. But with Siyavash by her side, it took them only an hour. And then it took them two more hours to review all the exam materials.

Finally, she let herself enjoy his beautiful face as he wrote the meaning of each of the words in Persian in her notebook. When it was done, she said excitedly, "You are an angel, sent by God; it would take me all night to be where I am now."

He gave her a big grin and said, "It is time for a break, then."

They went to the small coffee shop, which was located in the school of literature and science. There were many young men and women there, drinking coffee or eating cookies as they talked. They sat at a table and sipped on their coffee just looking at each other with pleasure. Neither of them wanted that moment to end, but eventually, she fought to control her emotion and looked at her watch.

He said with a smile, "You have to go, right?"

"Yes," she answered softly.

"I will take you to your dormitory and then go home; I will have a long day tomorrow."

"I can go with the shuttle, do not worry about me," she said.

He looked at her boyishly and said, "If it was up to my heart, I would stay up all night with you, but my brain tells me to go home for both of our sakes. But please call the hospital after your exam. I would like to know how it goes."

That night in her bed her thoughts went over the past two days' events. The more she knew him, the more she loved him, even though she had been raised to be skeptical of men's attention and behavior. Although her father was supposedly modern and had helped her to achieve her educational goals, in her house even as she was free to converse with their guests, so many of them single men, she was watched every minute so she would not cross the line. Shaking hands and conversing with them was fine, but she was told that men are there to cheat, and that they are always looking to satisfy their lust, not caring about the effects this may have on a girl's life.

The magazines' romances were full of the same messages. Those stories were all written by men which scared her so much more. Since she was too excited to sleep, she got up and studied more until she fell asleep on her books.

The next day she called the hospital and told Siyavash that she thought she would get an A and thanked him for helping her.

"Well we have to celebrate then; I will see you at 11:30 tomorrow," he replied.

She wore a green dress with her hair gathered on top of her head, and as usual, she did not wear any makeup. He met her in front of the dormitory in blue jeans and a short-sleeved light blue shirt, her favorite color. They went to a small but beautiful place close to her dormitory. It was a clean and cozy restaurant. Its dimmed light gave it a poetic atmosphere. They sat by the fountain, which was built into the wall of the restaurant.

"Do you like this place?" he asked.

"Oh, yes, it is beautiful." She could not tell him that she had never been in a place like this! The romantic atmosphere and his deep black eyes were giving her the feeling of sunshine. The food was delicious and their conversation pleasant. But neither of them could believe that the long month of separation and sadness had now been replaced with the freedom of seeing each other anywhere and anytime they wished.

After lunch, he asked her if she would like to see Eram Garden. She did. The many times she had been to Shiraz were always for some purpose, either to take an exam or because a member of her family was ill; she had never been able to see the beautiful city like a tourist or know it like the natives.

As they entered through the big gate with their student IDs, she could not believe the beauty she was seeing. There was a white building, which was surrounded with thousands of roses; row after row of them in different colors. In front of the building, centered in the huge courtyard was a rectangular pool, with sparkling clean water pouring in from the fountain in the middle. The pool was surrounded with garden after garden full of pansies.

"This is really like heaven," she told him as she thought, how does he know what I like? The blue shirt, the restaurant, and this garden—she would choose herself if she wanted to choose.

His reply interrupted her thoughts. "This was the property of Ghavam, but was confiscated by Reza Shah, and now it is one of Shah's palaces in Shiraz. But the garden is open to students." The garden was immaculately clean and the beauty of the place made her feel like she was dreaming.

They passed the beautiful landscape in front of the building and headed toward the old and tall cypress trees, which stood so tall that one could not see the top without looking straight at the sky. These were planted on each side of a wide street that took them to a round opening, which was covered by shaded trees. She could imagine the gatherings its original owner had in that place. She realized that they were all alone; no one was in sight.

He was standing beside her. When she raised her head, her eyes met his and they both felt their souls fall into each other. He stood in front of her with his deep eyes still fixed in hers. He felt her love burning inside and the thirst of kissing her lips filled his heart. He pulled her to his arms, but got her instant resistance.

She pulled back and said," Oh, I am not that kind of a girl!"

He felt shocked, and forgot all the pleasant time they had just spent together. The same feeling he had gotten after her message from Mahnaz crept into his heart. Heading toward the entrance door, he said, "What are you talking about?"

Nosha did not know what she was talking about. She was in love and desperately wanted to hold him and be as close to him as possible. But tradition had fastened an invisible chain around her such that she could go no farther than the chain permitted her to. She had to constantly fight her inner desire to be the good girl she knew she was supposed to be. But at that moment, she was thinking more of him than she was of herself. *What is he thinking about? If I let him kiss me is he going to be as loving, or will he conclude as everyone does at actions like these—that I am a bad girl, and not worthy of trust?* All the doubts she had about men and all the horrible stories had come to her mind and she had pulled back. Then, seeing him quiet she grew sad, assuming that their relationship would be over. He was obviously not happy and she could not say anything to change it.

There was a thick air between them as they walked side by side. They were in the middle of the garden when he began to talk.

He started talking about politics and the fact that they had a dictatorship. She did not agree with him and asked, surprised, "Why do you think that way?" A son of an Iranian general was telling her that Shah was not a good leader!

"Well, can not you see all the corruption everywhere?" he asked.

"Yes," she replied, "there is corruption, but you can not blame Shah for that."

"Who is responsible then?"

"All of us," she replied. "If every one of us would be good and honest, there would not be corruption. If you go to a government office and they ask you for a bribe, you should refuse to give it, and if nobody gives the bribe, the corrupt individual can not survive."

He looked at her again; he did not know what attracted him to this primitive girl who was so different. "What you are describing here is Plato's best city. The idea is correct in theory, but it can never be a city like that in reality," he said

Nosha felt a little better. She knew that Plato was a Greek philosopher, but did not know anything about his ideas and his city. His remark that compared her idea to Plato's was an honor that made her smile again.

When they got to her dormitory, she shook his hand warmly and thanked him for the wonderful day she had.

That night she was wondering if he ever would invite her again. But she had such a dreamy day!

For Siyavash, she was strange and mysterious. When he was going to kiss her, he felt that she had as much desire to kiss him as he did for her. But her reaction and her words told him a different story. He felt rejected and unloved, but what about her warm handshake? She told him that she had a wonderful time with him! All the times they were together and when she looked at him, he saw admiration and even desire in her eyes. Was all that only his imagination he wondered. He wanted an open-minded and modern wife. She was beautiful and was going to be a doctor soon. But was she not too traditional for him?

He was unsure that night, but he found himself calling her the next morning to see how she was. They ate at the cafeteria anytime he did not have his shift. They went to the movies whenever they had time. They walked in the romantic streets of Shiraz whenever they both had time. They enjoyed each other company, but no touching or closeness.

Two years passed and with his last year in college, he was very busy, but still found time here or there to see her. Her friends called him the best one. They jokingly kept asking her when was their wedding date? But she kept telling them that they were only friends.

"Can I date him then?" one of her friends asked one day.

"You can ask him, not me," she answered. "He does not belong to me to give you my permission!" But inside she was furious. She did not know how he felt. He came to see her, called her regularly, and worked with her when she had difficulty in her school. But there was no deep look in his eyes or any love letter or even the slightest remarks about her beauty anymore. You lost him, stupid, she told herself after her friend asked her if she could date him. Can't you see that so many girls are dying to get his attention? But why does he keep seeing me? Why does he call and why is he so concerned about my well being? Isn't that love? She asked herself, tired of waiting.

Oh, it would be so much easier if she could have fallen in love with one of her suitors in Pasargad. So many men sent their parents to propose or asked their friends to intervene. All she had to do was to say yes, but she had wanted Siyavash to be like one of them from the beginning and he was not. Nevertheless, she loved him every day more than the day before and was so fearful of losing him to someone else. She always knew at which hospital he was working and, whenever she had time, she went there to see him. He managed to take a ten-minute break at these times and always came out with a warm smile, to see her anytime she visited.

He told her about his patients and his ideas. And when his father died, she was there for him. When she went to pay her respects, she met his mother, a tall beautiful woman whose beauty had not vanished with her old age. She handed a big bouquet of flowers to her and gave her condolences. Siyamak introduced her to his mother.

"This is Nosha, one of my classmates."

"Oh, I am so happy to meet you," she said with tears in her eyes. Siyavash left for the mosque, and she stayed there with the other women for a little while, then said goodbye.

That night her phone rang. It was Siyavash.

"Hello Nosha, I am calling to thank you for the flowers."

"Oh, do not mention it; I am sorry for your father, are you okay?"

"Well you know, I was trying to tell my mother and sister that it is a natural thing that happens in our lives, and as doctors we see death every week, if not each day. But I can say, even with all the reasoning I give everyone, it is hard to lose my father."

They talked for hours that night. It seemed that he was acting bravely for the sake of his family. But at that moment he was only a small boy who had admired his father and looked up to him for everything, only to realize that he lost him and missed him badly.

Nosha could understand his sad feelings and told him, "Do not torture yourself to be practical! As natural as the loss, it is also natural to be sad and miss him badly. You should not hold your feelings because of practicality. I can imagine how much he meant to you. You are the kindest man I have ever seen in my life, and I am sure you learned it from him. Tell me about him and your childhood."

He told her all the good memories of his childhood. She sat listening to him, riveted, because she felt his pain like it was her own.

"I wish you were here, and I could put my head on your shoulder and calm down," he said at the end.

"How do you think I could make such magic?"

"I know because you always calm me down... Oh my God, it is late and I am keeping you up! Do you not have any classes tomorrow?" he asked suddenly worried.

"No, only in the afternoon, right now you are the priority."

"Am I?" he asked, laughing.

Oh, how much she liked his laugh at that moment.

"Well," he continued. "I think I've taken much of your time tonight. Thanks for the time you spent on me, have a pleasant night."

She went to bed with a smile. She was able to calm him down. She heard his laughter and he told her she always calmed him down. *Is he going to be romantic again?* she was wondering when she fell asleep.

In the weeks that followed, they talked only at nights, which were very short due to his busy schedules and then their final exams started. They could see each other only briefly in the cafeteria, and several times, he took her to live theaters, which were performed by the students of the art center. Even though she was happy with their time together, she still wondered if he loved her, or if he was just being a polite friend.

Siya's Graduation

One day Siya looked at Nosha as they walked together on campus.

"How is your schedule Monday?" he asked.

"My mother has an operation at ten o'clock," she replied. "Why do you ask?"

"I am graduating that same day."

"Your graduation is on Monday?"

"Yes."

She froze, then grew silent, feeling terrible. He was going to ask her to attend his graduation and she was going to be busy.

"What kind of operation is it?"

"They are going to take her gallbladder out since it is creating stones," she replied, with a worried voice.

"And you are going to be with her most of next week?"

"Yes, I am."

"Too bad," he replied. "That is the only week I am going to be free."

"What do you mean?"

"Well, my military service will start next week."

She felt a sharp pain in her heart. *Oh my God, I am going to lose him forever,* she thought. "But," she whispered, "But, where?"

"Here in Shiraz," he looked at her, laughing. "What is the matter? You look pale, are you all right?"

She wanted to tell him all about her dreams and her fears. She wanted to tell him that she was sick—that only one doctor in the world could help her, and that was him. But she couldn't; she just sat there and looked at him. The initial shock was gone; he was going to be in Shiraz for at least the next four months and that was at least a small comfort to her.

"What is the matter?" he asked again.

"Nothing; I am worried about my exam tomorrow."

"Do you need help?" She nodded.

On the bus, he said, "A few years ago your mom had another operation right?"

"Yes, and that was the time I could not talk to you. I had accidentally left my notebook at the hospital and my father found your letters after Fariborz paged me in the hospital but ran away when my father came instead of me."

"Was that really what happened?" he asked.

"What do you mean? Of course it happened," she replied, frowning.

He said calmly, "All this time, I thought you said that to have a reason to avoid me."

She looked at him and said, "It was hell for me, not being able to say goodbye to you; why would I do such a thing?"

"Well, first you told Fariborz that you would not call me again and then you closed the door on me when I had come to see you. I didn't know what to think; all I could do was wonder what I had done to deserve such treatment," he continued.

She said, "You did not do anything. I told him I would not call anymore to frighten him, but I didn't know he would come to the hospital! He paged me, but ran away when he saw my father, instead of introducing himself and saying he was there to see how my mom was! After all, he was our neighbor and none of the problems would arise then. You do not understand how much pressure I was under when my father found out."

He interrupted her and said, "So that's why you didn't bother to tell me yourself not to write you and instead sent a message through your friend?"

Her heart filled with sadness. He was deeply hurt and all these three years he did not say a word. *Why?* she asked herself. *Why did he not mention all this when he saw me again? Why now?* Then, she felt a real pain in her chest, to her this was the end of their relationship and he was giving her his reasons. She said desperately, "But I could not call myself!"

He looked at her, seeing her obvious discomfort, and said, "But why? I would like to know why you were so afraid of your father."

"Oh, you do not understand!"

"Tell me," he said, with his voice calm and his smile beautiful, and as he turned he looked at her intensely, his deep majestic black eyes staring into her green ones.

"Well, my father was not like any other father in my town. He was kind and understanding about my needs. He prevented my mother from pushing me into unwanted marriages. He paid for tutors to come so I could home study for three years and then brought me here to take the final tests. I could not bear to see him disappointed or sad."

He was puzzled now. "What do you mean by home study?"

"Our city did not have a high school for girls," she replied matter-of-factly.

"But it is a big city!" he said, surprised to hear this.

"Yes, it is, but before the land reform, nobody was interested in girls' education, so there was no high school," she said again.

"So your father hired a tutor to come teach you at home every day?" he asked, trying to imagine her situation.

She laughed and said, "Oh no. He could not afford it. And even if he could, there was no teacher available to do such a thing. He paid two teachers. Each one came only two hours per week to teach me math and science."

"What about the rest of the subjects?" he asked.

"I studied them myself. I read all day in our house. I started to look around to see the world differently only after I received your letter that hot summer afternoon."

The shuttle stopped and they got out; he asked if they could go to get a cup of coffee. He was so curious to know more. "If you had such an understanding father, then why was he so furious with my letters? They did not contain anything bad, only the fact that I loved you."

Her heart started beating again. The sentence "I loved you" shook her. It was a distant time since she had heard it from him, even though she felt so much closer to him now than at that time. *He loved me, but is he still in love with me?* she wondered, not finding an answer. But she broke her disturbed thoughts by trying to answer him. "The situation was more complicated than you can understand."

"Try me," he said, still staring into her eyes with his beautiful black ones. He wanted to know everything about her and it seemed that she was finally ready to open her heart and tell him about herself.

She shrugged her shoulders and said, "In our city, like any small town in Iran, a girl has suitors as soon as she reaches the age of puberty; it does not matter how old she is. As soon as they see that her height has reached that of an adult, they start coming. My father had the excuse that I was too young for them since they all were educated and much older than me. About a year before I met you, I met another young man who was just graduated from the college when I was in Tehran to take my final tests. When I got back to Pasargad, he was my new suitor. He was only four years older than me and from a rich family, and he had lost his father at the age of six. That unfortunate event made him a wealthy man, though. He was good-looking too, and my father could not find any excuse; but to tell me to decide for myself. He even left town for hunting trip when the young man and his mother came to our house to propose, which was an odd behavior that signaled that he did not want to interfere in any way. What made the matter worse was that his mother was my mother's childhood friend and she was pushing me to get married. I did not have anything against him except my educational goal. I did not want to get married and be prevented from going to school to pursue my dreams. But the young man did not want to hear no for an answer. He said he did not mind me studying, but I could read between the lines that he was not as open-minded as he wanted me to believe. So after several months of acquaintance, my answer was no, which made my mother very unhappy. But my father took my side and told her to leave me alone, that it was my life, and for her to let me decide for myself. It was not strange that he became furious to find me writing to a stranger none of us knew much about, just a few months later!"

She was quiet. His face opened up with delight. He was drawn to her without knowing why. In fact, there were many calls from different girls and much effort from his female classmates and the hospital nurses to get his attention. But without knowing much about her, he still wanted only Nosha. He had spent most of the past three years with her in social gatherings, but until that moment, he still did not know much about her. She was certainly beautiful, and like a magnet. Whenever they were out, so many heads were turning to look at her as they passed other young men in the streets of Shiraz. He remembered once a boy that was trying to sell him a lottery ticket, assuring him that if he bought it, he would win! Then another young man passed by them with his eyes fixed on Nosha, and overheard the ticket boy. He told him, 'Can't you see? He already has won the lottery!' Siyavash could not stop laughing that day; he knew that man's remark was the fact that he was with Nosha.

But that night, sitting across the small coffee shop's table looking at Nosha, his sentiment was not only an admiration of her beauty or her intelligence, but her persistence and perseverance toward reaching her goals. *She is so delicate, but inside she is like the mountain rock, one that is not afraid of heavy storms, one that stands tall to see the next morning's sunshine. She is a woman worth worshipping,* he told himself.

Then they left to go to the library. In the library they tried to study but both found themselves just looking into each other's eyes, and her face flushed several times seeing the love in his face. Again, she wanted to tell him how much she loved him and how desperately she wanted to be with him. But again, she stayed silent. She was too shy to tell him how she felt.

On Monday, she stood in front of the operating room again with her father but unlike the last surgery, it did not take more than the scheduled one hour. Her mother was fine and regained her consciousness soon. As she sat beside her mother, she found herself thinking about Siyavash's graduation ceremony. It is all over now, she told herself. She was so busy with her mother's admission and her surgery that she had missed his calls. Then the hospital operator paged her over the intercom, and she went down to see who wanted to see her. When she got at the desk she did not see anyone waiting.

She asked the clerk, "Who paged me?"

"Oh, I did," she replied, pointing to the big bouquet of flowers sitting on the front desk.

As she picked it up, the clerk also gave her a small envelope and said, "Dr. Afras. He asked me to give this envelope only to you, but the flowers to anyone coming down from your mother's room."

She took it and went to her mother's room, thinking, *oh, why didn't he stay so I could see him?*

"Who is this from?" her mother asked.

"A friend of mine that heard you were having an operation."

Then she left the room and opened the envelope with shaking hands:

Dear Nosha,
I came to the hospital to see how your mother was. I talked to her

doctor too. He was pleased with the operation. I am happy that she is fine. I missed you during my graduation. I am going to another party which is planned for me, and since I got a surprise ticket to Isfahan by my brothers, I will be leaving for a few days. But I will call you as soon as I return.

Love,
Siyavash

She put his card on her heart. She felt a ray of hope shine in her soul. *He sent her flowers and signed love under his card. Is he in love with me? God, why didn't he stay? I wish I could go with him to this party.* Then she felt a butterfly in her heart; *what if he sees a beautiful girl in this party or on his trip to Isfahan?* She felt scared to death. But what could she do? *He is going to his station this coming Saturday and will be leaving for Isfahan tomorrow. Am I going to see him before that?* She doubted it.

A week passed. She missed him so much. Then after his trip, he called her on Friday and talked to her but didn't mention going to see her. He told her that he would be going to his training the next afternoon.

Then another week passed and finally they were able to see each other again. They went to Sadi's Tomb, which was surrounded by all kinds of flowers and beautiful scenery. As they walked, he held her hand in his and began talking about his time at the military training. She felt vibrantly happy. He was back to the same romantic creature she knew three years ago. Only now, she knew and loved him so much more. Her dream was finally becoming reality after three years of waiting. An old woman was walking from the opposite direction in her traditional clothes, a white sheer scarf held tight under her chin with a safety pin, and her white *chador* with small blue flowers all over it loosely covered her head. When she saw them, she was overwhelmed by their beauty; the distant memory of her youth entered her mind, and she started clapping her hands, singing one of the love songs they usually sang in the weddings. She continued her singing, looking at them until she passed them. Both were amused by her action; they looked at each other and started laughing. Tragically, those beautiful times together could not be frozen and they had to be separated again. Friday afternoon came too soon, and he had to go back to his station. They met every Thursday afternoon and were together until late at night and came back together again for the last half of Friday.

On one of these Thursday nights, the night they spent together was especially beautiful; the moonlight lightening the lonely streets of Shiraz, and with their tall trees surrounding them, they walked hand in hand and side by side, enjoying every minute of the divine evening. As they reached Eram Dormitory, they crossed through the beautiful landscaping full of summer flowers and plush rose gardens in full bloom. When they reached the grassy hills and the willow trees, they sat under one of the willow trees and looked into the deep night lit blue with full moonlight.

"How are you feeling these days?"

"Missing you," she answered.

"Oh?"

"Yes," she stressed. "I miss eating with you at the cafeteria, and seeing you on a daily basis." She was ready to tell him how lonely she had been lately, telling him of her love for him, but his answer startled her.

"Oh my darling Nosha, you have to get used to it, it is not going to be the same anymore!"

Her heart felt terrible. What was he trying to tell her? Was he going to tell her their relationship was going to end? She said, "But why?"

He looked in her eyes, the same look that always melted her heart and said, "My assignment is set and I am leaving tomorrow."

"Oh, no! Where now?" she whispered.

"I am going to be stationed in Bohsheher."

"Why there?" she shouted. "Isn't it horribly hot and humid?"

He laughed and said, "Yes, but it is a military assignment. I have been drafted and have to go wherever they send me."

She frowned and said, "But you are from Pars, and there are so many remote areas that can use your expertise."

He held her hand, still looking in her eyes and said, "Do you know how much you mean to me?"

She gave him a big smile and said, "Do I? Do you have to ask?"

His head was so close to hers that she could feel his breath. "So much, in fact, that I want to spend the rest of my life with you," he continued. They were so close, her heart seemed to stand still, but as she felt his lips touch hers, the sound of a few steps and the voices of some girls and boys stopped them. He looked at her blushing face, as pretty as rose petals and asked, "So will you?"

She was in shock and as if she had not heard him asked, "Will I what?"

"Will you marry me?"

Tears of joy dropped on her cheeks; she had been waiting for these words for so long!

He put his strong arm around her shoulder and brought her closer to him, and with his other hand wiped her tears away, asking worriedly, "What is wrong?"

She put her head on his shoulder and said, "Oh, darling, it is nothing; they are tears of joy."

Their eyes met again, and this time her lips reached for his, as they immersed themselves in the passion they felt for each other. When they finally broke the kiss, they could only sit looking at each other, and neither could stop smiling. He brought his arm up to show her the time. It was late, without a word they went toward her dormitory.

But before she went in, she threw herself in his arms again and kissed him, she did not care who saw them anymore. For the first time she felt that she was free of the invisible chain that had surrounded her for so long. She did not care anymore! She was in love and her heart could not see anything or anyone but him. She was too exited to sleep. She looked at the picture she took of him the last time they were together, in his green military suit, which made him even more handsome. Then she started dreaming about their wedding until she fell asleep.

The telephone ringing woke her up. It was 9:30 a.m., too late for her usual day. It was Siyavash's warm voice. "Good morning sweetheart, what are you doing?"

"Dreaming about you!" she replied.

"I was too exited to dream, so I grabbed a book to read but saw you in the following verses, would you like to hear?"

"Sure," she replied, laughing.

Oh my darling, it was a wonderful kiss,

> *How much are your beautiful lips?*
> *I want the carafe full of sugar, which I found in your lips.*
> *Oh my clever laughing angel, I know your habits,*
> *You taste like sugar, please laugh, to lighten my days.*
> *Oh dear master, are you selling that carafe?*
> *Please don't close your door.*
> *I am a businessman buying your carafe full of sugar,*
> *For my sake start dancing in my dreams,*
> *With your love you kill me with your words,*
> *Oh the best of best, oh my laughing angel*
> *Show me your face and give me your lips.*[45]

Her laughter filled the air and she said, "So sweet! I didn't know you read poetry." He replied:

> *From one side love arrived into my heart,*
> *And from the other wisdom flew*

She continued,

> *I thanked god a hundred times that*
> *This stranger my heart no longer knew.*[12]

They both laughed.

"Nosha, I can sit here and read you poetry and let my heart beat so feverishly that I want to faint, but when can I see your beautiful face?"

"I like the idea, but I am not sure I will be alive not seeing your deep black eyes within the next hour or so," Nosha replied.

"Well there is a problem here, we do not want you to die, but I am not ready yet. I can leave in half an hour and if you can meet me in front of the medical school we will prevent your death, definitely!" he said humorously.

"Sure, I will be there in forty-five minutes," she said laughing. She looked at her closet and thought. *He likes blue, what if I wear blue today?* Most of her clothes were green to match her green eyes. But she found a dark blue short sleeve shirt with beige collar. *This is good with blue jeans*, she thought. She took a quick shower and was ready in less than twenty minutes. *I have enough time to get a taxi and get there*, she thought.

When the taxi stopped, she saw him waiting for her, lean and tall wearing his usual lovely smile. He took her hand and went inside the school under the tall trees where nobody was around; then he pulled her in his arms and kissed her. When they heard steps coming toward them, they parted and as they headed toward the gate he said, "I do not think sugar is as sweet as your lips."

"Where are we going?" she asked.

"It is a surprise for you, but you'll know soon."

They walked down the street across from the medical school and went down to Bagheh Shah Street. They turned to Hedayat and he stopped in front of a house and rang the door. Where was he taking her? She felt uneasy now. A woman's voice asked who it was and the door opened.

"Where are we?" she asked, hesitant to go in.

"My house; I would like to introduce you to my mother as my future wife," he said.

"Oh my God, why didn't you tell me?"

"Why?"

"I wanted to buy some flowers, besides, is it okay?"

He pulled her hand, brought her in, and said, "I love everything about you except these traces of old-fashioned traditions. Be the brave young modern woman you are and do not worry about traditions."

"But we are living in a traditional society."

"Yes we are, and that is why it took me three years to kiss you!"

She could not say anything. A tall slender woman with a white complexion, deep black eyes, and straight hair welcomed her.

"This is my mother."

"I am glad to see you again," she said, noticing how he got his beauty from his mother. She looked so much like Siyavash that she fell in love with her instantly. And like him, she was informal and kind. They went into a clean, well-furnished room.

Siyavash told his mother Nosha was upset. "I did not let her know we were coming here and she wanted to bring you flowers."

"Oh my dear, you brightened my day by coming here." Then she said, "I have seen you before, too."

Nosha replied, "Yes, we met briefly some time ago."

Mrs. Afras said again, "Siyavash and Siyamak have told me so much about you and I would like to get to know my new elegant daughter-in-law."

She smiled and a warmness wrapped around her heart; she remembered their first meetings! She did not know that Siyavash had told his mother about her, but all of the sudden she felt safe and happy. Lunch was delicious and the company was wonderful.

After Nosha helped her clean the table, she gave her a package and said, "I gave one to each one of my daughters-in-law; this one is for you." Nosha was so surprised to hear her call her daughter-in-law and to see her giving her gifts. When she opened the small white box, she was stunned. There was a beautiful white gold necklace and a ring that was covered with diamonds.

"Oh my God," she said, "this is too much!"

Siyavash winked at his mother as she said, "I know your family is quite traditional. When Siyavash comes back on his vacation we will visit your parents and propose."

Nosha was speechless. She just sat there and looked at her first gift from the mother of her love. Siyavash took the necklace and fastened it around her neck; then he put the ring on her finger.

She blushed and said, "It is so beautiful." Her shyness was back and she could not say much. He left the room and the two women were alone.

"I am happy he brought you here, dear. My daughter is in Dezful and my sons and their wives are in Isfahan. Siyavash is going to Bohsheher now. I will be alone here with only Siyamak. I do hope you will come and see me," she continued.

Nosha smiled warmly, "Of course I will."

"You are in the same class as Siyamak right?"

"Yes I am. I admire you as a mother. All your children are wonderful in every way; they are so smart, polite and accomplished" Nosha said shyly.

She smiled and said, "Yes, I am proud of them." Then she looked at her deeply and said, "But I think you accomplished more than my children. They had all the opportunities but you did not. Yet you still reached so high."

"Thanks, Siyavash must have told you a lot about me then."

"Oh yes, he cannot stop talking about you," she said with smile.

She looks so much like him, I must make sure to come to visit her, in order to calm my heart in his absence, she thought.

Siyavash appeared in his uniform with two small suitcases.

"Are you ready to go, dear?" his mother asked, suddenly looking sad.

"Yes mother," he replied, and Nosha's heart sunk with sorrow. The past two days were so full of surprises and excitement that she had completely forgotten about his trip to Bohsheher. She said goodbye to his mother and left with him.

"Your mother is so beautiful," she told him.

"I am glad you liked her," he replied with a wide smile, showing his white, well-arranged teeth. "You were not comfortable at first."

"Oh, I was frightened to death."

"Why?" he asked.

"I did not know if she would like me," she replied honestly.

"Are you out of your mind? Who can resist your beauty and your charm?"

An empty taxi stopped in front of them.

"Should we say goodbye?"

"No, I'll come to your station; I cannot say goodbye yet."

In front of the army station there were so many soldiers coming in and out. A bus was standing in front of the door.

"Is this going to Bohsheher?"

"Yes," replied the driver. He put his two handbags in the bus, and told her, "We still have almost twenty minutes; let's walk."

Holding each other's hands, they walked away from the crowded station and went down toward the tall shade trees on the opposite end of the platform. Surprisingly, there were not too many people and they found themselves alone in the romantic street with only a few people walking by.

He said, "We can say our goodbye now," and gave her the longest kiss of her life. She had strange feelings, a mixture of joy and sadness. She was sad that she would not be able to see him for several months, but at the same time, in his arms she felt secure and loved. She did not see any reason for her sadness, the fact that she knew he loved her and the surprise engagement ring he put on her finger that day contributed to the most magnificent day she had ever had in her life. But she could not help it, and despite herself, a tear fell down and wet her face.

He held her face between his hands and looking into her wet green eyes, said, "What is the matter? Why are you crying now?"

She wiped her tears and said with a smile, "I don't know; good-byes always make me sad."

Caressing her face, he let it go and held her hand again. As they headed back toward the bus and he jokingly said, "If I knew how much you loved me we would have been married long time ago."

She frowned, "You knew I loved you!"

He shook his head and said laughing, "No, I did not see even a sign. Your original reaction made me cautious and I didn't want to say anything to offend your traditional values. Besides, why are you sad now? We will be married soon and you will move with me to Bohsheher."

She froze. "What are you talking about?"

"Well when we marry you move wherever I move. Isn't that the tradition?"

"Yes, but..." she looked at him imploringly, frightened to death. If he wanted her to choose between her career and his love, certainly she would choose him since she was immersed in his love so much that she did not see herself anymore. But her mind was not as blind as her heart was. *One of the reasons you loved him so much was because he was modern and helped you to reach your goal,* she told herself.

She stopped and looked at him with disbelief, "You are joking, aren't you?"

He frowned and said, "What is the matter, darling? Are you telling me you are not going to leave your school and those hard courses for me?" Her head started spinning and she could not believe her ears. This was so unlike him. She looked at him in disbelief. He was still frowning and seemed quite serious.

"Can we talk about it some other time?" she begged desperately. Then his laugh filled the air. Oh, she loved the sound of his laughter so much, but why was he laughing?

"You believed me, didn't you?" Then he shook his head and said, "I thought you knew me better."

She made a fist and hit him jokingly and said, "You scared me to death."

"Why? Because I wanted to deprive you from pursuing the dream you fought all your life for? No wonder!" he said laughing. "But seriously, I will be back in no time. I am not going to a war zone, you know. I will be doing what I am trained to do," he continued with his usual kind voice.

"Oh, I know that," she looked at him affectionately. "But I will miss you so much!"

"I will too, honey, but I will write you every night all about my life and experiences there."

"Will you," she asked, joyously.

"Of course," he replied. They reached the bus.

"Are all these people assigned to Bohsheher?"

"Yes," he replied, "they range from high school graduates to post-doctoral ones; they are going to the remotest villages to help care for the basic needs of the people there." Some of the soldiers' families who were present started to hug their loved ones; she too hugged him and said goodbye when he turned to enter the bus. She stood there until the bus started to move and he waved to her from the window; then watched as it left, taking away the love of her life, and with him that beautiful smile and those big black ethereal eyes.

She was standing alone now with conflicting feeling of missing him combined with the excitement that the day brought her. She wandered down the lonely street that seemed so empty after all the young men left. She continued down and reached the crowded streets of Sadi and then turned left, heading towards her school. She went up Zand Avenue and entered Eram Boulevard to reach her dormitory. She passed this route so many times shoulder to shoulder with Siyavash, remembering all the times they spent together smiling, and enjoying each other.

When, two hours later, she got to her dormitory, she was dead tired. She lay down in her bed and became lost in her thoughts, to the point that she did not realize the passing of time until her phone rang.

"Nosha, what happened to you? Aren't you coming?" Her friend from the other end of the phone line asked. Wow, she had forgotten all about their group study she was supposed to be at that evening.

"I will be there in about twenty minutes," she assured her.

When she got to the library and started to open her books, her friends immediately noticed the ring on her finger, with its big impressive stone.

They all said together, "Who is that from?!"

"We are in the library," she whispered back.

"That is no excuse," said one of her friends.

She closed her books and stood up. "Let's go to the coffee shop. There we can chat as much as you like."

It was almost 7 p.m. and she was hungry. As soon as they stepped out of the library and started towards the coffee shop, their questions started. "Tell us! Who is he? The whole story!"

"Okay," she smiled and said, "Siyavash."

"The good one!" they shouted.

"I told you," one of her friends said.

"Oh, be quiet okay!" she shouted back, "I will tell you the story if you let me."

They reached the coffee shop after she got a small sandwich, she began telling them of his proposal the night before and her surprise ring that day.

"It looks like such an old piece of jewelry! Where did he find it?" they asked.

"Actually, he did not give it to me, his mother did."

Shahla, the most beautiful of her friends, was jealous and said, "All this time you were telling us that he was just a friend!"

"Well," she replied, "I always loved him, but I did not know that he felt the same way. We spent so much of our time together, but there was no romance."

"Oh, come on, we all could see the love in his eyes, why didn't you?"

She frowned and said, "How did you see it?"

"Well," she replied frankly, "I had a crush on him and tried my best to get his attention, but each time I tried, I saw him looking at you like Majnoon looking at Lyle so I finally gave up."

Nosha laughed and said jokingly, "Maybe I should not trust you to be with him anymore."

"No honey, have your guard up! You better be good with him or I will steal him from you!" she teased back, as everyone laughed.

Far and Away

School started again, and she grew busy with her classes and the sudden arrival of her sister. She was a senior in high school and their father brought her to Shiraz to attend the school there in the hope of getting accepted to the college.

"She can stay with me in the dorm until you can find a rental," she told her father.

But to her surprise, he told her, "No, I think we are better off buying a house. We divided the lot I bought some time ago and sold two of the new divisions. I would like to give the money to you and your sister toward your first house."

They began to look to find a house that was close to her school, or at least the shuttle route, and modest enough to meet their initial assets. But when that Thursday arrived, she felt the pain of not seeing Siyavash again. She wandered around the city hoping to clear her mind of sadness and she found herself at Hedayat Avenue, where his house was.

She saw a flower shop nearby so she stopped and bought a big bouquet, then went to ring his doorbell. His mother opened the door and her face lit up when she saw her guest.

They sat and talked together about Siyavash, a man they both loved and already missed. She felt so much better being with her future mother-in-law and seeing her young fiancé's face in his older and beautifully aged mother's.

Siyamak came in and told her, "You are missing Siyavash aren't you?"

Tears filled her eyes and she told him, "Yes, very much. In fact I came here to see your mother, she looks so much like him."

He grinned and said, "Yes, my mother gave all her beauty to my three older brothers!"

She replied, "No, you are not bad looking yourself. But well, Siyavash looks much more like your mother than you."

"Would you like to see his childhood pictures?"

"Yes, please!" He brought an album full of his pictures from his early childhood to his graduation day.

"You can take as many of these pictures as you like," he told her.

"Oh really? I only have one picture of him."

"Well, you did not need each other's pictures since you practically spent all your time together," he said with a smile that resembled Siyavash's. After couple of hours chatting with them, she said she had to go.

"Why are you leaving so soon, dear?" Mrs. Afras asked.

"I have so much to do, but it was so nice seeing you again."

"Oh my dear girl, I loved your visit; will you come back again?"

"Of course I will."

"What if you have lunch with us on Fridays?" Siyamak suggested.

"Yes, we would love to have you. The cafeteria is closed on Fridays and with your busy schedule you need to have a warm meal," stressed Mrs. Afras.

"I will come back next Friday, but I can't promise lunch. My parents might come into town."

"Well, see what happens, we cannot wait to have you over again."

That year all of Shiraz was busy getting prepared for the party of the year. The Shah decided to have a big party to celebrate the 2,500 year anniversary of the kingdom. There were many students involved in the preparations. Nosha was too busy to be involved in it herself, but she saw the bustle of the city everywhere she went.

One day, she was shopping on Zand Street with her sister and her friends and she saw a big line of students walking toward the medical school. Someone whispered, "They are on strike." Nosha did not know what the strike or walk was about, but as a student, she told her companions that she needed to go with the students.

They entered the medical school and the president came out and asked what they wanted.

"We want to go to the Mehr Saloon," screamed the crowd. The doors opened and they went to the big Mehr Saloon and sat down. There were some students she knew; two of them had black shirts on.

She sat like the others on one of the chairs. The speakers came and went, all reading from the Koran Moslem holy book and translating them and then quoting from Imam Hossein, Prophet Mohammad's grandson, and the Shiite third Imam!

She did not understand; what kind of strike was that? All the speakers talked and the gathering ended. They scattered around.

She had a pink short skirt on with a pink jacket, which looked very pretty on her. She went to the cafeteria to eat her lunch, still confused as to what was the gathering about.

Bijan, one of her classmates, came to her and said politely, "We are mourning our fellow students' deaths, and it would be more appropriate if you would be conscious of what you are wearing these days."

She looked at him surprised and said, "I was on Zand Street when I saw your walk and joined in, but I did not know someone was dead."

"Oh I know," he replied, "I am just asking you to wear darker clothes for a few days."

He left and later she heard that there were two students making a bomb in their dormitory, which burst in their hands and killed them that day; the bustle earlier was due to the fact that the students wanted to have a memorial service for these two. It was clearer to Nosha now why they were reading Koran verses in the ceremony. But she could not understand why they had been making a bomb in the dormitory! In the cafeteria, too she saw the walls were filled with religious slogans. But they all disappeared the next day and so had some of the students, Bijan and Mohammad among them. But the situation seemed to calmed down and everything looked normal.

His first letter arrived and she opened it with shaking hands.

Dear Nosha,

I am not satisfied, I am not satisfied,
From your laughing lips,
Oh a thousand praises to your teeth and lips,
How can one taste enough of your soul?
You are my life; your soul is my soul,
The thought of your soul combined with mine,
The clear memory of your face.
Day and night in my mind,
Anywhere I go I see you.

If I drink a cup of water I see you in there,
And without you I fly to the sky, painting pictures in the clouds,
I find myself crying like a darkening storm,
And even gardens full of roses, holding their beautiful sweet poses
Seem like a prison to me without you.
It will be such a beautiful day
When we sit down side by side in our house,
With two faces, and two figures but one soul,
All the angels will gather to see our love consummate,
When we show them our passion unfurled.
All the parrots will have their sugar, hearing the sound of our laughter.
We hold each other's hands with so much completion,
Happy, and joyful with no regard toward tradition,
Such a pity that I am in this crabby corner,
While you are in Shiraz so far away! [46]

The above poem tells you how I feel about you, and in reality in this muggy humid place I can survive only with the pleasant memory of my thoughts of you. You can not imagine the extent to which I have witnessed poverty, and the misery I have seen in the past few days. One can not imagine in the twentieth century we have so much poverty and lack of services in the villages of our land, with all the money from oil being wasted in the hands of a few. I have seen so many people who are sick, simply for the lack of hygiene. There is no water or electricity in most of these areas, and you tell me that our monarch is not at fault! Then who do you think is responsible? Oh, I am complaining to you since you always calmed me down whenever my emotions piqued these heights, as has been the case lately. Forgive me for my complaints.

Love always,
Siyavash

She wanted so much to talk to him right then but he was not there; their only way to communicate was to write. So she took her pen and started to write to him:

My Dearest Love,

Come back come back where are you?

Your mine of gold gave me so many signals.
Why aren't you showing me those beautiful jewels of your eyes?
Oh, you are so good and beautiful, so quick and elegant,
Oh, you, the king of beauty, all good and beauty,
I am away but holding your memory.[47]

My love,
You have not seen Persian villages until now. A boy from a city born in a well-to-do family of course can not imagine the extent of poverty we have in our remote villages. To understand it means you have to have been in these remote areas and have studied the history of our land. Yes, in the twentieth century it is hard to believe they still do not have electricity. But I ask you a question which might be irrelevant to our conversation. How long does it take you to build only one house? Let's assume that you have all the materials and money and man power. Is it going to take six months or one year?

Now let's assume you can build Iran to become a model in our region. How long do you think it will take you to do the job? Remember that we have more than sixty thousand remote villages whose population ranges from as small as five hundred families to thousands. They are separated by huge mountains, deserts, and seashores. There are not many good roads to reach most of these areas, let alone services. The young educated men and women in the country are not willing to go there to serve. What kind of magic will you play?

To me, our monarch did wonderful magic. His magic was to send thousands of city youth to these remote areas to help these people who need our help in the areas of education, health, and other services, practically for free. The exposure of the youth to the drama of our country is a double-edged sword. On one hand the people of these areas will get the services long due to them. On the other hand, they will realize that there is a possibility of better life after all. And you my darling, who would not know what was going on in other corners of your country, begin to understand their needs and will work hard to reach the goal of building the house we call Iran. But we need to be patient. It is a huge country, that will take years to build. Ever since the white revolution and the land reform, I have seen improvement in all areas of our lives.

Our country started the turn of the century with only few modern schools, now only forty years later, we have elementary schools even in the remotest region. Look at the data, talk to your elders and those who came from those regions and then, if you really believe what the leftists are telling us are true, put the fault on our monarch. The irony is that our monarch was not doing much for his first fifteen-year reign and nobody complained, and now that he is working on the problems that are bothersome to you and me, we are screaming about the obvious problems of our country. The leftists are calling him names and telling us not to believe his propaganda. They are ignoring the fact that he implemented a land reform in which all peasants became owners of their own land, the lands they have toiled on for decades. He distributed the company's profits between the workers. And last but not least, this free education we are enjoying. Everywhere from elementary schools to universities are free. There are so many scholarships available to bright students to study abroad that even Hegel and Marx would not be able to accomplish it in such a short time.

Yes, there is much more to do. The implementation of electricity and water reticulation, as well as wider health insurance, but I am sure we will reach those goals soon. Remember that my hometown population lacked electricity and water reticulation ten years ago. These services will be provided to the villagers too if they demand them. With education and exposure they will and will get these services.

So my dear, be proud of yourself. You are serving your country so patriotically that this is more honorable than if you were serving as a soldier in wartime. You are curing the wounds of a country instead of making them. You are preventing death instead of creating it. I am proud of you even as I am missing you so much. I love you every day more than yesterday and less than tomorrow.

Love,
Nosha

After sending the letter Nosha was a little ashamed of herself for talking so much about politics, rather than her burning love for him. The good thing was that she could talk to Siyavash about everything, even if her views were different than his. She understood his angst though. The country was going forward very fast, but propaganda against the regime had skyrocketed in recent years. There were so many pamphlets coming from leftists, who ironically were living in European countries, to Iranian universities; she got the booklets from Mao and Lenin, which were written on one-inch pages that she had to use a magnifier to read. They were distributed by students regardless of the danger. These materials were illegal and they could be put in jail for having them, but that did not stop her or her fellow students from reading them. She had a big fight with her mom last summer when she went back to Pasargad. She had taken some of these booklets with her to read away from the curious eyes of SAVAK agents (the secret police, or people working for the Intelligence and Security Agency of Iran). Her mom somehow found out what they were and, as usual, made a big fight and said she would disown her if she participated in the political struggles.

She felt sad for her mother, who did not see her rights. She was reading them in the privacy of her home, to know what these articles were talking about. But she was not attracted to the Marxist ideas. Although she believed in social justice, she accorded personal freedom a higher status and could not believe in forced economic justice. The newspapers were full of rosy statistics, but the leftist propaganda was calling them all lies, and false statistics that the regime was spreading with no reality behind them. She did not see any numbers to counter what she read in the newspapers, but there was obvious discontent among the smartest students in her generation. Her fiancé was among them.

She asked her father once for guidance, and he told her if the Pahlavi dynasty did not bring anything, they at least brought us stability and security; we need to cherish them. But even her father was not willing to get involved; since his retirement he had been asked to run for mayor or the House of Representatives; he refused both.

Nosha asked him why he refused to get involved. His answer stunned her. "If I want to change all the corruption running deep in our city hall, I will be ousted right away, and if I do not end that, then what's the use of being mayor?"

Then there was bad news of terrorist acts against armies in several locations, which caused SAVAK to push harder to crack down the student movements.

She shook her head; she was happy to have Siyavash. She could talk to him freely without him getting upset at her. She had her opinions, and he had his, but always they managed to get along and accept the more powerful evidence of their shared connection.

So as her sister was in her senior year, she moved to Shiraz, and their father bought a house for them to stay in. Her mother and her youngest brother would visit and stay with them often. She spent most of her time studying, and her free time was spent with her family or with Siyavash's mother, who she now visited often. Her only joy was Siyavash's love letters and counting the minutes until his return. When her mother noticed the ring on her finger, she had to tell her about her love for him. To her surprise, her mother was happy to hear that she was going to get married soon. It seemed like her mother's main priority in life was to ensure that her daughter would not end up an old maid, and as a result she was delighted to see the ring on Nosha's hand.

Siyavash Retuns

It was winter and the snow covered everything. The sun shining on the falling white snowflakes made that day brighter than usual. She came out of her classroom and heading toward the yard, she reveled in the magnitude of nature's beauty. Suddenly, she saw him. He stood in front of the building wearing his military uniform and his ever-present beautiful smile. She was so happy to see him that she forgot where she was and ran toward him, dropping her books in the snow, and opening her arms to embrace him.

He laughed as he caught her and said, "Calm down, we will have time for that; let's save your books," holding her tightly in his arms.

She looked down and realized her books were scattered around. They both bent down and picked them up from the ground and went inside to dry them before they became damaged.

Leaving her books in the library, she looked up and asked him, "When did you get here?"

"Oh, just an hour ago. I went home and left my suitcase there, then came here to see you."

"Why didn't you let me know?"

"I wanted to surprise you," he said smiling broadly.

"Oh, you did! I am so happy to see you." She looked at him, her desire was strong just to hold and kiss him; it was so unfortunate that she could not do it in public.

"And thank you for visiting my mother so frequently; she loves you so much," he told her.

"That is my pleasure, I love you, but your mother is really an angel. No wonder you all are so good and successful!" Then she looked at him and asked, "How long are you going to be here?"

"About two weeks." She jumped up and clapped her hands in joy. He put his arm around her waist and said, "I am hoping to set up our wedding date on this trip; do you think it is possible?"

"Oh, absolutely!" she answered joyously.

They walked out and started walking in the fluffy snow, which sat like a blanket on the walkways.

She looked around and said, "It is such a beautiful day."

"Yes, the days we have snow in Shiraz always are beautiful and radiant, aren't they?"

She pushed herself closer to his body and said, "Yes, and it is pleasant weather, not too cold either. I could walk in the snow forever."

"Do you want to walk to our house then?"

"I would love to, but in an hour I have another class."

"Then we walk in the snow till your next class, if only you promise me we'll go to our house afterward."

"Is your mother back from her trip to Isfahan?" she asked.

"No," he said smiling, "that is the beauty of it."

"What do you have in mind?" she asked, looking up at him.

He replied, "Nothing but being alone with my fiancé. Will you spend tonight with me?"

She looked startled and said, "No, you know I cannot."

He replied, "Come on, you are a medical student; you know what we need and want, why not?"

Her cheeks turned red making her only more beautiful. She replied, "Yes I know, but I cannot, even if I wanted to give in to my temptation, I cannot."

"Why not?" he asked, frowning.

"Well my parents are in town and I am not living in the dormitory anymore."

He asked, "Since when?"

She said, "A few months after you left. I was missing you so much and being with my sister and seeing my parents more often was a relief for me."

"Of course, but we will be married soon and there will not be any obstacles right?"

"Yes," she smiled.

The sun went away and the snow began to come down harder. There were not too many people in the street and the walk was so romantic and pleasant. They were like two morning doves immersed deep in each other's adoration, forgetting everything but the love they held for each other. On Eram Boulevard with nobody in sight, he pulled her in his arms and they lost themselves in each other's lips. After a few moments of heavenly joy, they parted, afraid of being seen by strangers. They both felt so happy having each other and wanted to freeze the moments they had together before their once again inevitable separation.

It was time to turn around when she said, "I wish I was an ordinary girl and I could be with you in Bohsheher, not here with all these classes."

He laughed and said, "You must love me very much to wish that you did not have to pursue your career, after all you have done to reach this point in your life!"

"Yes, I do," she sighed.

"Nosha, when can I meet your parents?" he asked.

"Well, I have a test and need to study tomorrow night, but tonight is fine; we will eat dinner and then we can wander around the streets again," she replied.

"It will be cold and you need your rest to be ready for your test. I too am tired from the long trip, but I would really like to get married before my vacation is over. Do you think that is possible?"

Her heart pumped heavy through her veins and a strange warmth spread throughout her body. She had been waiting for this moment for so long, and since she had met his mother and got the ring she was thrilled at being engaged, but he had not been introduced to her parents yet and she did not know in the short two weeks if it was possible to be married. "Oh I don't know!" she replied, "With your mother away and only two weeks to prepare!"

He interrupted her and said, "I called her and asked her to come back. She will be here the day after tomorrow."

She smiled in relief and said, "That is good, but the traditional family I have will probably want a big wedding."

"Oh yes," he replied, "we can have a big reception later; I am only talking of our wedding ceremony. I can not be away from you even a moment when we are in the same town!"

"Neither can I, but first things first; let me introduce you to my parents, and then we can talk about the details."

He looked at her with concern and said, "I am nervous!"

"What for?" she asked.

"What if they oppose our wedding?"

"Oh don't be silly, you are the best son-in-law anyone could wish for," she replied, laughing.

"I am serious; do you remember your father's reaction when he found my letters?"

"Yes, of course, but then he thought you were trying to take advantage of me. To them you were a wolf trying to catch me, not the kind beautiful angel that you are." she assured him.

"Thank you, but that is your opinion not theirs. Have you talked to them about me yet?" he asked worried.

"Yes, my mom asked me about the ring and I told her that we are planning to get married; she was happy to hear that. Siyavash, you are an educated, smart, handsome young man; they will love you." she assured him again. Then she gave him the directions to her house and said, "I will be waiting for you there."

"Can we go together?" he asked.

"We can, but I prefer to talk to them first and let them know you are coming to see them beforehand. I did not know about this until now, and I don't even know if they will be home!"

"Oh, you are right; I guess I am just anxious, but what if they are not home?"

"No problem, you will be visiting me."

"Sounds good, I will be there at 6:30 then." He waved and she went to her class.

She was too excited to be able to absorb any of the material in class; seeing Siyavash after a few months of separation was exciting enough, but getting married made her blood boil strongly. She never thought that one day she would be so excited about marriage. She had been afraid of marriage for so many years, but now she could not wait to get married, even two weeks seemed too long for her.

She bought some flowers and went home around 4:30 p.m.. Nonchalantly, she told her parents, "One of my friends is coming to meet you tonight."

Her father looked at her curiously and asked, "Your friend coming to meet us?"

"Yes he is."

"Who is he?" her father asked.

"Siyavash Afras," she answered.

"The same boy who wrote you love letters a few years ago?"

She was frightened now. "Yes *Baba*, he is the same one, only he is a doctor now and a very good man, please give him a chance."

He looked at her and said, "When is he coming?"

"I asked him to come at 6:30."

Then she went to the kitchen to help her mother prepare for the dinner. Time grew lazy again and the minutes seemed hours to her. When the hands on the clock finally reached 6:30, the doorbell rang.

He had a black suit on with a white shirt, and a striped tie, which complemented his stark black hair. He looked so handsome. In his hands he held a big flower arrangement, which he handed to her mother before kissing her hand. Then he handed Nosha a small gift bag. After he was formally introduced to her parents, he started talking with them as if he had known them forever. He then spent some time playing with her youngest brother, remarking how handsome he was.

"Yes he is," she replied.

When she opened the gift he gave her, there were a pair of earrings and a necklace set made of pearl. "These are so beautiful!" she cried with excitement.

"Yes, they are from the Persian Gulf. One of my patients, who is a pearl hunter, sold them to me and I gave them to a jewel shop to make them for you. They look like the snow you like so much and remind me of your skin," he said with much affection.

Then he told her parents that he wanted to come back with his mother if that was okay with them.

Her father said, "Of course, you can come to our house anytime you wish."

"We will come on Monday evening."

He stayed until 10 p.m. and then reluctantly left.

Her father looked at Nosha and said, "He seems to be a very nice person; I congratulate you on your choice." She nodded in agreement then lost herself in daydreams of her marriage ceremony.

The next day he called her, she told him her break time, and she went out of the hospital to see him. They wandered around under the trees—the same places she used to walk with him when he was in the hospital and on his shift.

He asked her impatiently, "So what did your parents think of me?"

"Oh, they loved you, as I predicted. My father especially was very happy to meet you," she replied.

"I liked him so much; he is very charming and easy to talk to. I was so nervous at the beginning, but I felt like I was talking to my best friend after a few seconds!" he continued.

"Yes, that is my father. He has friends from all classes and occupations, but he is very fond of doctors, as the majority of his friends are doctors."

"I noticed that he had much knowledge of medicine; do you talk to him about the medical news?"

"Oh no, he knows more than me. When he was young, one of his friends told him if he had known him a few years earlier, he would've acquired a license for him to practice medicine with his scope of knowledge on all the diseases and cures. He is a loyal subscriber of medical journals too."

Siyavash told her that he was very impressed with her father. She knew that her father was charming and was very proud of him, but her mother was a different story. She had to be sure that she did not talk too much when his mother came to their house, she thought. She did not know why, but her mother had a way of making things messy by saying some thing that did not make sense or that made people upset.

They saw each other a few times that day for ten to fifteen minutes. The next day she was very careful to clean the house. She cleaned the windows and arranged flowers in vases. She could not wait until they arrived. When they finally did, he was accompanied by his mother and his two older brothers who had come from Isfahan just for this occasion.

After the usual talk about the marriage was over, he asked her father if they could get married that Thursday, which was just four days away.

Babak looked at him and said, "My dear son, we have friends and family who have been waiting long for this day. How can we have the wedding without all of them? Besides, even my sons are in Pasargad. I came for just a few days before going back. I postponed my trip to see you today, but we can not leave our children alone for too long."

"Oh, I understand that, but can't they come here too? We will have our reception on my next trip in Hotel Korosh. All your family and friends will be welcome. We will give you invitations to send to anyone you would like to invite; no restriction on their numbers," he said hesitantly.

Babak frowned and asked, "What is the rush? Why can you not wait?"

Siyavash replied honestly, "It is hard to be away and when I am close to my fiancé I have to be careful and obey society's rules. Your daughter is perfect in every way, except she is very traditional and that is why waiting is hard."

Babak laughed and fell back into his own memories. He could see the love in his eyes and understood his frustration, but he also knew that the reception in the hotel would not suit his extended family. But that did not matter to him. The most important thing was that his beloved daughter had found a good and handsome man who she loved.

So after a long pause, he said, "Okay, we will have the wedding on Thursday of this week."

Nosha and Siyavash clapped their hands in excitement. The reception was set up for the last day of the year, the day before their New Year. That way they could have a short honeymoon and attend the party in Pasargad that her father wanted to have.

They both were so happy and began their wedding preparations. They had only four days to acquire the necessary licenses and they also had to do it while she was attending her classes. But the excitement of getting married to the most wonderful man she had ever met gave her more energy than she thought she had. As the big day approached, she could not help but lose herself in the blissful excitement of spending the rest of her life with a man that she loved, more than life itself.

The Wedding

Thursday arrived. She was wearing a white gown with the pearl necklace he had brought her from Bohsheher. She looked exquisite. The ceremony was modest. Her brothers came to Shiraz with Naneh. His brothers and their families arrived from Isfahan and his sister from Dezful. Only a few close friends of theirs and her parents were present as well. Their happiness was enormous and everyone could see the blissful radiance in their faces. She felt like she was flying in the sky and constantly thanked God that all her wishes had come true.

She asked "Siyavash, do you remember when you gave me Lonely Patricia?"

"Yes, why?"

"Well finally after four years, I got my prince charming, unlike Patricia who got hers in a few months."

He laughed and said, "No darling, you got me the first day you put your feet inside that rental house and I saw you. It took me days to get your attention and years to marry you, but that is you, the wild traditional girl I love so much."

The day after the wedding both of their families were leaving Shiraz and they spent most of the day going to the airport and bus station to say goodbye.

But then they were alone and relieved. They had a week to enjoy each other. They spent every minute together, he even attended her classes and a few of them she skipped altogether.

"I do not want you to get behind. Are you sure you can afford it?" he asked.

"Yes I am, do not worry. This is a precious time for me. And skipping a few classes does not do me much harm. After your departure I will have so much time to study."

Those enchanting days passed so fast that they could not believe it was already time for him to leave. She went with him again like the last time, and like the last time, she could not stop herself from crying.

He held her in his arms and caressed her hair, saying, "Do you want me to cry too? You should know that I can not see your beautiful green eyes so full of tears."

That was their life; they had to be separated, living in two different cities. In the effort of pursuing their careers, they had to tolerate the pain of separation. When he left she felt a deep sadness in her heart. The height of her joy over the last few days was the cause, maybe. She was alone again and she missed him desperately.

She pushed herself to study more as she always did when she was depressed. That technique always worked; she would come out of her sadness and she accomplish more. But that day she was not able to.

She started writing a letter to him. She wanted to talk to him and writing a letter would calm her down, she thought:

Dear Siyavash,

Without you, I am sitting alone in the corner of my space
Without you, I am trying so hard to study but I am lost in space
I can see in my mind the beauty of your face,
The smile you give me which illuminates my days,
The love and understanding you bestow upon me,
I can feel the warm memory of your arms around me.
I still have the sweet taste of your kisses on my lips.

You exist so beautifully oh my soul, don't go without me,
Oh my life, don't go to the rose garden without me,
Oh my earth don't turn without me,
Oh my moon don't shine without me,
Oh my earth don't be without me,
Oh my time don't pass without me,
This world is incredible with you,
Don't be without me in this world,
The nights are light with your moon-like face,
I am like a night; you are the moon in my sky,
Don't shine without me.

The thorns escaped the fire because of the flower's beauty,
You are a beautiful flower and I am your thorn,
Don't go to the garden without me,
The others call you love but I call you my king,

Oh, you are better than both, don't go without me.
What am I talking about? You have gone without me,
But you will be back and soon will be with me!

Oh my darling I love you so much,
I wish you did not have to go so long without me.[48]

Love, Nosha

She mailed the letter and felt much better; then she came back to reality and started to study. She received two letters full of love from him that week. The second one was a reply to her letter:

Dear Nosha,

It was such a delightful surprise to see your letter just two days after my arrival. I wrote you a letter the first night I was here, but I could not mail it right away, since we have to go to the post office here to mail our letters. I had asked a friend to mail your letter for me since the clinic was packed with patients that had not had a doctor for two weeks! My friend came back an hour later and told me that your reply came by airmail! That was a good joke since this remote village barely has a road to travel to by car. So I laughed and did not believe him until he gave me your letter, which surprised me so much! I opened it and wished I had wings to fly and be with you. So unfortunate that I don't have any wings and could not fly to you. But your memory is in my heart and everywhere I go, whether it is by the ocean looking at the deep blue water, which seems a translucent green sometimes like your eyes, or looking at the evening sky full of thousands of stars. I see you everywhere. I can hear your soft voice and see your engaging smile. I am happy that I have such a breathtaking wife; you are perfect in every aspect of being. I love you so much that there are no words to describe my admiration of you. I can not wait to see you again and once again become drunk from the wine of your lips and your love.

Love evermore,
Siyavash

She felt wonderful. *I am the luckiest woman in the world*, she thought. She was busy deep in work that she loved, and she had somehow found the most beautiful man on earth. She was happy and thankful for all the blessings she had. But she felt heavy-hearted without him nearby. So she drowned herself in work and study. She even volunteered to work whenever she had extra time on her hands. Work made her busy and she did not feel the loneliness without her husband. Time passed and finally the trees gave her the good news of spring. As soon as she saw the burst of the first buds on them, her heart started beating harder.

Spring is coming and my love with it, she thought. Spring is beautiful everywhere in the world, but in Iran, it has a different meaning. The first day of the spring brings with it the New Year, and soon everyone grows busy preparing to celebrate months ahead. Old poets wrote so many poems about spring, and the first buds on the trees reminds people to get prepared. They have to buy new clothes for themselves and their family if they have one. They also need to buy gifts for their loved ones. Sending cards before *Norooz* is another job to be done.

Nosha, like everyone else, had to go shopping. Besides her family, she needed to buy some gifts for her new family too, her husband especially. She knew that her mother was very busy with baking cookies; she still could smell the aroma of the cookies they made in their yard. But this year for her was going to be different. Her wedding reception was to take place the day before *Norooz* (the New Year) at the Hotel Korosh. So her wedding reception was on New Year's Eve. She did not worry about her dress since she was planning to wear the same wedding gown she had worn for her ceremony. She had thirteen days off for the New Year holiday, but her husband had only one week.

Luckily, *Norooz* was on Sunday that year and the sixth day was Friday, the official weekend in Iran; furthermore, one of the religious holidays happened to be on Saturday, so they had about nine days to be together. Her father planned a big party in Pasargad for the second day of *Norooz*, and they decided for their honeymoon to go to the Caspian Sea side afterward. That would give them around five days alone together. The days passed fast leading up to the festivities and every day she saw the beauty of spring growing, her excitement increased.

Her parents arrived in Shiraz two days before *Norooz*. All their families and their friends were invited to her wedding reception, but her father told her only a few could attend. Her uncles and cousins who were living in Tehran were going to come though. Then a day later her big day arrived and she saw her husband again after so many months of separation. Her joy was boundless.

"Shouldn't we go shopping?" he asked.

"What for?"

'Well, I just remembered that we did not buy a dress for your reception, here and in Pasargad! Did you buy anything?"

"No, how many wedding gowns do I need? You bought me one last time and I am not going to wear it only once," she replied.

"You are a very practical lady," he told her.

"What do you mean?"

"Well, I know most ladies want to have different dresses in different occasions. But you want to wear the same dress in three different parties?" he asked.

She said, "Yes, because all three parties are supposed to be my wedding and you get only one wedding gown."

He laughed and said, "The way you are! We will be rich soon."

"Well maybe, but waste not want not!"

The night was wonderful, the beautiful springtime weather in Shiraz and the dining hall with the majestically beautiful arrangements all held a feeling of enchantment for her. All the tables were covered with white tablecloths and combinations of white and red rose bouquets, which made them perfectly beautiful. Dinner was delicious too. Nosha and Siyavash were so happy together. After the dinner the live music invited the couples to dance. This was new to Nosha; she did not know how to dance and was very uncomfortable when he pulled her in his arms to dance with her.

She whispered, "I don't know how to dance."

He could not believe it! Nosha was very talented but he never took her to any dance clubs, which were opening all over town. He himself loved nature better than the halls full of smoking fumes so he had no idea. "Well my darling, it is time for you to learn," he whispered back.

"How?" Nosha asked full of embarrassment.

"I will hold you in my arms and we move that is all, in this crowd nobody will notice us," he replied.

"Are you kidding? We are the center of attention!"

"Yes, but you are so beautiful that everyone will see your beauty, not your dancing."

They danced with that song only and he did not push her anymore. He was so happy to have her, and did not want to make her uncomfortable. The rest of the night, they mingled around, thanking everyone for coming to share their happiness.

Early the next morning her family left to be home at the time the New Year started. It is customary for the Persians to sit by the *sofreh haft seen*, the symbol of the Persian New Year, in their homes at the exact time their new year starts. This was the first year she was not going to be with them. The exact time was 4:32 p.m. that year, and she knew that many people would stop by their house. She had so many memories of those festive days, she never missed it even though she had lived far away from them for the past five years. But being with her husband was much more important.

They spent a lazy but wonderful day together. Then she got ready around 2 p.m. to go with him and see his mother. She took the gifts she bought and wrapped for her husband and his family and went to his mother's house. They put the gifts by the *sofreh haft seen* and waited until 4:30, watching TV, which was showing dances and famous singers singing happy new year songs. As she kissed her husband's family members and wished them a happy new year, she felt heavy-hearted, and as she realized that she belonged to a new family, she felt how much she missed her parents and her siblings.

The next day they all were packed to go to Pasargad. The desert between Shiraz and Pasargad was covered with wild red anemone which made it quite beautiful. At one point, they stopped by a few trees that had grown near a spring with clear running water. They all were so amazed by nature's beauty that they stayed there for almost half an hour.

Finally, they arrived at Pasargad in the evening. As they arrived, the breeze brought them sweet perfumed air.

"Wow! What is this beautiful scent?" he asked.

Nosha replied, "The orange blossoms." *It is the best time to visit Pasargad*, she thought. Their house was prepared to be host of a big party and her father tried his best to make everyone feel good. The party was going to start at 5 p.m. and they had to get ready.

When all the guests arrived, the bride and groom went to the orchard.

The den in the left side of the building was prepared to host the religious men who did not want to be mixed with women. Nosha and the other women changed in the living room and went to the garden from a small hallway. The street in front of the house was designated for women only. Her aunts and very religious family members were seated there.

When Nosha and Siyavash arrived, all of them started the cheers with clapping. She thanked everyone for coming and went toward the main avenue of the garden. The white and blue irises were in full bloom on both sides of the trail, and they looked like they were there to welcome them.

"So many irises! Does your father sell them?" Siyavash asked while they were walking.

"Oh no, they are all for his parties and his friends. In fact every New Year Eve's he sends a bouquet of irises and a tray full of his best oranges to his friends," Nosha replied.

"They are so beautiful!" he whispered.

The main street was designed for their modern guests who preferred to sit with their own family rather than separate from each other. Their immediate families and all her father's friends were amongst them. Chairs were put on both sides of the street and a few rectangular tables that were decorated with blue and white iris bouquets and trays full of fruits and cookies were placed in the middle. Several people were serving tea and cookies. When they arrived, everyone cheered and they started clapping. Her sister and his were dancing to the happy songs coming from the music player.

A few lamps, which were decorations between the nearby orange trees, gave the party a poetic atmosphere. The guests could see rose trees, which were loaded with pink and red roses and white irises at their feet. Although it was a modest party compared to the ceremony, which had been arranged in Shiraz by her husband, Nosha felt proud since this was the home she had been raised in and to her it all had a wild natural beauty.

Nowhere else in the world would give her such a calm feeling of belonging. She was used to all her homeland customs, good or bad. All the women who covered themselves as soon as she entered their gathering with her husbands, all the gossip she hated so much, the orange blossoms scents, or the dirty streets of her town—all were part of her past and therefore part of her future.

The next morning, she went back to the garden with him. He was enjoying the good scenery of the spring wherever they went. The roses took his attention with their beauty and scents.

"The roses in Shiraz do not have such a strong scent. Why is that?" he asked.

"They are hybrid roses coming from abroad. These are the grafted roses produced a hundred years ago. They are beautiful and scented too. Their full blossoms come in spring, but they bloom all year round, though not as many as you see now " she replied.

They went up the horizontal street and past the street that witnessed their wedding reception the night before and turned left when he said, "Wow!"

She knew he would love that spot. There was a canopy with a climbing yellow rose tree covering it and the bright yellow roses were hanging from top and its side in abundance. Thousands of dark blue irises between white ones covered its foot while wild pansies covered its footsteps. A big tree trunk made a natural chair farther up.

He sat on it and pulled her toward him; she sat on his knees. He shook his head and said, "You know, this is like heaven and you are like the angel queen of this heaven."

She laughed and said, "And you are the god." They looked at each other and she bent down and kissed his beautiful lips.

The happy times pass us fast and so did that unforgettable trip to her homeland; before she knew it, Nosha found herself sitting in a bus leaving Shiraz to go to the Caspian Sea with her new husband. The north was so much different than Pars. From Tehran to Ramsar the roads were covered with lush green foliage. Nosha had never seen a road that green before and was so excited to see that from the top of the mountain to down in the alley everything was green! She knew her country had many different regions with different climates. From the hot desert of Kavir to the cold days in Tabriz, there it was, the green lush region of Mazandaran, which left her breathless.

They went to a hotel in Ramsar, which was beautiful. In front of their bedroom was a heart-shaped pool, with blue tiles and sparkling clean water.

She was amazed and said, "My God, it cannot be!"

He asked, "What is the matter?"

She whispered as if she had not heard him, "It is the same exact place!"

He was worried now. "What are you talking about," he asked her again.

She heard him this time and said, "You would not believe it. I dreamt for a long time, more than several years now, that I was walking and then stopped in a place and I did not know where it was, but it was a heart-shaped pool with tall green trees surrounding it. This is it! This is the place I used to walk once in a while in my dreams to relax and did not know where it was!"

He smiled and said, "Interesting! You have what they call the sixth sense."

"What is the sixth sense?"

"Well, I was reading in some journals that a few people have a sixth sense which allows them to predict the future."

"Oh, you don't believe that nonsense, do you?" she asked.

"Well my darling, either I should believe what you just told me to be the truth or a lie. If it is the truth then there is no other explanation, is there?"

She said with a sigh, "I guess you are right. Sometimes my dreams come true, and I do not have any logical explanation for them either. But this place is so beautiful, is it possible that my sixth sense knew I would spend the most important time of my life here?"

"Maybe, who knows," he replied laughing.

Their trip was full of fun and excitement. They went to the shore, which was by the hotel and looked at the deep blue water, walking, and conversing, holding hands.

"Do you swim?" he asked.

"Oh, I love to swim," she replied.

"Then let's go swimming."

"You want me to swim in front of all these people?" she asked.

"Why not?"

"Oh, don't you know how Persians look at modern women that do not pay attention to the norms?"

"Wow, that again!" he cried. "There are so many women here who are swimming."

"They are not swimming," she replied. "They just get in the water and stay there. If I want to swim I want to go all the way up where my feet do not reach the sea floor and then swim." She looked at him petulantly, hoping that would be the end of the conversation.

"Well, we can rent a boat then. Put on your bathing suit and let's go."

She could not argue any more. She loved to swim and the fresh clear water of the Caspian Sea was inviting. But the invisible chain of morality still had a deep hold on her and made her uncomfortable to be in public in only her bathing suit! But her husband's smile, as she said okay changed her hesitation, and she went in to put on her bathing suit, and then wore a dress over it.

They got into the boat he rented and sailed on the water. The sun was up and the cool breezy spring day felt good. The boatman was singing a love song and they leaned into each other as they enjoyed the sparkling water and the mild weather. When the boat was far away from the shore, the boatman stopped the boat and told them it was time to jump in the water. They both jumped in the water and started swimming away from the boat. The boatman started screaming that they had to stay close by. But she did not like swimming around the boat. It was making too much of a wave which made swimming difficult. But they found a way to make the boatman shut up and do their swimming. They swam away from the boat until he screamed, then floated on waves, which were going toward the boat, and then repeated the ritual. She enjoyed the cool water and riding the waves so much; she had never swam in a sea nor an ocean before.

After an hour of fun and play, they stopped and went back to the boat. She lay down on the bench to dry out. After a while, he broke the silence and said, "You are a good swimmer! Where did you learn it?"

"In our small pool in Pasargad," she replied.

"Really? That pool is very small!"

"Yes, but I was only seven years old when my father started teaching me how to swim."

"Wow! Most people do not know how to swim until they're adults! Your father must love you very much."

She laughed and said, "They had no choice. They did not want me to drown so they had to teach me. Actually I fell down in the pool three times by age seven and they had to rescue me!" she continued.

"My! You must have been a handful then. Is it usual for the children to fall in pools?"

"Yes, very usual. I always loved the water and would sit by the pool any chance I got."

He looked at her. "Tell me about the incidents."

"Well, I don't remember the first two times I fell in the pool or how was I rescued. But I know they were scary enough for my father to try to teach me how to swim. They did not have all the plastic tubes they have these days, so they had to improvise. The palm tree leaves when dried and cut at the end are very light and float on the water. So my father and the gardener made a hole in three of these leaves and put a rope through them. Then they fastened the rope around my waist. That way I could float and I started to learn how to swim.

"A few days later I was playing under the sour orange tree, when a long branch caught my eyes. This is a good branch to swing with, the thought crossed my mind and immediately I grabbed the branch and started swinging. The branch was young and flexible and it was swinging a few yards from the pool to the middle of it. I remember the joy I felt. Little did I know that the branch was too weak to hold my weight. Once, when I was in the middle of the pool, the branch broke and took me down into the pool! My joy did not vanish entirely; there was a new adventure waiting for me. I was in the bottom of the pool, and then I was floating. I had no problem breathing yet. I was happy that I was able to swim and could come up without any problem. I felt the edge of the pool when someone pulled me out.

"Out of the water my joy disappeared fast. My mother was in the pool and *Naneh*, Nooshin, and a little later my father were worriedly looking at her; she was fainting. They took her out of water and a doctor was called in. My mother was in her ninth month of pregnancy!

"Apparently when the branch broke my sister saw me going down, and she started screaming. My mother heard her screams from the other side of the yard and ran toward the pool, but according to her, she fell down couple of times until she reached the pool and pulled me out. *Naneh* and my father heard my mom scream, one from the kitchen and the latter from the orchard, and came. I could not believe that all this activity happened while I was having fun and was swimming. I still cannot believe that was enough time for my mother to fall couple of times and then get me out! But nevertheless, I was rescued instead of being able to get out by myself and that was disappointing to me. Apparently, the falls and the scariness of the event were the reasons that my mother's water broke and she was ordered bed rest for couple of days until my brother was born."

He started laughing and said, "I never thought you could be such a trouble making child for your parents! But who knows, maybe you were right and you were almost out when she jumped in to pull you out. Besides, it shows that you always were daring and smart," he continued with obvious affection.

"Oh, thanks," she replied.

They stayed in the boat for a couple of hours, then went back to shore. Their stay in the Ramsar Hotel was full of fun; and both were saddened when it had to end and each had to lead their separate lives again.

※

Her days were spent with study, work in the hospitals, and writing to her husband whenever she had time. But not everything in Shiraz was as calm as her life. In the last few years, Shiraz had witnessed several festivals. The cultural and art festivals in Shiraz were full of controversy; festivals that fueled anger in the student community.

The 2,500 Years of Monarchy celebration was the current point of controversy that was to be celebrated that year. Millions were spent on this party—why couldn't he spend it for the poor people of the villages, the opposition demanded. However, Nosha's pride told her it was not such a bad idea anyway. The Persians had been very humiliated under the Ghajar when the colonization was at its peak and Iran was divided into two powers spheres, the Russian sphere in the north and British sphere in the south. The foreigners who went to Iran those days did not have anything good to say about Persians. Most of their books were full of memories of which some parts were true, but since it was so one-sided, it made most Persians feel very bad about their country and culture. There was no mention of the rich culture that they thought they gave to the world, but only bad parts of the society that were caused in part by colonization and also by greedy individuals who were thinking more about their own pockets than the well-being of their country. So the Persians were now eager to tell newcomers that they had a rich culture in the past and that they were not the wild animals that Westerners thought them to be. Most Persians who traveled abroad were met with questions like do you speak Arabic? Or, do you ride a camel? They wanted to change that image, and more than anything else, the king himself, who was very sensitive to these images, wanted to show the world the rich culture that Persians enjoyed in the past. The 2,500-year celebration was only for that purpose. To tell the world that Iran was not a backward country, that Iran was same as the Persia that most Westerners only read about in their holy books. And to tell the world that their official language was Persian, which had been spoken and enjoyed extensively over a large area of Asia in the early ages.

The party employed thousands of students, civilians, and soldiers. They built the road from Shiraz to Taghteh Jamshid (Persepolis), as nice as it could be in the most developed world.[1] There were nine kings, three ruling princes, two crown princes, and thirteen presidents from all over the world attending the ceremony. But the results turned out to be opposite of what the Shah wanted to create. The foreigners could not understand or appreciate what had been done; on the inside, students who could see that they were not allowed in the ceremony became outraged. Nosha once went with one of her friends who was working in one of the sites. But they refused to let her in, and she was sent back.

Another problem was the poor people of the villages who did not have electricity, water, or good roads. The young armies who went to the villages to help them were the loudest opposition to the monarch. Why can we not spend all this money to build roads for the remote villages or on hospitals for all these needy people, or electricity and water circulation systems, they would demand. The Shah should not be spending people's money to have fun with his friends. Although the older generation who saw the problems before Pahlavi were still behind him, the younger ones were falling away from him.

Was the party a mistake? Probably. It could have been held after his ambition of taking the country to the twenty-first century had been fulfilled, and not for the kings and presidents of the world, but for his own citizens; they could celebrate their long civil history and invite all the foreign journalists to see and publish the event. His goal would have been fulfilled much faster and his people would not call him a foreign stooge. If the Shah knew the trouble it would cause him, he probably would not have done it, or the way he did would have been different. Nevertheless, the uneasiness started right away, even before the party.

Yet another incident made Nosha deeply concerned. A group of seventeen people were arrested for the charge of conspiracy to capture/kill the crown prince. Two of their leaders, who were Marxist and refused to accept the court, were sentenced to death, but the strange thing was that one of the women in the group was from the royal family. She said in the live interview that she joined the group when they took her to south of Tehran and showed her how people were living there! Nosha wondered if she was thinking right in her understanding of the opposition. *If the sons of the generals and the royal family think our ruler is bad, then maybe they know some thing I do not know*, she thought. However, nobody knew of extent of the coming storm, which ruined so many lives in the years to come.

As she started her sixth year, she grew very busy with all the shifts and patients in every hospital she was working. They were very poor and some were neglected entirely until they were too sick, finally brought to the free hospitals where she was working. She could not understand why they did not have more knowledge of hygiene or any medical doctors in their villages to help them and have them diagnosed earlier.

"Yes, we are a wealthy country but our citizens do not even have basic necessities in their lives," her husband told her when she complained about it on one of his trips to Shiraz. He told her that he had seen even worse scenarios in the places he was working.

"I was in my station one day when a man came to me with obviously worried face and begged me to go with him to his remote village. I could not leave with all the patients waiting, I told him. He begged harder and said he might lose his wife if I did not go. I asked my assistant, the paramedic who was there to do his military service, to check if we did not have major emergencies among my patients. He came back and told me that there was nothing serious. So I told him to help whoever he could and reschedule the rest of them for the next day.

"I went to his village. It was a long, hard road that we had to climb almost halfway by foot. We went toward the clay rooms, which were built close together; the place they called home. In one of them was a young woman surrounded by several other women who were beating her. My arrival made them stop."

"'What is going on here?' I asked. They told me there is an evil spirit in her soul that is preventing the baby from coming out. 'But why are you beating her? She is in pain already!' I said.

"They wanted to drive the evil spirit out. After an examination, I realized that the baby was bridged and there was no way I would be able to help her. She needed a cesarean and I was not sure if the baby was alive anyway. I told them to move her so we could reach my car and take her to Bohsheher. We did and that saved her life but not her baby's," he said with a sigh.

Nosha said, "I do not know when we are going to have enough to develop those remote villages."

Siyavash smiled and said, "Either you are right and we will build enough roads and facilities in those villages in the near future or, as the opponents of the government are saying, the monies will be spent on unnecessary things and they will never get the basics in their lives as long as we have the same political party."

He was very careful not to attack her ideas, but instead spoke of facts, which were clear to her too. Should she believe the older generation who were telling her that the rosy picture of their country was true and she was going forward, or the opposition who discarded even the obvious and believed anything that the government was telling them was a big lie?

Reality Time

Then came the day when one day Parviz, one of her quiet fellow students, went to jail; his crime was that he was reading one of the forbidden books outside in the garden of the hospital. This time, Nosha and others knew his whereabouts and they did not have to wonder why he was not in his classes anymore.

Among some of these forbidden books, along with the Marxists and the communists, were a few Iranian writers. The first writer was an elementary school teacher who wrote children's books and in it argued that stealing was okay if the robber was poor and was stealing from the rich. This book was not okay for the children at all and was banned, but the college students were reading it admiringly and passed it to each other. Nosha could not believe how they could not understand that stealing is bad no matter what. But was that not one of the communist ideals?

The other writer was a doctor of theology whose books were very popular among students. She could not even finish one of them without getting bored or falling sleep, something that never happened with other books.

He wanted a society run by pure Islam. Although he very cleverly interpreted lots of Islamic beliefs very attractively to the youth, he was not clear about what his Islamic government would be like, and none of the students who were in love with his idea asked themselves why the Islamic governments of the past eras could not achieve what he was claiming was possible to achieve. But still, Nosha was not against religion. She was raised by Moslem parents and even with her busy class schedules managed to pray five times a day.

She did not cover herself because she was not used to it. She also did not go to the mosque or the religious ceremonies. While she obeyed almost all other religious aspects, she did not like the interpretation of religious leaders about women in society. She also could not believe that after fourteen centuries they could change that much. The

Islamic laws were good and sound; the problem was their interpretation by the clerics, who called taxation illegal and considered going to school a sin. After the white revolution, the number of students going to school had increased dramatically, but still there were a few very devoted people who did pay attention to the call from mullahs.

She remembered a vivid and exciting scene one day. She was walking in the orchard in Pasargad when she saw Oujan's daughter Sedigheh sitting by the tree near the pool doing her homework. What was strange was that her foot was fastened to the tree and her father was working nearby.

"What is going on?" Nosha asked. "Why did you fasten her foot to the tree?"

Oujan replied, "Because she did not do her homework and her teacher told me."

Nosha was amazed and asked, "But your son did not finish his middle school and it did not bother you; what is the difference between him and your daughter?"

"Oh dear Nosha, there is a difference. My son could go and work as a construction worker, but she cannot do that. She will get abused by her husband if she does not get an education and does not work!"

Nosha could not stop laughing. "But tell her your reason and she will study harder; fastening her to the tree will not solve the problem."

Then she opened the rope from the child's foot and talked to her for a minute, asking her if she would promise to study harder.

"Yes, Miss Nosha, I will," the child replied.

She was so happy to see that their illiterate gardener saw the value of education for his daughter.

But the news was not so good all over. Just two days ago, she had heard bad news. Her father told her that Fereshteh, her second cousin, whose butler had told her when she was two years old that she was going to be a doctor, had quit school because she was told by her father that going to school was against their religion! Nosha replied that she could not finish school since she had a low IQ.

Her father frowned and said, "What are you talking about, do you mean she is worse than Oujan's daughter?"

"Yes Father, I was tutoring both of them, don't you remember?" she replied.

But inside she wondered, what is happening to people? Fereshteh's father had been a communist at a young age who had denied god altogether. He would tell everyone that if God exists then I will plant a tomato plant and let it go without water; if it survives then there is a God! Everyone knew that in the dry climate of Pasargad tomatoes did not have a chance of survival without any water. This same person told his oldest daughter that going to school was against his religion!

More disturbing news came in the form of Ali, another cousin of Nosha's, who had been accepted to the university but his father refused to pay for his tuition for the same reason. Poor Ali had to rely on his older brothers who were working and some small money from his uncle, Nosha's father, until he finished his first year, but the free tuition for all college students helped him a lot from the second year onward.

For students in the universities, those days were very good ones. The girls especially had very high morality standards. They did not drink, smoke, or have sexual relationships; the few who were in love had limited relations, which did not exceed kissing or hugging each other. That was the exact reason Nosha did not like the writer who was promoting the pure Islamic government. But she heard to her dismay one day that a high school student went to jail for supporting Khomeini, an exiled cleric who had risen against the Shah for giving women the right to vote. He said that this would cause women to become prostitutes. How could anyone with a right mind take the risk of going to jail for following him or advertising for him? she asked herself.

With Parviz gone, Nosha now knew three boys who had gone to jail for different political reasons. Bijan, a tall lanky boy with brown eyes who was very polite, was one of them; he disappeared from all her classes and the cafeteria after the long walk they had for the dead students. Almost six months later, she saw him in the cafeteria.

He came and sat at her table and said, "Hi."

"Oh hello Bijan," she replied. "Where have you been? Long time no see."

"Oh yes, I know," he answered. "I was in jail," he continued frankly.

"Why?"

He laughed and said, "Well, I was stupid enough to distribute pamphlets against our government. They could not prove it though; I denied every thing." he continued. He could not continue his career in medical field, because of poor grades, and was forced to study social science.

She learned from other students several years later that he had joined SAVAK, so she asked him point blank. He denied it and said, "Since I am doing volunteer work for the government they are assuming I am part of SAVAK."

Mohammad was the second one who disappeared about the same time as Bijan. He was, according to himself, the son of a merchant whose father was bankrupt, and the Shah had pardoned him so he was able to continue his merchant work. Nosha did not believe him that much. She knew him from before her college years, even before she met Siyavash. When she had been looking for a tutor in Pasargad, she was introduced to Mohammad, a college student who came from Shiraz to teach at the local school. She asked him to teach her English while her father paid him. He was a good teacher and she was able to pass the entrance test with his guidance.

But he also had a crush on her and had invited her to go out with him several times. He would bring poems from both Persian and English languages in his teaching sessions. He also told her that he did not date the students at his college; she did not ask him why then, but he acted very strange after her acceptance to the university. He started to act like he did not know her. But then one day he told her he needed some money and asked if she could lend him five hundred toman. She did and after that he avoided her completely until he vanished.

A year later when she was going to the library to study, she saw him standing in front of the door and he came over to talk with her. *Strange*, she thought, *has he changed his mind or is he maybe ready to pay me back the money that was due more than a year ago?*

She looked at him. "Where have you been?"

"Let's walk, I will tell you," he answered. She got up, curious about what he wanted to tell her. As they walked, he began.

"I was in jail," he said.

"Why?"

"Oh, I do not want to put the body of my past memories in front of my eyes and stab it again. I only do not know what to do now. Without an education, I cannot do much in my life. You are lucky, you are going to be a doctor and you are going to be successful in life! Do you know how much I admire you? There are beautiful things in our lives that we wish to have. And you are one of those things I always wished to have."

Nosha did not know what to say. She did not trust him at all. Maybe if, at the beginning when she became a student, he had told her, she could have responded more favorably, but why now?

"Is that why you were hiding yourself from me?" she asked sarcastically.

He did not reply to her comment but instead continued, "I am leaving tomorrow! I do not have any money, otherwise I would stay longer."

Oh, she thought, *that is why I am one of the beautiful things he wishes to have; he thinks I will pay him more money!* "Are you coming back to school?" she asked.

"If God wishes, of course!"

She had to go back to her studies and so she said goodbye to him. She felt sorry for him and did not ask for the forgotten money he borrowed from her.

Are these the people who want to rescue our country? she wondered. *He does not believe in anything and does not show any sign of religious morality in his life, but he says "if God wishes" for something he could achieve himself!*

She later told Siyavash about it. She was confused at the differences between the opposition propaganda and reality, between the government statistics and ones of the opposition. The newspapers were full of promising statistics about every area of life, everything from the number of schools, roads, and factories to the per capita income was increasing. The colleges paid the students some money, which was plenty to have a good and modest life.

One day, while chatting with some of her classmates, she heard a British student who was doing research in Iran say, "I know an Iranian guy in England who is getting all his expenses paid; he has been studying there for several years now!" Then she continued bitterly, "When is it coming to an end?"

"What?" Nosha asked.

"The oil money."

"Are you jealous of him?" she asked, surprised.

"No, but…"

Nosha, disturbed by the British student's comments, interrupted her and said, "So when the British were taking all the oil from our land and did not even employ any Persians, you were not waiting for it to end, but now it is so bad that the students are benefiting from oil money, that you cannot wait till it dries out?"

The British girl was startled and said, "Well I didn't mean it that way. I meant that the poor people should get some part of this wealth too."

Obviously, that was not what she meant, but Nosha did not continue the discussion and left the group.

The same thing was happening everywhere. She had a foreign teacher in her first year that was very popular among the students and they all said he was very good. She took his class and realized out he was not in fact a good teacher but a political one. He told everyone in the class things like, "I met an American worker who was paid a much higher salary than me, and on top of that, the government paid all his rent. When you and I want to rent a place then we will not be able to afford it."

Well, that probably was a true story, but years later when she was in the United States, she realized that with all the freedom in that society people did not know each other's salaries; even if they did the same kind of work in the same company, they could have a different salary.

However, with all the uneasy feelings there seemed a calm and prosperous future in sight. By the end of the year, her husband came back and opened a small clinic on Afras alley, the same place where his old house was located and started to work. Her happiness was boundless; she was finally living with her husband and he did not have to take long trips away from her. He also was very busy studying to continue his education and become a specialist.

Her seventh year was just started when one morning she went to the hospital, and her supervisor gave her a letter to sign. She became furious after reading it. The letter stated that all the Persians had to be registered in one party called *Rastaghiz*, and anyone who did not like it was free to leave the country!

"This is unbelievable!" she shouted. They'd had two parties in Iran for some time, and they would write some articles against each other. Most people, including Nosha, were not part of either party, but she did not like the tone of the letter. "I am not signing this," she told her supervisor.

He smiled and said, "You have a student's soul—opposing everything!"

"What do you mean?" she asked the older doctor.

"You remind me of myself when I was your age," he continued with a kind voice. "I was a fool then; I was one of the *Todeh* party members and was shouting in the street for *Mosadehg*."

"You had more freedom then," she interrupted him.

He shook his head and said, "No, not really. There was chaos, not freedom. Everywhere you went there were groups shouting, long live Shah or death to him. There were clashes daily between the pro-Shah movement and pro-*Mosadehg*. It was not good at all. We have security now and peace of mind. We are free to choose our outfits, our professions, and our religions. We are free to do whatever we like in our homes. There are abundant jobs with good pay. Free education everywhere; what more do we need?"

"Insurance for everyone!" she told him.

He shook his head and said, "We will have that too. But can you please sign this letter so they know you have seen it?" He was kind and sounded right. He reminded her of her own father. But she still did not want to register for the party when she had no idea what it was about.

So she said, "I do not want to be part of this new party, though."

He said calmly, "You do not need to. You have seen this letter and it is up to you if you would like to join the party or not. All I am asking to sign it, which shows all the hospital personnel have seen it."

She signed the letter and continued with her busy schedule. She once again became immersed in her thoughts; although everything was calm, she could see discontent in the air. She could not understand how their king could make such a mistake; asking the citizen of a country to leave their country was not a wise decision! But she shrugged her shoulders and fell into her work with the arrival of her first patients.

Before she knew it, she was done with medical school and was now officially a doctor. All of her family and her husband's family attended the graduation ceremony, as her brother-in-law was graduating at the same time too. They all enjoyed the ceremony. She had tears of joy in her eyes; she finally achieved what she had wanted since she was a child, and not only that, had a good man beside her as well. Nobody was as lucky as her, she thought.

That night in his arms, he asked her after her graduation what she wanted to do.

"Be a good wife for you and cure the people to the best of my ability," she replied honestly.

"Would you like to help me in my office? My MGEMS exams are next month and I can use some help."

"Yes, I would love to!" she told him. "Are you sure is it okay?"

"After all, we both graduated from the same school; why shouldn't I be sure?" he asked.

"Well, you did practice for almost two years in Bohsheher and have more experience than me," she said shyly.

"I think you have everything you need to be a great doctor in my office. Stop being so silly. You will be wonderful."

"Ok," she answered. "I would love to."

Leaving the Homeland

He was glowing when she saw him. He opened his arms and as he held her in them he said, "I did it! I got accepted for my residency and a postdoctoral degree." She jumped up with joy too. She knew how hard he had been studying for the exams and how much he wanted to specialize.

"Oh, congratulations darling! Where did you get accepted?"

"Duke University; they have all kind of specialties and you might be able to start there too after passing the exams."

"Duke University in the United States?"

"Yes! Can you believe it? One of the top ten medical schools in the country!" he continued excitedly.

There was immediate sadness pushing on her heart that she tried very hard not to show. That meant that they were going to a faraway land and leaving behind everything that was dear to her! She was very happy and proud of him and did not want to ruin his happiness with her concerns. But in the days that followed as they began the packing process, she felt more sadness. When their departure day arrived, her father was down; it seemed that he knew this was going to be a long and painful separation. Her feelings were no easier to bear than her father's. She felt uneasiness in her heart and shared it only with her sister.

She told her, "Well, you always wanted to get your post doctorate too. Go finish your education and come back. If you think of it this way then you will not feel so bad."

The rest of the family wished them a good trip and they finally departed from the land they loved.

It was the first time she had ever flown and the excitement of it calmed her sadness a little. When the airplane raised up and could see the last glances of their capital city, a tear fell on her cheek, which she wiped away quickly. Siyavash was very happy and she did not want him to feel bad. She loved his excitement and jubilant behavior. He was very happy for being accepted to Duke medical school and she did not want to ruin it for him.

After an hour or so, he asked her to look outside; she saw the clouds spread beneath them like a pile of fluffy soft snow.

She said, "It's so beautiful." He asked her to sit by the window and enjoy the scenery.

She did; then he broke the silence and said, "You are so quiet, what is the matter?"

She looked at him and said, "I do not know. We are going to a faraway land and I feel there will be some very big changes before we come back, which is disturbing me."

"Yes, there will be changes darling, but for the better," he replied.

But even despite her disturbing feelings and the fact that she already missed her family, the trip was pleasant. The plane stopped in London for an hour to get fuel, which gave them enough time to walk around and see the London airport. He took several pictures of her until it was time to leave.

They arrived in Kennedy Airport in New York City. One of Siyavash's cousins lived there and was waiting for them at the airport. They were going to visit him and see New York City for a few days before going to North Carolina.

New York to her was a huge city, full of fun and surprises. The clover leaves on the highway caught her eyes and she remembered how hard it was to read about them in their English books back home. She understood Shakespearean English better than that article about highway cloverleaves. But after seeing one, everything she read came back to her mind and did not seem so hard anymore.

The subway was so interesting and she enjoyed being able to get all over the city without having to drive or take a taxi. They walked around the city and enjoyed their time together in one of the United States' biggest cities. At night, they spent time talking with Siyavash's cousin and his wife, both of whom were very friendly and hospitable. They left for their destination a week later.

The day he registered at the Duke medical school she started some classes to prepare for the required exams. She felt so homesick, especially because her husband was going to be very busy, and she wanted to be busy too so she would not feel lonely. She also wrote several letters back home to her sister, friends, and her parents. Her father's letter was the first to arrive, which followed with the others, but gradually they diminished and only one letter would come each week, from her father. He wrote her beautiful handwritten letters filled with many poems and beautiful compositions, which reminded her of the jasmine perfumes she enjoyed in her summer bed. In one of his letters, he wrote:

My darling Nosha,

The daffodils and narcissus are giving us the promise of colorful spring. The almond trees are bursting out of their buds with their first blossoms and the birds are coming back from the south to sing us love songs. I can not stay in the garden too long anymore since I used to go there to pick up flowers for you and now you are gone. You are gone to a land far away and I am here, old and wondering when I will see the light of my eyes again? You are away and I want so much to see you close by. I want to pick these beautiful flowers, and make bouquets to send to you, but you are in a land that is too far away to send them to. The jasmine tree is giving more flowers too, but to what use; your beautiful face is too far away to be poured upon with them. Your mother and I are missing you so much. But we know that you are happy and with a wonderful man by your side.

We should have no complaints but to wish that this time of separation shortens quickly, for us to see you again.

Love,
Babak

She found some new friends and realized that there was not much difference between the people of different countries. The kind ones were the same everywhere and she felt lucky to know only the kindest ones. At this time, there were questions of when they would have a child from both of their families. She was concerned too; she was reaching twenty-seven, and was concerned about getting pregnant after the age of thirty. She wanted to have children and being home was a good time for her to get pregnant. He agreed that it was a good time too. Then, the day came when their joy skyrocketed and they found that she was pregnant. Her parents told her they would come to see her and help her with the baby and they did in her ninth month of pregnancy.

It was a cold winter night when their daughter was born. She was a beautiful healthy baby who got his family's dark black hair and from her side, bright blue eyes; they called her Nasim. Their joy was endless and she was so happy that her parents were with them. They stayed two months and then it was time for them to leave. She was not happy seeing them leave, but that was her destiny and she had to accept it, as her grandmother used to tell her.

Nasim was a year old when she was accepted in the residency program. They arranged time to be with her, but the arrangement meant that they did not see much of each other; however their love and affection did not diminish; to the contrary, they appreciated each other more and more.

Two years passed without any important incident and soon he was done with his residency. She had only two more years to go and was pregnant again when the storm started.

The Storm

It was spring of 1978 and they were busy as usual, but the news around them was not so good. The Carter administration was pushing democracy, and human rights were his aim. Meanwhile, the news was full of story after story about the cruelty of Iranian régime. Was it really true? In the whole world did only the Iranian régime not pay attention to human rights? Was this a CIA plan or the work of the Iranian opposition who had convinced Washington and the U.S. media that the Shah was a bad dictator? He was indeed a good friend of United States of America, but in the media everywhere there was talk of the violations of Iranian human rights.

In November of 1977, the Shah had come to visit the United States of America to meet Carter. There was a demonstration by hundreds of the Iranian students who were for and against Shah. A fight broke out between them, and police had to use tear gas, which caused both Carter and Shah to have tears in their eyes when talking to each other.

In the summer, when her parents visited them again, Laiya told Nosha that her conservative cousins were distributing pamphlets against the government.

"Since when did they become political?" Nosha asked.

"I don't know," her mother replied. "They are saying that they want Khomeini."

Nosha froze inside, and said, "If a religious government replaces the current ones it will be worse."

"Oh, I do not know, but both the Shah and his prime minister are saying no matter what, they are committed to democracy."

She thought a little; but she could not understand the relationship between democracy and spreading pro-Khomeini pamphlets by her conservative cousins!

Her parents departed at the end of the summer and her mother promised to come back when the baby was going to be born. "I have to go to Mecca for a pilgrimage, so I have to go but will be back," she promised.

In the days that followed, there was more bad news. There was strike after strike in Iran, which collapsed the economy. Her father wrote her, "There is a storm here that is ruining everything; one that has been unheard of since I was born!"

Democracy and human rights were being replaced by theology, gradually and calmly. Khomeini was in Paris sending out thousands of tape-recorded speeches all over the world. Now there was no question of who he was. But what did he want? Thousands of students studying abroad were watching the events in their homeland from their western TVs. Some with disbelief and others with joy and the hope of a better future for themselves and their country. Nosha and Siyavash were in the first group.

There were heated discussions between a few Persian students at school. Azam was one who was not so concerned. Nosha looked at her one day; she was wearing a beautiful dress and makeup, her hair gathered behind her head nicely, which made her even more beautiful. She was the wife of one of the resident students and had a master's in political science. She was from Tehran, where she did not have to fight clerics to get the simple right to be able to achieve her goal.

Nosha thought, *but why doesn't she see the obvious facts?*

Then she asked, "Azam, Islam is asking all the Moslem women to cover their heads and says divorce is the men's right. Do you agree with them?"

Azam, who seemed annoyed, said, "No, but Khomeini is not talking about that; he is talking about colonization and our rights to stand up. Have you listened to his tapes?"

Nosha was not satisfied with her answer so she continued, "Dear Azam, I do not need to listen to his tapes. I know the laws and regulation of Islam. I have no problem with those who are following those laws, but if we get an Islamic government, the first thing that will go is the women's rights to wear the clothes they like to wear. The second one will be the family law, which prevents polygamy! Do you understand what I am saying? Are you supporting this?"

"No, of course not."

"But you are supporting Khomeini! And to me there is no doubt that those two subjects will be his first priority."

Azam replied after a pause. "I do not think that is true; nobody will go backward in history!"

"But our nation is screaming for an Islamic government, isn't it?"

"Yes, but that does not mean backwardness."

Nosha shook her head; obviously, Azam was reading many *Shariati* books and thought Islamic government meant heaven on the earth and nothing bad would come out of it! But she did admit that she was not well informed about the man that the Western media called a spiritual man who wanted democracy in his homeland, and did not want any financial rewards for his efforts.

Nosha, with a three-year old and all the work in the hospital, did not have time to read any books or listen to any tapes. Her only window of information was the CBS and NBC news every night, which introduced them to Khomeini and his assistants. There was Dr. Yazdi, Dr. Banisadr, and others—all western-educated, who talked logically and very democratically! They all stressed that Khomeini was not going to be part of the future government. He will go back to the city of Qom, they said.

One night, Nosha looked at her husband and said, "They might know more than us."

"Well, if he does not have any power, nothing will change," he replied.

Little did they know it was all lies. In fact, the main reason that schools were outlawed by the religious leaders was that they did not have power over them. They did not approve of teaching that was based on secular society. A Khomeini power in Iran became Washington's policies for the whole region.

Nosha heard from the national news that *Brzezinski* declared that it was good to encourage the religious feelings in the third world countries so that they could combat communist ideas. It was the middle of Cold War and the West was very much against communism. But did they know what they were doing? Was it a plan? Or lack of it? NBC quoted the CIA as saying that the Shah was their baby who had grown up. The statement was good propaganda for the opposition to Shah. Persians are proud people and they do not like their leader to be any agency's baby! But why was he the only one in the Middle East who was their baby? Most of the Arab leaders in the Middle East had the same friendly relations with the United States, and most of them were tyrants of their nations. But CIA only called Shah their baby, not anybody else! And Carter only pushed for human rights in that land? Nosha did not understand this logic.

The suspicion of every movement is part of the people's nature. Since the rise of colonization, every movement and every leader in Iran was looked at suspiciously, and everyone thinks of those movements motivated by foreign entities.

Nosha was deep in her thoughts of politics when Nasim, her three-year-old daughter, ran to her laughing. "Mommy, Daddy is trying to catch me!" she shrieked, trying to hide in her arms. Nosha realized that she was losing her precious time with her family by being drawn into politics that she could not do a damn thing about.

She smiled at her husband and said, "You can not catch Nasim since she is in my arms."

Siyavash smiled back and said, "Oh really, I will see," and came toward them. Nasim's laughter got louder as Siyavash came closer and started tickling her. Nosha told herself again, sternly, *I should enjoy my family*. Between study, work, and thinking about the politics of her homeland, she had forgotten to enjoy life. And on that fall afternoon she decided to forget about the bad feelings she had about these turbulences in her homeland and enjoy her life as it was supposed to be.

Nasim was so beautiful and smart at age three; she could read simple words and knew all of the English alphabet. In addition, Nosha sang a few simple Persian poems and songs to her that she had memorized and could recite them when her mother asked.

They worked on her English first, since they thought that when they went back home, she would master the Persian language, and it was wise to perfect her English while they could.

"Let's go and see the trees," Siyavash told Nosha. Autumn was magnificent and they enjoyed the afternoon watching nature's rainbow on each tree. Nasim was giving them more joy by her sweet talk and her laughter.

Days were passing and revolution grew closer by the day to the land they loved. Obviously, they were looking at the events with worry, but they were giving themselves hope that it was going to get better eventually. By the end of fall, all the mail stopped coming. Navid called Nosha from England and told her that the money their father sent for his tuition had never reached his school! There was no way of communicating with Iran any more at all. No telephone calls or letters could come or go through.

"There are strikes and nobody is working; that is why there is no mail and banks can not send the money parents were sending their children," one of their friends explained.

On September 8, 1978, crowds gathered to demonstrate in Jaleh Square in downtown Tehran. Government troops opened fire on the protestors. Hundreds of people were killed, the newscast announced, although its truth was challenged later and the numbers disputed as being too many.[38a] Nevertheless, seeing the events and all the bloody bodies of her fellow countrymen brought tears to her eyes.

It was the end of November when she went into labor and went to the hospital. Their son Nima was born a few hours later. She was so happy seeing him with his dark soft black hair and beautiful white skin, which resembled his father's. Next day, when Siyavash came to visit her, he had a very special surprise for her. After a couple of months not receiving any letter from her father, he brought her five letters at the same time.

Wow, she was so happy to see his pretty handwriting! She read each word with delight. Then she hugged her husband and kissed him with tears of joy in her eyes. She felt that she was a lucky woman, with her husband and her two children. But she missed her family so much, especially with so much uncertainty in her homeland.

Since Siyavash had just started his new job, she decided to stay home that year. She had more time to watch the news. But the news was getting worse day by day. To distract herself, she played with the children and listened to Nasim's laughter, which made her forget about all the troubles around her. Nima, too, kept her busy and relaxed with his constant smiles. January arrived and with it an unbelievable event.

On January 16, 1979, Nosha, with millions of others, witnessed a shift of power that would change their lives forever. She turned the TV on and saw the ruler of her country in tears getting ready to leave his homeland. That was the promise of calm and happy days for Persia; at least that was what opposition leaders claimed! The Shah, who looked very thin and pale, was standing in the airport with a few army generals, who cried as they kissed his hands. Tears were in his eyes when he bent down and took a handful of Iranian soil—the same gesture his father took when was forced to depart from Persia by the

Allies three decades before.

There was a rush of sadness into Nosha's heart and tears gathered in her eyes. She was surprised by the extent of her sadness. *Why am I so unhappy?* she asked herself. It was a cold afternoon and dark outside with thick grey clouds covering the sky. Both of her children were asleep, so she let her tears come and wash over her face. She felt like she was losing someone dear to her and she did not know the reason! She did not think the king was a cruel dictator who did not care about his land, but she knew firsthand that there were problems in her homeland. The Shah could have done so much more! He also could have prevented a lot of what was happening. *Did you forget all the bloodshed that happened last month?* she asked herself and knew how upset she had been with the event. *Do you agree with the corruption that is choking this country? Do you agree with the torture of the people and with what SAVAK does?* Her answers to all these questions were no, but why did she feel so miserable?

She had to find the answer; one logical explanation was that she had been raised to love the Shah as her beloved country's ruler, and now that he was departing, she was sad. *But if all the TV shows in United States about him are true, or if all the writers' descriptions are true, then why should you love such a man?* she asked herself again. She could remember vividly how furious she was when she found out her classmate was taken to prison for just reading a book, and she also remembered the order Shah sent to all government employees to join his party or leave the country! *Now that he is leaving you are crying; why?* It did not make sense.

Yes, she knew all the problems but she did not know the solutions. She did not think the clerics would be able to do better than him, and thought that they might even be worse in some cases. That was a better explanation. She knew for sure that she did not like the idea of a theocratic government. She loved to study her homeland's long history, and in any decade that there was theocratic government in her homeland, there were complaints and there were problems, that had almost destroyed Iran and her people. She was purely secular and liked the Pahlavi dynasty since theocracy was minimized and there was a secular society. Iran had always been quite diverse. There were Jewish, Christian, and Zoroastrian groups, plus several different Islamic sects in Iran, who were getting hurt anytime that there was a theocratic government. Besides that, Nosha was very devoted to women's rights, which had been ignored throughout the centuries, but with the rise of Reza Shah, they enjoyed relative freedom.

For over an hour, she was drawn deep into her thoughts and the sadness overcoming her mind, until the happy voice of Nasim brought her to reality. Nasim ran to her and said, "Mommy! Nima is up and smiling!" Nosha held her in her arms and tried to quickly wipe her eyes dry with her fingers so her daughter would not see her tears. Then she said, "Oh, is he really? Then let's go see him."

Two weeks later they were witnessing another historic event in their country; Khomeini made a triumphant return to Iran. Nosha felt the same overwhelming sadness she had felt two weeks before with Shah's departure, and as tears rolled down her cheeks, she grabbed a tissue to wipe them.

Siyavash, who noticed her tears, pulled her in his arms and asked, "What is bothering you?"

She looked at him, "If you want to stay here I do not mind."

"Oh really? What happened to your patriotic feelings? I thought you were a nationalist."

She sighed and said, "That is gone. There is no room for patriotism or nationalism any more! It is a theological time, which to me is a poison to nationalism."

"So are you giving up so fast?" he asked.

"Don't you see the reality? Look at the crowd welcoming his arrival. I am not even there and from what I see, people like you and I are minorities. We can not do a damn thing and he is going to destroy our beloved country."

He asked, surprised, "How do you know? He is saying he will not be taking any role in government and there are so many intellectuals around him!"

"Yes, but don't be fooled, darling. They want an Islamic government! That means a theocracy. I have been very sad in the past two weeks. I can not put my finger on anything, but I feel that our destiny is not Iran anymore; we should stay here."

Nasim tried to sit between them. Nasim had been trying very hard to get their attention since Nima was born. Pushing herself too close to Nosha when she was nursing Nima was another thing she was doing. Siyavash picked her up, put her on his knees, and told her, "Your mom is making this decision for you."

She said, "Is that true, Mommy?" Not knowing what decision she was talking about, she was visibly happy that her mom was doing something for her. Nosha smiled and kissed her as she told Siyavash, "That is right; as a woman I don't want my daughter to be raised under a theocratic government. There will be too much restriction!"

"What about your family? You were obviously unhappy, even when you knew that we were living here temporarily," he said.

"Oh, I do not know, Siya. I feel things are going to be bad, very bad there!" She really did not know why. Was it her sixth sense, as her husband told her on their honeymoon? She wished that was not true. She wanted to believe that all the joy her people were showing in the welcoming ceremony when Khomeini arrived would be truly good for them.

All the opposition groups from right to left were optimistic that things were going to be better. But her heart was telling her to be prepared for the worst. The event that followed proved she was right; her feeling was right again.

Nine months later Iranian students would take dozens of Americans hostages at the U.S. embassy in Tehran. U.S.-Iranian relations grew sour and the death of Iran was observed around campus. There were some Iranians and Arabs, who had no relationship to Iranian government, who were beaten badly. But Nosha's American friends were so kind that she did not have any worry about getting hurt. There were people she knew only as someone who lived in the neighborhood, that she had said hi to a couple of times. They rang their door and asked if they were okay. Their embassy has been taken and their flags are burning in my country and they are worried that someone would harm me. *Oh, that is so noble*, she told herself. She did not experience any hostile behavior, even in the hospital since she had gone back to her residency. These actions moved her deeply and she understood the reason people from all over the globe wanted so much to be living in the United States of America. The fact that the people of United States welcomed newcomers and the infinite opportunities that awaited them were some of the main reasons.

It was a cold winter afternoon when they got the news. Siyavash's brother-in-law and his cousin had been executed in Iran by the new Islamic republic of Iran. They did not know what his crimes were. They were told that he was involved in the Nooje Coup d'etat (the plot that some air force generals planned to overthrow the Khomeini government). There was an informer who told the new government about the plot, and before anyone could do anything, hundreds of the top generals and the best pilots were killed.

Siyavash was very sad and she could see pain and tears in his big beautiful eyes. She went to him and hugged him. He put his head on her shoulder and told her all about his memory of him.

"He was like a big brother to me. Why should they kill him?" he asked her. But she did not have any answer; nobody had any logical answer to all those killings. Surprisingly none of the media were talking about it. They all forgot about Iran and human rights. He talked for hours and she listened.

She tried to calm him down by telling him, "He is going to be in your memory and you should remember that he did not want you upset."

"Oh, I know," he said, "but I am worried about my sister! What is she going to do with all her children and no job?"

"Well, you have five brothers and only one sister. You should try to help her both financially and emotionally."

"How can we do that? She is so proud that I do not think she will accept any help from us."

"I know, but I am sure that she is also smart enough to accept your help when she needs it."

Then he looked at her and said, "You knew it! Didn't you?'

"What did I know, dear?" Nosha asked.

"Do you remember when told me? 'I feel things are going to be bad, very bad there!' How did you know?" he stressed.

"Oh my dear Siya, I did not know anything. I did not even think of people being killed in the name of Islam. I was frightened of the tight laws and regulations for women. But I did not think the religion that taught us kindness, helping, and compassion would be used to kill hundreds of innocent people. I did not know that there would be courts without jury or even the just judges, who try people in the name of God. No, do not give me any credit on this, even I did not see all these problems. I was only unhappy and did not know why."

Siyavash shook his head and said, "Yes, of course you can see and predict the future without knowing. Your sixth sense told you the trouble ahead of us. Is it going to get better?"

Nosha shook her head and said, "No, I feel we will have worse days ahead of us, but I hope I am wrong."

But she was not; the new Islamic republic of Iran not only made the world angry at the Iranians, who were caught between a rock and a hard place, but also started to sing another song, one that talked of exporting their revolution to other Moslem worlds.

The first country, which was Khomeini's priority, was Iraq, with more than half of her population Shiite Moslem. His preaching apparently had stimulated that population and as a result, Saddam killed many of them and sent thousands to the refugee camps in Iran. Since the killing of this population made matters worse and the resistance continued, Saddam took advantage of Iran's isolation in the world and their weak army. With so many of Iran's top generals and almost all of her air force pilots killed, he attacked Iran. The southern providence of Khozestan fell before the Persian youth started to register to fight against Saddam.

The hostage crises finally came to an end with the election of Reagan as president, which coincided with Nosha's graduation. She specialized in psychiatry. But the fight with Iraq had only begun.

Going Back

In winter of 1981 she got bad news in the form of her father's illness. He did not feel too good and was asking her to come and visit him. The advice from the U.S. government was that no one should go to Iran unless they got a reentry visa. Nosha, Nasim, and Nima got their tickets to go. Siyavash was advised not to go.

"The situation is very dangerous and you might lose your job since there is no way of knowing when you can leave the country," Nosha told him. But Siyavash was very worried since the war was going on and he was afraid of losing them. It was a tough decision not to go with them, since it was commonplace news to hear of Tehran being hit by bombs and Iraqi attacks. Nosha told him not to worry since they were going to Shiraz, where there were not too many attacks.

"But you are going through Tehran, anything can happen," he replied.

Then, in the final days, he looked at her intensely and said, "You know what, I have made my decision. I cannot let you go alone! You and the children are all I have and if I lose you, I will be dead. If something happens to you I want to be with you to the last minute."

Nosha, who was moved by his decision, told him, "But what if we can not come back on time and you lose your job?"

"It is okay, Nosha. I am an expert doctor whose experience is needed all over the world. If I can not come on time and this hospital does not let me work, I am sure there is another hospital that will. Even if we are stuck in Iran, we will be together and we can pay our dues to our country by working there. I heard that since the revolution thousands of doctors have left the country and in wartime, they need us, so we do not have to worry." Then he took her in his arms and told her with his usual smile, "Please don't try to change my mind. I am coming with you."

She held him tight and said "Okay."

Even as she thought of all the trying times and problems in her homeland, she constantly reminded herself how lucky she was to have him. With him, all the problems seemed small and she could survive anything.

Their tickets were with Swiss Air, and they had to stay there one night. Then they left for their homeland, a land they had left more than six years ago. Her heart was filled with the joy of seeing her beloved land. When the airplane entered Iranian air, she could not breathe, for her excitement.

They arrived at Mehrabad airport in the morning. Then there was an announcement in the airplane that all the women should cover their hair and body before it landed. Nosha had a knitted hat and a suit with an overcoat that was long and wide. However, she had a scarf too in her handbag in case they did not like the knitted hat. She was very nervous.

They had heard so much bad news that they were prepared for the worst. There was a long line but then there was an announcement that all the women with babies should get in front of the line. That was a relief to Nosha who had her four-year-old Nasim and one-year-old Nima. They went ahead of the line and they were the first one to emerge from the crowded airport.

Siyavash told her, "Go out with the children; I will get our suitcases and join you." She was eager to go out. She knew that her sister-in-law and her brother were waiting for them.

When she finally made her way out, she saw black robes everywhere. They were women who were wearing black *chador*; she could not believe her eyes, and how much women's' clothes had changed. With so much black in front of her, she could not see anyone she knew. It took her more than ten minutes looking through the crowds waiting for their passengers before she saw Navid's golden hair.

She opened her arms and hugged him tightly. She was so happy to see him after so many years. He was more handsome than ever. Navid, who had studied in England for past five years, had come back when he got his MS degree, for his father's sickness. Then they saw her sister in-law, Sima. She had aged so much within the last six years that it was hard to recognize her. The stress of the revolution was probably the reason, Nosha thought. Sima was so happy to see the children. Nasim was not so friendly and refused to let her hold her, but Nima was smiling and went into her arms right away.

Soon Siyavash joined them and the emotion was so high seeing them together with tears of joy in both of their eyes. They had airplane tickets to go to Shiraz so they took their suitcases to the internal flight section and waited while talking of the past and present times until their flight time. When they got to Shiraz airport, she saw her sister Nooshin waiting. Nosha again was stunned by her appearance. She looked much older than her age and was very sad looking.

Oh my God, she thought, *what is happening to everyone?* Nooshin had been a very happy outgoing girl who had been one of her hometown's great beauties. Although she had not lost her beauty, even with a black loose Manto and scarf, she still looked much older and seemed exhausted.

When they got home and arrived, she started crying while hugging her father. He was thinner and was laid down in his bed. As he hugged her and looked at her children, he said, "Thanks God, I can die peacefully now."

Nosha could not hold back her tears and said, "Baba, don't talk this way. I wish you a healthy life and fast cure."

He replied, "Oh my dear Nosha, I am in pain day and night; I do not think I will be cured; I want to go. But I wanted so much to see you, your children, and my dear son Siyavash again. Now I am in peace. I will be okay."

The Revolution

The Persians have a custom of visiting the ill and elderly. All the extended families and friends will stop by to visit you and wish you a rapid recovery if you get a simple cold. Babak was not any exception. He had terminal cancer and every day there were so many people coming to wish him a rapid recovery or to tell him they love him. In the visitors Nosha could see the sample of their society that included women, men, children, religious and nonreligious, Moslems and non-Moslems. And as they visited her father, Nosha could hear the heated debates about the way things were running in their country. It was wartime, but most of the population was angry with all the killings and the martyrs.

The first scary episode happened the day she arrived. Her younger brother Nozar had joined the revolutionary guards. He came to see their father and visit his older sister who he had not seen for six long years. He politely said hello, wearing his revolutionary clothes. Nosha felt a sharp pain in her heart and started to cry.

"Why are you crying?" He asked as his bright blue eyes looked at her with concern.

With tears falling down her face, Nosha said, "I see you in these clothes and think either you will be killed or will kill someone."

He did not answer her but instead only smiled and went to his father to sat down by him. Nooshin and Nader were sitting there too. The conversation soon turned to politics and government. Nooshin was saying that the revolutionary guards were spies for the government and don't have any mercy even on their own families.

Nozar disagreed and said, "If that were true then I would tell on you as well, for not wearing the *hejab* when strange men are in the house." But Nooshin stressed again that most revolutionary guards were spying on people including their own families.

Then she said bitterly, "Our neighbor is a revolutionary guard. If I had a gun I would probably kill him."

Then Nader continued to look at Nozar with anger, "If I had a gun

I would kill you first." There was a long silence. Nosha looked at Nozar, who only smiled again, then said goodbye and left.

Nosha could see pain on her father's face. It was not a physical pain but an emotional one that she could understand. He loved both of his sons and hearing one wishing he could be able to kill the other son was painful for sure. Nosha could feel his pain in her own heart too. She also knew that Nader could not kill anybody, especially his own brother; nevertheless, his words hurt his father, his sister, and his brother without him realizing it. Their family was divided just like her country was!

The conversation continued with Nader and Nooshin complaining about the new revolutionary government. Nosha was curious and asked why Nozar had joined the revolutionary guards.

"He is stupid," said Nooshin.

But Babak interrupted her, speaking with a deep sadness, "My dear children, he is young and he has been brainwashed for the past four years. Even before the revolution they were being brainwashed by the propaganda." Nosha was surprised to hear this. Her father always was a devoted Moslem, he was kind, generous, and prayed five times a day. He never lied and he avoided taking bribes when he was working. He taught them to be honest and generous, to be kind to all of humankind. She heard that after her departure he even started to go to the mosque to pray regularly. Nosha thought that all the devoted Moslems were pro-Islamic government but hearing her father saying that his son was brainwashed to join the revolutionary guards meant that he was not so happy with the government or their version of Islam.

When Nooshin and Nader left, he could not stay silent and told her how distressed he was about Nader's remarks. "Nozar has not done anything to him and he wants to kill him! How can I bear this?" Nosha told him to calm down and not worry about Nader. When he gets mad, he says things, which he does not mean. But the diversity of opinions was so great that she could not avoid becoming depressed.

Beside the external war, which was killing thousands of young soldiers, there was an internal war between one of the opposition groups and the government. There were bomb explosions, which had killed hundreds of top officials, and there were arrests of thousands of young girls and boys who were accused of joining the *Mojahedin Khalgh*.

The group had recruited young people age ten to thirty and had been instrumental in ousting the Shah from power. But when the theological government of Khomeini was established and their goals had not been achieved, they started to combat the new government with firearms and bombs. That was indeed a foolish act of their leader who was only thirty years old, and so filled with pride that he had ousted the Shah with his big armies. But he did not think about his actions and the timing! There was a war going on and everyone was worried about the foreign invasion that could divide the country. Even those who hated the government did not like their tactics. Besides, their ideology was not appealing to the majority. The *Mojahedin* wanted a government that was Islamic but did not have any classes.

In other words, they wanted an Islamic and communist government combined. The State would be governed by the Islamic laws, but there would be no private state or upper or lower classes. Most of the looting and some of the killing of rich people in the early years of revolution had been done by them, some believed. The majority of the population was against communism, and Islam itself honored private ownership, so devoted Moslems did not consider this group as Moslem, and those who were annoyed with Islamic government and Islamic law also did not like *Mojahedin*, since their women were the first to wear the *hejab*. *Mojahedin* are worse than Khomeini's regime, they were saying. But there were thousands of young people who were willing to die for their ideologies! They were from the most educated and most conservative families of Persia. They joined the *Mojahedin* because they did not like the Shah's westernized society, combined with the fact that they either could not understand or did not like Khomeini's rule.

That evening they had a visitor that Nosha never met before. She was *Naneh*'s sister-in-law, who came to visit her father. She had a scarf under her *chador*, which expressed how traditional she was, and also was working as a servant in a family house in Shiraz, which put her amongst the *Mostazafin* (poor), whom Khomeini was purporting to be in good condition under his reign.

So what was wrong here? Why was she so mad at Khomeini's government and his many mullahs? One in particular was *Dastgheib*, the top cleric in Shiraz. She was asking the Almighty to come cleanse them of these people.

"Please God, make him pay for the blood he has on his hands killing all those children!" she begged. According to her and many other visitors, there had been thousands of executions of their youth happening in every city. Their parents did not have permission to bury them in the ordinary cemetery, and instead, they were buried in cemeteries that did not have any gravestones or identification. The cemeteries' names also were different and very offensive to those who lost their children. 'He/she is buried in *Lanatabad* (the cursed place),' the families were told. Two days later, Dastgheib was killed by a suicide bomber, a woman who was the mother of one of the students that had been executed by his order.

It was so disheartening to hear all the stories. Anyone who was coming to see her father, had a story to tell. Usually their stories were about those who were executed by government; people they thought to have been killed wrongly. One particularly alarming story was about a Jewish woman who was pregnant and had been executed as a prostitute! Nosha's friend who told the story was saying that they knew the woman's husband, and were sure that his wife was no prostitute.

One day her father was a little better and was not so pained from his aches, so she asked him. "Why are they doing it? Why should people be suffering so much?"

Babak shook his head and said, "They asked for it."

Nosha was stunned. "What are you talking about, Baba? How did they ask for such a thing?"

"For the fifty-five years of the Pahlavi dynasty we got everything, prosperity, justice, and security. But people started screaming and went on their roofs to sing the *Azan*."

"What are you saying?"

"They asked for this government. They chose this government, so now they have to pay for the consequences of their actions."

Who is happy with the new government? she asked herself. For one thing, one of her brothers was. Nozar was a revolutionary guard and for sure he was pro-Khomeini, but as her father said, he was very young and a true believer. Who else? Out of all those who were visiting, she had heard everyone complain. Then her aunts came from Pasargad. Nosha knew they were pro-Khomeini, as they had always belonged to a very conservative sect of religion.

Her aunt Ozra told her father about a man they both knew. He had only one son who had become an engineer, but last week had gone to a team house and was arrested immediately. Apparently, the government knew about the house and arrested the people who were living there; then they stayed in the house and waited there until all the team member came and arrested them.

"What happened to the son? Is he in jail?" Babak asked.

"No," Ozra answered, "he was allowed one phone call to say goodbye before his execution!" At this, everyone fell into a stunned melancholy, which resulted in a deep silence among them all.

No wonder my father said, now I can die peacefully! You hear so much bad news that you give up easily. If all the young and the beautiful die in war or in jail, why should an old man suffering from constant pain both physically and emotionally have any wish to survive? Nosha thought.

Her father's deep voice broke her thoughts. "Oh God, that must be so hard for him. God help him to bear such a pain! How is he now?"

"Well, he is broken, the boy was his only son," she replied with a sad voice.

Nosha said, "I do not understand why our government is killing so many people!" She looked at Ozra almost aggressively, "What do you think? Which kind of Islam is this? It is not the compassionate religion we knew."

Her aunt Ozra did not answer, but Mr. Abasi, her son-in-law, and the son of a top cleric in Pasargad, replied, "You are wrong; all of Islamic history consists of bloodshed. Islam needs blood to grow and become pure."

Nosha looked at him in disbelief and said, "Wow, so that is the analogy you are making to clear your conscience! Blood does not bring love or devotion. You can not force people to believe what you do, especially through bloodshed like this!"

She was so angry, but just then another group of the visitors arrived, interrupting their heated discussion. As the new guests sat, she looked back at Mr. Abasi still feeling the heat in her face from their argument. He was a man she truly detested. For some reason she had never liked him, but his wife was not just her cousin, but also her best friend.

The feeling is mutual, she thought. He was a religious man, and to him, women like Nosha were nonbelievers who deserved to die. But yet Nosha was sitting in the same room beside her husband and her father wearing a short sleeve shirt with her golden hair gathered neatly in the back arguing with him about Islam! *He would report me if he was not afraid of his wife*, she thought.

The day passed and soon it became night. Nosha went to bed only to be awakened by Nasim who wanted a glass of milk. The eight and half hours' difference in time zones was hard for Nasim to adjust to. She slept most of the day and at night, she was up keeping her U.S. hours, while for Nosha it was impossible to sleep during the day with all the people coming to visit. Then at night, she had to be woken up by Nasim, who wanted different things as excuses to talk to her.

Tired and very depressed, she got up, went to the kitchen, and gave her a glass of milk. After Nasim finished her milk, they went back to the bedroom. But Nosha could not sleep anymore. All the problems in her country kept running through her mind and the heavy feeling of sadness overtook her heart. Tears started running from her eyes. She did not want to disturb her husband's sleep, so she got up to leave, but Nasim's voice had her stop.

"Mommy, can you kiss me please?"

She sat next to her daughter, and as she kissed her she said, "Please go to sleep; you are going to wake your father and your brother." Her tears were running freely now, and she could not talk clearly, so she ran out of the room and went to the kitchen.

She sat down and let her tears wash over her face. With her head between her hands, she sat crying, when suddenly she felt strong hands take hold of her arms and Siya's warm voice whispering in her ear, "What is the matter darling?"

She looked up and said, "Oh, did I wake you up?"

Siya sat on the chair next to her and said, "No, Nasim woke me up and told me you were crying."

"Did she really? How did she know? It was so dark."

Siya smiled, held her hands in his, and said, "She is your daughter, she senses things! But when I asked her the same question she told me she felt your wet face when you kissed her."

"Oh, I am sorry. I didn't..."

Siya squeezed her hand and said, "No, I am glad she woke me up. I like to know when something is bothering you. What is wrong?"

"Well, everything. You know how much I love my father and my country and now they both are ill and I cannot do a damn thing about it. I am upset that Nozar has not come back to see my father after

Nader threatened him, and I am upset about all the stories that are so horrifying that I want to believe they are just horror stories, not reality."

Siya replied with a sad voice, "I understand, I feel the same way. It is hard to believe people's problems and how they have changed. There are stories of mothers telling on their children and sisters telling on their brothers. It is so sickening, but you have to remember that we are living in a country that has just gone through a revolution. If you look at any revolution, you will see injustice and lots of killing. You also will see division even among family members. It is hard, but we have to adjust to the environment we are in."

Nosha interrupted him and said, "Siya, please go, get out of the country while you can."

He put his head down and said, "I am sorry, I cannot."

Nosha put her hand on his shoulder and said, "But we will be okay here. I will join you. I would like to stay with my father while he is alive, but you should go."

He replied, "But even if I wanted to go, I cannot!"

"What do you mean?" Nosha asked, frightened.

"Well, I went to the Sadi Hospital to see my friends and they told me I was crazy to come back. There has been an edict issued that states because the war is going on no doctor can leave the country."

Nosha felt frozen. "But we have an exit visa! They gave it to us in the United States."

"Yes, but my friend who told me about the new law also had an exit visa."

Nosha was silent for a few moments and then said, "So we are stuck here, aren't we? I told you to stay back."

Siya put his hand on her face, and in his usual calm and kind voice said, "Even if I was there I would fly here to be with you. It seems that you forgot that you are a doctor too, and used the free tuition to go to school!" He paused a little, looked at her face that expressed how unhappy she was, and said, "It is not that bad, we are after all in our own country and there are so many here who need us."

"It is very bad, if you get killed!" Nosha exploded.

He kissed her and said, "I think we should talk about this some other time. You should get your rest now, but I promise you that I will not do anything to risk my life. I want to live for you and my children as long as I can."

They went to the bedroom and found Nasim sitting up in her bed waiting.

"Are you okay, Mommy?" she asked.

"Yes honey, now you can sleep."

They lay in their bed, but Nasim got up and came to their bed asking, "Why did you cry?"

Siya took her up and said, "Have you seen when your brother cries, your mother puts him in his bed and he falls sleep" She nodded her head. "Okay, you too get cranky when you are sleepy. That is why your mother was crying. She is very tired since she is up all day and you wake her up at night."

"Oh Mommy, I am sorry that I am waking you up," Nasim said, looking at her mother.

"My sweet Nasim," he told her, "you should try to sleep at night and stay up during the day so your mother can sleep. If you do that then your mother will not cry anymore."

"Okay," Nasim replied. They both kissed her and she went to her bed. The dark night started to lighten when they finally fell into deep sleep.

The next morning Siya asked her if they could all go to visit his mother. She was so happy to see her grandchildren. Nosha asked him what his plan was now that they were going to stay.

"Well," he replied, "I am going to apply for a job and this house probably is a good place for us and the children. I know that you were independent for the last six years and understand if you would not like to stay in this house, but—"

She interrupted him and said, "Oh, no, I love your mother and it is fine. We can live on the second floor, that way we will not be interfering with her life either."

"She will be happy to hear that," he said, obviously pleased by her answer. Then he said, "If it is all right with you, we will stay here starting today, and every morning I will take you to your father's place, then will come at night to take you back. You can leave the children with my mother too, so that you can help your mother a little more."

She said, "Yes, I think it will be much more comfortable here. We can put the children in their own bedroom and that might let us sleep better, but I do not know about leaving the children, it might be too much for her."

Her mother-in-law came in and said "Oh, no, they are so cute, and I would love to have more time with my grandchildren. I do not mind at all."

Nosha replied, "I do not think Nasim will stay, though, and she is the one who is a handful."

Siya told her, "I will stay here with her for a few days until she gets used to my mother; then I think she will stay. You are so tired from being there and not being able to do anything because you have to keep an eye on her. This will make things easier for you." Nosha kissed both of their cheeks and thanked them.

She then remembered the episode of two days ago. Nasim was crying and since Nosha did not want her father to hear her screams, she asked her mother if she could leave Nima with her for half an hour to take Nasim out.

"Sure," she said. It was hard for Nosha to take both of them. They had not brought Nima's stroller along and holding him for half an hour while holding Nasim's hand was an impossible task. Also, Nima was a very calm child. If you fed him and changed his diaper on time, he played with anything you gave him without much complaint.

She looked around. It was morning and no guests were there. *Naneh* was in the kitchen, and her uncle and Navid were sitting in the living room. They both loved Nima and played with him often. Okay then, she was safe.

She left the house and walked around with Nasim for twenty minutes, bought her a few toys, and went back. When she got home her mother immediately started screaming hysterically.

"Why did you leave your kid here when I have so much to do?" She looked at Nima who smiled at her. She picked him up and asked, surprised at her anger, "This child is no trouble for anyone. He is sitting and playing. Why are you so mad?"

She was still complaining, "He was crying and I had to give your father a bath." She completely ignored Nosha's remarks. She complained constantly until afternoon when she was a little calmer.

Nosha asked her again, "But why did he cry? Did you not say that it was okay to leave him when I asked?"

Her mother said, "Well his diaper needed to be changed, and when I changed it I saw that he had diaper rash! I did not anticipate that!"

Siya's voice brought her back to earth. "Are you ready to go back?"

"Oh yes," she answered. Nima was in her grandmother's arms. She looked at them and asked, "Are you sure it is okay to leave him?"

"Yes, of course," they both replied. She kissed her son and her mother-in-law again and left the house.

When they got to her sister's house, they found Nooshin arriving as well, in a wide scarf that made her look like a beautiful nun, her light skin looking much whiter under the black scarf.

"Where is everyone?" Nosha asked.

"Well, Mom left for Pasargad. *Naneh* is in the kitchen and *Baba* has gone for his radiation therapy with Navid," Nooshin replied.

Siya told Nosha that he had to run some errands and would be back to see her father in the afternoon, then took Nasim with him and left.

When they were alone Nosha asked, "Why did Mom go back to Pasargad?"

Nooshin, taking her scarf off to let her long brown hair free of the black cloth, replied, "She does not stay here too long. She says she cannot take care of the old man!"

Nosha, obviously annoyed, said, "But she does not even do much. *Naneh* cooks and Navid takes him to the hospital and back. He goes to the bathroom himself. What is left to do?"

"The support of her being here," Nooshin replied. "No, not much in fact except helping him to take a shower once every few days." Then she continued telling stories that showed their mother's selfishness.

Nosha listened to her younger sister patiently, and told her that she understood the pressure she must be under, both from the changes in society and from their father's sickness. She also said that she should try to accept their mother's shortcomings.

"As much as we love our father, you have to understand their age difference and the fact that she is not happy in her life. She was complaining when he was healthy and caring. You cannot expect her be happy when he is sick. When a person gets ill, they complain and have no patience whatsoever."

Nooshin shook her head and said, "But do you remember all those days that she was sick and he was there for her? He would take her to doctor, give her medicine, and stay with her in the hospital when she had her surgeries."

"Yes," said Nosha, "he did it because he is a caring person. He did it for her and he did it for his brother too. He also took care of the villagers who were sick and needed help. That is his personality and that is why we love him so much. But, Mom is not that way. She probably never knew how to take care of anyone. Her hard childhood made her stone-hearted.

"She is not a normal person as our father always told us. Her depressed personality makes her just sit down and only remember the bad times. In her eyes, everyone is trying to hurt her. All this pain she is complaining about is real pain. So don't take it personally, Nooshin."

Nooshin asked, "What is the solution? Are you telling me she is suffering from some kind of illness?"

"Yes, she is mentally troubled. If she did not have a pampered life as she has now she would be labeled as mad. She does not have much responsibility, she can sleep as much as she wants, there are not too many people arguing with her so her illness does not get out of hand."

Nooshin asked, "Is there any medicine that can cure her?"

"Yes, but first she has to accept her mental problem. She likes to think her problems are all physical and does not accept mental problems, but with the right medicine her physical pain may vanish too. Most medicines, though, have side effects which cause patients not to continue their treatments."

Their conversation was interrupted by their father's arrival.

It was much easier for Nosha to attend to her father now that she was living with her mother-in-law, since the children were usually either with her or with their father. It had been almost a month since they arrived when her father's illnesses got worse and he was admitted to the hospital. And around the same time, Siya started working.

He told her, "There is a shortage of doctors and supplies in his hospital. The nurses do not have time to take care of the patients; each has to care for ten patients in any given hour. The problem was that most doctors left the country and the nurses that stayed were barely enough for the population. "

Without new nurses or doctors, the number of emergencies were tenfold because of the war. "There are children between ten to fifteen years old who are losing a limb or two every day!" Siya told her. He was a surgeon and did surgery on those who were wounded in the war. "They need moral support," he said. "We need psychologists to talk to them and prepare them for the harsh life they will encounter after the war."

Nosha could see his concerns but was not ready to work for the government she detested. "I understand you have to take a morality test to be able to get hired!" she said. "I hate them with their morality values and do not want to submit to their demands to wear a *chador* while working!"

"But you are a trained doctor and they are the patients who need you! Besides, you always wore a uniform while working, the shape of your uniform has only changed with the law," he reasoned.

"Your uniform did not change with the law and you are not obliged to wear a scarf!" Nosha replied angrily.

Siya pulled her into his arms, and with a loud laugh said, "Please do not get mad at me; I did not change the law!"

Nosha, who realized the tone of her voice had grown loud and offensive, said, "I am sorry, I was wrong. You did not change the law and if you could we would be living in heaven instead of this hell."

"Thanks, but I am not a politician, I am a doctor like you. I know that we became doctors because we cared about people and that is why I think you should think about your career too. I know you want to be with your father while he is alive, but there are so many people that need your help. You do not need to believe in governmental morality to help them either. Look at your sister. She hates our government more than you do but she goes to school and teaches the children, even despite the long black scarf."

"Help who? The soldiers who believe in what the government tells them? That is hard; I am not a surgeon like you, where I can just do a surgery and not have a conversation. I have to talk to those people knowing that my beliefs are different from theirs. To me, why should there be any war in the first place?!"

Siyavash replied, "Nosha, they are only children who were brainwashed to go over the mine fields; they all are our fellow citizens who pledged to fight our enemies. They could be my brothers or yours or some distant relatives. They have families who think the same way we do, who cannot cope with the fact that their beloved sons have lost parts of their bodies for an imaginary heaven! You can help them."

Then he said, "Take your time, though. Be with your father and your family and think of all of those who desperately need to talk to someone."

Mahnaz

One day while talking to her sister, all of the sudden Nooshin asked, "Have you heard about Mahnaz?"

Nosha paused a little and said, "No, what about her?"

"I heard from a friend that she is divorced and was seen crying in public!"

Nosha could not believe the rumor. Mahnaz was her best friend from childhood, who she had not seen since she left Iran six years ago. Their friendship was formed at an early age since their fathers were best friends. This friendship continued until Mahnaz left Iran. She was a pretty and light-hearted girl whose laughter made everyone around her happy. She was raised in a upper class family; her father was a physician and her mother a wealthy woman who ruled the household. She was the boss with no questions asked.

While she was very kind and warm to talk to, her husband did not do anything without her approval. Nosha admired her and wished she was her mother instead. She used to go to their house often. Mahnaz had a lover all through college whom she eventually married. Their wedding was the envy of all who attended, it was big and magnificent. They left Iran to pursue their education shortly after the wedding. When Nosha was in her senior year, Mahnaz came back. She visited her once. Mahnaz had two master's degrees from Harvard University in public broadcasting, while her husband, a mechanical engineer, had also gotten his doctoral degree from there. They had a beautiful son who was so cute that Nosha could not stop looking at him.

"What are you thinking?" Nooshin asked.

She shook her head and said, "Just running through past memories," then took the receiver, and dialed Mahnaz's old number. The voice that answered was the familiar voice of Mahnaz herself.

Nosha said hello, and told her who she was. A scream of joy filled her ears.

"Nosha! I was looking for you for so long! I heard your father does not feel good, but I did not have an address to go visit him."

Nosha gave her the address and asked how she was. "I will tell you in person. I will be there this evening, Mahnaz," replied.

Indeed Mahnaz showed up that evening with her mother. Their visit was very emotional. Babak had just come back from visiting his doctor, who told him that there was nothing he could do for him. He told them the news and everyone started crying.

The fact had been obvious for some time to his family that his illness was terminal, but it was very hard for all of them to accept the fact of losing such a beloved man. Babak was happy to see the daughter of his best friend, who had died several years before, and asked her how she was and what was she doing?

"Not much; I was working in the TV station with a very good salary, but after the revolution they fired all of us with false accusations!"

Azar who had come from Tehran to see her uncle, announced, "That is no surprise! Most women got fired from their jobs by false accusations after the revolution."

She had been a weather forecaster in Tehran before the revolution. "The only women that are working now are the teachers, nurses, and doctors, which they can not do without."

"That does not make sense," Nosha stressed.

"No," Mahnaz replied, "but what makes sense in the Islamic republic? Does killing, putting children in jail, raping young girls, or firing all the women employed by the government make sense? What does make sense?"

Their conversation was interrupted by arrival of new guests. Another family friend whose friendships spanned generations came to visit: Ali Masood. His son was the same age as Nosha, and he had been fired from his job too. As he told her his story, he added, "I swear I will fight *Mostazafin* and not become one!"

Nosha frowned and said, "But you were leftist; what happened?"

"I did not know what the mass illiterate poor would do to our country and our nation. But now I know they deserve to be poor! We did not know then, but your father knew. We were happy when Shah left the country and were showing our happiness." Ali paused a little, pointed to Babak, and said, "He told us, 'I will see you crying after his departure.' I asked him, 'But you are a devoted Moslem. Khomeini is going to bring us a pure Islamic government—so why are you telling me we are wrong for being happy?' He said, 'You are wrong! Islam is a frame. They will shape it the way they want, just wait and see.'"

Nosha looked at her father who was deep in his own thoughts. What was he thinking? Was he thinking about his beloved country that was going through turmoil, or his own health? Did he care anymore? No, had he not told her that people deserved what they got?

Her thoughts were interrupted as Mrs. Masood turned to Mahnaz. Her son had been a friend of Mahnaz's ex-husband's and now she looked at her and asked, "What happened, dear? I heard of your divorce and I was stunned, he was a good man!" All eyes fixed on Mahnaz's face. Everyone wanted to know what had happened to their passionate love for each other.

"Yes, of course, he looked and acted very good in public," Mahnaz replied. "But he had a very bad temper that he did not show me until I got married. He also was a compulsive gambler and womanizer!" she told them bitterly. That day passed and Mahnaz continued coming back to the house to visit her. She told Nosha how her husband divorced her, without her even knowing it!

"How could he do that?" Nosha asked.

"Easy, under Islamic law!" she replied. Then she started to cry as she told her that he had gotten custody of their son too.

"Do you have any visitation rights?"

"Yes, two times per week, but if he gets cross with me, he does not let me see him at all!"

Nosha was so sad to see her happy friend change so much, but she could not blame her! She was the smartest girl she knew, a woman who had everything a woman should have. She had a pretty face, happy personality, and a good education! She deserved to be happy, but the man who she loved so much and for so long not only divorced her but took her only child. To distract her she asked, "Well, what you are doing now that you are not working?"

"I am sewing wedding dresses, baby clothes, and their accessories for money."

"Do you really?"

Mahnaz started laughing, "Yes, why are you so surprised?"

Nosha said, "Well I knew you could sew but—"

Mahnaz interrupted her and said, "I know but I have to make a living!"

"Is it good enough?"

"Yes, of course. I am glad my father, bless his soul, sent me to sewing school, otherwise I do not know what would I do."

"Your family was wealthy; why do you need to work?"

"Well most of the lots I owned were sold; my ex asked me if he could while we were married, and I agreed. I saved lots of money from my salaries in an account that he opened for our son. But after the revolution, since he had opened the account, I was not allowed to take anything out. Once I needed some money and I asked him if he could give me small portion of it and he said that was our son's account and I would not touch it!" Then she paused and said, "I was stupid to trust him, though, do you remember what Azar said she did after she was fired?"

"Yes, she asked her husband to pay her the salary she made when she was working each month," Nosha replied.

"Yes, with the law of our land women should get smarter and protect themselves," Mahnaz continued.

Nosha smiled and told her, "I think Persian women are smart and you are one of the smartest. Things happens when we least expect it. You did not know you would get divorced or fired. Anyone else in your shoes probably would fall apart, but look at you. You are standing tall, have found your way out of misery, and are working for yourself. I predict a bright future for you, Mahnaz. You are not a loser."

Her prediction proved to be right a couple of years later when Mahnaz took her son and left the country illegally through the dangerous roads of Azerbaijan to Turkey, and from there to the United States, where they started a new life.

The Death of an Idol

A few days after her father talked to his doctor and found the disturbing news, they had several dozens of visitors come from Pasargad. All her cousins came and asked her father to go back to Pasargad. He accepted. Nosha took Nasim and went with him. In Pasargad the picture changed. There the visitors did not come with their families but groups of men would come to visit him, and Nosha and Nooshin had to stay hidden in the other room until their departure. Then another group would come and they had to leave their father's side.

During the whole day, they were able to be with him only a few hours. Since Nosha was not certified yet to write prescriptions in Iran, they had to ask the local doctor who was an old friend of his. He prescribed very strong sedatives for his pain. Babak was in bed and slept most of the time. Had he lost his will for life or were the sedatives too strong? She did not know. She missed Nima, who was staying with his grandma, so she decided to leave Pasargad for a couple of days and go back to Shiraz. Nooshin told her she would leave the next day, which was Saturday, since she needed to go to work. Navid accompanied her to Shiraz.

He did not see much need for his presence in Pasargad either, since the doctor was coming to their house and there were others who brought his medicine.

"You have your hands full with Nasim; I will not let you go alone," he said. When they sat in the bus, which was leaving Pasargad, Nosha told herself, *I do not think my father will be living more than a few more days*, and tears filled her eyes as she remembered the last words he had said to her when she said goodbye: "Go, honey. God be with you."

Tears ran down her face, which she tried to hide by turning her face to the window. Navid was quiet, only talking to Nasim in English once in a while. Nasim loved Navid, who was the only one that talked with her in English and as a result, she was very fond of him. *He is the kindest of my brothers*, Nosha thought. He was in the airport when she arrived and now he did not let her go alone and was coming to Shiraz with her.

When she got home she hugged Nima, who was so happy to see her after a few days, but he looked very happy with his grandmother. Navid had his lunch and went back to Pasargad. That night she went to bed and fell asleep peacefully, but about midnight she felt something was shaking her very hard. She sat up. "What was that?" she asked herself. She was shaking!

Siya woke up and asked, "What is the matter, honey?"

"I do not know; I just feel something had happened. My father! Is he dying?" Nosha replied, panicked.

"Come on honey, did you have a bad dream?"

"No, no, I felt that he will die in a couple of days and I felt that I would not see him again on the bus this morning. But just a few minutes ago, I was shaken in my sleep and felt something had happened."

He held her in his arms, kissed her softly, and dried her tears from her face, then said, "Calm down, darling. I will take you back tomorrow if you like."

"Should I call them?"

"You know they are sleeping and you will wake them up." She tried to sleep but she could not. Siya brought her a pill to calm her down. She took it and an hour later, she was in deep sleep.

She woke up around twelve. Siya was gone and the children were with their grandmother. Before anything, she called home and to her surprise, she heard Nooshin's voice.

"Nooshin is that you?"

"Yes."

"But why didn't you leave? You told me you would leave at twelve today."

"Oh no, I am off today and tomorrow morning, and I will leave tomorrow."

"How is father?

"He is the same; no change."

She said goodbye, confused.

She took a quick shower then went to the living room. Her mother-in-law, who was setting the table, asked, "How are you dear? I heard you had a bad night."

'Yes, I took a pill which made me sleep half of the day."

"That is okay; you need it," she replied.

Siya arrived and asked her how she was.

"Okay, but I need to go home."

"Yes, of course, we will leave right after lunch."

They asked her to sit and eat something. She did, but did not have much of an appetite, all the while thinking, *why didn't I stay there?* After lunch, Siya asked Nasim if she would like to take a nap.

Nasim was getting used to the new time a little, but she still loved to sleep after lunch, which was 9 p.m. U.S. time. She agreed immediately. Siya took her to her bedroom and stayed with her until she fell asleep. When he came back, he asked her if she was ready to leave.

"But Nasim is asleep."

"Yes, she will be staying with my mother. I will drive you there."

Nosha said, "No, Nasim will cry and it will be too much for your mother to take care of both of them."

Siya said calmly, "But she will stay here. We can not take her there with us."

Nosha felt an urge to cry and felt a lump in her throat, but she tried hard to control herself and asked, "Do you know something that I don't know?"

Siya sat on a chair, then took hold of her hand and asked her to sit down. "Dear Nosha, you were right! Last night your father died almost the same time you woke up."

Nosha broke into tears. Through them, she looked at Siyavash and said, "But why didn't you tell me anything?"

"I got a call from your sister ten minutes before I came home."

"I talked to her when I woke up! She lied to me?"

Mrs. Afras sat by her and told her, "I think you have been far from this land for some time, and have forgotten the custom. She could not tell you bad news by phone; she wanted a support system in place when you heard it; that is why she called Siya."

After she calmed down a little, Mrs. Afras helped her to change her clothes to black and they went to her hometown, where she had so many good memories of her father. Thoughts of the memory of jasmine perfumes by her bed and the poems he recited for her all her life passed through her mind as she travelled to the town she liked so much because of him. But now that she was going there, she knew that she would not see his kind face, nor would she hear his beautiful poems. He was gone and she felt lost without him.

They got there around 5 p.m. Siyavash went to the mosque where the memorial ceremony was held for the men. The house was filled with women. She was crying quietly when she heard a scream from other side of the room. She did not know most of the attendees, and except for Nooshin and her, there was not much loud mourning, since it was natural for a terminally ill seventy-five-year-old to die, especially in wartime when they witnessed so many young men's deaths.

So who was the woman who was screaming and crying so hard? She was curious. The woman was using foul language toward the government and was calling for justice from God. Nosha asked a relative who the woman was and why was she crying?

"Her son was executed by firing squad and she could not see his body," the relative whispered. "The other women were trying so hard to calm her down; some were saying it was God's will and she should submit to his will. The others said that is not God's wish to kill the best of our youth. It is the government who uses his name to kill them. There were some who were silent and there were others who were involved in discussion. The woman stopped her crying and started to listen to them." Group therapy worked, Nosha thought. Then Siya's words came to her mind: *there are so many who need your expertise. They lost brothers, sisters, or a child, you can help them.*

The next day she saw another disturbed mother whose son was killed in the war. She was proud of his sacrifice for the country, but was depressed since she did not have him anymore. She was crying constantly while she was there and nobody was able to calm her until she left. After her departure, someone told Nosha that she lost her son a week before and she was not allowed to mourn in his funeral. The government was saying the soldiers were fighting for God, and if they died, they went to heaven, so their family should be happy and they did not need to cry. This was unheard of in a culture in which there was a long period of mourning for the deceased!

The next day there were yet more complaints from a mother whose son was injured in the war. He lost both of his legs, in fact, all of his friends lost a limb or two. "Yesterday they came to visit, one was blind, and the second one lost his hand and the third one his leg. I guess our next generation will all be disabled," she continued bitterly.

With the dawn of the third day, Nooshin sighed with relief. "This process," she said, "is so long and boring. We have to sit and greet the people we do not know and listen to their problems. If we worked, probably we would not think that much about our loss."

Nosha replied, "While you are right I think this way it is out of our system. We cried as much we could, we heard other people's problems, which are much bigger and more painful than ours. That gives us a reason to be happier in our lives; our father's memory will be with us forever, but we know that we are lucky to have each other and cherish his life while he was with us."

There was a question of who would be in charge of the orchards. Nozar was going back to the war zone. Navid was registered in the army, and did not know when he had to leave for his service. Nooshin was working in Shiraz and could not move back to Pasargad like Nosha. Nader volunteered. He had a small shop in Shiraz and was living there with his wife (who was from Shiraz) and their son.

"What will happen to your shop?" Nosha asked.

"I will sell it," he replied.

Nosha knew that down inside he was not happy with his work as a small shop owner. He had graduated a couple of years before as an engineer, but after he finished his military service and got married it was revolution time, and he could not find a job since he was not a devoted Moslem, he was told.

Then they all left Pasargad, to return to their separate lives.

Navid's Disappearance

In Shiraz, Nosha accepted her husband's suggestion that she needed to work to overcome the depression caused by her father's death. She wanted to open a private office for women only, which she thought would not require her to wear a scarf, but the government rejected her request on the grounds that she needed to work for the government for four years to be able to open a private practice. So she applied to the same hospital Siyavash was working at and got the job.

The problems were endless, since the war and the revolution made so many changes that people were not able to cope well. First, there were economic problems; most women visiting her were depressed about losing their jobs, sons, or daughters. Other women were asking her advice about their husbands' job loss and their possible involvement with drugs. With the scarceness of medicine, she had to rely on psychoanalysis most of the time.

It was not two months after Navid went to his army station, that they realized that he was missing from the station. None of his fellow soldiers knew what happened to him. All of his siblings, Nosha especially, were worried to death. His missing meant only one thing, which was clear to all of them. He was in jail somewhere! But there was no way of knowing where and why. Hundreds of young girls and boys were being arrested each day; most of them the educated elites who were brave enough to say or do something. Nosha was wondering why Navid, though, since he was very quiet. Nosha knew that like Nader, Nooshin, and herself, Navid did not like the Islamic government's policies, but she also knew, like them, he did not belong to any special political groups. Why did he go to jail, she wondered.

Their mother was crying a lot and was going to different jails each day to find out if her son was there. Several months had passed and she was taking food and clothing for her son, asking the guards to give them to him. They took the items and said, we will, but nobody would tell her if he was there or not.

One day, one of Nooshin's neighbors went with her mother. She went up to a guard and begged him to let her know where Navid was. Outside, there were many women sitting at the entrance door waiting to find out what happened to their loved ones. When they saw Laiya, they grew angry and started using foul language against her.

"Why are you asking them? Don't you know that they are not human? They don't have any feelings," said a woman sitting next to her. But Laiya did not stop begging the guard.

"Please sir, I know you are a Moslem, please give me mercy and let me know. Where is my son?"

"Stupid jerk," said another woman, "if they were Moslem they would not put all these young beautiful people in jail!"

"They are wolves in sheepskin," said another woman.

The yelling increased as Laiya continued to beg, the other women telling her to shut up and stop begging these same people who left them miserable waiting at the jail door. "They are supposed to be in the universities teaching; their place is not in a jail," screamed several women, mad at Laiya for begging the guard.

There was a change in the guard's attitudes. There were so many who were mad at him for doing his job and now Laiya was being attacked for respecting him, so he told her, "OK. Come with me."

As they went in he asked, "What is your son's name?"

"Navid Pezejk Pour," Laiya answered.

He went and brought three thick books and said, "I do not know where your son is. But I know that all the people who are in a Shiraz jail and have a name starting with P are listed in these books. Look at them yourself and see if you can find his name."

They started with the first book, but they had only gotten through one third of the book when it got dark. So Laiya asked the guard if they could come the next day. Obviously, he wanted to do her a favor and show her he was not as bad as the other women had said, so he said yes. "You can come here as long as you need to." She came back for the next three days and they did not find his name.

She went to Nosha crying. "If he is not in Pasargad's jail or Shiraz's jails, then where is he?"

Nosha, who was disturbed herself, said, "Who knows?"

The thought crossed her mind that they might have already killed him. It was not strange either if they had. "Are there so many in jail that you needed to look at three books for three days to see only one letter of the alphabet?"

"Yes, there are," her mother replied. "You should see how many women are at the jails every day to find out where their sons are."

Navid's disappearance stirred further the family feud in Nosha's family. Nader and Nooshin did not want to see a glimpse of Nozar, and Nozar no longer came to visit any of them.

Furthermore, everyone was blaming Laiya for supporting the government and argued that her religious beliefs made Nozar a devoted security guard, but they did not think clearly that there was a difference between a guard who was going to the war zone for the last two years to fight their common enemies and the guards who were taking people to jail. Nader and Nooshin were denying there was a God altogether and they talked frankly about their beliefs with their own analogy. Laiya, who was very disillusioned with Navid's situation, became even more upset hearing blasphemy from her children.

Nosha could understand both sides. Her training told her to use the tools that would heal her patients' souls and religion was one of the tools. Her mother was so depressed about Navid's disappearance in which even her prescription drugs were not working. Nosha never thought that her mother cared that much about them, but with Navid's disappearance Nosha could see how much she cared, even if she might not always know how to show it. In this situation, her mother's religious beliefs could help her, but her siblings did not seem to understand that fact.

On the other side, she could see her siblings' anger toward the system that had messed up their lives. Navid was very highly regarded among all of them for his kindness and his intelligence. Losing him was very devastating for all of them. They could not help but expect to be able to talk in their own homes about the things they were not able to talk about in public or even among their friends.

It was strange to Nosha, too, how her mother could believe in a system that made her so miserable, the same system that took away her son and made her wander around the city jails. Nosha could understand her sensitivity for the religion. But she had a fanaticism for the same Khomeini that was causing all this misery in her country. To Nosha and those who thought like her, Khomeini was only a cruel leader who was doing what any powerful dictator did and nothing more. Her mother saw him as a symbol of religion, whose word came from God himself. It was hard for them to grasp this concept. Why can she not see all the problems? Why does not she see that there should not be any war between two Moslem countries? Islam prohibited killing another Moslem, they argued, then why are they killing so many Moslems? But there was no straight answer for all these questions. Boys were leaving for the war zone so eagerly to become martyrs, and the women were left stressed from either too much work or no work at all. The food ration preoccupied most of their thoughts. They had to stay in long lines with their coupons for hours to buy the necessary items for their families.

And time continued passing them by with no relief to the madness. They learned to adjust and adapt, but they never got used to the way things had become.

Two years passed since Navid had vanished into thin air when they got a phone call from Nader, who told them, "Please clean your house; unwanted guests will arrive soon!" That was a code to tell her that the secret police would be coming to their house and they had to clean from their house anything they could take as an excuse to put them in jail. Nosha was devastated; she liked to read a lot and did not want to part with her books, some of which were not to the government's liking. Siyavash told her not to worry. They took all their books and went to one of Siyavash's cousins and left them there until their house was searched and they were safe. They were not sure what triggered the authorities to search their home.

Nooshin, who was married then, took all her books, poured them in a sleeping bag, took them to a remote place out of town, and dumped them there.

Nosha asked her, "Why did you take the sleeping bags?"

"Well, they might accuse me of having a team house and letting *Mojahedin* in my house! I do not want any trouble."

Nader and their mom also followed suit. But the problem was all the old books left from their father, in a room full of books in Pasargad. The magazines, which had been miraculously kept clean for more than fifty years, had been transformed by their father into books with so much to tell about the past times. All of these books, along with the books that were published in the old regime were put into a fire by Nozar and his friends.

When she heard this, Nosha told Siyavash, "This time in our lives reminds me of the time Arab Moslems attacked Iran and burned thousands of books, ones that held important signs of our civilization. But this time book burnings are being done by our own people—not foreign forces."

Jail and Justice in Revolutionary Persia

They came in at midnight. A quick knock on the door and then they poured in. The children began crying and Nosha, Siyavash, and Mrs. Afras were all frightened to death. They were not told why they were in their house in the middle of night. The guards searched every inch of their house. They took a few of the medical books written in English that they still had in their house and they also took all their jewelry. Then they told Siyavash to go with them.

"What for?!" screamed Nosha.

But they shoved piece of paper at her and told her to sign it, saying, "Shut up or you will go too." Tears ran down her face. *Is he going to be like Navid?* she asked herself.

Siya, who was amazingly calm told her, "Why are you crying? I will be back in no time. I am serving my country and did not break any laws so I am not afraid."

She signed the paper as their guns were pointing at her and the childrens' heads:

> I, Nosha Afras, certify that security guards came to our house and were very polite and respectful. I have no complaints against them.

Nosha Afras

Then they left. Nosha tried to calm the children down and told them stories until they fell asleep again. But the two women were not able to sleep. They sat together, both women alternating between shock and tears, neither able to calm the other down. They were both worried to death. The night passed as it did, it brought an even longer day.

She was not able to function in the state of mind she was in, so she called in sick and started to investigate who she could talk to, anyone who could possibly be able to let him go. But the day passed without any ideas and it brought another long and hard night to endure.

It was midnight when she remembered a patient of his. "Oh, he had operated on a high-ranking cleric just two weeks ago," she told her mother-in-law.

"Let's go to his house," she told Nosha.

"But I do not know where his house is."

"Well, can't you find it in the hospital files?"

A ray of hope filled her heart. She jumped up, kissed her mother-in-law and said, "Oh, you are brilliant! I will find it and we will go to his house."

The next day she had something to look forward to. She went to the hospital, but could not get close to her husband's office. Apparently, that was under investigation too. She asked a nurse if his patients' files were in his office.

"Only the ones who were under his care," she replied.

"How about those he operated on in the last few weeks?"

"They are downstairs in the filing room."

"Can you get Hagi Abas's file for me?"

"Sure, I'll try," replied the nurse. She knew her problem and was very sympathetic to her.

It was late afternoon when she came back with the file. She was so excited that her hands were shaking. Quickly she took the man's address. When she got home she changed into a black outfit, scarf, with a black *chador* on her head and with her mother-in-law went to *Hagi* Abas's house.

They knocked the door and asked to see him.

"Who are you?" The woman at the door peered at them from behind the cracked door.

"I am Nosha Afras and this is my mother-in-law, Mrs. Afras. We are the wife and mother of the doctor who operated on him two weeks ago. We need to talk to him if it is possible, please." The woman went and came back a few minutes later and took them to a very high-class room with Italian furniture and Persian rugs.

After a few minutes, the man appeared at the door. They both rose and said hello. He returned the greeting formalities and asked them to sit down. "What has brought you here, doctor?" he asked her.

"Oh sir, you know that my husband and I came back to Iran after the revolution and are now living here, serving our country and mankind, just as God asks of us."

"Oh yes," replied *Hagi* Abas. "He saved my life! Your husband is a wonderful surgeon!"

Mrs. Afras leaned forward and said, "Yes, he is. That is why his place is not in jail."

"Which jail?" *Hagi* Abas asked.

"We do not know. The night before last night, they came to our house at midnight and arrested him. We do not know what his crime was, or why they came for him."

"But we do know that he is innocent," Nosha added.

"Yes," continued Mrs. Afras. "Siya was never into politics and he always was fond of our religion and its high standard of morality."

He shook his head, obviously troubled at this news. Then he looked at Mrs. Arfras and asked, "Are you the late Colonel Afras' wife?"

"Yes, sir."

"Ah, I have been to your house, God bless his soul; he was a good man."

"Indeed he was and so is my son," she replied.

"I will go and see what is going on. If he was not involved in any political activity he will not be there for too long."

Nosha wanted to tell him that Navid was not involved either, but he had been missing for more than two years, but she stopped herself. She only wanted her husband out of jail, that moment. They knew where he was and the time of his arrest, and knew that there was still a chance of finding him, using the Persian way of tapping into relationships with authorities to pull strings.

They left with hope but still were worried. When they got home, after two nights of no sleep, they fell asleep right away. The next day was Friday and she did not need to work.

The telephone rang the next morning and a polite man introduced himself. "I am *Hagi* Abas, hello doctor."

"Oh hello sir," Nosha replied.

"I have been talking to authorities; apparently there was an identity mistake and Dr. Afras will be home soon!"

She jumped up with joy and screamed, "Oh thank God and, thank you sir. I do not know how to thank you."

"No need," the man answered. "His place is not in jail; he needs to be in the hospital curing the ill and injured."

"Oh thank you a million times." She ran to the kitchen where her mother was preparing breakfast for the children. She screamed, "Good news! Siya will be home soon!" Siyavash's mother jumped up and hugged her; they both started crying, a cry of joy and relief.

It was about 1 p.m. when Siya came home. He looked very tired and was limping a little. Nosha and his mother rushed toward him with the happy anticipation of hugging him. But he pulled himself back from them and said, "My back and my body are hurting; do not touch please."

As they took him into the bedroom, Nosha asked him if he had been injured.

"Yes, I think my back is, I feel the burning of a cut."

She took his shirt off and he laid on his stomach. Both women's eyes filled with tears. His back was covered with long deep welts. Nosha quickly started washing his wounds and putting medicine on them. She also put bandages on those parts that had a deeper cut.

"They whipped you; why?" she asked.

"It is a normal procedure to get information from the prisoners. I was lucky that one of my patients came to jail and saved me!"

"Yes, we know."

"How do you know?" he asked.

"We went to his house last night and he called me this morning and told me that you would be released," she replied and asked, "what information did they want you to give them?"

"They wanted me to tell them about Navid."

Nosha frowned and said, "But you have not seen him for over two years now."

"Yes, that was the problem!" He got up.

"Wait, I am not done," she protested.

"I need to tell you something. I saw Navid in jail."

She froze. "Oh my God, really? How was he?"

"Well, he was not too good from what I saw."

"What happened?"

"Well, *Hagi* Abas came to my cell and asked, 'How are you, doctor?' I told him at the moment I was a patient without anyone to take care of me. He laughed and said, 'Can you come with us?' I said sure. He and the head of prison took me to another cell, in which a tall man was sitting alone. As soon as they opened the door, he started screaming and saying all the things I wanted to tell them for the past two days. I was so surprised, and wanted to know how could he say what he was saying without being killed? 'Do you know this man?' they asked me. I told them the voice was very familiar, trying to look at him more closely. He screamed again and said to me, 'Go to hell you agent of that devil. You are a devil yourself, otherwise you would not spy for him, you traitor!'

"'We think that he is your brother-in-law," *Hagi* Abas told me.

"It hit me then, yes, that he was. So I told him, 'Yes, he looks much different than two years ago with the long beard, but it could be him!' *Hagi* Abas told the prison head, 'See, I told you that a mistake was made. Dr. Afras has operated on hundreds of men who had some kind of injury in the war.' Then he looked at me, pointing at Navid and asked, 'Is his behavior normal?'

"'No,' I said quickly. I could tell that this may be the way to save him. 'He is getting worse. He had some mental problems then, but not so severe!' 'See,' he repeated again to the prison head. 'There has been some mistake.' We left the cell. Then I went through signing all kind of exit papers. I was to swear that I had nothing to do with Navid or any groups related to political parties. Then I was able to leave the prison. I asked *Hagi* Abas what my crime was, and he said that they found a notebook with Navid, in which it said I was his inspiration!"

Nosha could not believe her ears. "But that does not mean anything!"

"Yes, I know, but what makes sense in this government," he replied.

"What did Navid do?"

"The only thing they have is the notebook, his diary. They also said he was using all kind of foul languages toward their leader, that devil called Khomeini. But I told him again that Navid needed medical attention and that he needed to go to the hospital, not be in jail. I do not know, Nosha, maybe in a strange way my arrest was a blessing in disguise, that I was able to see him and use his condition to rescue him," he said, exhausted.

"Yes, I am sure it was. But can you lie down again so I can take care of your wounds?" He did. After she was done, she asked him, "You were also limping; what is wrong with your legs?"

"They kicked me a lot. It hurts."

"Do you think they broke your leg?"

He shook his leg and said," I do not believe so."

"But what if I call the ambulance and we go to hospital to see if it is broken."

"No, not now please, I am so tired and angry. I do not want to see any of those bearded men any time soon."

"Okay, I will call a private hospital; we need to be sure," Nosha stressed.

"Oh, honey, I know it is not broken. You can examine it yourself."

Nosha looked at his leg and bent his leg a couple of times. His pain did not worsen. So she agreed to let him sleep.

Soon he fell into deep sleep. Nosha was relieved. She was happy that her husband was okay, and that she now knew that her brother was alive. She needed to let her mother know. She called Pasargad. Her mother answered the phone, happy to hear her voice.

"I have good news for you; we found out that Navid is here in the Shiraz jail," she said.

Laiya paused a little then said, "Are you joking? His name was not among the prisoners in Shiraz."

"No Mom, I am not joking, and I can not talk on the phone. We will talk more about it when you are here."

Next, they had to know what they could do to help Navid. After seeing and talking to several officials they learned that he had been sentenced to eight years in jail. He was arrested in Kerman for no reason and they found his dairy, which put him in solitary confinement for over a year and got him a seven-year jail sentence. He was transferred to Qom's jail and then to Shiraz after his mental breakdown. Why Qom, they wondered, but soon understood that influential families had good friends who could change the course of events. That was why in the revolution often they executed people without any prior notice. They also kept the young men in the jails of different cities where nobody knew them.

Her mother arrived the next day. Nosha talked to her. She told her about the trouble Siya went through and the fact that Navid was in a very bad mental condition. After several days of agony, they let her mother visit him.

She was shocked to see her son not knowing who she was. A month later, they agreed to transfer him to a hospital where he could get some medical attention. Nosha went there and with the hospital, permission started giving her brother medication he needed. It was much better than prison and although there were a couple of guards in front of the door, her mother could visit him often. It took a whole month for Navid to gain his conscious mind and recognize his family members.

One day he asked his mother if he was going mad.

"Why are you asking that?" her mother replied.

"I can see, and everywhere I look I see mad people. I am here so I must be mentally ill also," he replied.

With medication, he was almost cured and went back to jail against his family's protests and his doctor's recommendation. However, they told them that he could have more visitors than others and Nosha could monitor his medicine. As the months passed, gradually Navid got better. Nosha visited him regularly, which created a strong bond between them. Navid was much younger than Nosha and she always admired his talent and loved his kind heart. Seeing him and talking to him was a pleasure she looked forward to, and was so happy seeing his beautiful smile when she went there. He was not complaining that much any more. He was optimistic and was looking forward to the day he would be free.

"I have so many dreams," he told Nosha one day. "The dream of being free. I have the dream of having a normal life and playing with your children outside of this crappy place," he told Nosha often.

"You will get all that. In a few years, you know! The time passes very fast and before you know you will be free and will see your dreams come true," she told him.

Amazingly, Navid's situation made his family come closer than they had ever been. One day Nosha complained and asked Siya, "How can Nozar see Navid's situation and still be loyal to this government?" Siya told her, "It is harder for him to cope with than any one of you."

"How is that?" Nosha asked angrily.

"Who gave you your degree?" Siya asked her jokingly.

Nosha looked at him, puzzled. He continued with his usual smile. "He is a devoted Moslem who sees conflict in his beliefs and the love he feels for his family."

"I don't see that much distress in his behavior," Nosha said bitterly.

"Well I am amazed, you should know better than anyone else!"

Nosha looked at him, "What do you know that I do not?"

"Well, he came to me for help to find a doctor. He did not want to disturb you with his problems, he told me. I introduced him to Dr. G. and he told me all about his conflicts and his confusion. He is so young but is bending under the pressure your family is putting on him and his own confusion. He needs your support. There is a corrupt government that we do not like, but also there are so many people who believe in eternity and Islam. We are directing our anger toward them while they are themselves victims. Look at all the disabled veterans and all who died for this country; they are all the believers who lost their lives and their limbs! They did not start the war, nor did they kill anyone. The corruption does not come from them!"

He was quiet. Nosha, who was listening like a student to her teacher said, "You are right, I guess. But the corrupt government can not survive with out their support and it is their beliefs that are destroying our country, their lives, and so many others who do not think the same way as them."

"Maybe, but what can we do about it? Destroying the most precious thing we had is not the answer. For so long family had been the backbone of our society. The family always had been important to us until this era. You cannot exclude one from your family because he does not think like you. What if he dies in the war tomorrow, will you be so mad at him still?"

Nosha felt a sharp pain in her heart. He was right. Nozar had been in the war zone for the past four years and he could be killed easily. Siya who was watching her realized her discomfort and started reciting a famous poem.

Come, come,
Let's appreciate each other
Before death will take us apart,
Since you will kiss my grave,
Kiss my cheeks we are the same.
You will be on my grave after my death,

Why are we loving the death but not life?
Let's be friends now and think I am death,
Since I am not hurting any one you can think I am dead.[49]

There was a deep silence. Nosha felt her tears come down her face, making her mouth salty. She went and hugged her husband, putting her face on his chest. She knew anything was possible and that she could lose Nozar any day.

The door rang and she welcomed Nozar, who came in with a smile. After that day, he came to their houses often. Talking to her siblings, she realized that in an amazing way Navid's situation had brought them closer together.

Persian Women & the Revolution

Mrs. Masood

Any time she visited Mrs. Masood, she was reminded of the handsome man named Ahmad who was her second son. He was the same age as Nader, and had gone to the United States shortly after high school to continue his education. He got his PhD but returned to Iran shortly after the war began; he told his mother that he wanted to defend his country. She told him of course, if you do not go then who else will? He packed his bags and went to the volunteer lines to defend his homeland but he never came back. She spent her time sitting by the door and waiting. She waited for the mailman every day to see if she had any letters from him. She asked her husband each time he went out to see if he saw any of his friends. They talked constantly about how maybe he was a prisoner of war. Nobody knew where he was. Or what happened to him.

"I dream about him often," she told Nosha. "I see his tall strong body and his light brown eyes fixed on me. I run toward him to hug him but then he is not there. He vanishes into the thin air and I remember that he went to war. I remember that we do not have any news from him. Day after day, I am sitting here waiting. I am waiting to hear some news—anything is all right as long as I know what is happening to him." She would then cry and tell her about how she went to see the soldiers who went to the war zone with him.

"His friend said they saw him one day from a distance and they know he got captured by the enemy. I am sure he is in prison there, but why does he not write me? Other prisoners write their families but I do not get any letters." Nosha was deeply affected by her sorrow and tried to comfort her, but she had so much trouble coping with the fact that Ahmad was missing. Mrs. Masood and her husband were her parents' friends and she had a good relationship with her sons, who were almost her age. Ahmad was a polite, kind, and smart person. She loved him like she did her brothers. One of Ahmad's cousins told Nosha one day that Ahmad was dead. That he was not the prisoner of war they want to believe that he was. Nosha felt pressure in her heart. The fact was so bitter that even she did not want to believe it.

Gohar

The amount of mental illness increased both in men and women. There was a sudden change for the intellectuals from bad to worse. The war and its aftermath, bad economy, and the rigidity of a religious society all were the cause of their mental illnesses. There was also a women's suicide epidemic, which was uncontrollable. Women had to cope with every problem men had in that society and be confined to rigid clothes and behavior. A total stranger had a right to tell them shut up if they laughed. Pull their scarf down if even a few hairs were showing under it, with her knowledge or without it.

The married women had other dilemmas to cope with. They lost all the freedom they had enjoyed under last regime and were forced to live with abusive or addicted husbands. All those problems emerged in the form of a number of suicides in which they set themselves on fire. The epidemic started a few years before when a young woman went in front of Tehran University and poured gasoline on herself, then took her *chador* and screamed, "I will die in the name of freedom! I do not want to wear this black robe,". Then she put it in the fire and as soon as the authorities went to get her for not wearing *hejab*, she jumped in the fire and went up in flames. She became the symbol of resistance to hundreds of women who were lost in the midst of the revolution and did not know which direction to go. Most of these women died before they got to the hospital and those who did survive faced a dreadful life with burned and disfigured skin.

With the mild weather, Nosha decided to walk to work. She was walking to work that early morning; when she got to the hospital, she saw a burning bush in flame sitting next to the green hollies, making a magnificent contrast. Then she saw the maple trees with their red, green, brown, and yellow colored leaves, which made a beautiful bouquet of flowers. Jealous of their beauty, she thought, *oh, nature is so beautiful and peaceful.* She wished she could just forget about all the problems and enjoy nature as she was supposed to. She went in when she saw Siya, who told her, "We have another suicide attempt; you might want to come with me."

"Sure," she said, and followed him.

There was a young woman burned beyond recognition. They took her to the emergency room to see if they could save her. Nosha began to flip through her file to see what she could do for her or her relatives. But the woman's name became big and bigger in her mind. Her heart began to pound very hard as an unbelievable pain overtook her entire body. *Gohar!* she whispered to herself as she ran to her office. She started to remember a distant past, a happy past in all its glory.

There she was, a young pretty girl with black eyes and hair and bronze skin. She was laughing and everyone around her was laughing too. Who was she? Her name was Gohar, Nosha's roommate from her freshman year. Then she remembered her sitting down praying with small picture of a young handsome man beside her prayer carpet. She finished her prayer, then picked up the picture, slowly bringing it to her lips to kiss it. 'Oh so romantic,' Nosha told her. She started laughing again. Her infectious loud laugh made Nosha very happy. Gohar was engaged and that was her fiancé's picture next to her prayer carpet.

They became instant friends as soon as they became roommates. Gohar's joyous behavior made her happy all the time. Then another picture of her and Gohar came to her mind, a picture of a snow day in Shiraz where the two young girls were walking in the snow giggling and admiring their surroundings. Then Gohar's voice rang her ears with excitement. 'I am the only one in my family to go to college but sometimes I feel that it is too much being away from my husband. I love him so much.' 'But he comes here every week to see you,' Nosha told her. 'Yes he does but still I miss him dearly. I want to be with him all the time!' And then it was Gohar's graduation day, with her screams of joy reaching the entire surrounding area as she held her husband's hands in hers.

A tear dropped from her eyes onto Gohar's file as she whispered to herself, *what happened to her? Where did all that energy and joy go?* She tried to concentrate on reading the file. A piece of paper got her attention: it was Gohar's handwriting. Simply explaining that she was killing herself since there was too much to handle, especially her husband's addiction!

Nosha sat down and let her tears to fall freely now. *I have this much right to cry for a friend,* she told herself. While so many women were under so much pressure, some lived remarkably well, like Mahnaz, who, against all the odds, took charge of her life, made money from a skill she learned when she was only a child, and gathered enough money to take her son and leave the country. Nooshin was another one whose husband lost his job and she was the sole provider of her family, so she found another job. She was teaching high school during the day as a full-time teacher. She found a night school and started teaching there full time too. All even as she was juggling the heavy task of taking care of her two children! But some, like Gohar, could not handle this tough life and tried to end it. The route they took was so odd and painful, though! *Why?* Nosha asked herself. The answer was unknown; maybe it was a sure way to go.

"What is happening now?" Siyavash's surprised voice interrupted her thoughts.

She looked up and said, "She was my roommate."

Siya, who had been wondering why she was crying, did not know who she was talking about, but then it dawned on him. "Who, the burned woman?"

"Yes," Nosha replied, breaking into tears.

Siya kneeled down in front of her and said, "Honey, I am so sorry. I did not know!" Then he frowned and said, "I thought her name was familiar."

"Yes," Nosha said through her tears. "She used to call you the good one."

They sat there together in the corner silently, both deep in their thoughts of sorrow and disbelief.

"What is going to happen to her?" Nosha asked, still crying.

"I am sorry to tell you she died in the emergency room. She was burned so badly," Siya told her, and then asked her if she wanted to leave the hospital.

"No, I need to talk to her mother and relatives."

"Did she have any children?"

"Yes, she had two young ones. My God, with a dead mother and addicted father what are they going to do?"

"Well, we have to trust nature that they will be okay."

"What a pity," she told him.

Zarin

That evening she had a patient who was coming to her regularly. She was an educated woman who was teaching in high school. She was married, but her husband was an addict. She was frightened for her children and wanted a divorce, but she was not able to get one. "I cannot leave my children with him," she told her.

"Can't you prove he is addicted and get custody of them?" Nosha asked.

"No, are you kidding? He says all the high-level officials are addicted to some kind of narcotic and I will lose. Without a divorce, I need to be able to be calm," she begged her. It was so common for women to be in between a rock and a hard place; she told her that her health was so important for her children' well-being and she should think of herself first. She also prescribed a mild antidepressant. *She has the same situation as Gohar,* thought Nosha, *I hope I could help!*

Ziba

The next day she had another patient. She was a proud woman under the last administration, educated and smart. She had been working as a nurse. She was married to an abusive man. He kicked her out of their house one day so she decided to move back in with her parents. Without getting a penny from him, she was managing her life, but she was not able to get divorce. The law did not give her the ability to file for divorce, so she went with what the law permitted her to do. She filed for divorce based on his refusal to take care of her financial needs. He replied that she was refusing to live with him, and he would provide for her when she moved back home. But, she told the judge, he kicked me out! How can I move back in with him?

But her struggle went nowhere. They refused her divorce and she stayed with her parents. She had to cope with this mess and so she was coming to see Nosha regularly.

"There has always been physical and verbal abuse in some marriages, what is different in this régime compared to the last one?" Siya asked her.

"The difference is that then women could get out of bad marriages and now they cannot. The law was protecting abused women then. But now they are taking men's side no matter what happens to women. That is why there are so many suicide attempts among women these days," Nosha replied.

"But I have heard different stories. Some of my patients complain that there are so many premarital agreements that it is hard to get married!" Siya replied.

"Well the parents are waking up now. They push for more rights for their daughters. If under the last régime a high *mehrieh* was the norm, these days they know that they have to put down the children's custody, the right to get divorced, etc., in their agreements. Persian women are smart; they find ways to get what they want. Our generation has a problem since they calculated for the laws they had, not the new laws."

"Hmm, so our daughter should not be worried," Siya said it jokingly.

"No, she should not; she will be living in the United States, where she was born."

"Oh, are you really thinking of sending her there?"

"Aren't you?" Nosha looked at him in surprise. "I do not think she will be happy here from what I see. Nobody is happy here and if she can be living in the free world, why not?"

Siya laughed and said, "It is so strange for you to talk this way. You were not happy when we left Iran, and for most of the time that we were there."

"You are right, I was not. I loved my country and had not seen so much injustice here. There were discussions about not being able to do or say anything, but I did not feel the fear I feel now. I had not witnessed the injustices I see daily now.

"I was so drowned in my nationalistic love for my country that I could not understand the pain that other immigrants had gone through to get there, and thought that they were betraying their old nations by rejecting their homelands and embracing the freedom of America. But now I understand what they were talking about. You have to be in a bad environment to appreciate the good one."

The End of Dreams

Days came and went, they got older, but the war still was asking for more sacrifices. It was hard to go out and to not notice the pictures everywhere. The pictures of young men killed in the war. There were funerals on each lane and street regularly. All the street names had changed to martyr this and that. In each cemetery you could see row after row of young faces that were framed on the top of the graves. People were trying to forget the hardship of war, the rationalizing, the long lines to buy the simplest necessities.

They had to stay hours in one line to buy milk, another to buy bread, and another to buy oil. Then there was bombing when Iraq attacked; they had to leave the city and run out to the suburbs. That became the ordinary way of living. "The human mind is great; it can adjust to the worst situation imaginable!" Nosha told her husband once.

There was a smart kid named Ali, who lived in Nosha's neighborhood. He lost his father at an early age and his mother had to work hard to raise her two sons. Ali was the smarter one. He was first in his grades all throughout high school and was accepted to a top university in Tehran when Nosha was in her senior year of high school. Apparently he was determined to succeed in every step of his life and was in the top one percent of his class when he won a scholarship to study in the United States.

Just before his departure, he came to see Nosha and her family. His big eyes and his bronze skin made him very attractive. His dark skin and light eyes made him look like he had been tanning under sun for days. His teeth were so white and straight with a smile that dazzled whomever saw it. He was warm and kind. He had big dreams, which he shared with Nosha. While talking to him she thought, my God, he is so handsome. He looks more like the Greek gods than a normal man. How can one have so much beauty and such a good brain?

She did not see him again and forgot him until that awful day. Iraq was bombing Shiraz and Nosha decided to take the children and go to Pasargad for a few days. Things were not that comfortable there either. With her father gone, her mother was unable to maintain a good clean environment and on the top of that, the kerosene they used for heating and warming the water was scarce.

That was the day she heard the news. Ali had been martyred. Her mother told her when she asked why there were screams coming from the alley. "When did he come back?" she asked, stunned to learn the news.

"He got back a few months ago and was sent to Kurdistan. He was killed by locals!" her mother told her. She could not help remembering his dreams and his long eyelashes on that bronze face. It was easy to pass the pictures of young martyrs and be indifferent, but it was not easy to know a person and admire their ability and stay calm.

She went to his funeral and saw his mother crushed; bent over as though she were dead herself. She had worked so hard to raise him, without any father, and now all her dreams were gone with the wind. One of his cousins whispered, "It was not the Kurds who killed him! The government killed him since he was giving money to *Mojahedin* when he was in the States! People who heard him going to Kurdistan told him he should refuse to go, but he did not want to hear anything about it."

Nosha thought, *what was the difference? A flower was flattened, did it make any difference how?* A true mind was gone; was the government so stupid to kill such a mind? She was not sure.

Upon her return to Shiraz, she told the story to Nooshin. Her husband shook his shoulder and said, "Now they are telling us that he was from one of the opposition groups? That is a lie, he was a member of the *Hezbollah*."

As if he was talking about an enemy and did not care if he was dead, Nosha thought. *What is happening to humanity? A smart and beautiful young man lost his life and dreams; should they talk about him like he was an enemy?*

The war had now been going for seven years, but it was still thirsty for blood and destruction. The news was too close to home this time. Nosha's second cousin (Parivash's first son) was martyred. She could remember his blue clear eyes from the time he was a few months old until his recent marriage. He was not a soldier. Nor was he working there. He was a sympathetic volunteer who was gathering blankets and clothes from donations and taking them to the war front. That day he delivered his goods and was talking to some of the soldiers when a bomb exploded and all of them died. Another dream was lost and another mother was left crying. Such a waste! What will his widowed wife and his newborn do? These thoughts crossed everyone's mind!

Nozar is there too, Nosha thought that bright spring morning when he arrived in the hospital. *Is he going to live a long time?* A group of injured soldiers were brought to the hospital and Siya went to see them. He came to her office and asked her to sit down.

"What is the matter?" Nosha asked.

"I have good news and bad. Nozar was hit. A mortar shell hit his neck, but only a little bit under his skin, you can visit him in an hour if you like. He was lucky, since all his compatriots died at once."

The color evaporated from Nosha's face.

"Is he alive?"

"I told you he is all right and will be conscious in an hour."

She could not say much. In that situation being happy that her brother was alive meant she was happy that his compatriots died. They all were from Pasargad and all young men age twenty or less! But with Navid in jail, she could not understand. Her brother had not realized how much his actions would hurt his mother. She was worried to death for both of her sons. Although he had resigned from the revolutionary guards shortly after they found Navid, he had been drafted as a soldier for almost two years now.

That year the war monster was getting wilder and too many youths' lives vanished. The big events were the chemical weapons used by the Iraqi government first on Kurdish people and then Iranian soldiers. It was late summer that she got the news from Nader.

She called him and he said Nozar was there, to relax, though he had been hit by the chemical bombs.

"Is he going to be okay?"

"We are not sure yet, but he has to be in total darkness for a while, otherwise there is possibility of going blind."

"How come he did not go to the hospital?" she asked.

"Well he did, and was treated, but they did not have space to keep him for recovery."

"How are you managing him?"

"He just sits or sleeps under a thick black robe. We give him food and drink that he has to take from us under the robe. I imagine that is very hard for him!" Days came and went and after a long period of time, Nozar recovered from the radiation, which made so many blind and killed so many more!

"It was my prayer," proclaimed her mother one day. "I was praying day and night and on two occasions, Nozar escaped from certain death."

Nosha told her how amazed she was by her beliefs. "On one hand, every day hundreds are getting killed though they have faith. On the other hand, you think God answered your prayer since Nozar survived. Do you think God is deaf to other mothers' prayers?" Her mother grew angry at this statement, telling her that she did not want to hear blasphemous talk and left her house.

Nosha's highlights were the times she went to see Navid. He was full of hope and joy. Being in that dark and dingy place made everyone depressed and with his past experience, Nosha was wondering every day if he would be bend down again and be crushed. He could go back anytime to the dark days of nervous breakdown. Each time Nosha saw him smiling, felt the world was smiling on her. She was expecting worse and was happy that he was okay.

One day she went to see him he told her, "I think it will be the end of our long terrible war."

"How do you know?" Nosha asked.

"I do not know, but I heard from the news that United States hit one of the Iranian ships!"

"Yes, they did."

"I think the world is getting tired of war and they are making both stupid jerks stop it."

"Hush," Nosha told him. "You do not want me to get prohibited from seeing you."

He smiled and said, "I am sorry, but I did not mention any names. Do not worry."

They continued talking about her children. Nasim and Nima were eager to see their favorite uncle, she told him.

He said excitedly, "This is my last year. I am going to be free soon. It will be such a beautiful day when I finally walk in the streets and watch the shops. I bet I will be stunned seeing the prices. I read in the newspapers that inflation has skyrocketed."

Nosha shook her head in agreement and said, "Even we get shocked when going shopping. The prices are changing on daily basis! It is okay if you are free and healthy—prices should not matter that much."

Nosha felt sadness creep into her heart. She also felt rage. *Why do they keep him in jail?* she asked herself while trying to change the subject. "Navid, are you okay here, dear?"

"Oh, yes. As long as you pray five times a day and do not argue with them, they leave you alone. I do everything they ask me to do; with the pills you prescribe me I do not have any energy to fight!'

Nosha kissed him and left.

※

A few months later there was another accident; one of the Iran Air passenger jets was hit by American missiles. Three hundred people died. The U.S. military claimed that they hit it by mistake, but nevertheless these people as well died with all their dreams. The news was very sad, but then there was good news. Khomeini told the Iranian people that he was drinking from a poisonous crate as he signed for the cessation of the eight-year-long war.

There was a joy in the air. It was going to be a new era, an era of peace and prosperity to come. But Nosha felt terrible. *Why do I feel this way?* she asked herself. *There will be no more martyrs, no more young men's pictures all over the streets, and no more food rationing*, she thought.

The day passed lazily and when she went to bed that night she was still uncomfortable and felt a butterfly in her chest. *I must be prone to depression too*, she told herself. *I need to do more exercise. Today I should be jumping up and down with joy instead of feeling this sadness!* But nobody was screaming in joy. The news was good, but people were drowned too much in their problems to be able to be happy and joyous.

It was midnight when she started to dream. No, she started to see her nightmare. She went to jail and they took her to Navid's cell, which consisted of a bathtub. He was laid down in the tub, which was full of blood. She started to scream. *No, no, this can not be happening!*

"What, darling? What is wrong? What cannot be happening?" It was Siyavash's voice and his hands that were holding her.

She looked around. She was in her bedroom. Tears ran from her eyes as she said, "They killed him."

"Who?" Siya asked again.

"They killed my Navid. He is gone, I know it."

"What are you talking about? Who killed Navid? He is all right and will be free any day now.'

"No, they killed him!"

"Honey, you had a bad dream, that's all! If they wanted to kill him they would have when he was cursing the revolution."

"They knew he was sick then, they wanted to give us hope and they wanted us see him happy and healthy, then destroy him." She started crying harder.

Siya could not calm her down. The more he tried to reason with her the less he was successful. Finally, he told her, "I do not know how you heard your news, can you tell me?"

She told him about her nightmare.

"Oh come on. We always dream but they do not come true."

"But I can not stop the feeling that tells me he is gone."

"Can I give you something to calm you down? Maybe your feelings are exhaustion or depression. You have no shred of evidence to prove you are right."

She paused a little; maybe he was right. Maybe she was exhausted, didn't she tell herself last afternoon that she was prone to depression? "Yes, you are right I have some tranquilizers in the medicine cabinet; can you give me one?"

Her urge to cry made her think that she was depressed too. She could not stop crying. They were up for a couple of hours and she had to take two pills until she fell asleep.

The next morning she woke up around 10 a.m. Siyavash and the children were gone. She did not feel like going to work. She tried unsuccessfully to call her mother, but no one answered the phone. She turned on the radio when Mrs. Afras came in with the breakfast tray.

"Oh thanks," she said, "but I am not hungry."

"I know dear. Siya told me you had a tough time last night. I told him that you are working too hard. You are a working woman and mother of two who wants to do all the work herself. You need relaxation and rest, dear. But more importantly you need to eat the right food."

Tears came to her eyes again, which she tried to control. She was right; she needed to eat something. While she was eating, her mother-in-law started talking to her about her past memories of the children. She always enjoyed her mother-in-law's stories, just like when she was little and her grandmother was telling her stories of her life.

It was noon when Siya came home. He kissed her and asked her how she was.

"Oh, I am a little bit better; listening to your mother's life stories is so calming." They were talking when she jumped up and said, "I need to call my mom again."

There was silence again. "Nobody is answering," she told them.

"Well maybe they are out or something."

Then Siya asked her if she felt any better.

"No," she replied, "but there is no bad news; I think I need to treat myself with antidepressants."

"Can you go to jail and see Navid?"

"No, it is not my visitation day," she replied trying to fight off another huge urge to cry. She ran to the phone again and dialed her mother's number. Someone said hello, but she heard crying in the background.

"Who are you and what is going on there?" she asked.

The woman replied, "I am a neighbor; are you Nosha?"

"Yes, I am. Who is crying?"

"That is your mother. She had a call that Navid was executed this morning and you should go and get his clothes."

The phone dropped from her hand and without a word, she sat down. Tears fell down her face as she blankly stared into the space in front of her.

"What happened?" Mrs. Afras asked. Siya took the receiver and listened to the woman's voice.

"Okay, we will." Then he sat down next to her and while tears were filling his eyes told her, "I am so sorry, what can I do to help?" She only put her head on his shoulder in response and continued to cry.

Navid's voice was in her ears: *I am going to be free soon and I will be able to play with Nasim and Nima.* Nobody could help her, nobody. Another flower was flattened and this time that was her beloved brother. And her mother's neighbor's voice was ringing in her ears: *you should go and get his clothes.* Did that meant that she could not even see his handsome face anymore? Only his clothes; they could not have his body. They were not going to see his grave either. What happened? What made them kill him? There were so many questions that she had no answer to.

Years later, she learned that they were not alone. They were all political prisoners who were killed in one night by the direct order of Khomeini himself. They were from all walks of life, old, young, religious or communist. They were ending a costly war of eight years with no significant advantage, and they did not want the prisoners to come out. There was no possible reason for it, just a waste.

Flying Back

Nosha was right; she was prone to depression and this time she could not seem to shake it. Losing Navid was the last straw. She wanted to cry all day and night. She knew that she needed to be strong for her children, but the urge to cry was constantly there. She was not working anymore, afraid of losing it in front of her patients. She could not cure anyone, she told her husband, who was worried for her health. Instead she was reading book after book about what to do. She was walking long hours every day and she was swimming more than an hour a day in their pool in their yard. But she could not stop her tears. Even in the water she could feel her tears were running. The only time she was not crying was when her children were home. She would take a tranquilizer to be able to stop her tears in front of her children. Siyavash watched all of this and was very disturbed. Nosha was his love and joy; he could not see her so depressed.

"Why don't you start writing articles like you used to when we were in the United States?" Siya asked her one day. "If you do not want to work, it is okay. But if you become busy, you will be able to get better." He was right and that worked; she prepared two articles. Siya wrote a few articles himself and sent all of them to the Duke Weekly News. They got published, and with the publication came an invitation to attend a conference at Duke University.

When she got the invitation, she said without emotion, "But we cannot go."

"Why?" Siya asked.

"Well, we are doctors and we are not allowed to leave the country!"

"Wrong," he said, "we could not during the war. We will go. Everyone who was someone had left the country already." Even her brother Nader left shortly after their brother's execution.

"I wish you could come too," Nosha said to Nooshin, when she said goodbye and left the airport to go to the airplane.

When the airplane went up, she looked down on the land she loved and felt her feelings relax, which made her wonder. She was leaving her homeland and she was breathing much more easily now that she was leaving her country. A strange feeling!

She remembered one of her classmates in medical school in Shiraz. She was talking passionately to him about the nationalistic feelings she had toward Persia. He said, "The land is the same everywhere, the soil is the soil; what makes one land more attractive to you than the other lands is the system you love, not the land itself!" How much she had disagreed with him then, but now after such a long time she could see his point.

She waved and said goodbye. She looked at her daughter Nasim. Was she going to have an easier life than hers? Was she going to cherish the fortune of living in a free country, was she going to take advantage of her opportunity, or take it for granted and destroy her life in this new free land?

Whatever the outcome, she thought, *her dreams will not be Persian dreams.*

Glossary

Choback ... Natural soap
Kozeh .... A clay container
Hakim .... Medical Doctor or wise man
Birooni .... The outside courtyard and house in which it has another door to another house
Darooni ... The inside courtyard and house in which it's door opens into another courtyard.
Bazar ..... Persian shopping mall
Naneh ..... Nanny or sometimes is used as a mother
Kalontar ... Police officer
Morshed ... Religious leader of mystic dervishes one of many branch of Islam
Mangal .... A charcoal heater
Mordeh ... Dead
Chadoor ... black sheet-like drop or robe, a piece of cloths which covers the women from head to toes and they hold it's side together to cover themselves.
Kaleh Ghor . Someone who is bad luck where whomever she meets dies
Mehrie .... money, like a dowery; the agreed money Moslem men put in the marriage contract on the wedding day
Baba ...... Persian slang word for father Dad
Bakrain ... A citrus tree which is used for grafting orange trees because of it's strong root and sweet taste.
Maktab .... A religion school which were teaching children Islamic rules and reading and writing.
Bargh ..... Electricity
Konkoor ... Entrance test taken before entering any universities or colleges.

Maman ... Mother or mommy

Sofreh haft seen .. A table set for the Persian new year with cookies, fruits, eggs, gold fish and flowers which the symbol of Norooz, the Persian new year.

References

[3] Author

[2, 40, 41, 42] Sadi the famous 13th Persian century poet

[1, 4, 17, 18, 19, 20, 21, 23, 24, 25, 26, 27, 28, 29, 30, 31, 32, 33, 34, 35, 44, 45, 46, 47, 48, 49] Molavi from the Ghazalyat Divan Shams: The 13th century Persian poet known as Molavi Rumi was a famous Persian poet and one of the leaders in Sufi's sect of Islam. He has two famous books of poems Divan shams Tabrizi and Masnavi. The poems in this book are a literal translation from Divan Shams by author.

[5, 10] Hafiz, the mystic Sufi Persian poet. Poems from 13th century

[6, 12, 13, 14, 22, 38] Iraj: 1872-1926 a Persian poet with new style, he was the prince of Ghajar Era

[7] Eraghi: 11th century Persian poet

[8] A song by Gogoosh

[9] *Baba* Taher: The oldest in Sufi's poet. Poems from 10th century.

[11] Khayam: Famous mathematician and poet of 11th century.

[15] Malekolshoara Bahar: A 20th century poet

[16] A Persian song, by Aref

[36] Iranmehr: September 2003

In 1941, Reza Shah was given a travel ship to take his family to India and the ship left Bandar Abbas to go to Babaie India. However, the British were worried that his stay in India might boil up the unrest of millions of Moslems in India. So they ordered the British navy to facilitate the abduction of Reza Shah and his family from the travel vessel to a navy ship and take them to Moris Island in South Africa. According to Sharam Javid Pour, this taught other countries and other groups to abduct people for political purposes

[37] January 20, 1981—History of Iran: Under Reza Shah's sixteen years of rule, the roads and Trans-Iranian Railway were built, modern education was introduced, and the University of Tehran was established, and for the first time systematically dispatch of Iranian students to Europe was started. Industrialization of country was stepped

up, and achievements were great. By the mid 1930's, Reza Shah's dictatorial style of rule caused dissatisfaction in Iran. In 1935 the country's name changed from Persia to Iran.

[38a] *kohan diyara* (191 people were killed in two way fight; 121 revolutionaries and 70 soldiers)

[39] Jami: A 10th century Persian poet

[43] Faridoon Moshiri: 20th century Persian poet

About the Author

Maryam Tabibzadeh was born in Darab, Pars, in Persia (known as Iran). She got her master's degree from Shiraz University and moved to the United States. She attended SUNY Binghamton to further her education in 1980.

Maryam has been writing short novels and poems in Persian for the past twenty years. Her short stories, published in the North Carolina Persian Newsletter, include *Omid va Bahar (Hope and Spring)*, *Az Shame Pors Gheseh (Ask the Candle about My Love)*, and *Rozi Keh Neyamad (The Day Which Never Came)*.

Maryam resides in Raleigh, North Carolina.